'SHALL I PROPHESY FOR YOU, MY LORD PRINCE?

Shall I show you what will come to be, no matter how hard you try to rewrite what the gods themselves have written?'

Trapped by the Ihlini's spell, I could not turn away as Strahan lifted his hand, forming shapes amidst the darkness. Colors poured from his fingertips: argent purple, deepest lavender, palest silver lilac. And the lurid red of fresh-spilled blood.

He painted a picture of living flame: a rampant Homanan lion and a compact Cheysuli warbow. They hung against the air as if they waited. As if I had only to pluck the bow from the darkness and loose an arrow at the lion.

'The Homanans want no Cheysuli shapechanger on the throne,' Strahan said above the hissing of the flame. 'The Cheysuli want no unblessed Homanan on the throne. But you are both and neither: what do *you* think will happen? Look to your people, Niall' he said. So softly he spoke; so gentle was his time. 'Look to your friends . . . your enemies . . . *your kin* . . . lest they form an alliance against you!'

Jennifer Roberson writes:

'The *Chronicles of the Cheysuli* is a dynastic fantasy, the story of a proud, honorable race brought down by the avarice, evil and sorcery of others - and its own special brand of magic. It's the story of an ancient race blessed by the old gods of their homeland, and cursed by the sorcerers who desire domination over all men. It's a dynasty of good and evil; love and hatred; pride and strength. Most of all it deals with the destiny in every man and his struggle to shape it, follow it, deny it.'

Also by Jennifer Roberson

CHRONICLES OF THE CHEYSULI

Book One: SHAPECHANGERS
Book Two: THE SONG OF HOMANA
Book Three: LEGACY OF THE SWORD

and published by Corgi Books

Chronicles of the Cheysuli: Book Four

TRACK OF
THE WHITE WOLF

Jennifer Roberson

CORGI BOOKS

TRACK OF THE WHITE WOLF

A CORGI BOOK   0 552 13121 0

First publication in Great Britain

PRINTING HISTORY
Corgi edition published 1988

This book is set in 10/11pt Plantin

Corgi Books are published by Transworld Publishers Ltd.,
61-63 Uxbridge Road, Ealing, London W5 5SA, in Australia by
Transworld Publishers (Australia) Pty. Ltd., 15-23 Helles
Avenue, Moorebank, NSW 2170, and in New Zealand by Transworld
Publishers (N.Z.) Ltd., Cnr. Moselle and Waipareira Avenues,
Henderson, Auckland.

Made and printed in Great Britain by
Cox & Wyman Ltd, Reading, Berks.

This one is for Mark O'Green,
who computerized me,
then married me.
So far, both experiments are working.

the Tuble Ocean

Valgaard

Atvia

Andemir

Rondule
Kilore

Homana

Mujhara

Erinn

Lestra

the Idrian Ocean

Solinde

Hondarth

the
Crystal Isle

©danforth 1984

THE HOUSE OF HOMANA

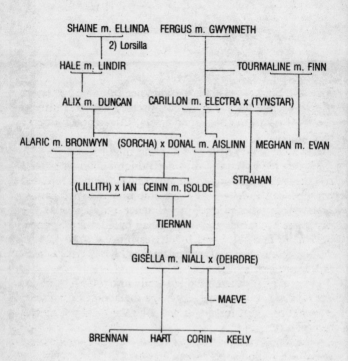

PROLOGUE

I knelt in silence, in patience, right knee cushioned by layers of rain-soaked leaves. Boot heel pressed against buttock; the foot within the boot, perversely, threatened suddenly to cramp.

Not now, I told it, as if the thing might listen.

My left leg jutted up, offering a thigh on which I could rest the arm supporting the compact bow. Support I needed badly; I had knelt a very long time in the misted forest, keeping my silence and my patience only because the discipline my father and brother had taught me, for once, held true. Perhaps I was finally learning.

How many times did Carillon kneel as I kneel, lying in wait for the enemy?

My grandsire's name slipped easily into mouth or mind. Perhaps for another man, perhaps for another grandson, it would not. But for me, it was a legacy I did not always desire.

—Carillon *would keep still for hours* – Carillon *would never speak* – Carillon *would know best how to do the job*—

Distracted by my thoughts, I did not hear the sound behind me. I sensed only the shadow, the *weight* of the stalking beast—

Even as I tried to turn on cramping foot, the bow was knocked flying from my hands. Half-sheathed claws shredded leather hunting doublet and, beneath that, linen shirt. Weight descended and crushed me to the ground, grinding my face into damp leaves and soggy turf.

In the cold, breath rushed out of my nose and mouth like smoke from a dragon's gullet. *Mountain cat.*

I knew it at once, even as the cat's weight shifted and allowed me room to move. There is a smell, not unpleasant, about the cats. A sense of *presence*. An ambience, created the moment one of their kind appears.

I rolled, coming up onto my knees, jerking the knife free of the sheath at my belt—

—and froze.

A female. Full-fleshed and in prime condition. Her lush red coat was a dappled chestnut at shoulders and haunches. The tail lashed in short, vicious arcs as she crouched. Dark-tipped ears flattened against wedge-shaped head as she snarled, displaying an awesome assemblage of curving teeth.

She hissed, as a housecat will do when taken by surprise. And then she purred.

I swore. Slammed the knife home into its sheath. Spat out mud and stripped decaying leaf from face and hair. And swore again as I saw the laughter in her amber, slanted eyes.

And suddenly I *knew*—

I glanced back instantly. In the clearing, very near the place I had waited so patiently, the red stag lay dead, the *king* stag, with the finest rack of antlers I had ever seen. And a red-fletched arrow stood up like a standard from his ribs.

'Ian!' I shouted. 'Ian – *come out!* It was not fair!'

The cat sat down in the clearing, commenced licking one big paw, and continued to purr noisily.

'Ian?' I looked suspiciously at the cat for a moment. 'No – Tasha.' Still there was no answer. It was all I could do not to fill the trees with my shout. 'Ian, the stag was *mine* – do you hear?' I waited. Wiggled my foot inside my boot; the cramp, thank the gods, was fading. '*Ian*,' I said menacingly; giving up, I bellowed it. 'The stag was *mine* not *yours!*'

'But you were much too slow.' The answering voice was human, not feline. 'Much too slow; did you think the king would wait on a prince forever?'

I spun around. As usual, with him, I had misjudged his position. There were times I would have sworn he could

10

make his voice issue from rock or tree, and me left searching fruitlessly for a man.

My brother sifted out of trees, brush, slanted foggy shadows into the clearing beside the dead stag. Now that I saw him clearly, I wondered that I had not seen him before. He had been directly across from me. Watching. Waiting. And laughing, no doubt, at his foolish younger brother.

But in silence, so he would not give himself away.

I swore. Aloud, unfortunately, which only gave him more cause to laugh. But *he* did not, aloud; he merely grinned his white-toothed grin and waited in amused tolerance for me to finish my royal tirade.

And so I did not, having no wish to hand him further reason to laugh at me, or – worse – to dispense yet another of his ready homilies concerning a prince's proper behavior.

I glared at him a moment, unable to keep myself from *that* much. I saw the bow in his hands and the red-fletched arrows poking up from the quiver behind his shoulder. And looked again at the matching arrow in the ribs of the red king stag.

Conversationally, I pointed out, 'Using your *lir* to knock me half-silly was not within the rules of the competition.'

'There were no rules,' he countered immediately. 'And what Tasha did was her own doing, no suggestion of mine – though, admittedly, she *was* looking after my interests.' I saw the maddening grin again; winged black brows rose up to disappear into equally raven hair. 'And her own, naturally, as she shares in the kill.'

'Of course,' I agreed wryly. 'You would never set her on me *purposely*—'

'Not for a liege man to do,' he agreed blandly, with an equally bland smile. Infuriating, is my older brother.

'You ought to teach her some manners.' I looked at the mountain cat, not at my brother. 'But then, she has arrogance enough to match yours just as she is, so I am sure you prefer her this way.'

Ian laughing – aloud this time – did not answer. Instead he knelt down by the stag to inspect his kill. In fawn-

11

colored leathers he blended easily into the foliage and fallen leaves. Another man, lacking the skills I have learned, would not have seen Ian at all, until he moved. Even then, I thought only the glint of gold on his bare arms would give him away.

I should have known. I should have expected it. All a man has to do is look at him to know he is the better hunter. Because a man, looking at my brother, will see a Cheysuli warrior.

But a man, looking at me, will see only a fellow Homanan. *Or Carillon, until he looks again.*

For all we share a Cheysuli father, Ian and I share not a whit of anything more. Certainly not in appearance. Ian is *all* Cheysuli: black-haired, dark-skinned, yellow-eyed. And I am all Homanan: tawny-haired, fair-skinned, *blue*-eyed.

It may be that in a certain gesture, a specific movement, Ian and I resemble one another. Perhaps in a turn of phrase. But even that seems unlikely. Ian was Keep-raised, brought up by the clan. I was born in the royal palace of Homana-Mujhar, reared by the aristocracy. Even our accents differ a little: he speaks Homanan with the underlying lilt of the Cheysuli Old Tongue, frequently slipping into the language altogether when forgetful of his surroundings; my speech is always Homanan, laced with the nuances of Mujhara, and almost never do I fall into the Old Tongue of my ancestors.

Not that I have no wish to. I am Cheysuli as much as Ian – well, nearly; he is half, I claim a quarter – and yet no man would name me so. No man would ever look into my face and name me, in anger or awe, a shapechanger, because I lack the yellow eyes. I lack the color entirely; the gold, and even the language.

No. No shapechanger, the Cheysuli Prince of Homana.

Because in addition to lacking Cheysuli looks, I also lack a *lir*.

Part I

CHAPTER ONE

I think no one can fully understand what pain and futility
and emptiness are. Not as *I* understand them: a man without
a *lir*. And what of them I do understand comes not of the
body but of the spirit. Of the soul. Because to know oneself
a *lirless* Cheysuli is an exquisite sort of torture I would wish
on no man, not even to save myself.

My father was young, *too* young, when he received his
lir, and then he bonded with two: Taj and Lorn, falcon and
wolf. Ian was fifteen when he formed his bond with Tasha.
At ten, *I* hoped I would be as my father and receive my
lir early. At thirteen and fourteen I hoped I would at *least*
be younger than Ian, if I could not mimic my father. At
fifteen and sixteen I prayed to all the gods I could to send
me my *lir* as soon as possible, *period*, so I could know myself
a man and a warrior of the clan. At seventeen, I began to
dread it would never happen, never at all; that I would live
out my life a *lirless* Cheysuli, only half a man, denied all
the magic of my race.

And now, at eighteen, I knew those fears for truth.

Ian still knelt by the king stag. Tasha -- lean, lovely,
lissome Tasha — flowed across the clearing to her *lir* and
rubbed her head against one bare arm. Automatically Ian
slipped that arm around her, caressing sleek feline head and
tugging affectionately at tufted ears. Tasha purred more
loudly than ever, and I saw the distracted smile on Ian's
face as he responded to the mountain cat's affection. A
warrior in communion with his *lir* is much like a man in
perfect union with a woman; another man, shut out of either
relationship, is doubly cursed . . . and doubly lonely.

15

I turned away abruptly, knowing again the familiar uprush of pain, and bent to recover my bow. The arrow was broken; Tasha's mock attack had caused me to fall on it. A sore hip told me I had also rolled across the bow. But at least the soreness allowed me to think of things other than my brother and his *lir*.

I have never been a sullen man, or even one much given to melancholy. Growing up a prince and heir to the throne of Homana was more than enough for most; would have been more than enough for me, were I not Cheysuli-born. But *lirlessness* – and the knowledge I would remain so – had altered my life. Nothing would change it, not now; no warrior in all the clans had ever reached his eighteenth birthday without receiving his *lir*. Nor, for that matter, his seventeenth. And so I tried to content myself with my rank and title – no small things, to the *Homanan* way of thinking – and the knowledge that for all I lacked a *lir*, I was still Cheysuli. No one could deny the Old Blood ran in my veins. No one. Not even the *shar tahl*, who spoke of rituals and traditions very carefully indeed when he spoke of them to me, because – for all I lacked a *lir* – I still claimed the proper line of descent. And that line would put me on the Lion Throne of Homana the day my father died.

That, at least, was something my brother could not lay claim to – not that he would wish to. Being bastard-born of my father's Cheysuli *meijha* – light woman, in Homanan – attached no stigma to him in the clans. Cheysuli do not place such importance on legitimacy; in the clans, the birth of another Cheysuli is all that counts, but as far as the Homanans were concerned, Donal's eldest son was tolerated among the Homanan aristocracy only because he was the son of the Mujhar.

And so Ian, as much as myself, knew what it was to lack absolute acceptance. It was, I suppose, his own part of the discordant harmony in an otherwise pleasing melody. It only manifested itself for a different reason.

'Niall—?' Ian rose with the habitual grace I tried to emulate and could not; I am too tall, too heavy. I lack the total ease of movement born in so many Cheysuli. 'What is it?'

I thought I had learned to mask my face, even to Ian. It served no purpose to tell him what torture it was to see my brother with his *lir*, or my father with his. Most of the time it remained a dull ache, and bearable, as a sore tooth is bearable so long as it does not turn rotten in the jaw. But occasionally the tooth throbs, sending pain of unbearable intensity through my mind; my mask had slipped, and Ian had seen the face I wore behind it.

'*Rujho*—' so quickly he slipped into the Old Tongue – 'are you ill?'

'No.' Abrupt answer, too abrupt; I inspected the bow again, for want of another action to cover my brief slip. 'No, only—' I sought a lie to cover up the pain '—only disappointed. But I should know better than to match myself against you in something so—' I paused – 'so *Cheysuli* as hunting a stag. You have only to take *lir*-shape, and the contest is finished.'

Ian indicated the arrow. 'No *lir*-shape, *rujho*. Only human form.' He smiled, as if he knew we joked, but something told me he knew well enough what had prompted my discomfiture. 'If it pleases you, Niall, I will concede. Without Tasha's interference, you might well have taken the stag.'

I laughed at him outright. 'Oh, aye, *might* have. Such a concession, *rujho*! You will almost have me believing I know what I am doing.'

'You know what I taught you, my lord.' Ian grinned. 'And now, if you like, I will go fetch the horses as a proper liege man so we may escort the dead king home in honor.'

'To Homana-Mujhar?' The palace was at least two hours away; rain threatened again.

'No, I thought Clankeep. We can prepare the stag there for a proper presentation. Old Newlyn knows all the tricks.' Ian bent down and with a quick twist removed the unbroken arrow from between the ribs of the stag. 'Clankeep is closer, for all that.'

17

I shut my mouth on an answer and did not say what I longed to: that I much preferred the palace. Clankeep is Cheysuli; *lirless*, I am extremely uncomfortable there. I avoid it when I can.

Ian glanced up. 'Niall, it is your home as much as Mujhara.' So easily he read me, even by my silence.

I shook my head. 'Homana-Mujhar is my place. Clankeep is *yours*.' Before he could speak I turned away. 'I will get the horses. My legs are younger than yours.'

It is an old joke between us, the five years that separate us, but for once he would not let it go. He stepped across the dead king stag and caught my arm.

'Niall.' The levity was banished from his face. '*Rujho*, I cannot pretend to know what it is to lack a *lir*. But neither can I pretend *your* lack does not affect me.'

'Does it?' Resentment flared up instantly, surprising even me with its intensity. But this was intrusion into an area of my life he could not *possibly* understand. 'Does it affect you, Ian? Does it disturb you that the warriors of the clan refer to me as a Homanan instead of a Cheysuli? Does it affect you that if they could, they would petition the *shar tahl* to have my birth-rune scratched off the permanent birth-lines?' His dark face went gray as death, and I realized he had not known I was aware of what a few of the more outspoken warriors said. 'Oh, *rujho*, I know I am not alone in this. I know it must disturb *you* — a full-fledged Cheysuli warrior and a member of Clan Council — in particular: that the man intended to rule after Donal lacks the gifts of the Cheysuli. How could it not? You serve the prophecy as well as any warrior, and yet you look at me and see a man who *does not fit*. The link that was not forged.' It hurt me to see the pain in his yellow eyes; eyes some men still called bestial. 'It affects you, it affects our sister, it affects our father. It even affects my mother.'

Ian's hand fell away from my arm. 'Aislinn? *How*?'

His tone was unguarded; I heard the note of astonishment in his voice. No, he would not expect my lack of a *lir* to affect my mother. How could it, when the Queen of Homana

18

was fully Homanan herself, without a drop of Cheysuli blood?

How could he, when there was so little of affection between them? Not hatred; never that. Not even a true disliking of one another. Merely – toleration. A mutual apathy.

Because my mother, the Queen, recalled too clearly that what love my father had to offer had been given freely to his Cheysuli *meijha*, Ian's mother, and not to the Homanan princess he had wed.

At least, not *then*.

I smiled, albeit wryly, and more than a little resigned. 'How does it affect my mother? Because to her, my lacking a *lir* emphasizes a certain other bloodline in me. It reminds her that in addition to looking almost exactly like her father, I reflect all his Homanan traits. No Cheysuli in me, oh no; I am Homanan to the bone. I am Carillon come again.'

The last was said a trifle bitterly; for all I am used to the fact I look so much like my grandsire, it is not an easy knowledge. I would sooner do without it.

Ian sighed. 'Aye. I should have seen it. The gods know she goes on and on about Carillon enough, linking her son with her father. There are times I think she confuses the two of you.'

I shied away from that idea almost at once. It whispered of sickness; it promised obsession. No son wishes to know his mother obsessed, even if she is.

And she was not. She was not.

'Clankeep,' I said abruptly. 'Well enough, then let us go. We owe this monarch more than a bed of leaves and bloodied turf.'

A muscle ticked in Ian's jaw. 'Aye,' he said tersely; no more.

I went off to fetch the horses.

Once, individual keeps had been scattered throughout Homana, springing up like toadstools across the land. Once, they had even reached a finger here and there into

19

neighboring Ellas, when Shaine's *qu'mahlin* had been in effect. The purge had resulted in the destruction of Cheysuli holdings as well as much of the race itself; later the Solindish king, Bellam, had usurped the Lion Throne and laid waste to Homana in the name of Tynstar, Ihlini sorcerer, and devotee of the god of the netherworld. With Carillon in exile and the Cheysuli hunted by Solindish, Ihlini and Homanan alike, what remained of the Cheysuli was nearly destroyed completely. The keeps had been sundered into heaps of shattered stone and shreds of painted cloth.

My legendary grandsire had, thank the gods, come home again to take back his stolen throne; his return ended Solindish and Ihlini domination and Shaine's purge. Freed of the threat of extirpation, the Cheysuli had also come home from secret keeps and built Homanan ones again. Clankeep itself, spreading across the border between woodlands and meadowlands, had gone up after Donal succeeded to the Lion on Carillon's death. And though the Cheysuli were granted freedom to live where they chose after decades of outlawry, they still preferred the closeness of the forests. Clankeep, ringed by unmortared walls of undressed, gray-green stone, was the closest thing to a city the Cheysuli claimed.

As always, I felt the familiar admixture of emotions as we entered the sprawling keep: sorrow – a trace of trepidation – a fleeting sense of anger – an undertone of pride. A skein of raw emotions knotted itself inside my soul . . . but mostly, more than anything, I knew a tremendous yearning to belong as *Ian* belonged.

Clankeep is the heart of the Cheysuli, regardless that my father rules from Homana-Mujhar. It is Clankeep that feeds the spirit of each Cheysuli; Clankeep where the *shar tahls* keep the histories, traditions and rituals clear of taint. It is here they guard the remains of the prophecy of the Firstborn, warding the fragmented hide with all the power they can summon.

And it was here at Clankeep that Niall of Homana longed to spend his days, for all he was prince of the land.

Because then he would be Cheysuli.

The rain began again, though falling with less force than before. This was more of a mist, kiting on the wind. Sheets of it drifted before my horse, shredded by the gusts. It muffled the sounds of the Keep and drove the Cheysuli inside their painted pavilions.

Except for Isolde. I should have known; 'Solde adores the rain, preferring thunder and lightning in abundance. But this misting shower, I knew, would do; it was better than boring sunlight.

'Ian! Niall! Both my *rujholli* at once?' She wore crimson, which was like her; it stood out against the damp grayness of the day as much as her bright ebullience did. I saw her come dashing through the drifting wet curtains as if she hardly felt them, damp wool skirts gathered up to show off furred boots of sleek dark otter pelt. Silver bells rimmed the cuffs of the boots, chiming as she ran. Matching bells were braided into thick black hair; like Ian, she was all Cheysuli. Even to the Old Blood in her veins.

'What is this?' She stopped as we did, putting out a hand to push a questing wet muzzle from her face; Ian's gray stallion was a curious sort, and oddly affectionate toward our sister. But then, perhaps it was the magic in her showing. 'The *king* stag!' Yellow eyes widened as she looked up at Ian and me. 'How did you come by this?'

'Solde seemed untroubled by the rain, falling harder now, that pasted hair against scalp and dulled the shine of all her bells. One hand still on the stallion's muzzle, she waited expectantly for an explanation.

I blew a drop of water off the end of my nose. ''Solde, you have eyes. The king stag, aye, and brought down by Ian's hand—' I paused '—in a manner of speaking.'

Ian glared. 'What nonsense is this? "*In a manner of speaking.*" I took him down with a single arrow! *You* were there.'

'How kind of you to recall it.' I smiled down at 'Solde. 'He set Tasha on me the moment I prepared to loose my own arrow, and the cat spoiled my shot.'

21

'Solde laughed, smothered it with a hand, then attempted, unsuccessfully, to give Ian a stern glance of remonstration. At three years younger than Ian and two years older than I, she did what she could to mother us both. Though I had my own mother in Homana-Mujhar, 'Solde and Ian did not; Sorcha was long dead.

Rain fell harder yet. My chestnut gelding snorted and shook himself, jostling all my bones. I was already a trifle stiff from Tasha's mock attack; I needed no further reminding of human fragility. ''Solde, do you mind if we go into Ian's pavilion? You may like the rain, but we have been out in it longer than I prefer.'

Her slim brown fingers caressed the crown bedecking the king stag's head. 'So fine, so fine . . . a gift for our *jehan*?' She asked it of Ian, whose stallion bore the stag before the Cheysuli saddle.

'He will be pleased, I think,' Ian agreed. ''Solde, Niall has the right of it. I will shrink like an old wool tunic if I stay out in this downpour a moment longer.'

'Solde stepped aside, shaking her head in disappointment, and all the bright bells rang. 'Babies, both of you, to be so particular about the weather. *Warriors* must be prepared for anything. *Warriors* never complain about the weather. *Warriors—*'

''Solde, be still,' Ian suggested, calmly reining his stallion toward the nearest pavilion. 'What you know of warriors could be fit into an acorn.'

'No,' she said, 'at least a walnut. Or so Ceinn tells me.'

The stallion was stopped short, so short my own mount nearly walked into the dappled rump, which is not something I particularly care to see happen around Ian's prickly stallion. But for once the gray did nothing.

Ian, however, did. 'Ceinn?' He twisted in the saddle and looked back at our smug-faced sister. 'What has *Ceinn* to say about how much you know of warriors?'

'Quite a lot,' she answered off-handedly. 'He has asked me to be his *cheysula*.'

'*Ceinn?*' Ian, knowing the warriors better than I, could

22

afford to sound astonished; all I could do was stare. 'Are you sure he said *cheysula* and not *meijha*?'

'The words do have entirely different sounds,' 'Solde told him pointedly, which would not please Ian any at all. But then, of course, she did not mean to. 'And I do know the difference.'

Ian scowled. 'Isolde, he has said nothing to me about it.'

'You have been in Mujhara,' she reminded him. 'For weeks. Months. And besides, he is not required to say anything to you. It is *me* for whom he wishes to offer.'

Ian, still scowling, cast a glance at me. 'Well? Are you going to say nothing to her?'

'Perhaps I might wish her luck,' I answered gravely. 'Whenever has anything we have said to her made the slightest amount of difference?'

'Oh, it has,' Isolde said. 'You just never noticed.'

Ian shut his eyes. 'Her mind, small as it is, astonishes me with its capacity for stubbornness, once a decision is made.' Eyes open again, he twisted his mouth in a wry grimace of resignation. 'Niall has the right of it: nothing we say will make any difference. But – why Ceinn?'

'Ceinn pleases me,' she answered simply. 'Should there be another reason?'

Ian glanced at me, and I knew our thoughts ran along similar paths: for a woman like our sister, a free Cheysuli woman with only bastard ties to royalty, there need be no other reason.

For the Prince of Homana, however, there were multitudinous other reasons. Which was why I had been cradle-betrothed to a cousin I had never seen.

Gisella was her name. Gisella of Atvia. Daughter of Alaric himself, and my father's sister, Bronwyn.

I smiled down at my Cheysuli half-sister. 'No, 'Solde. No other reason. If he pleases you, that is enough for Ian and me.'

'Aye,' Ian agreed glumly. 'And now that you have taken us by surprise, 'Solde, as you intended all along, may we get out of the rain?'

23

'Solde grinned the grin that Ian usually wore. 'There is a fire in your pavilion, *rujho*, and hot honey brew, fresh bread, cheese and a bit of venison.'

Ian sighed. 'You knew we were coming.'

'Solde laughed. 'Of course I did. Tasha told me.'

And with those well-intentioned words, my sister once more reminded me even she claimed gifts that I could not.

CHAPTER TWO

The rain began to fall a trifle harder. Isolde flapped a hand at us both. 'Go in, go in, before the food and drink grow cold. I have my own fire to tend, and then I will come back.'

She was gone, crimson skirts dyed dark by the weight of the rain. I heard the chime of bells as 'Solde ran toward her pavilion (did she share it now with Ceinn?) and reflected the sound suited my sister. There was nothing of dark silence about Isolde.

'Go on,' Ian told me. 'Old Newlyn will wish to see the stag now in order how best to judge the preparation. There is no need for you to get any wetter. Tasha will keep you company.'

Ian did not bother to wait for my answer; much as I dislike to admit it, he is accustomed to having me do as he tells me to. Prince of Homana – liege man; one would think Ian did *my* bidding, but he does it only rarely. Only when it suits that which he believes appropriate to a liege man's conduct.

I watched him go much as 'Solde had gone, fading into the wind and rain like a creature born of both. And she had the right of it, my *rujholla*; warriors did not complain about the weather. Warriors were prepared for anything.

Or perhaps it was just that they knew how to make themselves look prepared, thereby fooling us all.

I grinned and swung off my gelding, looping the reins over a wooden picket-stake before the pavilion doorflap. As I pulled the flap back, Tasha moved by me into the interior, damp fur slicking back against muscle and bone as she pressed briefly against my leg. I wondered if she hated the rain as most housecats did; but then, she would hardly thank me for comparing her to a common creature such as knew the tame freedom of Mujhara's alleys and the corridors of Homana-Mujhar.

Ian's pavilion was dyed a pale saffron color. The exterior bore a stylized painting of a mountain cat in vermilion, honoring his *lir*. The interior was illuminated by the small fire 'Solde had lighted, but because of the gray of the day the shadows lay deep and thick. Trunks merged with walls and tapestries, the divider curtain with the faint haze of silver woodsmoke. Nothing seemed of substance except the fire in the cairn.

Tasha wasted no time. She stretched her damp, substantial length upon the silver-blue pelt of a snow bear and began to lick herself dry. Unfortunately, I could not do the same with my own soaked skin, not having the proper tongue.

Wet leathers smell. So do wet mountain cats. Between myself and Ian's *lir*, there was little left that did not offend my nose. And because Ian and I were not at all of a size, me being both a hand-span taller and at least thirty pounds heavier, I could not borrow dry leathers from one of his clothing chests. So I wrapped myself up in yet another bear pelt, this one chestnut-brown, and hunched down beside the fire with my back to the doorflap. I poured a cup of hot honey brew and inhaled the pungent steam.

'Ian.' The voice outside startled me into nearly spilling my drink. 'Ian, we must talk. About your *rujholli*'s future and the future of the Lion—' Without waiting for the word admitting entrance, the man who spoke jerked aside the doorflap and ducked inside. 'Your decision can wait no long—'

He broke off at once as I turned on my knees to look at him. He was a stranger to me; clearly, I was not to him. And neither was his subject.

I rose, shedding bear pelt, and faced him directly. He was young, but several years older than I. Quite obviously all Cheysuli and just as obviously all warrior. He wore leathers, damp at the shoulders, dyed the color of beech leaves. His

26

gold bore the incised shapes of a rock bear, a breed smaller than that most commonly found in Homana, but doubly deadly. I had not heard of a warrior bonding with a rock bear for years.

By the *lir* I judged the man. And by the look of him, he was not one to allow another man time to speak when he had words of his own in his mouth. Even in all its youth, his face was hard, made of sharp angles, sharper than is common. His nose was a blade that sliced his face in half. There was the faint tracery of an old scar cutting the flesh at the corner of one eye. Though not so much older than I in years, I knew he was decades older in self-confidence.

But I have learned how tall men can occasionally intimidate shorter men. I reached out and took up the weapon. 'Aye?' I asked. 'You spoke of me?'

I waited. Dull color stained his dark face darker, but only for a moment. The yellow eyes veiled themselves at once; he was not a man I could intimidate with height *or* rank. But then I should have known better than to try; Cheysuli are intimidated by no one.

''Solde said her *rujholli* was here.' He gave up nothing in manner or speech.

'He is,' I agreed. 'Did she not say – *both*?'

He judged me. I could see it. He *judged* me, as if he sought something in my face, my voice, my eyes. And then I saw the brief glance at my left ear, naked of gold, and knew the judgment reached.

Or perhaps merely *recalled*, as if it were no new thing. 'No,' he said smoothly. 'She mentioned only Ian.'

My fingers clenched briefly on the cup; carefully, I unlocked the stiffened joints. With effort, I kept my voice from reflecting the pain his casual words had caused. That much I had learned from my father; kingcraft often requires delicacy of speech as well as subterfuge. This meeting would afford me the chance to practice both. 'My *rujholli* is with Newlyn. But if you would prefer it, you may wait here for his return.' I paused. 'Or leave your message with me.'

27

I knew he would not. I could smell it on him: a great need for confidence, secrecy; his manner bespoke an arrested anticipation. Whatever news he had for Ian was important to them both. And would therefore be important to me as well, I thought, a trifle mystified; I wondered anew at the stranger's attitude.

'With you?' He nearly smiled. And then he did, clearly, and I saw he was not so much older than I after all. 'My thanks, but no. I think not, my lord; it is better done in private.'

He spoke politely, but I knew well enough what he did. Cheysuli warriors only rarely give rank to another, and then only to a Homanan such as my grandsire had been. To another *warrior*, never, because Cheysuli are born and remain equal until they die. And so he reminded me, as perhaps he meant to, that he viewed me as nothing more than a Homanan.

An unblessed man, as lirless Homanans are called. Well, perhaps he is not so wrong.

Politely, he bowed his head in subtle acknowledgment of my rank. It grated in my soul, that acknowledgment; I would trade every Homanan rank in the world for acceptance in all the clans.

'Tell your brother Ceinn has words for him,' he said quietly, using the Homanan tongue as if I were deaf to the Cheysuli. 'And forgive me for interrupting.'

He was gone before I could stop him; before I could say a word about my sister's marriage. It was not my place to say nay or yea to the union; Cheysuli women are free to take what warrior they will, but there was little good in making no effort to like the man she would wed.

Well, the effort would have to wait.

The cup was cool in my hand. It would be easy enough to pour out the cold liquor and refill my cup with hot, but suddenly I wanted no liquor, no food, no pavilion filled with my brother's *lir*. Thanks to Ceinn and his careful words, I wanted nothing to do with anyone.

Tasha still lay on the pelt. She had interrupted the

28

grooming ritual to look at me with the fixed, feral gaze of the mountain cat, as if she sought to read my mind. That she could read Ian's I knew, but mine was closed to her. As much as hers was to me, and always would be.

Abruptly, I set down the cup and went back out into the rain. At once I shivered, but did not allow it to turn me from my intention. I jerked the reins from the picket-stake and swung up into the wet Homanan saddle.

Homanan this, Homanan that – it is no wonder the Cheysuli look at me with doubt!

'Niall!' Ian, coming through the rain, lacked both stallion and stag. '*Rujho—*'

I cut him off. 'I am for Mujhara after all. I have no taste for Clankeep today.' I reined my fractious chestnut around. 'Ceinn came looking for you.'

Black brows rose a trifle; what I looked for in his face was missing. There was no guilt in my brother, no embarrassment, that he discussed me with others behind my back.

But I wonder . . . what does he say?

Ian shrugged, dismissing Isolde's warrior. 'Niall, stay the night, at least. Why go back in this rain?'

'The rain has stopped.' It had, even as we spoke, but the air was heavy with the promise of more. 'Ian, just – just let me be.' It came out rather lamely, which irritated me even more. '*Rujho . . .* let me be.'

He did. I saw the consternation in his face and the brief tightening of his mouth, but he said nothing more. One brown hand slapped my chestnut's rain-darkened rump, and I was away at last.

Away. Again. Away. Gods, how I hate running—

—and yet, as always, it seemed the only answer.

I stopped running at sunset because my horse went lame. Not far from Mujhara – I could see torchlights just ahead – I pushed myself out of the damp saddle with effort (wet leather against wet leather hinders movement considerably) and dropped down into sucking mud. I swore, jerked boots free, slipped and slid around to the right foreleg to inspect

29

the injured hoof. The gelding nosed at me and snorted as I insisted he lift the leg. I tried to ignore damp questing nostrils at the back of my neck as I dug balled mud from his hoof.

A stone had wedged itself in the tender frog of the hoof. Cold, stiff fingers did not accomplish much; I unsheathed my knife and dug carefully at the stone until I pried it loose. The frog was bruised. It was nothing that would not heal in two or three days, but for now riding him would only worsen the lameness and delay recovery. And so I took up the reins and proceeded to lead my horse into the outskirts of Mujhara.

The city is centuries older than I. My father once told me the Cheysuli originally built Mujhara, before they turned from castles and houses to the freedom of the forests. But the Homanans claimed their ancestors had built it, though artifacts of Cheysuli origin had been found in old foundations. I could not say who had the right of it, as both races had lived in Homana for hundreds and hundreds of years, but I thought it likely the Cheysuli had built at least Homana-Mujhar, for the palace was full of *lir*-shapes carved in rose-colored stone and rich dark wood.

Mujhara itself, however, resembles little of the city that once held court upon the land. Originally curtain walls had ringed the city, offering protection against the enemy. But Mujhara was like a small boy growing to manhood all at once, without warning. It had burst free of childhood's bones and sinews with new adult growth and strength, as I myself had so dramatically two years before; now the city walls and barbican gates lay nearly half a league yet inside the outskirts, leaving hundreds outside the Mujhar's official protection.

But we had not been at war for nearly twenty years, and all the treaties held. Homana was at peace.

The gelding limped behind me as I led him through the narrow, mud-clogged streets. Inside the walls the streets were cobbled. Outside they were not, since no one could say what dwellings might go up overnight, thereby creating

30

new streets. Ordinarily the ground was dry and hardpacked, or frozen solid in winter. But now it was only fall, too early for true winter. And so I slogged through the mud with my limping horse behind me.

I headed straight toward the nearest gate leading into the inner city, but nothing in Mujhara is straight. Streets and alleys and closes wind around and around like Erinnish knotwork, lacking beginning and end. So the Prince of Homana and his royal mount also wound around and around.

In fall, the light dies quickly. With the sun gone the streets lay shadow-clad in deepening darkness. I frowned against those few torches that threw inadequate illumination from dwellings into the street, for they played tricks on the eyes by hiding real obstacles even as they created others.

Your own fault, I reminded myself. *Ian offered a warm pavilion, dry pallet, good food, company, drink.*

Well, so would Homana-Mujhar, providing the horse allowed me to reach it before the night was through.

The rising yowl of an angry cat broke into my thoughts. The sound came closer still, rising in volume as well as tone; I turned, searching, and saw the dark streak come running at me from out of the shadowed wynd. Behind the cat came a dog singularly dedicated to catching his prey. Neither animal paid mind to me or my horse, both intent upon the moment. The cat flew by me, closely followed by the dog, and as I turned to watch them go I came face to face with a cloaked and hooded man.

I stopped short. So did my horse; he nearly walked over me. As it was, I felt hoof against heel before I could step away.

The cloaked figure did not attempt to move out of my way, nor did he offer apology. He stood his ground. I thought perhaps he mistook me for another; when he put out a restraining hand as I made to go on around him I knew he did not, and I closed my free hand around the hilt of my knife.

'A moment of your time,' said the cloaked figure quietly.

The gelding, so close behind me, snorted loudly into my left ear and showered me with mucus as I jumped and swore. The stranger pushed the hood from his head and let it settle on his shoulders. I could see his face dimly in the diffused light of the torches. He was smiling; my horse's response had amused him.

I let the merest hint of knife blade show and hoped my voice sounded steadier than I felt. Thieves and cutpurses abound in any city, even Mujhara, and I was not in an area I knew well. For that matter, only rarely do I go into the city alone at all. Ian is almost always with me, or others from the palace.

'I carry no wealth,' I challenged, attempting to sound older and more confident than I was. 'I have only this horse, which is far from a valuable beast at the moment. Else I would be riding.'

The smile widened a little. 'If I wanted your horse and your wealth, my young lord, I would take both. As it is, I desire only a moment of your time. But first, let us have better light. I would let you see to whom you speak.'

I opened my mouth to repudiate his arrogance and his demands upon my time; I said nothing. I said nothing because I *could not*, being struck dumb by the illumination he conjured out of the air.

A hand. The merest flick of eloquent fingers, sketching, and a rune glowed in the air. Deepest, richest purple, swallowing the darkness and creating light as bright as day.

I thrust up an arm to block the sudden flame and fell back two steps. Briefly I felt the bulwark of my horse's chest behind me. But then he, too, took fright from the fire and shied badly, lunging away so quickly he jerked the reins free of my hand. I whirled, trying to catch him, but for the moment his lameness was forgotten. He wheeled and went back the way we had come, spraying thick clots of mud into the air and liberally daubing my clothing as well as my unshielded face.

But the horse was the least of my worries. Much as he had spun I also spun, but not away. Not yet. I faced the man instead, though admittedly only through utter astonishment and no particular measure of courage. But I could hardly see him through the brilliance of his rune.

The hand dropped back to his side, hidden in woolen folds of darkest blue. The rune remained: hissing, shedding tendrils of brilliant flame . . . and yet there was no heat. Only the bitter cold of harshest winter.

'There.' He was content with what he had wrought. 'Light, my lord. Illumination. Not in the manner to which you are accustomed, perhaps, but light nonetheless. Which would lead me to believe there is no Darkness in my sorcery if I can conjure Light.'

Illumination filled out the details of his face. He was an immensely attractive man, as some men are; not precisely *pretty*, but more than merely handsome. As a child he would have been beautiful. But he was no longer a child, and had not been for years.

Suspicion flared much as the rune flared, blinding and all-consuming. At once I looked for the telltale eyes and found the stories true. One blue. One brown. The eyes of a demon, men said of people with mismatched eyes; appropriate, in this case, for his name was linked with such. With Asar-Suti himself, the god of the netherworld, who made and dwells in darkness.

Black hair, worn loose and very long, was held back from his face by a narrow silver circlet. He was clean-shaven, as if he wished all to see his face and marvel at its clarity of features. No modest Ihlini, Strahan; he wore pride and power like a second cloak, and finer than any silk. I saw the glint of silver at one ear. His left, as if he mocked the *lir*-gold of the Cheysuli.

But then perhaps he mocked no one; he could not wear an earring in his right because he lacked the ear.

I took a single backward step. Stopped. Again, not because I found a sudden spurt of courage, but because I found I could not move. Facing him, seeing for myself what manner of man he was, I could not go immediately out of the sorcerer's presence.

Ensorcellment? Perhaps. But I choose to call it consuming fascination.

I licked my lips. Breath was harsh in my throat. It was difficult to swallow. A weight was pressing on my ribs. The contents of my belly threatened to become discontent with their surroundings.

The odd eyes watched me. Strahan judged, as Ceinn had judged. And, like Ceinn, the Ihlini saw I had no gold of my own. But then, undoubtedly, Strahan already knew quite well of my lack.

He smiled. I wondered how much of Tynstar was in him, his father, whom men claimed a handsome man. And his Solindish mother, Electra, who had been Carillon's wife and queen before Carillon had slain her. Oh aye, I wondered how much of Electra was in him, because she was in me as well.

'Kinsman.' Coolly, he acknowledged the blood between us. 'You must tender my regards to your father when I am done with you.'

I did not care for the implications in the statement. And yet I knew I stood little chance against him, whatever he chose to do. *Lirless*, I lacked the magic of my race. Nothing would turn the Ihlini's power if he chose to use it against me.

Strahan smiled again. Women, I knew, would be at once swallowed whole by the magnitude of his allure. *And* men. For a different reason, perhaps, but the results would be the same. Where Strahan had need of loyal servants, he would find them. He would *take* them. And use them up before he ever let them go.

'I have heard stories of you, Niall.' *That* did not serve to settle me at all. 'Tales of how the Prince of Homana, young as he is, bears a striking resemblance to Carillon. Of course it is in the blood, you being his grandson, but I wonder . . .' The smile showed itself again. There was speculation in his ill-matched eyes. 'When I knew him, he was an old man made older by my father's arts, and he was ill. Ill and dying, slowly, as the disease devoured him. But still a strong man, as strong as he could be.' Black brows

34

drew down a little beneath the silver circlet; he was judging me again, and using my grandsire as the point of comparison. Like my mother. Like so many *Homanans*. 'He was the enemy, of course, a man I desired to slay – *especially* once he had slain my father,' the cool voice hardened, 'but in the end, Osric of Atvia did the slaying for me.' Briefly, one corner of his beautiful mouth twisted in an expression of irritation. 'And now, in some strange manner, I see I must face Carillon again.'

'No.' Inwardly, I drew in as deep a breath as I could. It did not dull the fear, but it filled the emptiness of my belly with something other than utter panic.

Strahan's arched brows rose. 'No?'

I wanted to clear my throat before I tried my voice again. I did not, because I knew he would take it as a sign of my fear. And then, looking into the sorcerer's face, I no longer cared what he thought or what he knew.

This man is kin to me . . . Ihlini, perhaps, and powerful, but still a man like me.

'You face *me*, Strahan,' I told him as evenly as I could. 'Not my grandsire. Not my father. *I* am the one you face.'

The Ihlini smiled a little. '*You*, then.' Casually said, as if I hardly mattered. So easily was I discounted by Tynstar's son. 'Again; you will tender my regards to your father, the Mujhar.'

I smiled. I felt it stretch my lips a little, and heard the steadiness of my voice. As even as I could want it. 'Be certain I will, Strahan. And know he will be pleased you have shown yourself in Mujhara. He has sought you many years.'

'And will seek me many more.' He was patently unruffled by my bravado. 'What is between Donal and me will be settled one day, but not tonight. Tonight I came seeking you.'

'And if I said I had neither the time nor the inclination to trade empty threats with you?'

Strahan laughed. The rune hissed and spat and pulsed against the darkness, as if it laughed as well. 'The wolf's

35

cub hackles, snapping; the falcon's hatchling spreads his wings and tries to fly.' The laughter stopped as quickly as it had begun. Softly, he said, 'A suggestion, my lord prince: waste no effort in displays of dominance when you have no *lir* to mimic.'

From a Homanan, from a Cheysuli, the taunts were bad enough. But from an *Ihlini sorcerer*—

Rage roared up from inside my head. I heard a voice shouting at Strahan, calling him foul names in Homanan and Old Tongue alike. That much I knew of the language. I felt my body take two steps forward, saw my hand rise up as if to clutch at the Ihlini's throat. And then my hands struck through the flaming rune and the bones filled up with pain.

Cold. Not hot. *Cold.*

I cried out. I felt myself crushed to my knees in the mud of the streets. The rune ate through leather and flesh to my bones and turned my blood to ice.

Through the haze of pain and the glare of living flame, I saw the Ihlini's inhumanly beautiful face. Dimly, I saw how he watched me, glinting eyes narrowed, black brows drawn down as if he studied a specimen. Waiting. Watching. Examining the results of the specimen's foolishness.

I watched him watching me and remembered who he was.

As well as *what* he was.

At last, he spoke. 'Not now. Not yet. *Later.*'

No more than that. A fluid gesture of one hand and the rune ran away from my body, spilling out of my flesh like blood from an opened vein. It ran down my thighs to splash against the mud, pooling like rancid water. Puddled. Ran in upon itself. And then hurled itself upward to renew its form in the shadows of the night.

Strahan looked down upon me as I knelt in the mud of the street. Once again he smiled. I saw genuine amusement and a trace of pleasure in his eyes; a look of contented reminiscence.

'Your father once knelt to me,' he said in a perfect contentment. He did not gloat. I think he did not need to.

36

'Did he never tell you?' A nod of his head as I held my silence; it was the least I owed my father. 'No, he would never say it; not to you, but it is true. And now his son as well.' Strahan paused. 'His *Homanan* son; the Cheysuli would never do it.'

So easily he reached into my soul and touched that aspect of my character which I hated. Not my brother. Never Ian. No – *myself*, for resenting the gifts Ian – and others – claimed. Gifts I should claim myself.

I wrenched myself from my unintended posture of obeisance. A small thing, to face the sorcerer standing, but the beginnings of rebellion. It was the least I would offer him.

'State your business,' I said flatly. I have learned something of royal impatience from my father, who hates the demands of diplomacy. Too often he is trapped by endless petitioners.

Strahan's eyes narrowed a trifle. 'You are betrothed to your cousin, Gisella of Atvia: *do not wed the girl.*'

Stunned, I waited for something more. And when he offered nothing, I laughed. It was unintended. The situation hardly warranted levity, but he caught me so off-guard there was nothing else I could do.

I laughed at him. And Strahan did not like it.

'You *fool*,' he snapped. 'I could grind you into the mud before you could utter a word, and never bestir myself.'

Suddenly, he was no longer so awe-inspiring. I had touched a nerve. 'Do it,' I challenged, emboldened by his unexpected vulnerability. 'What *better* way of keeping me from wedding my Atvian cousin?'

Something hurled me flat against the ground, pinning me on my back. Half-swallowed in mud, I lay there, staring up at the angry sorcerer. 'Drown,' he said between clenched teeth. '*Drown* in all this mud!'

I could not move. I felt the ground shift beneath my flattened body. It heaved itself up from under me, lapped over my limbs and began to inch up my torso. I felt it in my ears; at the corners of my eyes.

But even as I drowned, I was aware of a nagging question. Why did it matter to *Strahan* if I wed Gisella or not?

The mud was at my mouth. My body was nearly swallowed whole. I felt the first finger reaching into my nostrils. I shouted, but my mouth filled with the mud.

Drowning—

Insanely, I did not think of dying for itself. I thought instead of disappointing others by the helplessness of my dying. *Ah gods, not like* this *– Carillon would* never *die like this – in such futility.*

Abruptly, the rune winked out. Darkness filled my head.

I thought it was the mud. I thought it might be death. And then I realized that though I lay flat on my back in the street, I was free of the drowning mud.

I lay there. All was silence, except for my ragged breathing. The abrupt disappearance of the brilliant rune left my eyes mostly blinded; I saw nothing, not even the light from nearby dwellings. Only darkness.

I twisted. Thrust one shaking hand into the ooze and slowly pushed myself up. Mud clung to me from head to toe, but it no longer threatened to drown me. I was weary unto death, as if all the strength had been sucked from me. I was cold, wet, filthy, stinking of my fear . . . and angry that I was so inconsequential a foe for the Ihlini.

'Why should *I* do it?' Strahan asked. 'Why should I trouble myself with *you*?'

I twitched. Spun again to face him. I had believed myself alone; that Strahan had gone into the darkness. And then I saw the ghostly luminescence of his face in the light of the quarter moon, and I realized the clouds had broken at last.

I spat out mud. My reprieve made me momentarily brave. 'I think I understand, Ihlini. If I wed Gisella and get sons on her, I have added yet another link to the chair. Another yarn to the tapestry of the Firstborn.' A muscle jumped once in his cheek. 'Aye, that *is* it! Atvian blood mixed with that of Homana, Solinde and the Cheysuli brings us decidedly closer to fulfilling the prophecy.' Suddenly, I laughed; I understood it at last. 'By keeping me from wedding Gisella you break the link before it is truly forged.'

'*Wed* her,' he said sharply, abruptly changing course. 'Wed the Atvian girl; I do not care. One day you will come to me; *I invite you now to do it*.' His odd eyes narrowed a little. 'If you have sons, I will make them mine. I will *take* them . . . but I think you will never get sons upon Gisella because the others will see you dead.'

'*Others*?' I could not help the blurted question. 'Who but *you* would wish me dead?'

It was Strahan's turn to laugh. 'Has your father taught you nothing? Do they keep you in ignorance, thinking to ward your pride? Not any easy thing to know, is it, that you are the center of the storm.' Silver glinted at his single ear. 'Better to ask: who would *not* wish you dead.'

'Not—?' I whispered hollowly, as if I were a puppet and he the puppetmaster.

Strahan pursed his lips in consideration. Black brows rose below the circlet. 'Or, if not *dead* . . . at least replaced by another.'

Replaced. Me? But it was not possible. I was the Prince of Homana, legitimate son of Donal the Mujhar and Aislinn the Queen, Carillon's daughter. The proper blood was in my veins. There were no other legitimate children; the Queen was barren, the physicians said. There was and always would be only me. How could they think to replace me, and – by the gods! – with *whom*?

One hand parted the darkness and filled it with light again. 'Shall I prophesy for you, my lord prince?' asked the compelling tone. 'Shall I show you what will come to be, no matter how hard you try to rewrite what the gods themselves have written?'

He did not wait for my answer. He lifted the hand again and lent it the fluid, eloquent language of brush against living canvas. I saw the fingers move, forming shapes amidst the darkness.

Colors poured out from Strahan's fingertips: argent purple, deepest lavender, palest silver lilac. And the lurid red of fresh-spilled blood.

He painted a picture of living flame: a rampant Homanan lion and a compact Cheysuli warbow. All rich in detail, even to the curling tongue of the gape-mouthed lion and the ornamentation of the warbow. They hung against the air as if they waited. As if I had only to pluck the bow from the darkness and loose an arrow at the lion.

I stared. Swallowed hard. There were no words in my mouth. All I knew was a sense of awed, awful discovery: the picture he painted was a true one, regardless that the artist was enemy.

'The Homanans want no Cheysuli shapechanger on the throne,' Strahan said above the hissing of the flame. 'The Cheysuli want no unblessed Homanan on the throne. But Donal's son is *both and neither*; what do *you* think will happen?' The parti-colored eyes were eerie in the light of the glowing shapes. 'Look to your people, Niall,' he said. So softly, he spoke; so *gentle* was his tone. 'Look to your friends . . . your enemies . . . *your kin* – lest they form an alliance against you.'

Smoothly, he bled together the shapes of bow and lion. And out of the flame I saw born the face of my brother – and the face I knew as my own.

'I think I need not trouble myself with you,' Strahan said in quiet satisfaction. 'I will let the others do it for me.'

CHAPTER THREE

'You should have come to me *first*.' She had both temper and tongue to complement the red-gold brilliance of her hair. 'Do you know how I have worried since that horse returned without you?'

That horse had indeed returned (without me, of course) and my absence had set the palace into an uproar. Rather, my lady mother had. Most of the Mujharan Guard had been stripped from better duty and sent out looking for me, as if I were a foolish, spoiled child gone wandering in the streets. And they had found me, some of them, just as I approached the gates of Homana-Mujhar. It had been a humiliating experience trying to explain how my horse and I had come to be separated. Especially since I could say nothing of Strahan's presence in the city. Not to them. Not at once. Not until I faced my father.

But now, looking at my mother's pale face, I knew it had been worse than humiliating for her. Always she worried. Always she fretted, saying Ian alone was not enough to guard me against misfortune. This would give her fuel for the fire.

Deep down, I was touched she cared so much, knowing it arose out of insecurity because she had borne only a single son, but mostly I was resentful. Oh, aye, she meant well by it, but there were times the weight she placed upon me was nearly too much to bear.

You may not be his son she often said, *but you bear his blood, his bone, even his flesh. Have you not looked in the silver plate?*

Oh aye, I had, many times. And each time I saw the same thing: a crude vessel lacking luster, lacking polish. But no

41

one saw the tarnish because it was overlaid with the shining patina of *Carillon*.

Even now she gave me no time to explain; to say a word to my father as he came into my chamber and shut the heavy door.

And so I let the resentment speak for me. 'Would you have me remain in my befouled state, then? *Look* at me!' I had gotten as far as shedding muddy boots, soaked doublet; I faced her in filthy leather leggings and damp linen shirt. Thin rivulets of muddied water ran down to stain the carpeted floor.

'Niall.' That from my father; that only. But it was more than enough.

I looked back at my mother's taut face. 'I am sorry,' I told her contritely, meaning it. 'But I wanted to bathe and change first, before I came to you.'

'It *could* have waited. I have seen men in worse conditions, and they were not my son.' The strain showed at the corners of eyes and mouth. She was still beautiful in a way harpers and poets had tried to describe for years, but it was a fragile, brittle beauty, as if she might break with the weight of who and what she was. Aislinn of Homana, daughter of Carillon; once a princess, now a queen, and the mother of her beloved father's grandson.

I think she judged herself solely by the fact she had borne Carillon an heir. A *true* heir, that is; a man with much of his blood, not a Cheysuli warrior handpicked because Carillon had no choice. No, my mother did not view herself as woman, wife, mother or queen. Merely as a means to perpetuate her father's growing legend.

The resentment died as I looked at her. I could not name what rose to take its place, for there was no single emotion. Just a jumble of them, tangled up together like threads of a tapestry; the back side, not the front, with none of the pattern showing.

I released a breath all at once. 'I am well. Only wet and dirty. And more than a little hungry.' I looked at my father, longing to tell him at once of my confrontation with Strahan.

42

But I would not so long as my mother was in the room. I saw no good in giving her yet another thing to fret about.

'Ian?' he asked.

I shrugged, turning away to strip out of my clammy shirt. 'At Clankeep. I think he will stay the night.' I heard the servants in the antechamber, filling up the cask-tub with hot, scented water. Oil of cloves, from the smell of it.

'Niall—' It was my mother again, moving toward me, but she did not finish. My father put his hands on her shoulders and turned her away from me. He did it gently enough, but I saw the subtle insistence in his grasp.

'Leave him to me, Aislinn. We have guests to entertain.'

Womanlike, she instantly put a hand to the knot of red-gold hair coiled at her neck to tend her appearance. There was no need. She was immaculate, as always. The bright hair, as yet undulled by her thirty-six years, was contained in a pearl-studded net of golden wire. Her velvet gown was plain white, unadorned save for the beaded golden girdle and the gold torque at her throat. My father's bride-gift to her some twenty years before.

'So we do.' Her voice was flat, almost colorless. 'But I wonder that you choose to host them at all.'

'Kings do what kings must do.' I heard an edge in my father's voice as well. 'We are at peace with Atvia, Aislinn; let us not break the alliance with discourtesy.'

Her eyes flicked back to me. Great gray eyes, long-lidded and somnolent. Electra's eyes, they said, recalling the mother's beauty. But in conjuring Electra's name they also conjured Tynstar's.

'This concerns you as well, Niall,' she said abruptly. 'More so than *us*, when it comes to that. And if your father does not tell you the whole of it, come to me. I will.'

The tension between them was palpable. I looked from mother to father, but his face was masked to me. Well, I could wait all night. One thing he had bequeathed to me was more than my share of stubbornness.

My mother went to the door and tugged it open before either my father or I could aid her. She lifted heavy skirts

43

and swept out of the door at once, leaving me to shut it and face my father alone at last.

My father. The Mujhar of Homana he was, but more and less than that to me. He was a Cheysuli warrior.

A son looking upon his father rarely sees the man, he sees the parent. The man who sired him, not the individual. I was no different. Day in, day out I saw him, and yet I did not. I saw what I was accustomed to seeing; what the son saw in the father, the king, the warrior. Too often I did not see the *man*.

Nor did I really know him.

Now, I looked. I saw the face that had helped mold my own, and yet showed nothing of that molding. The bones were characteristically angular, hard, almost sharp; even in light-skinned Cheysuli, the heritage is obvious in the shape of the bones beneath the flesh. The responsibilities of a Mujhar and a warrior dedicated to his *tahlmorra* had incised lines between black brows, fanned creases from yellow eyes, deepened brackets beside the blade-straight nose. There was silver in his hair, pale as winter frost, but only a little; we age early only in that respect, and with infinite grace.

For the first time in a very long time I looked at the scars in his throat and recalled how Strahan had once tried to slay my father by setting a demon-hawk on him. Sakti, her name was, and she had set her talons true, even as she died. But my father had not, thanks to Finn, my kinsman, and the gods who gave us the earth magic.

Earth magic. Another thing I lacked.

He was tall, my father, but not so tall as I, with all of Carillon's bulk. He lacked my weight, though no one would name him a small man; Cheysuli males rarely measure less than six feet, and he was three fingers taller yet. He was certainly more graceful than I, being more subtle in his movements. I wondered if that total ease of movement came with the race or age. The gods knew I had yet to discover it.

Beneath lowered lids, as I began to undress, I watched my father, and wondered how he had felt as Carillon bequeathed him the Lion Throne. I wondered what he had thought, knowing so much of Cheysuli tradition would have to be altered to fit the prophecy. To fit *him*: the first Cheysuli Mujhar in four hundred years.

I would be the second.

He said nothing of my mother to me. A private man, my father, though open enough about some things. Just – not about what I wanted to hear.

'Well?' That said, he waited.

I stripped out of my leggings and walked naked into the antechamber. Steam rose from the cask. The scent of cloves drifted into the air. And then I waved away the servants so my father and I could discuss things privately.

I considered telling him the whole of it, from the beginning of the hunt to my arrival, on foot, at Homana-Mujhar. But that would be unnecessarily perverse of me, and I thought the circumstances warranted more seriousness. So I took a shortcut straight to the matter of most importance to us both.

'I met a man tonight,' I began. 'A stranger, at least to me. But he had a message meant for the Prince of Homana.' I took up the soap and began to lather my muddy skin. 'He said I was not to wed my Atvian cousin.'

My father's motion to hook a stool over with one foot was arrested in mid-reach. He did not sit down at all but faced me squarely, an expression of astonishment mingled with genuine bafflement on his face.

After a moment of startled speculation, he frowned. 'How odd, that such a thing is said today.'

I dipped under the water to soak my hair; came up with water streaming down my face. 'Why only odd *today*?' I spat out soapy water and grimaced at the taste.

'Because the Atvians we host tonight are here upon business concerning the betrothal.' This time he finished hooking the stool over and sat down. 'It seems Alaric has decided it is time the betrothal became a marriage.'

I stared at him. The scent of cloves filled my nostrils. Water still ran down my face. But I did not try to wipe it away. 'Now?'

45

'As soon as can be.' He sighed, stretching out long legs. 'Alaric and I made an agreement nearly twenty years ago. He has every right to expect that agreement to be honored.'

His tone was a trifle dry. My father has no particular liking for Atvians, having fought them in the war; he has less affection for Alaric, the Lord of Atvia himself. For one, Alaric's brother had slain Carillon, making my father Mujhar. And Alaric himself, upon swearing fealty to Donal of Homana, had demanded my father's sister in marriage as a means to seal the alliance. Though my father had hated the idea, he had agreed at last because, in service to the prophecy of the Firstborn, he saw no other way of linking the proper bloodlines.

And to link them further, he had declared his firstborn son would wed the firstborn daughter of Bronwyn and Alaric.

Oh, aye, Alaric got the match he wanted. He even got the daughter, called Gisella. But no other. For Bronwyn died while birthing my half-Cheysuli cousin.

I looked at my father's face. He is a solemn man, the Mujhar, not much given to impulsiveness or high spirits. Once he might have been different, but responsibilities, I am told, can often change even the most ebullient of men. The gods knew he had known more of them than most, my father. He had had mother, father, uncle and Mujhar all stripped from him, in the name of the prophecy. In the name of Ihlini treachery.

Lir-gold shone on his bare arms. He was Mujhar of Homana, but he did not forsake his Cheysuli customs, even in apparel. Certain occasions warranted he put on Homanan dress, but mostly he wore the leathers of his race.

Our race.

I slid down against the curved wood of the cask and flipped the soap into the water. 'Well, I expected the marriage to be made one day. You never hid it from me, my *tahlmorra*.' I grinned; it was an old joke between us. 'Just – not *yet*.'

My father smiled. No man would call him *old*; he is not

so far past forty, but neither would a woman call him young. Still, his smile banished the gravity of his title and set him free again. 'No, not *yet*. But soon.' A glint of amusement showed in his yellow eyes. 'You have a little time. Atvian custom demands a proxy wedding before the true marriage is made.'

I frowned in distraction at a purplish bruise on my right knee. 'How soon will this proxy wedding be performed?'

'Oh, I think in the morning . . . I did say you had a *little* time.' The glint in his eyes was more pronounced.

'In the *morning*!' I stared at him in dismay. 'Without warning?'

He sighed. 'Aye, I would have preferred it myself. And that is what upsets your *jehana*. She swears it is a purposeful insult and that we should send them home at once until proper homage is made, along with a respectful request, since Alaric owes *me* fealty, and not the other way around.' His smile was wry; my mother, born to such things as royal rights and expectations, was much more cognizant of details my father thought less important. 'But Alaric's envoy says a message was sent some months ago, though it never arrived. Perhaps it was.' He shrugged, patently dubious. 'Regardless of that *and* the lack of proper homage, the betrothal was made in good faith. Alaric has the right to ask the wedding be performed. At seventeen, Gisella is old enough. Once the proxy ceremony is completed, you will go to Atvia to bring your *cheysula* home to a Homanan wedding.'

Cheysula. He used the Old Tongue word for wife. But his mouth shaped it differently than mine; like Ian, he had been keep-raised. They were very alike, my father and my brother. I was like neither of them.

As Strahan had taken infinite pains to point out.

Almost at once I forgot about *cheysulas* and proxy weddings. '*Jehan*,' the Cheysuli word slipped out more easily than usual. 'The man who told me not to wed Gisella—' I broke off a moment, not knowing how to say it. 'It was the Ihlini. *Jehan* – the man was Strahan.'

47

He stood up at once, my father; so quickly, so abruptly he overset the stool. I heard the thump of wood against stone. The hiss of his indrawn breath.

But 'Strahan' was all he said.

In the heat of the scented, steaming water, I was cold. To see that look in my father's eyes—

'Aye.' Mostly it was a whisper. '*Jehan*—'

'You are certain.' The tone was a whiplash of sound. No longer did I face my father. Nor did I face the Mujhar. What man I saw was a warrior filled up with a virulent hatred, dedicated to revenge.

'Certain,' I echoed. 'I saw his eyes: one blue, one brown. And he lacked an ear.'

'*Aye*, he lacks an ear! Finn made certain of *that* much before he died!'

He broke off. I saw the spasm of grief contort his face. Almost as quickly, the mask was back in place. But he did not veil his eyes. Perhaps he could not. And what I saw sent an icy finger down my spine. '*Jehan*—'

'By the gods, I have prayed that *ku'reshtin* would come within my grasp.' Both hands were extended. Fisted. I saw how the sinews stood up beneath the flesh; how the nails dug into the palms. 'By the *gods*, I have prayed for this!'

I had not known such hatred could live in my father. He can show anger, aye, and irritation, and more than a little intolerance of things he considers foolish, but to see such bitter hatred in his eyes, to hear it in his voice, made me a child again. It stripped me of size and confidence and made me small again.

I sat in the cask with water lapping around my chest and stared at the warrior who had sired me. And wondered what manner of man *I* might be had the Ihlini served me such pain and grief upon *my* platter.

'He did not harm you?'

Slowly, I shook my head. 'He – gave me a taste of his power. But he did me no lasting harm.' I thought again on his parting words to me and the vividness of his painting. True? Or false? A trick to undermine my trust in Homanans

48

and Cheysuli? More than likely. It was the Ihlini way.

And I knew it might succeed.

I looked away from my father. Replace me, Strahan had said. With another. Friends, enemies, kin. An alliance uniting them.

'Niall.' He reached down and caught my left arm, gripping me by the wrist. 'He *did not harm you?*'

'No.' I said it as calmly as I could. 'He said I was to tender you his regards.'

After a moment, my father released my arm. He swore beneath his breath. 'Aye, he would. Ever polite, is Strahan. Even when he kills.'

'But why *did* he let me live? Surely it would suit his plans better if I were not *in* his way to the throne?'

'You are not *in* his way, not really.' My father, looking infinitely older, shook his head and sighed. 'The gods know why, but it is an Ihlini trait to play with an enemy before the kill. They twist the mind before they twist the body, as if it makes the final snap that much more satisfying. Tynstar did it with Carillon for years, though in the end, as you know, Carillon slew Tynstar.' Of course I knew. It was all a part of the legend. 'It may be a perverse manifestation of the power.' He shrugged again. 'Who can say? Strahan did not let you live out of kindness. No. More like – anticipation.' His expression was very grim. 'It means he has other plans for you. It means you are part of his *game*. And when he is done playing with you, he will end it. As he ended it for Finn.'

When he is done playing with you, he will end it. I shivered. My father's tone was so matter-of-fact, so certain of Strahan's intentions. He did not shout or bluster or claim we would put an end to Strahan's plans. And it emphasized the Ihlini's power.

I recalled how Strahan had invited me to come to him, one day. I recalled how he had said he intended to take my sons. And I wondered how he could be so certain there would be sons to take, as well as that he would take them.

But mostly, I looked at my father. *What does Strahan mean to him?*

49

His face was stark. The man was a stranger to me. '*Jehan*.' I straightened in the cask. 'If − if I had known how much you hated him . . . I would have tried to slay him.'

He did nothing at all at once. He only stared down at me, as if he had not heard what I had said. In perfect stillness, perfect silence; a statue carved out of human flesh.

And then he said something in the Old Tongue, something that came out of his mouth on a rushing of breath, and I saw the tears forming in his eyes as he knelt down on one knee to grasp my hand in both of his.

'Never,' he said hoarsely. 'Never, *never*, Niall. He would slay you. He would slay you. He would take you from me as he has taken all the others, and I would be *alone*.'

I stared at him. His hands were cold, so cold, and I realized he was afraid. I had meant to comfort him, to offer what I could of loyalty. Instead, I had broken the fox from its den and set the hounds upon its trail.

By the gods, my father is afraid . . .

'How?' I asked, when I could. 'How could you be *alone* when you have so many others?'

'Name them,' he said unevenly. 'Say their names to me.'

'My *mother*!' I was amazed he could not do it for himself. 'Taj and Lorn. General Rowan. Ian and Isolde.' I stared at him. '*Jehan*, how could you be alone?'

His breath was harsh. 'I have them, aye, I have all of them: *cheysula*, *lir*, children, trusted general. But − it is not the same.' He rose abruptly, turning his back on me. His spine was rigid beneath leather jerkin and human flesh. Then, just as abruptly, he swung around to face me. 'Look what I have done to your *jehana*. I would offer her the sort of love she craves, if I could, but so much was burned out of me when Sorcha − died.' Even now, he could not speak the truth: that his Cheysuli *meijha*, Ian's and Isolde's mother, had slain herself because she could not bear to share him with a Homanan. 'There is much affection between Aislinn and me, of course, and honor, regard, respect − but that is not what she wants. Nor is it what she needs.'

50

His anguish was manifest. 'But I cannot offer falsehood to her when she is deserving of so much better.'

I listened in shocked silence, grateful I knew the truth at last, but unsettled at the hearing. He was an adult speaking to an adult, man to man, and yet I still felt so very young.

My father sighed and scraped a lock of black hair out of his eyes. 'As for Taj and Lorn, aye – I share everything with my *lir* a warrior should. But they are *lir*, not men. Not kin. As for Rowan—' He grimaced. 'Rowan and I work well together in the ordering of the realm, but we will never be easy together in personal things. I am not Carillon, whom he worshipped.' He bent and righted the stool. 'Ian and Isolde are everything a *jehan* could desire in his children. But I am the Mujhar of Homana, and the Homanans perceive them as bastards. It makes them different. It soils them in Homanan eyes, and that perception affects me. And so it leaves me only you, Niall.' He smiled a little, but it had a bittersweet twist. 'None of them are you. None of them are born of the prophecy.' I saw the trace of anguish in his eyes. 'None of them will know the things I have known. Not as *you* will know them.'

For a long moment I said nothing at all, being unable to speak. But when I could speak again, I asked a thing all men might desire to ask of warriors and Mujhars. 'Would you have it differently?'

My father laughed, but there was no humor in the sound – only pain. 'What warrior, looking fully into the face of his *tahlmorra*, would not?' His smile was twisted; wry and regretful. 'I would change everything; I would change nothing. A paradox, Niall, that only a few men have known. Only a few men *will* know.' He sighed. 'Carillon could tell you. So could Duncan and Finn. But all of them are gone, and I lack the proper words.'

'*Jehan*—'

But even as I began, he turned and walked out of the room.

CHAPTER FOUR

In my dreams I was a raptor, circling in the sky. I felt the buoyant uprush of warm air beneath my wings lifting me heavenward, carrying me higher yet. But higher was not where I wished to go. And so I angled outspread wings, tilting toward the ground, and swept downward, downward, in an ever-tightening spiral, until I drifted in idleness over the walls of the castle garden, and saw the two girls plainly.

Young. Very young, yet much the same age. They knelt upon the lush grass of a new spring, surrounded by a profusion of brilliant blossoms, and shared a game of their own devising. I heard sweet soprano voices rising on the sibilant breeze. And yet the sweetness was tempered by an odd possessiveness.

Closer. My shadow was a winged blotch upon the ground, darkness itself sweeping across the grass until it swallowed both girls whole. Enough, I thought, to make even a man shiver from the omen. But the two small girls took no notice of my shadow, or of me. Instead, they fixed one another with feral, angry glares and tugged in opposition at something held between them.

My shadow swept onward, turned, then hastened back again. More closely yet I drifted, raptor's eyes caught by the glint of something on the thing they shared. Closer still; the thing, I saw, was a cloth doll, nothing more, with a cheap gilt brooch fastened to its forehead in a child's mimicry of a crown. But only one doll and two girls; no good would come of it. Sharing does not always serve.

A glint from the brooch. A sparkle, bright as glass. Ravenlike, I yearned to make that brightness mine. But I was raptor, not raven; if I stooped to claim a prize it would never be a bit of tin or glass. No. Something worth far more.

Angry, accusative voices, filled with hate and scorn. I had heard the like in my childhood, had shared the tone with Ian and Isolde once or twice. But those days had long passed and the girls below me were strangers.

I saw no faces, only the color of their hair as they knelt stiffly upon the grass with the doll clenched in their hands. Each was the antithesis of the other: blue-black hair/thick gold hair. Young skin the color of copper-bronze/young skin the color of cream.

Antithesis, aye. As Ian and I to one another.

'Mine, mine!' cried the black-haired girl.

'Mine, mine!' cried the gold-haired girl.

Closer. Closer. I saw how the doll's arms and legs were spread and pulled taut, tugged at until the seams threatened to split. Beneath the gilt brooch-crown someone had stitched on a face with colored thread. The red mouth smiled. The blue eyes gazed vacantly into the heavens, blissfully blind to the fate I so clearly foresaw. And even as I opened beak to cry out a warning, the tortured toy split apart and spilled out its dried-bean blood onto the grass. I heard the hiss and rattle as the beans poured out and a shriek from each of the girls.

My shadow slanted across them both. Now they saw me. Now they took notice of my nearness. Now they threw down the two empty halves of the ruined doll and turned their faces toward the sky.

And I saw clearly, as I had not from the beginning, that neither girl had a face. Only blankness, endless blankness amidst the black/gold hair, devoid of a single feature.

Weight descended upon me. In a panic, I tried to sit up and could not; I was pinned to the bed too securely. Even as I opened my mouth to cry out, the warm, pungent breath of a mountain cat rushed in to replace the sound I sought to make.

Tasha loomed over me. I heard the deep staccato rattle of her rumbling purr. Her cool nose touched mine briefly, then she set tongue to flesh and began to lick.

'Ian!' Most of my strangled shout was muffled beneath Tasha's tongue. I did not dare move. Forepaws on shoulders pinned my upper body; hind ones were thrust between my

53

naked thighs. No; it *was not* worth the risk. 'Tasha — *enough!*'

I felt the rap of tail against kneecap. The licking halted momentarily, but the tongue, resolute, remained attached to cheek and chin. My flesh, abraded, stung; shaving would be painful.

The licking renewed itself, but only for one more swipe. Undaunted by gauzy summer bed-hangings, Tasha sprang through them to the floor and left me free once more.

I sat up at once, yanking the bedclothes over my nakedness. 'Ian! What—'

'You needed waking,' he interposed smoothly. Through the creamy gauze I could see him standing alone at the foot of my bed, blurred by the texture of the hangings. 'Torvald meant to come, of course; I told him I would see to the preparations for your wedding.' Ian grinned. 'I am no *proper* body-servant, of course, but I know where the arms and legs go. I should do well enough.'

The sudden waking on the heels of an ugly dream left me with a headache. I glared at Ian and rubbed my forehead, trying to draw out the pain. 'Better I go naked to my wedding than leave the dressing to *you*.'

'Your choice.' Ian, still smiling, shrugged. 'No doubt the bride, proxy or no, might prefer it that way.'

I grunted. 'Only if Alaric sends me a well-used girl in Gisella's place . . .' I frowned at him through the draperies. 'What are you doing here? I thought you would stay at Clankeep.'

Ian shook his head. In the thin pink light of dawn the cat-shaped earring glowed against the blackness of his hair. '*Jehan* sent word through Taj late last night; I left before dawn.' Briefly, he frowned. 'Did you think I would miss your wedding?'

'*Proxy* wedding.' I fought my way through layers of gossamer gauze and stood up beside the bed. Spring or no, it was cold; Torvald's absence meant an absence of heat as well, since Ian had not tended braziers or fireplace. I squinted toward the nearest narrow casement. 'Dawn, just.

54

Time enough for food and clothing before this ceremony.'

'You will eat *at* the wedding breakfast, not before.' Ian laughed as I swore beneath my breath. 'Fasting might improve your temper.'

'As much as Tasha improved my face.' I glared sourly at the mountain cat sitting silently near the door. Amber eyes were slitted; the tip of her tail twitched once. 'Your idea, *rujho*?'

'Tasha is fond of you.' Ian, considering that explanation enough, sat down on the nearest of my storage chests, leaning against the tapestried wall, and brushed at a smudge upon an otherwise spotless boot toe. Wedding finery: he wore supple doeskin jerkin and leggings dyed a soft honey yellow. The boots he tended matched, worked with copper-colored thread. Tassles trembled as he worked at the smudge. Bare-armed, the *lir*-gold shone.

Looking at him, I saw what I was not; what I could never be. *Ah gods, I wish you would give me the right to claim a lir and wear the gold on my arms and in my ear.* But I did not say it aloud. Instead, I answered Ian's comment.

'Fond of me,' I echoed dryly. 'If she loved me, would she use her teeth instead?'

'And plenty of claw, as well.' Thoughtfully, Ian looked at an old scar on the underside of one wrist.

Even as I started to move toward my clothing chests, I stopped. Swung back. 'Ask *her*,' I said tersely. 'Ask Tasha why I have no *lir*.'

I had never asked it of him before. The bond he and Tasha shared was intensely private, and even another warrior knows better than to ask of private things better left between human *lir* and animal. And yet I could not put off the request a moment longer. Something drove me to it.

If Ian was surprised, he hid it well. At first, I saw only a new rigidity in the line of his shoulders. He sat upright on the trunk, no longer leaning against the tapestry. And as he spread fingers against the wood of the trunk in a silent and subtle plea for strength from someone other than me (the gods, perhaps?) I saw the tension in his hands.

'I have,' he said tonelessly. 'Repeatedly. Did you think I would not try?'

'And her answer?' Consumed, for the moment, with discovering Tasha's response, I ignored the faint undertone of pain in Ian's voice. I had wounded him somehow, but I thought his cut lacked the infection of my own.

Ian looked away. Plainly troubled, he stared at the floor. The uncarpeted stone beneath his boots was red, rose-red, as were the walls of Homana-Mujhar. A shaft of light working its way through a blue panel of stained glass in the casement painted the rose a deeper red, until the shade was nearly purple.

I stood barefooted on the Caledonese carpet by my bed and waited, naked, for my answer.

'I have asked,' Ian said again. I saw how the muscles jumped once beneath the firm flesh of his beardless jaw. Sharp as a blade, the bone beneath the flesh. And aye, beardless. Because the Cheysuli cannot grow them.

But I had to shave each morning, or look more like Carillon than ever. 'And the answer?'

When he could, he met my eyes and shook his head. 'I have no answer for you.'

'Not from *you*,' I said roughly, 'from *her*.' I jerked my head in Tasha's direction. 'She is *lir*. The *lir* have all the answers. They know much more than any warrior can ever know. Ask her *again* for an answer!'

Ian drew in a deep breath. 'No.' Flatly said, with no room for urging or argument.

I opened my mouth to urge, to argue, to plead. And closed it again, because I saw there was no point. All the anger spilled away as I looked at my older brother. Aye, he had asked. More than once. But saying nothing to me, until now, because to tell me was to hurt me.

Liege man. *Rujholli*. And more. *Ah gods, I thank you for my brother*.

'Niall.' He stood up and faced me. I was taller, heavier, fairer – two puppies sired on different mothers, but sharing kinship ties stronger than full-blooded brothers. '*Rujho*, I

56

swear I would take the pain from you if I had the arts to do it.'

'I know.' I could not look at him. His pain reflected my own, and that I could not bear. 'I do not mean to berate *you*.'

'Nor should you berate yourself.' He did not smile. 'Do you think I do not see it? I know the nights you cannot sleep, cannot eat. I know when you drink too much. I know when you look to a woman to ease the pain. I am your *rujholli*, aye, and liege man as well, but I am not always with you. And yet − I can tell. I can see the marks on your back though the whip be invisible.' He reached out and caught my arms above the elbows, where the *lir*-bands ought to be. 'It does not make you less a man to *me*.'

The emphasis was eloquent, though he did not mean it to be. To him, I was a man. But to the warriors in the clan, I was merely a Homanan.

I looked at him directly. 'What did Ceinn wish to say to you?'

He had not expected it. His fingers tightened in reflex before he could release my arms. 'Ceinn?' I saw the brief loathing in his eyes. 'Ceinn is a − fool.' He wanted to say more; he did not.

'It had to do with me.'

'More to do with me.' He shook his head. 'No good would come of it. *Rujho*, let it go.'

'And if I do not?'

He tried to smile, but it came out less than amused. 'When have you ever been able to make me speak when I have decided against it?'

True enough. Glumly, I gestured toward one of the brass-bound clothing chests that lined fully two of my chamber walls. 'What do I wear for this, *rujho*? What finery do I put on?'

Ian's look was level. 'It depends,' he said calmly, 'on what man you choose to be.'

I stared. 'What man?'

'Cheysuli,' he said, 'or Homanan.'

Ian and I were directed to one of the smaller audience chambers. Somehow I had expected the ceremony to take place in the Great Hall, so full of ambience and history. But the Mujhar, we were told, had selected the smaller hall, to promote intimacy rather than intimidation.

'Possibly a mistake,' Ian said in a low voice as we entered the audience chamber. 'I know little enough of statecraft, but I think the Atvians may require what intimidation we can offer.'

'They shall face Cheysuli,' I said lightly. 'That should be enough.'

Ian laughed. 'A good omen: my *rujho* jests on his wedding day.'

'*Proxy*,' I reminded him as the servant shut the door behind us. Though considerably smaller than the Great Hall with its Lion Throne, the chamber was impressive enough in its own intimate way. Here the rose-red walls had been whitewashed. Stained glass tableaus of Homanan history filled the deep, narrow casements and lent the white walls a subtle wash of countless colors. The stone floors were bare of rugs, but here the natural rose-colored surface was allowed to go unpainted. Sunlight and stained glass filled the chamber with a pastel nacreous glow.

'Proxy,' my father agreed. 'And as binding as a proper Homanan wedding.' The Mujhar rose from the cushioned chair on the low dais at the far end of the chamber. Lorn sat slumped against one wooden leg as if his sole responsibility in life was to hold up the chair. On the back perched the golden falcon, Taj, and beside the chair stood another for the Queen of Homana; at present, however, it was empty.

I glanced around quickly, searching for Atvians, but saw none. Only my mother, by one of the narrow casements, staring out into the inner bailey.

She turned abruptly. Yellow skirts swirled around her feet. I saw the sheen of silk; heard the sibilance of fold caressing fold. 'Binding!' she said bitterly. 'What binds us now is *idiocy*. Niall would do better with another.'

'Aislinn, we have been through this,' my father said in weary exasperation. 'As for doing better, *how* better? Gisella is his cousin, and *harana* to you by your marriage to me. Throw a stone at Gisella, Aislinn, and you splatter its mud upon yourself.'

Gold glittered at my lady mother's neck. Her hands were clenched in the folds of her silken skirts. There was gold on her hands as well, threading from the heavy girdle through rigid fingers to clash against the fabric. Her rich red hair was bound up against her head, and resting against her brow was a circlet of twisted gold wire.

'It is not *Gisella*,' she said tightly. 'It is her father. *Him*. The Lord of Atvia himself. Do you forget it was Alaric's *brother* who slew my father?'

'I do not forget,' he told her plainly. 'You do not *let* me forget.'

She wanted to go to him. I could see it in her face; in the great gray eyes that harpers sang of, making her beauty into legend. But she did not go to him. She stood instead by the casement and faced him, proud as the Mujhar himself, and equally inflexible.

I glanced briefly at Ian, still standing next to me. His face bore the polite mask it always wore before the Queen of Homana and Solinde. But I wondered what he thought. I wondered what my mother's terrible pride in heritage did to the man who was not her son.

I sighed. My headache threatened to return. 'Does it go on, then, this ceremony? Or do I go back to my chambers and take off my finery?'

My mother still looked at my father, even as he looked at her. I wondered if they had heard me at all. I wondered if they even recalled Ian and I were in the chamber. They waged some private battle, and I could not begin to name the stakes.

'No.' My mother, at last, still looking at my father, though the answer was for me. 'No, you do not.'

There was neither triumph nor relief in my father's face.

59

Acknowledgment, I thought, of my mother's surrender. And perhaps, a trace of compassion, because he knew why she fought so fiercely.

'You look well.' My father turned to me. 'I approve the selection of Cheysuli leathers.'

I shrugged a little. 'It – there was no choice. But – I could wish my arms were not so naked.'

'And *do* wish it,' my father said. 'I know, Niall. Better than you think.'

The pain renewed itself. I had chosen, but the choice did not feel right. It made my belly churn and stab at me with a familiar burning pain. But I had not earned the leathers.

'You are Homanan *also*,' my mother began, as always; it was her litany. 'Put not so much weight in ornamentation and think of the blood in your veins.'

'Carillon's blood?' Through the pain I could not smile. 'Aye, lady, always. As you would have me recall it.'

Color stood high in her flawless face. The gray eyes flicked to Ian. 'Was it your suggestion?'

'No, lady,' he said gently. 'I merely offered him the choice.'

Briefly, she shut her eyes as if to shut out his words. But almost immediately they opened again and she looked at him unflinchingly. Her tone lacked the bitterness of moments before. 'No, no, you would not thrust one or the other upon him. I know you better than you think, Ian. It is *myself*—'

But she did not finish, because the liveried servant who had shown us into the chamber was opening the door yet again. And this time there came Atvians into the room.

A man and a woman. The man was tall, elegant, garbed in understated blue velvets and an attitude too well-trained to betray anything other than respect and graciousness, and yet I sensed a power in him, leashed, as if he were a hawk waiting for the jesses to be cut. His hair was very dark, nearly black, and his eyes were an odd pale brown. The only ornamentation was a silver ring on his left hand and matching earrings in his lobes.

His outstretched left hand offered escort to the woman. Though her right hand met his palm, they hardly touched one another. An odd dance by two magnificent animals. A bizarre sort of courtship rite, I thought, when the woman was meant for me.

Looking at her, I reminded myself at once the ceremony was proxy only. What I knew of the custom was no less than anyone else: I would wed the woman in Gisella's place to make certain the alliance between Homana and Atvia was sealed by the blood of our respective Houses, but I would not bed the woman. That was left for Gisella.

And yet I found I regretted it.

She put me in mind of a harp string, capable of a poignant, subtle power. Plucked this way, plucked that, she would still emit a tone that would bind each man to its strength, resonating in his soul. I thought almost at once of my mother's mother, Electra of Solinde, whom legend said could ensorcell men with a single glance from lambent eyes. And yet what I knew of that woman did not apply to this one. The white-blond hair was black. The ice-gray eyes were also. The velvet gown was brilliant crimson.

Smiling faintly, she allowed the man to lead her forward. The hem of her skirts brushed the stone of the floor; I heard its subtle song. A woman's song, that sound, and incredibly powerful. But it was not at her skirts I looked.

Her head was bowed in a perfect humility, but there was pride in her posture as well, and a comprehension of her strength. Beautiful, aye, and claiming that power as a matter of course, but there was more to her than simple beauty. There was confidence as well. An acknowledgment of her place in the world of kings and princes.

My mother moved smoothly to my father's side. They stood together on the dais before the padded chairs, united in titles and goals, and waited to receive the Atvian envoy and Gisella's proxy bride.

Silver glittered. The woman wore it at hip and brow. A chain of interlocking silver feathers formed a girdle. A plain silver circlet touched her brow, then flared out at each

61

temple to form delicate downswept wings, curving back to encircle her head. Black hair, unbound except for the winged silver circlet, fell in a silken curtain to girdled, crimson hips.

'By the gods,' I whispered to Ian, 'is there a way I can wed the *proxy* bride instead of the genuine thing?'

His answering smile was wry. 'It might discompose Gisella.'

'As well as the alliance.' I sighed dramatically. 'Ah, well . . . *tahlmorras* must be obeyed.'

'Such sacrifice,' Ian mocked. '*I*, however, am not already bound to such a course.'

I opened my mouth to return a suitable retort, but the envoy was speaking and I shut my mouth on my answer.

'I am Varien, ambassador from the Atvian court to yours,' the Atvian said quietly. 'My lord Mujhar; Aislinn, queen of Homana and Solinde; Niall, prince of Homana – may I present the Lady Lillith, sent from Alaric himself, Lord of the Idrian Isles.'

Shea of Erinn would dispute that particular title. And did, I knew, even now. A petty thing, to fight over petty titles, but it was not Homana's problem.

Varien's voice was a smooth, cultured baritone. He spoke with a fluent, meticulous courtesy in accentless, flawless Homanan. Envoys are required to speak many languages, but for a moment, oddly, I wondered how he would do in the Cheysuli Old Tongue, which defies those not born to its cadence and lyricism.

Lillith. An odd name not unpleasing to the ear. I rolled it over on my tongue silently and found it more difficult to say than to hear.

Crimson skirts flared and settled as she dropped into a curtsy before the dais. I saw her nails were tipped in silver, and her mouth was painted red.

Beside me, Ian drew in his breath in a sudden hiss of shock. I looked at him sharply and found him staring rigidly at the woman as she rose from her eloquent obeisance. Yet it was not the stare of a man struck by a woman's beauty, but by realization instead.

And then I heard Tasha's growl.

Almost at once, the chamber was filled with tension. Tasha still growled, tail whipping at Ian's right leg. Lorn rose to stand before the chairs, hackled from neck to tail. And Taj, still perched upon the chair, bated in agitation.

My brother's hand was on his knife. My father was off the dais and standing before the woman. 'You *dare* to come into my hall?' His anger and astonishment were manifest. 'You *dare* to come into my city?'

'My lord Alaric sent me.' Her voice was low and husky. The Homanan words had a foreign lilt.

'Does *he* know what you are?'

After a moment, Lillith smiled. But only a little smile. 'My lord Alaric knows everything about me.'

I could not be as calm as the woman so obviously was, but neither could I experience the same measure of shock as everyone save my mother. 'Ian – what *is* she?'

'Ihlini,' he hissed in an undertone. Then, more loudly, 'By the gods, she is *Ihlini*!'

'What is the meaning of this?' my mother cried. 'Alaric sends an *enemy* to show what he thinks of the betrothal?'

'Not at all,' Varien said smoothly. 'He sends a lady he holds very highly in his esteem.'

'I am Ihlini,' Lillith said quietly. 'I do not deny it. But what is between your race and mine has nothing to do with the betrothal. Be assured, Alaric desires the marriage.'

'Ihlini and Cheysuli do not treat with one another.' My father's tone was deadly. 'Is this some trick of Strahan's?'

Arched black brows rose below the silver circlet. 'My lord Mujhar, I say again: Alaric desires the marriage. Strahan has no hand in this. Was it not you yourself who agreed to this alliance sealed by a marriage between your son and your sister's daughter?'

'It was agreed by Homana and Atvia,' the Mujhar said. 'There was no mention of Ihlini.'

'He did not know me then.'

She was deadly serious. But I wondered if she was as calm as she appeared. An Ihlini in the halls of Homana-Mujhar?

63

No more calm, I thought, than I would be within the halls of Ihlini Valgaard.

'Did he know, when he sent you, he gave us every opportunity to break off this betrothal?' my father demanded.

Lillith's eyes were unwavering. Her expression did not alter. 'The enmity between Ihlini and Cheysuli is known to all men, my lord. But Alaric intended no insult. He sent me because he wished to, regardless of my blood.' Briefly, black eyes narrowed. 'Are the Cheysuli so hostile they cannot set aside their hatred for the sake of realms and children?'

'Ask us where our hostility comes from,' my father commanded. 'Ask us how we came so close to being annihilated by our own Homanan allies. Because of the Ihlini, *Lady Lillith of Atvia*. Because fear and hostility were fostered by the Ihlini, who reaped the benefits of a mad king's attempted extirpation of my race.'

Lillith did not answer at once. I had seen my father this angry only once or twice, and I liked it no better this time. A man of iron control; it is painful to see him let it go.

Varien made a movement as if to speak, but Lillith put a hand upon his wrist and he said nothing after all. Instead, she took a single step forward toward my father. They were close. Very close. She had only to put out her hand to touch him. Uneasily, I thought of Strahan and his cold Ihlini fire.

I heard the metallic scrape of a knife pulled from its sheath. Ian's lips were moving in silent prayer or silent curse as he clenched his hand upon the hilt; I could not say which. But I saw how the swollen pupils turned his yellow eyes black. I saw how he watched the Ihlini woman, and knew she would live no longer than was humanly possible if she sought to slay our father.

'My lord Mujhar,' she said quietly in her honeyed, husky voice. 'I see no Ihlini within the halls of Homana-Mujhar. I would say we *lost* the battle for the Lion.'

Donal of Homana merely laughed. 'Oh, aye, you lost the

battle for the Lion. But never, *never* do us the discourtesy of thinking we are foolish enough to discount the Ihlini so long as they serve the god of the netherworld.'

Lillith met his steady gaze. She did not so much as blink. 'And do you think, my lord Mujhar, that *I* serve Asar-Suti?'

After a moment, my father smiled. 'Lady, I would wager you lie down with the dark god himself.'

It was Lillith's turn to laugh. The husky sound filled up the chamber. 'Oh, *no*, my lord Mujhar . . . I only lie down with Alaric.'

CHAPTER FIVE

My mother recoiled a single step, then caught herself, as if she preferred not to show the Ihlini woman she could be taken by surprise. 'You are Alaric's whore?'

Lillith looked at her calmly. 'Whore? In the Cheysuli Old Tongue women such as I are called *meijhas* and offered honor. In the Homanan language, the proper word is *light woman*. Yet the Queen herself resorts to the low speech of the streets?'

'If it is the *truth*,' my mother answered. 'You insult the Mujhar, *Lady Lillith*. Do you forget his sister was Alaric's wife?'

'Bronwyn has been dead nearly eighteen years,' Lillith told her calmly. 'Before she died, she gave my lord little welcome in her bed. And once she *had* conceived, she denied him utterly. Do you expect Alaric to keep himself faithful when he is wed to a woman like that?'

My father's hand was a blur as he reached out and caught one of Lillith's velveted wrists. 'That is *enough* from you, Ihlini! You will keep your mouth from my *rujholla*'s name!'

I was a little surprised by my father's vehemence. He and my aunt had parted on unhappy terms when Alaric came awooing from Atvia. My mother had told me Bronwyn wanted nothing to do with the marriage, but because of politics and the prophecy, my father had seen fit to wed her to Alaric even against her wishes. They had neither seen one another nor corresponded again, though I knew my father would have given the world to make peace with his sister.

Lillith's chin rose a little. Sunlight set the winged circlet aglow against raven hair. 'Plain speech, I freely admit; I meant it so, just as the Queen meant her question. But I ask you this, *my lord*: if the Cheysuli are so dedicated to the tolerance of *all* races — as claimed in the prophecy of the Firstborn — then why am I renounced for mine?'

'Alaric's whore,' my mother repeated distinctly. 'Oh, aye, I use the low speech of the streets. Because you are not worthy of better.' She stepped down from the dais and moved to stand next to her husband, confronting Lillith directly. The first shock had passed; she faced the woman possessed of a quiet dignity and an equally eloquent air of command. 'You may return home to Atvia, Lady Lillith, and tell Alaric he will have to look elsewhere for a husband for his daughter.'

'Take your hand from me.' Lillith did not acknowledge my mother's words, looking steadily at my father. '*Take your hand from me.*'

After a moment, my father did so, as if he could not bear to touch her.

'My lord.' Varien, smiling, still couched his words in unruffled courtesy. 'My lord Mujhar, I well understand the Queen's feelings in this matter. But I think she may wish to reconsider what she has just said.' He inclined his head to my mother. 'It is true that Lady Lillith is Ihlini. But it is as I said; my lord Alaric esteems her highly.'

'In his *bed*.' It was Ian, shocking us all with his virulence; I stared at him in surprise.

Lillith turned her head far enough to slant him an inquiring glance out of eloquent eyes. A delicate silver wing glittered against her hair. 'In his bed *and* out of it. Why? Do you wish to share it as well?'

Ian's laugh was a gust of air expelled with all the force of disbelief. 'I would sooner lie down with a leper!'

Lillith's eyelids lowered as if she consulted an inner voice. It gave her a shuttered, secretive look of incredible insularity. It made me wish to ask aloud what she thought; what she intended to say. But I did not. What Ihlini would tell a Cheysuli the truth?

Shut up within her thoughts, she presented an incongruous picture of maidenly decorum. I knew better. She was *Ihlini*; I had faced Strahan. And as for maidenly decorum, she had already proclaimed herself Alaric's light woman. It gave her a passkey to vulgarity, if she wished to use it.

But apparently she did not. When the kohl-smudged lids lifted again, baring her eyes to all, I saw nothing but resolute innocence.

Her head lifted minutely. Her chin and jaw were distinctly molded, so that a tilt of a head this way or that divulged a multitude of things otherwise left unsaid. Someone had schooled her well in the use of her body.

Or perhaps witches such as Lillith and Electra are born to manipulate men with a smile, a look, a sigh.

Pale hands gathered heavy velvet. Smoothly she put her back to the Mujhar and the Queen of Homana and turned instead to face Ian and me, hair swinging, skirts swirling, silver nails flashing against the rich texture of the velvet.

She looked at me, but briefly; her attention was blatantly fixed on Ian. 'Are you kin to the Prince of Homana?'

Somehow, it was not what either of us expected. I frowned; Ian answered because of innate courtesy, though the tone did not reflect it. 'We share the same *jehan*.'

It was clear she knew the word. The painted lips, still smiling, parted in silent comprehension. 'Then you are the *bastard* son.'

It took us all by surprise, her pointedly casual comment, but Ian more so than anyone else, I think. I saw the color drain out of his face until it was chalky-gray. He was not one generally much perturbed by insults – being so obviously Cheysuli, he was used to occasional Homanan curses – and bastardy bears no stigma in the clans. But this was from a woman, emphatically unprovoked, and an Ihlini woman at that. Somehow her precise explicitness honed the words more sharply. Without a doubt the knife cut more deeply than ever before.

Angrily, I swung back a rigid hand, fully intending to

68

bring it across her lovely face. But Ian stopped me by reaching out to catch my wrist. 'No.'

'*Rujho—*'

'No,' he said evenly. 'Do not soil your hands.'

'Lillith.' My mother's voice, calm, cool, supremely in command of the situation. She was all queen now, standing tall in yellow silk and royal gold. What I witnessed was Carillon's legacy.

I saw the instinctive response in the Ihlini woman as she turned almost at once; saw also how that reaction surprised her by its alacrity. And how much it sat ill with her.

'Lillith.' My mother smiled her lovely, deadly smile. 'I will allow you to insult my husband's son no more than I will allow you to insult my own.' Her face was smooth, untroubled; I saw a glint of satisfaction in her eyes. 'Or, regardless of *whose* bed you sleep in, I will have you cast bodily out of this palace.'

I nearly gaped in surprise. To hear her protecting Ian so definitively was shocking as well as welcome; they said little enough to one another, being uneasy companions at best, and certainly nothing in the past had warranted such loyalty on the part of my mother. And yet she sounded as fierce as if she defended *me*.

Smiling inwardly, I flicked a pleased glance at Ian. His color was back, though a little more flushed than normal; shock had been replaced by anger at the Ihlini. No doubt my mother's defense startled him as much as it had me, but he did not show it. He showed nothing but a mask.

Lillith inclined her head. 'As you wish, lady. No more insults. I offer choices instead.'

The mask slipped. 'Choices?' Ian demanded roughly. 'What choices could an *Ihlini* offer us?'

Lillith looked at the Mujhar. '*Your* choice, my lord: send Varien and me back to Atvia, and have the betrothal broken.' She tilted her head a little to one side. 'I have given you reason enough.'

'Purposely,' he said lightly. 'Aye, I have seen that clearly. There is a purpose to all of this.' He smiled. It was not the

69

smile of a man he showed her, but of a predator whose attention is fixed upon the spoor of lively game. 'Now, Lady Lillith, give me the other half so I may know the choice.'

But it was not Lillith who answered. Varien spread his hands. 'Simple, my lord: ignore the lady's heritage and allow the ceremony to go on.'

My mother laughed aloud. 'Do you expect us to overlook what she has said, let alone what she *is*?'

No. My instinctive response was immediate. *If for no other reason than the pain she brought to my brother, I would send her back to Alaric.*

'Choices,' Varien said. 'My lord?'

My father did not answer at once. I saw the fine-drawn tension in my mother as she waited, and felt it in myself. Not because I particularly wanted to marry Gisella – cousin or no, I did not know the girl – but because some deep-seated instinct told me the choice facing my father carried more weight than usual.

He knew it as well as I, perhaps better, being who he is. I saw him smile again, mostly to himself, and then he turned it fully on the Atvian envoy. 'Alaric and Shea have made a truce.'

I frowned. It made no sense; none of it. What had a truce between Alaric of Atvia and Shea of Erinn to do with my marriage?

Varien's lips tightened. Briefly, oh so briefly, I saw anger in his eyes, and then he covered it. He was himself again, urbane, diplomatic, yet I knew my father's response was not what he expected.

I looked immediately at the woman, knowing instinctively she was a truer diviner of emotions. But if Lillith was angry, she hid it well. Instead, she smiled, and nodded once to herself. As if she had won a wager.

Or understood us better than anyone wished to believe.

'A truce,' my father repeated. Still smiling, he sat down at last in the padded chair and gestured for my mother to do the same. After a moment's hesitation, she did so. But I knew she understood my father's manner no better than

I, even as he laughed. 'Let me speculate aloud, envoy, for a moment. Please correct me if I am wrong.' He straightened a little and tapped one finger against the wooden arm. 'Alaric and Shea, regardless of their respective reasons, have agreed to a truce. I think it unlikely Shea would ally himself with Alaric for any reason, judging by the turbulent history of the islands; nonetheless, a cessation of hostilities leaves Alaric in possession of a united warhost for the first time in decades.' He paused, and I saw he no longer smiled. 'Have I the right of it thus far?'

Varien's schooled face exhibited neither resentment nor regret; he merely acknowledged my father's summation with a brief inclination of his head.

'What is he doing?' I whispered to Ian. 'What has a truce between Alaric and Shea to do with anything?'

I saw the ironic curling of his mouth; Lillith's insult had not banished his sense of humor. 'If you would close your mouth and open your ears, perhaps you would find out.'

But my father went on before I could respond. 'If I broke off the betrothal for reasons well known to all of us in this chamber, Alaric would have the right to consider the alliance shattered; the right to levy war.' The Mujhar's face displayed no tension, only calmness. He had the right of it. Wars had been started over more trivial matters than this. 'The past has proven Atvia incapable of defeating Homana in battle because her armies have been divided. Shea's *meddling* made it necessary for a portion of the warhost to be left at home to protect Atvia, and so it was that much easier for Homana to defeat her enemy. Now, of course, with Erinn and Atvia at peace, no matter how brief the duration, Alaric can levy half again as many men against Homana.'

'My lord.' Varien said nothing more; nothing more was needed. Even I began to see.

'And so if the betrothal is broken and Alaric comes against me, as would be his right, it is potentially possible that Homana could be defeated . . . and Alaric made Mujhar.' My father shut his mouth on that; patently, he was finished discussing the thing.

71

Varien said nothing. He did not dare to in the face of his supposedly neutral commission.

But Lillith did. 'Enough Erinnish knotwork, my lord Mujhar. Let us speak plainly.' She did not so much as look at Varien as she stepped in front of him to face my father. 'You may interpret the reason for my presence here in any way you choose. You may even be correct. But bear in mind that *if* war came of a broken betrothal, Atvia might well lose all. There is always that chance in war. I think you realize, my lord Mujhar, that Alaric has more to gain by seeing your son and his daughter wed than by breaking the betrothal.'

'Then why this elaborate farce?' my mother asked. 'By the gods, woman, Ihlini or no – have you an explanation?'

Lillith smiled. 'Of course. But I leave that for you to divine.'

'Insult,' my brother murmured to me. 'No more than that; a petty attempt by a petty man to irritate his overlord.'

I frowned. 'All of *this* just for *that*?'

'United army or not, Alaric would be a fool to believe Atvia could defeat Homana. But he cannot accept continuing vassalage graciously; he is sly, he is resentful. His pride aches, so he offers this idiocy merely to slip the nettle into our bed.' Ian shrugged. 'I doubt Alaric is stupid enough to believe we would fall for this foolishness.'

My father looked at me. 'I will let the Prince of Homana make the choice. It is *he* who must wed Alaric's daughter, not I.'

Varien had not expected that. Neither, I thought, had Lillith. They had discounted me early in the game as too young, too unimportant to consider. It was the Mujhar for whom they had set the trap.

Well, *I* had not expected it, either.

Nothing would please me more than to pack Alaric's light woman back to Atvia in disgrace. But I think it is not worth a war.

I inclined my head briefly to acknowledge my father's trust. And then I crossed the chamber to the woman

72

dressed in crimson and reached out to take her hand.

Silver-tipped nails glowed. The painted lips smiled a little, waiting for my answer. Close up, she was lovelier than ever. But it was a hard-edged beauty with nothing of softness about it.

No, she would never be the prey. She would wear the hunter's colors; she would run the prey to ground . . . and follow him into his burrow.

'Lady Lillith,' I said evenly, 'nothing would please me more than to have this wedding go forth.'

Kohl-smudged lids flickered minutely. I saw the brief, considering glance slanted at me out of eloquent eyes, black as the unbound hair. The smile widened. And then she laughed her husky laugh. 'You know the game after all.'

'No,' I returned, smiling. 'But I am a passable student.'

My father looked to my brother. 'Will you have the priest sent for?'

Silently, Ian did so, even as Lillith continued to laugh.

Laughed as if she had won.

CHAPTER SIX

' "Will you, the Prince of Homana, promise to provide all things necessary to the station and well-being of the Princess of Atvia," ' my brother quoted. ' "Will you, Niall, clan-born of the Cheysuli, promise to provide succor and honor, respect and regard, to Gisella of Atvia?" And so on, and so on.' He laughed. 'You notice he left out the word *love*. For a Homanan priest, he has surpassing sense.'

'Proxy or no, it was hard to say the words.' I swallowed sour red wine to wash away the taste of the vows I had made. 'I kept telling myself it was for Gisella the promises were meant, but I had to look at *Lillith*.'

'And now you are bound to her forever,' Ian mused. 'Homanan law is an unforgiving thing, allowing no man – or woman – the chance to end a marriage that does neither any good.' He shook his head. 'Foolishness. Look at Carillon. Surely he more than any man should have had the right to end his marriage. Had he been able to set Electra aside permanently and wed another woman, he might have sired a son. And you would not be Prince of Homana, in line for the Lion Throne.'

No, I would not . . . and undoubtedly I would not be bound forever to Gisella.

I turned from the stained glass casement and faced my brother. We were alone in the audience chamber. The ceremony had been completed an hour or more before. I had not left because a servant had brought wine to us all, intended for celebration. But none of my kin wished to share wine with Varien or Lillith past the customary nuptial cup; everyone, including Tasha, had departed, and

74

now Ian and I kept company in the presence of emptiness.

He sat in my father's padded chair. I had not drunk so much wine as to weave fancies of my thoughts, but I could not help but mark the appropriateness of his position. He resembled our father more and more with each year, as if his flesh grew more comfortable with his bones. His mother, Sorcha, had taken her life before I had been born, I had no one to compare him with except the Mujhar. And now, looking at him, I saw Ian possessed the same mouth in repose. It was only rarely that I saw my father this relaxed.

I swallowed more wine. It went down so easily, too easily; I would have to stop soon, or I would suffer for it in the morning. 'Have you ever wondered what life would be like for you if *you* were heir to the Lion?'

Like me, he held a cup of wine. Unlike me, he did not drink. He stared at me fixedly over the rim. 'Why do you ask?'

I shrugged. 'No reason, save curiosity. We are so different; I merely wondered how you would feel if you were in my place.'

'Deceased,' he said succinctly.

'*Why?*' I was horrified. 'Why would you feel *dead?*'

'Because I would probably *be* dead.' Ian straightened a little. 'Do you think the Homanans would allow *me* to succeed to the throne?'

'Why not?'

'I am a bastard, for one. Cheysuli for another.' He paused. 'More *blatantly* Cheysuli.'

I waved a hand. 'Let us dispense with the first and say you are not a bastard. How would you feel *then?*'

He smiled a little. 'You dispense with it so *easily* . . . well enough – I am legitimate. I am the Prince of Homana. I would still be dead, because the Homanans would see to it I was slain.'

'Assassinated?'

He shrugged. 'If it was not an *accident.*'

I felt a cold finger brush my spine. 'Because you are Cheysuli.'

75

'Aye.'

'Our father is Cheysuli.'

'Carillon chose our *jehan*. From him they would accept any man.' He did not look away from me. 'Niall, *you* are in no danger. You are Aislinn's son. You bear the blood of the man.'

'As well as the man's *flesh*.' I swore and stared into the blood-red wine. 'So I survive on sufferance.'

'Do not mistake me, I do not accuse all Homanans of wishing to see Cheysuli dead,' he said pointedly. 'More and more are reconciled to the reinstatement of our people, even to the succession. But there are *some* who would prefer it otherwise.'

'Oh. *Those*.' I grimaced. 'The zealots.'

'*A'saii*,' my brother murmured into his cup. 'Like Ceinn.'

'What?'

He blinked and looked up at me. 'The Old Tongue word, *a'saii*. It means *zealot* in Homanan, or something close to that.'

'What has the word to do with Ceinn?'

'Nothing.' The mouth was taut as wire. Ian began to drink his wine.

I set my own cup down in the casement sill and went to my brother. Before he could speak, I caught his wrist and kept the cup from his mouth. 'I am not deaf, *rujho*. Neither am I stupid. At Clankeep, Ceinn came to your pavilion seeking word with you. He made a mistake: he began to speak before he saw I was there. You yourself said he was a fool. Now you call him *a'saii*. I want to know what it means.'

'It means what I said: Ceinn is a fool.' Ian twisted away from me and rose, leaving me with his cup of wine. 'He is more devoted to the old ways – the old *days* – than others in the clan.'

'The days of the Firstborn?'

'Directly after, when the prophecy was first discovered.' Ian turned to face me. 'In those days, the Cheysuli bred only with Cheysuli, to keep the blood clear of taint. In the end, that is what nearly destroyed us; we *need* the new blood promised in the prophecy.'

I nodded. 'I know this. Ian—'

'I am answering!' he said sharply. 'Gods, Niall, must you have it carved for you in stone? Ceinn adheres to the beliefs of the early days, when our women only lay down with our men. To keep the blood pure.'

'And mine, of course, is not.' I smiled tightly, though the relevation of Ceinn's beliefs did not particularly shock me. 'He thinks I should not be in line to inherit.'

'Aye.' It was clipped; Ian was angry with himself for letting me learn the truth.

'Let me guess: Ceinn believes *he* should inherit the throne.'

'No,' Ian said. 'He says the Lion should be mine.'

I shut my mouth so as not to resemble a simpleton. 'You,' I said. '*You?* But – I thought surely *he* would want it. Is that not why he pursues Isolde? To make his claim stronger?'

'No.' Ian drew in a breath and released it through taut lips. 'The *a'saii*—' he stopped short. 'Ceinn feels I have more right than you. That my blood is purer.'

'He forgets Sorcha was half Homanan,' I said bitterly. 'You are no more *pure* than I!'

'We have a *jehan* who claims the Old Blood from Alix, our granddame. That ensures *my* right. But on your *jehana*'s side there is Solindish blood in you; Electra was *your* granddame, never mine.' Ian's face was a mask. 'There. I have carved it out for you. Can you set the stone into place?'

'Electra, my mother's mother, was also Tynstar's *meijha*,' I said flatly. 'Aye, I can set the stone into place. So, the blood that endears me to the Homanans – the Queen is Carillon's daughter, and for that they will overlook even *Solindish Electra* – devalues me to the Cheysuli.' The pain rose up to swallow my belly whole. Grimacing, I spun and threw Ian's cup at the closest wall. Instead, it shattered the nearest casement.

Colored glass rained down against the floor. I stared aghast as the shards splattered down like blood, spilling across the stone. Sunlight gaped through the lead frame: naked light filled my eyes until the tears spilled over.

My clan will not accept me. My race reviles me.

'Niall.' Ian's hands were on my arms. 'Sit down – *sit down!*' He guided me to one of the chairs and pushed me into it. '*Shansu, rujho, shansu.* Such anger can harm the soul.'

As well as gripe the belly. Hunched over, I leaned against one of the padded arms. 'How many, Ian? How many of the *a'saii?*'

'Too few, I promise you. And the canker is very small.'

'Cankers grow. Cankers can overtake the healthiest of men.'

'And cankers can be cut out.' He knelt down in front of me. 'Do you think I would ever allow Ceinn or any other warrior to harm my *rujholli?* What manner of liege man am I? What sort of brother am I to you?'

Brother. The Homanan word was accented. Ian was more accustomed to the Cheysuli. *While I only rarely resort to the Old Tongue.*

'Would you want it?' I asked. 'The Lion?'

Surprising me, Ian smiled. 'If I ever laid claim to the Lion, the Homanans would have my head. Do I look like a martyr to you?'

My laugh resembled a gasp. 'No, nor a particularly ambitious man.' I leaned back in the chair as the pain in my belly began to subside. 'I need you, Ian. Liege man, *rujholli*, companion . . . I need you with me, Ian. Here or in Atvia.'

'Atvia,' he said. 'I thought it might come to that.'

'Even now the Homanan Council hammers out trade agreements with Varien as part of the marriage settlement. In a week the ship sails. And I must go with Varien and Lillith to claim my Atvian bride.' I forced a smile. 'I have no intention of going there *alone* with that Ihlini witch.'

He sighed. 'I suppose I have no choice.'

78

The smile came more easily. 'You never have. Your *tahlmorra* lies with me.'

Ian sat down in the other chair. 'A long trip,' he predicted. 'Tasha hates the water.'

The week before sailing was both the longest and the shortest of my life. The thought of the trip itself was exciting, regardless that my future wife lay at the end of it. I had never been out of Homana before, and the idea of a sea voyage was almost intoxicating. At first there had been some disagreement over whether I should go. It would be easy enough for Alaric to send his daughter to Homana, but it was agreed at last that I would go to fetch her myself, as a mark of honor.

But now I had other things to think about; other things to gnaw at the back of my mind, even when I tried to keep my attention on matters of more importance.

A'saii, Ian had called them. Cheysuli warriors *too* dedicated to the refinement of the Old Blood.

And there was Lillith. Varien's overtures of friendship were easy enough to brush off: he was envoy, not prince; his rank did not match mine, and I found myself using an impatient condescension I had not known I possessed. But with Lillith, it was different. Being a beautiful woman, she knew how to manipulate men. Being Ihlini witch, she had recourse to more arts than most. And so I found myself agreeing to accompany her into Mujhara to show her the sights of the city.

'Alone?' I asked as we walked the length of the corridor. 'You and I?'

She retied the wine-red ribbon threaded through her single braid. 'We are wed. There is no law against it.'

She was solemn-faced as we neared the main entrance, but I saw a glint of amusement in her eyes. It irritated me as much as she meant it to.

'*We* are not wed,' I pointed out. 'The union was never consummated.'

Lillith smiled. 'We could take pains to see that it *was*.'

'No.' I said it coldly, banishing any attempt at politeness or diplomacy.

Lillith's husky laugh rang out. 'If you are *frightened* of me, my lord, why not have your warrior brother accompany us? His magic will prevent me from using mine.'

Another man might have instantly refused the chance to gain an ally, being too proud and too full of himself; *I* was not a fool. Strahan had already impressed upon me how easy it was for an Ihlini to level sorcery against me, and I was not about to give Lillith the opportunity. I rousted Ian from conversation with one of my mother's ladies, ignored his muttered threat, and explained matters to him. He stopped complaining, summoned Tasha from his chambers, and went with Lillith and me into the city streets.

In the thirty-five years since Carillon had returned from exile and made the Cheysuli welcome in their homeland again, most of the Homanans had learned to coexist with warriors and *lir*. Tasha's presence no longer alarmed Mujhara's citizens to the point of taking action against her as they once would have against a mountain cat who happened into the city. While no one precisely *welcomed* her – she is large, lethal, and incredibly powerful – neither did they hunt weapons with which to slay her.

Ian and I flanked Lillith out of good manners, nothing more. Tasha preceded us, clearing a path through the crowded streets as passers-by made way immediately. Though the streets were cobbled, a thin layer of dust rose to film Lillith's wine-red skirts and turn them a faded ocher-red. But she hardly appeared to notice. She observed everything around her with calm, discerning eyes, as if she fit the city into a private ordering. She did not appear aware of the stares she received from men, or the mutters from the women. They could not know she was Ihlini, but her vivid *apartness* made her a beacon in the streets.

Ian and I took her to Market Square, the hub of every city or country village. In Mujhara the Square is huge, hedged by buildings at every turning. It was here everyone brought wares to trade and sell, commodities meant for competitive distribution. Canvas stalls filled up the Square, narrowing the alleys and streets to winding walkways hardly wide enough for three to walk abreast. Even Tasha found the going more difficult.

'Is it always like this?' Lillith asked.

Ian was ahead, I behind. Jostled, I stumbled a step closer to her. 'It is Market Day today. Another time it is not so bad, although the Square is always crowded.' My foot squashed a sodden sweetmeat someone had dropped; grimacing, I shook the remains from the sole of my boot. 'It is worse at Summerfair.'

Lillith held up her skirts with both hands as Ian broke a path through the throngs of people. 'Rondule is not so big as this. But then, neither is Atvia as big as Homana.'

'Do you not come from Solinde?' I nearly had to shout over the babble of the crowds.

'Originally.' She slanted a glance at me over a shoulder. 'Atvia is now my home.'

'Because of Alaric.'

'Because I *choose* it as my home.'

Ian was brought up short by a man on horseback, always questionable transportation in the Square. Lillith, still looking at me, bumped into him. Ian turned, intending to steady her; he stopped himself. For a moment they merely looked at one another, as if offering mutual challenges.

Then Lillith laughed. Ian looked away.

'*Rujho*,' I said sharply, 'look.'

Ian turned. We had been stopped by the stall of a furrier, and the smell of freshly-dressed hides was pungent. There were pelts of every sort: coney, fox, beaver, bear, wolf and mountain cat, countless other kinds. The largest pelts were tacked upon wood and hung from the back of the stall. Tails depended from nails. The plusher, finer pelts were piled upon benches and over the counter itself.

My hand had automatically gone down to brace myself against stumbling. It was buried in sleek softness; one look told me the hide had once clothed a living cat.

I recoiled. The color was Tasha's, lush red tipped with

81

chestnut brown. Though there is no tenet in the clans against trapping or slaying animals who are not *lir*, the likeness of Tasha sent a shiver of distaste and superstition down my spine.

Ian's face was stark. Here we saw hundreds of pelts, and all the animals dead.

'Lovely,' Lillith said, and her hands caressed the remains of the mountain cat.

A man stepped forward from behind his racks of pelts. He was small, quick, authoritative. 'A discerning eye,' he said, smiling warmly at Lillith, but not *too* familiarly. A shrewd glance at Ian and myself told him we could afford the price of any one of a hundred pelts; his smile became obsequious. 'A fur-lined mantle, perhaps? A bit of coney for the collar?' He snatched up a night-black mountain cat pelt and swept it around Lillith's shoulders. 'Black on black,' he said. 'Lady, you are lovely.'

But Lillith looked past the man and lifted a slender hand. 'No,' she said, 'the white.'

The furrier glanced over his shoulder. His brown hair was tied back with a length of blue-dyed leather. His clothing also was of leather, with strips of fur at collar, cuffs and doublet hem. Red fox, I knew. I thought it fit his manner.

'Lady, that is not yet ready for sale.' Still smiling, he took the black pelt from Lillith and offered a silver one instead. '*This* one suits you well.'

'*That* one,' Lillith said, and there was no mistaking her tone.

The furrier pressed palms against his leathers. 'It has only just come in. There are treatments. I must first render it suitable.' He bobbed his head toward Ian and then myself. 'Perhaps something else for the lady?'

'There is nothing here for her,' Ian said flatly. 'I hunt and skin animals when I must, for food and warmth and shelter, but I do not slay – or *sell* – so many as to make my living at it.'

The furrier slanted a nervous glance in Tasha's direction.

The cat's amber eyes were fixed on his face, as if she intended to leap on him momentarily.

'I wish to see it,' Lillith said, and threw down the silver pelt.

The furrier complied. He settled the white pelt down in front of Lillith and folded his arms across his chest.

'Wolf,' she said, and I thought I heard satisfaction in her tone.

'Aye,' the furrier agreed. 'Brought in this morning. The trapper gave it only a bit of a cleaning.' Deft fingers peeled back an edge of the pelt to show the hide beneath. 'It wants softening, brushing, dyeing; all the things I do to the pelts to make them lovely enough for a lady as lovely as you.' No more merchant's chatter; he meant what he said, profoundly.

Lillith fingered a fur. 'Will it be white again? True white?'

'Wants cleaning.' He bobbed his head.

She smiled. 'The wolf must have been a lovely animal, alive.'

'Wanted killing,' the furrier said. 'Plague-ridden beast.' Uneasily he glanced at me. 'No more, of course. I'd never be selling a plague-ridden pelt.'

'What plague?' I frowned. 'There is no plague in Homana.'

'North, across the Bluetooth River,' he said. 'Herders took sick after a white wolf got into their sheep.'

'*This* wolf?' Ian asked.

The furrier shrugged. 'Trappers are taking every white one they can find, for the coin. Herders are paying good silver.'

'What are *you* paying?' I demanded.

He did not look away from me. 'Copper,' he said, and smiled. 'There is no plague in Mujhara.'

'And what will you sell it for?' Ian asked.

'Gold,' the furrier answered. 'White wolves are rare; there are people who crave the unusual.'

'Lovely,' Lillith murmured, burying fingers in the pelt.

'Enough,' I said abruptly, 'there is more for you to see.' I put a hand on her arm and turned her away from the stall.

'Nothing for the lady?' asked the man. 'Nothing for either of you?'

'We do not crave the unusual,' Ian answered, 'when purchased at the price of an animal's life.'

'It carried *plague!*' the man insisted, then shut his mouth as if he realized he might lower his asking price.

'Plague,' Ian said in disgust as we threaded our way through the throng. 'More likely the *sheepdogs* carried the sickness.'

'Or the herders themselves.' Lillith smiled. 'I have seen enough. I would like to go back to the palace.'

'You have seen nothing,' I said, surprised. 'You have hardly tapped Mujhara—'

'I have seen enough,' she repeated distinctly. A slim hand insinuated itself in the crook of my arm. 'Will you escort me home, my lord?'

The emphasis as she singled me out was slight, but still apparent, and certainly so to Ian. I saw the slight twist at one corner of his mouth; amusement or irritation, perhaps both. He glanced at me, smiled, gave in graciously. But I thought he and Tasha fell back a few steps with an undue amount of alacrity.

Lillith said little enough as I escorted her back to Homana-Mujhar, keeping herself in companionable silence. Ian and Tasha followed, but she ignored them both. The hand still rested in my elbow; I could hardly strip it away, though I longed to do it. Common courtesy denied me the pleasure.

Ihlini or no, she is Alaric's representative – in bed or out of it, as she says. What little I have learned of statecraft from my father forbids outright rudeness unless I have no choice. And for now, there is a choice.

Still, I wondered if Lillith had truly seen enough. Or if, more likely, she had seen precisely *what* she had come to see.

CHAPTER SEVEN

We took ship from Hondarth, bound for Atvia. It was possible to go overland through Solinde to the western port of Andemir, then set sail for the island, but the fastest way was to go by sea entirely. Besides, we had no wish to enter Ihlini environs with Lillith in our company.

Aside from Varien, Lillith, Ian, Tasha and myself, there was an escort of sixteen Homanan men handpicked from my father's personal Mujharan Guard. Ian, less inclined to approve of such things as royal escorts and decorum, was amused by it all. I felt a mixture of pride and resignation. I was content enough to accept my role as Homana's heir with all attendant traditions, but I realized, somewhat belatedly, that never again would I have the freedom to flee my princely concerns. The marriage, proxy or no, had locked the circlet around my head.

The weather, as we sailed out of Hondarth, was good. The rains had lifted entirely, leaving clear skies and a more temperate climate behind. Only a faint cool breeze snapped the blue sails of our ship and set the scarlet pennons flying.

Behind us lay the whitewashed city and lilac-heathered hills. Ahead of us floated the Crystal Isle, wreathed in silver mists. Ian, standing beside me at the taffrail, nodded toward the island. 'All the history, *rujho*. Do you ever think of it?'

'I thought of it enough when the *shar tahls* made me memorize all the stories.' Cautiously, I eyed the whitecaps slapping against the prow. I had not yet decided if I was born to sail or to keep myself to land.

Ian laughed. 'I, as well . . . but now those stories seem more alive. I think we should have come here *then*.

85

Immediacy makes the lessons more comprehensible.'

'I have no intention of reciting those lessons *now*,' I declared. 'Still . . . you have the right of it. Perhaps we should have come.'

'Why not recite those lessons to me?' inquired the husky voice from behind us. 'Surely you know I learned a *different* history.'

I turned to face Lillith. Ian did not. Beside him, with paws spread, Tasha snarled and pressed against Ian's leg.

She wore an indigo mantle. The edges, stitched with gold thread, snapped in the rising wind. Her unbound hair blew freely about her shoulders. I was put in mind of a shroud. Black. Silken. And all-encompassing.

'Then shall I tell you what *I* know of the island?' She slipped between Ian and me, touching neither of us, yet I was as aware of her as if she were a wine too heady for my wits. As for Ian, I could not say how he responded, save to see how rigid was his posture. 'It is the birthplace of the Cheysuli,' Lillith told us. 'The heart, if you will, of Homana.'

Whatever I had expected of her, it was not that. Never the truth. Sidelong, I looked at her, and saw the distant smile. 'The Ihlini rose out of Solinde,' I said; it was common knowledge.

A thick strand of hair was whipped into her face. Slender fingers caught at it and pulled it away from the questing grasp of the wind; silver-tipped nails flashed. 'The Ihlini rose out of *Homana*.' The smile was gone, but there was no hostility in her tone, merely matter-of-factness. 'I am certain Tynstar told Carillon, probably even your father. It is the truth, Niall; once the Ihlini and Cheysuli were as close – *closer* – than you and Ian.'

She had never said my name before. Accented, the syllables had a different sound. The sound of intimacy, which did not please me at all.

'Lady,' deliberately I denied familiarity, 'I think you mouth lies we would rather not hear.'

'Then tell me your truths,' she invited. 'Both of you: tell

86

me what all Cheysuli children are told, when the *shar tahls* share the knowledge contained in the histories.'

Ian turned abruptly. 'What do you know of Tynstar?'

He took her by surprise. Arched brows rose slightly. Then she smiled, and the corners of her eyes creased. The wind put color into her cheeks. But before she could answer Ian, I asked her a question of my own.

'How old are you, Lillith?' In my intentness, I hardly noticed my use of her given name. 'I have heard the stories of aborted aging.'

Lillith laughed. 'Along with other arts.' She looked at each of us, one by one, and her smile grew wider still. 'I shall answer both of you; I am more than a hundred years, and Tynstar was my father.'

Ian physically recoiled. Behind him, Tasha growled.

'Tynstar!' I blurted. 'How is it possible?'

'How is it *not* possible?' she countered. 'Oh, I know, you are thinking of Electra, Tynstar's mistress. Your granddame, was she not?' Lillith nodded before I could answer. 'Well, I can only say that when a man such as Tynstar lives for more than three hundred years, he will take more women than only one. Electra was the *last* one, perhaps, but hardly the first.' She raised her head against the wind and let it caress her face. 'My mother was Ihlini. We do not weigh the value of people by rank, only by power . . . but in your terms, she would have been a queen. As my father was the king.' Lips parted in sensual pleasure. Eyes closed, she bared her flawless face to the rising wind.

'Strahan is your half-brother.' I thought again of the man I had met in Mujhara, who had nearly drowned me in the mud.

'My younger brother,' Lillith agreed. '*So* young . . . and so newly-come to his arts.' She opened black eyes and looked at me. 'There is much left for him to learn.'

'But not so much for you,' Ian said harshly. 'Is that what you seek to say? To warn us of your power? Do not bother, lady. I have no intention of ignoring who or what you are.'

'No,' she said, 'that is obvious. But why must you assume I bear you or your brother ill will?'

'You are Ihlini.' It was explanation in itself.

'And kin to you, somewhere ages and ages ago.' Lillith gathered in flying hair and contained it in a slender hand. 'I am, albeit unspoken, Queen of Atvia. I am content with Alaric. What would I do with Homana? Why do you assume I *want* it?'

'You are Ihlini.' This time from me, and equally inflexible.

'Ihlini,' she said. 'Second-born of the First, and therefore a threat to you.' Lillith shook her head. 'Not all of us seek to hinder the prophecy.'

Ian's mouth opened, closed. I saw him visibly gather his thinning tolerance. 'Lady,' he said finally, with the infinite patience of a man who despises his opponent, 'you have the right of it when you say Tynstar must have spoken to Carillon and my *jehan*. Aye, I know the truth that drove the demon: fulfillment of the prophecy means the end of the Ihlini. How can you *not* work against us?'

Lillith stood very still. Mostly she faced Ian now, but in her profile I saw a look of exalted triumph. 'Aye,' she said on a breath of accomplishment, 'I think you begin to understand.'

Ian shook his head. 'Understand an Ihlini? I think not.'

She backed away from us both; wind-whipped wraith, suddenly, indigo blue and black. And magnificent in her pride. 'Why should we be any different?' she asked. 'Why should we be hounded by your dogs of righteousness until no one in all the world can see the *sense* in what we do — why we fight for our survival! Do you see? Do you see it at all?' Her eyes searched my face and Ian's. '*Evil*, you claim us; *demons* you call us; seed of the dark god himself. And why? Because we do what we must to survive. *Survive!* Would *you* do any differently if promised demise by the fulfillment of a prophecy?' The mantle cracked in the wind. 'Words,' she said bitterly. 'Words. And with them, you destroy an entire race. Even as you were nearly destroyed. Will you do the same to us? Unleash a Cheysuli *qu'mahlin?*'

'Enough,' Ian said, white-faced. 'You have said *enough*.'

'Have I?' Lillith demanded. She glanced at me, then met Ian's baleful, yellow-eyed glare. 'Looking at you, I say I have not. But then *you* are fanatic enough to be *a'saii*.'

The last was bitterly said. But before I could ask her how she came to know so much of the Old Tongue, Lillith turned her back on us both and took herself out of our sight.

A'saii. Ian? I knew better. Until I looked at his face.

'*Rujho—*' I began.

Ian's face was the mask I knew so well. But his ashen color was not. 'She has the tongue of a serpent.'

'Can a serpent tell the truth?'

His head snapped around as he looked at me in shock. 'You *believe* her?'

'No,' I told him, troubled, 'I think no Ihlini would ever bear us anything but ill will. But what if she tells the truth about their *reasons* for hating us so?'

'Truth, lies, what does it matter? Their knives are just as sharp.' Ian shook his head. 'Would it make you less dead if the man who slew you believed he was serving his race?'

The taste of salt was in my mouth. The tang was bitter-sweet. 'No, *rujho*. No.'

'See that you remember it,' Ian told me flatly. 'See that you never forget.'

I watched him as he took Tasha with him to the other side of the deck. Alone, *incredibly* alone, I stood against the taffrail and wondered if there was, beyond the obvious, any real difference between Ihlini and Cheysuli.

We love and hate and fight with equal certitude. But then, so can brother and brother; so can sister and sister.

I shivered. The wind was decidedly cold.

The Idrian Ocean is a fractious beast, tame one day, wild the next. As we passed the crumbled headlands of south-western Solinde, nearing the two islands known as Erinn and Atvia, the beast turned definitively disagreeable; I discovered I was a good sailor in good weather, a poor one in bad.

I stayed below much of the time, studiously ignoring what I could of the pitching ship, but when the swells deepened and the timbers began to groan alarmingly, I dragged myself up the slippery ladder to the sea-splashed deck above.

The sun was swallowed by clouds. I could not tell if it were evening or afternoon. Wind-wracked, sea-swept, I could not even tell if it rained, or if the water came from the ocean. All I knew was I was soaked through in an instant and the deck was incredibly slick.

'Ian?' He was somewhere on deck, I knew; he spent as much time above as I did below. 'Ian!' Slipping, sliding, swearing, I made it to the taffrail and clung with all my might. Spray nearly drowned me; the wind tried to batter me back.

I spat out the taste of salt. All around me the light was odd, an unearthly, ocherous green. My belly began to dance within the confines of my flesh.

'Gods,' I muttered aloud, 'if this is but a gentle blow, I would not care to see a gale.'

The wind snapped the words back at me, along with the salty spittle of the sea. Eyes stung, mouth protested; I spat back, making certain I did it *with* the wind, and not against.

Ian came up behind me, looming out of the lowering sky. 'The captain suggests we go below.'

'No,' I blurted instantly. 'At least up here I can breathe.'

Ian smiled as I turned to spit again. 'Can you?' The humor faded as he squinted past me into the wind. 'Niall – perhaps we should do as he says. The waves will surely swamp us.'

I looked at the rolling ocean. The swells were watery mountains; the troughs a common grave.

I glanced back at Ian. Wet black hair was flattened against his head. Bare-armed, the water polished his gold. His leathers were soaked, but no more so than my woolen breeches and padded doublet.

'Where is Tasha?' I asked.

'I sent her below. She hates the water so, I could not bear

to keep her with me.' Ian squinted into the slanting rain. 'Gods, Niall – look at *that!*'

I looked. Out of the pewter-green skies came a tracery of lilac. Delicate fingers touched here, touched there, insinuating themselves between the lobes of heavy clouds. It spread; spreading, it began to swallow the waves as well as the sky.

'I have seen nothing like *that* before,' I declared.

'Nor have I,' he agreed grimly, 'but neither of us is a sailor.'

No, we were neither of us a sailor. But it does not take a sailor to know when a storm is a bad one, or when the waves are more than *water.*

Gods – how they rise – how they prepare to swallow us all—

And then I forgot the waves and stared only at the heavens. 'By the gods, the sky is *alive!*'

The ship dropped, prow-first, into a deep trough. It seemed almost to stand on end. I clutched the rail and braced myself against the slippery deck.

'Niall – the wave – *hold on—*'

Crushing weight descended upon me. It drove me to the deck, battering at flesh and bones, until I slid freely across flooded decking and came to rest, however briefly, against a pile of massive rope. I clutched at the nearest coil, locking rigid fingers as the huge wave rolled over the deck. Timbers groaned and shuddered. Like a surly stallion, the ship bucked beneath my body.

The water lived. It tried to swallow me down a sea-dragon's gullet, sucking, *sucking*, threatening to chew, until I lodged against a sore tooth and kicked, *kicked*, still clutching my coil of rope. Heaving, the sea-dragon spat me out; exhaled bleeding, screaming debris as well as silent bags of broken bone and shredded flesh.

My mouth was filled with blood and salt. My ears, deafened by pressure as well as by sound, throbbed painfully. Water and blood was streaming from my nose.

'Ian,' I mumbled thickly. 'Ian – *where are you, rujho?*'

The mast snapped. Spars broke and were flung through

91

the air, skewering flesh and canvas. Sheets and shredded sail collapsed across the deck, tangling men within heavy folds and the deadly embroidery of knots and coils.

'Niall!' Distantly, I heard him. 'Niall – *where are you—?*'

'Here!' But in the heart of the storm I could hardly hear myself.

Something pierced my leg. With the pitching of the ship I tried to pull myself onto hands and knees, but the slippery deck denied me proper purchase. Face down, I slid from my coil of rope toward the skeletal silhouette of the taffrail, fragile promise against the violence of the storm.

And heard the scream of a mountain cat.

Ian? No. More likely Tasha, searching for her *lir*.

Pitch, roll, heave . . . I slid nearer the side of the ship, knowing a negligent slap of the dragon's tail could sunder the wood and sweep me into the seas beyond.

Tasha. Screaming. Ian?

I lurched upward, lunging for solid wood. Found it; what it was I could not say, knowing so little of ships. It creaked. Groaned. But it held.

Lurid lightning spilled like blood through the blackened clouds and lit up the drowning ship. In its glare I saw Tasha, huddled against a heavy sea chest. Wedged, the chest showed no signs of giving itself over to the storm. Timing the swells, I let go of my handhold and ran.

The ship rolled, wallowing like a drunken man in a pool of urine and vomit. I fell to both knees, skidded, slid into the terrified cat, apologized silently, and peeled myself up from the deck. The chest had brass handles; I grabbed one and held on.

Tasha's amber eyes were dyed yellow-green in the livid light. Tufted ears flattened against her head. Tightly, so tightly, she clamped her tail around quivering haunches. Diminished by the storm, she was little more than a terrified housecat.

It made me tremendously angry, that gods – or demons – would play with the mountain cat so.

'Tasha, Tasha – *shansu*. Be easy, my lovely girl . . . the

storm will come to an end.' A hand against soaked shoulder found rigid flesh and hardened sinew. She shook, even as I did; from the rain, from the cold, from the fear.

'Tasha, where is your *lir*?' I knew she could not tell me, but I could not hold back the question.

The cat snarled, baring lethal teeth in rage and pain. In the lightning I saw the gaping hole in her flank.

'Oh Tasha – *no!*'

It was deep. Jagged. It bled freely, but the rain washed it open again. And again; I watched her life spill onto the deck.

'No!' The shout tore out of my throat. 'Gods, Tasha, *not you* – if you die, *Ian* dies—'

A heavy line slapped across my face, knocking me to the deck. Stunned, I felt the stinging spring up in my cheek and the pain growing in one eye. Groping fingers sought the welt and found it, as well as the cut over my eye. Already the lid swelled closed.

'Tasha—' I saw the cat's third eyelid rise. Sluggish, weakened, she panted, exposing slack pink tongue. From deep in her chest I heard the ongoing wail of pain and fatigue. Rising, dropping; a song of death and regret and futility.

If Ian was not already dead, Tasha's death would destroy him completely. Drive him into madness. Drive him into seeking the death-ritual.

Briefly, I thought of my grandsire, Duncan. Tynstar had slain his *lir*, Cai, the hawk. And so he had also slain Duncan.

Oh gods, if my brother must die, I beg you – let him die in another way . . . Not a petition I was proud of, but I could not bear to lose him twice.

I crawled to Tasha. Peeled off my padded doublet, sodden and dripping with rain, and folded it, pressing it against the wound in Tasha's flank. My linen shirt plastered itself against my battered body. I shivered. My cheek and eye hurt; vision was restricted to my left eye only.

The ship rolled. Caught. Shuddered like a man expending himself in a woman. Stopped dead.

I was thrown to the deck, flung completely away from Tasha, and saw the taffrail tilt eerily. Beyond it lay the horizon, backlighted by saffron and silver. The moon, I realized, balanced itself on the blade of the horizon.

Free of trunk, of handle, of Tasha, I slid toward the maw of the dragon. Stiffened fingers and boot toes scrabbled against wet wood.

Shuddering again, the ship tilted farther yet and slid more deeply into the sea. Another wave drove it deeper, scraping the deck free of debris. At the broken rail I was caught by rigging; dragged up again as the ship wallowed, foundered, tried to pull free of the sea. As I grabbed for rope and spar, I saw Tasha swept by me into the dragon's mouth.

In shock, I could not grieve. I could only mouth the names of my brother and his *lir*.

The ship shuddered again, groaning as the hull splintered against jagged rocks. I felt the vibration through my body and realized what it meant.

'Land?' I croaked aloud. 'But – how can there be land?'

I flailed in the rigging, trying to right myself. The ship, solidly aground, no longer pitched or wallowed. But it had tilted to an alarming degree; no more was there a deck on which I could stand. Knees grated against the rigging, lapped about with water, and slipped loose in the force of the waves.

'Niall.'

I wrenched my head around and saw the woman clinging to a spar. It slashed a diagonal wound across the fabric of the sky. The storm had broken; behind her, the moon bled silver light.

'Lillith.' The name was hardly a sound.

Sodden hair tangled at her hips. She had shed the indigo cloak. The gown she wore was deepest black, so that except for face and hands she was a part of the darkness itself.

I saw her reach out a hand. I saw the silver flash of her painted nails. But mostly I saw her beguiling smile, promising life, survival, continuance.

'Your choice,' she said. 'I will not make it for you.'

I drew in a trembling breath. 'And the price of Ihlini aid?'

'Whatever your life is worth.'

I tried to swallow and found the task too painful. 'My brother,' I croaked, 'and his *lir*.'

Lillith smiled. And then she laughed. 'I am sorry,' she said at last. 'His choice is already made.'

I spat. And then I cursed her.

The pale hand rose. I saw a line of purple flame come hissing from out of the darkness to dance in the palm of her hand. In its lurid light her face was thrown into relief, hollowed: a fragile mask of death.

She carried the flame to her mouth, pursed her lips and blew. In the explosion of smoke and fire, Lillith disappeared.

Alone, alone, I cursed the woman. And then I threw back my head. 'If you want me, *if you want me* – then, by the gods, you must *take* me!'

For a moment a hushed silence descended upon the ship. A quiver of fear and awe ran through my body.

The spar Lillith had clung to broke. Falling, it tangled me in its rigging. The weight of it crushed my chest.

I tumbled helplessly into the sea.

CHAPTER EIGHT

I roused to the taste of salt in my mouth, my teeth, in the crusted cuts on my lips. It burned. I sought to spit it out, but my mouth would not form the proper shape.

My flesh also burned and itched. The cloying touch of salt was in every crease of my skin, in every crease of the rags that remained of my clothing. One hand twitched. I pushed it weakly to and fro, relieving an itch by scraping the back of my hand against damp, rounded rock. Once done, my hand fell limply into water.

Water.

Realization awoke knowledge within my sluggish mind. Water. All around. It dampened my clothing and puddled beneath my cheek.

Asking nothing else of my battered body, I tried to open my eyes and found only one answered my bidding.

Sand and pebbles grated beneath my face. I tongued my lips and tasted salt, the ever-present salt, and felt the swollen dryness of split flesh and crusted sores.

Move, arm. The arm moved. It lifted and carried wet fingers to my face. The fingers awkwardly brushed away sand from my good eye and peeled back crusted salt.

Dimly, I saw tumbled rocks and rounded boulders. And the sea. Waves lapped gently at the stone nearest me, and I realized the tide was coming in.

I must move.

The pain was exquisite. Never had I felt such before, not even when the barber had jerked out a rotten tooth; the intensity astonished me. My hand, searching gently, felt damp cloth on my chest and shredded flesh beneath. My linen shirt was badly torn. The bones within bruised flesh ached with a fitful ferocity.

I twitched all over, once. The involuntary movement awoke dull fire within every limb and brought full consciousness rushing in. I remembered it all.

Ian—

I sat up carefully, hugging my sore chest with one arm. The other I braced against the sand, holding myself upright. Dazedly I stared out to sea and saw the ship was gone.

Rujho—?

The crying of a seabird pierced the dullness in my ears and drew my burning eyes. Clusters of fellow gulls swooped and circled in the air, crying shrilly. I saw I was not on land at all, but a craggy fingerbone of stone. Sand clogged some pockets, water pooled in others. My salvation was but thirty paces from the shore; still, I felt too weak to make the attempt.

Ian.

Waves lapped at my feet. One boot was missing, sucked off by the sea-dragon's spite. I shuddered. The sea was my enemy, as it had been my brother's.

Oh gods, you have taken my brother from me—

But I was too dry for tears.

I felt at my waist and discovered my belt was whole, as was the silver-laced sheath; the knife itself was gone. But the ruby signet ring on my right hand glowed brilliantly in the sunlight, and I realized I had managed to keep my deliverance. For the worth of this ring, surely *someone* would give me aid.

I pressed myself to knees, then feet, and wavered alarmingly. My bones were brittle, hollow things; I feared they might shatter at any moment. My right eye ached and burned. The pain in my chest made me hunch, to relieve the strain on my ribs.

The tide is coming in. If you do not move, the sea will finish what the Ihlini witch began.

Slowly, with infinite care, I waded across the shallow inlet to the shore. By the time I reached it, the sea had swallowed

97

my rocky perch. And so I stared inland, knowing my safety lay there, and wondered if I had come, however tragically, to Atvia at last.

Maps.

I thought back on the maps I had seen in my father's council chambers. I recalled the rugged coast of western Solinde, and even the channel separating Erinn and Atvia. But no matter how hard I thought back, I could not recall if Rondule lay north or south, east or west. For that matter, I could not begin to say where I was in relation to the city.

Ian would say I deserve it, for shirking my geography. Oh, Ian, I would give anything to have you present. Your reprimand would be welcome.

I heard hoofbeats before I saw the riders. I turned immediately south toward the sound. Mounted men pounded toward me, garbed in plain, badgeless clothing that clearly was not household livery. The men wore caps on their heads. Baldrics dyed bright green slashed diagonally across their chests.

Perhaps some manner of household badge after all.

I waited, holding myself stiffly upright, and tried to think of what to say.

Twelve men. They surrounded me almost immediately at lancepoint. Somewhat startled by the reception – I was a single bedraggled man – I stared first at the gleaming points, then looked at the men who bore them.

Strong men all; I saw it at once. With all of Carillon's youthful height and bulk, I am hardly what one might regard as small. But, even on horseback, I judged very few of the men would have to look up at me when they dismounted. They were bearded, toughened soldiers, fully experienced in what I believed had to be the Erinnish/Atvian war; I knew, looking at them, even clean, fed and whole, I would offer them little threat.

I summoned what dignity I could. 'Is this Atvia?' The croak I emitted was hardly human; a second try produced a hoarse but recognizable question.

Eleven men remained perfectly still atop wary horses; the

twelfth rode slowly forward until the tip of his lance rested against my vulnerable, sunburned throat. He wore an age-polished leather cap fastened with a strap beneath his jaw, which was forested by heavy blond beard. His green eyes were shrewd. His expression was unrelenting.

'Atvia,' he said softly. ''Tis Atvia you're wanting?'

Swallowing was painful. What I needed was water, but would not ask for it from him. 'My ship was bound for Atvia. It went down in the storm. I do not know where I am.'

A humorless smile carved deep creases at the corners of his eyes. 'Not Atvia, lad. 'Tis Erinn, held by Shea himself, and Lord of the Idrian Isles. Erinn, lad, not Atvia. Atvia's *enemy*.'

'You have a truce,' I blurted, startled.

The green eyes narrowed consideringly. 'What would *you* be knowing of a truce between your betters?'

'Betters,' I muttered. I ached. I did not need this inter-rogation. 'Take me to your lord, if you will. What I have to say will be for him.'

The lance dug a hole in my neck, but did not cut me, quite. 'What would *you* be saying to Lord Shea, ye bedraggled pup?'

I wanted to laugh, but could find neither strength nor voice. So I tried to strip the signet from my finger, to prove my right to a royal audience, but discovered my joints too swollen for the effort. Finally I extended my arm toward the man. 'If you will look at the stone, you will see a rampant lion. I am Niall of Homana.'

'Niall of Homana,' the Erinnish man mocked. 'What would Homana be wanting with Erinn?'

I wavered. 'Nothing in particular, except aid for a bedraggled pup of a prince.' I tried to smile disarmingly. 'I did not intend to come here. It was the storm.'

'Aye, the storm,' the other interrupted. ''Twas a fierce one, was it not?' He grinned, showing strong white teeth. 'We are accustomed to a bit of weather, now and then, here in Erinn. How is it with you in Homana?'

I glared up at him, too weary to care about impressions. 'In Homana I am treated better, being heir to the Mujhar.'

The man exchanged grins with his fellow riders. 'Heir, are ye, to the Mujhar? Is it Donal ye mean? And ye say you are his son?'

'Aye.' The word was all I could manage.

'Legitimate, too, or is that too much to expect?'

'*Ku'reshtin*,' I swore feebly, 'I said I was his heir—' There was more I wanted to say and could not, being overtaken by a painful racking cough. I bent over at once; some of the sea I had swallowed came up to scour my teeth and throat.

I saw the sun glint off the lance tip as the man at last lowered the weapon. 'Have ye had a hard time of it, puppy?' he inquired in mock solicitude. 'Well, I'll be seeing to it you are treated befitting your rank—' as he paused I glanced up and saw his green eyes narrow '—once the rank is proven.'

'*Ku'reshtin*,' I muttered again. 'Look at the ring, you fool.'

The soldier frowned down at me. 'What is that? That word? What name did you call me by?'

I summoned an ironic smile. '*Ku'reshtin*? It is Cheysuli, of course. The House of Homana is Cheysuli – or did you not realize that?'

I had expected further questions, or at least a mocking comment. Instead the soldier turned and gave a quiet order to one of his companions. In weary surprise, I watched as the man dismounted and brought his horse to me. The reins were held out in invitation.

'Take the horse,' the leader said. 'I'll be escorting you to Kilore.'

'Kilore.' I frowned. 'Shea's castle?'

''Tis my father's home.'

Reaching for the reins, I froze. I looked sharply up at the blond-bearded man.

'Aye,' he said, when I did not bother to ask it. 'Had ye not heard Shea has himself a son, even in Homana? 'Tis not *that* far away!' He grinned. 'I am Liam. Prince of Erinn. Shea himself's own heir.'

'No.' I said it distinctly.

He laughed. 'Oh, I admit I'm not looking much like a prince at the moment. Still, I am; underneath this soldier's garb is princely flesh, I swear. But 'tis enough to fool the Atvians, when they try to land their boats.' He jerked his head toward the horse. 'There is your mount, puppy; let us be going home.'

Sluggish resentment rose. 'Puppy,' I muttered wearily. 'When I am no longer so sore, I will knock that word from your mouth.'

Liam of Erinn laughed and shoved the leather cap from his head. Blond curls fell around his face and I saw the years fall with it. Capped, bearded, with his weathered, wind-chafed cheeks, I would have said the man claimed at least forty years. But now he shed them easily; he was no more than ten years my senior.

I wavered, and Liam's laughter died. 'The sea has treated you poorly, lad, and I no better, have I? Mount your horse, Homana's heir, and I will see to it you're given the honor a prince deserves.'

I turned to the horse in silence and clutched at pommel and cantle, hoisting myself from the ground. But if the Erinnish prince had not reached out and caught my arm, I would have fallen again.

Drooping in the saddle, I hunched forward over the pommel. 'Ian,' I mumbled, 'where are you?'

'Here, lad,' Liam told me, thinking I said his name.

'No—' I meant to explain, of course, but the light spilled out of the day.

Ropes fell away from wrists. Belatedly, I realized my face was buried in a horse's braided mane. I spat out the acrid taste of horsehair and pushed myself upright carefully, wishing I could neglect to breathe until my ribs had healed.

Liam stood by the horse, ropes dangling from his hands. 'I tied you on because I thought you might fall off.'

Undoubtedly I would have. I blinked, squinting, and peered around the cobbled bailey of a castle. The eleven soldiers – a prince's guard, I realized – arrayed themselves around me. 'Kilore?' I croaked.

'Kilore. The Aerie of Erinn, my lord.' Liam grinned and swung his cap by its leather strap. 'Before you ask: I looked at that gaudy ring. I know the rampant lion, puppy, as well as I know my dogs.' He rumpled brassy, tumbled curls. 'Are you really Cheysuli, then? You lack the yellow eyes.'

A chill washed over me. *Even here they know the difference.* 'I *am* Cheysuli,' I muttered, 'but I look like Carillon.'

Liam's heavy brows rushed upward to hide under hair that needed cutting. 'Carillon, is it? I have heard of him. Was he not one of your heroes?'

'A man,' I said crossly, having no desire to debate my grandsire's merits in Erinn any more than in Homana. 'No more than that; a man.'

Liam eyed me without expression. 'A man who hacks away at legends builds little of his own.'

'I have no *wish* to build a legend,' I said in weary disgust. 'All I want is a *lir*.' I shut my mouth almost immediately; was Liam a sorcerer to bewitch such admissions from me?

'A *lir*?' he asked; no sorcerer, then, or surely he would know. 'A charm, is it? A spell?'

'Animal,' I answered. 'A gift from the gods themselves. Without them we cannot shapechange.'

Liam's escort muttered among themselves. Liam himself stared intently up at me. 'And you are missing a *lir*.'

'I am.'

'So you lack all Cheysuli magic.'

'I do.' I said it between my teeth.

Grimly, he shook his head. 'Not a wise admission, lad. Some men might be wishing to use you for their gain. 'Twould be better you made them think you have the magic.'

''Twould be better you let him get off that horse,' said a resonant, growling voice, 'before he falls on his head.'

102

I looked toward the castle and saw a tall, big-shouldered man in fine woolen dress descending the steps of the cavernous entrance. He was considerably older than Liam, but his manner and movements were those of a younger man. His blond hair and beard had silvered heavily, but still showed signs of the richness of youth. Green eyes were bright beneath an overgrown hedge of brows.

'Shea,' I mumbled, 'at last.'

'Have him down,' the old man said. 'Unless he be Atvian, he is due some words to me.'

'Homanan,' Liam told him, moving forward to help me down. The dismounting was painful. I shut my mouth on a curse. 'He says his ship went down in the storm.'

'Accursed Ihlini storm,' Shea growled. 'Alaric's witch, again.' He looked more intently at me. 'Homanan, are ye? What word have you for me?'

'Nothing *prepared*, my lord. I was not originally coming here.' I managed a weary smile. 'Still, I have no doubts my father would wish you well.'

Shea glared. '*Why* would your father wish me well, and who is he to wish it?'

'Donal,' Liam told him. 'Donal the Mujhar.'

Shea's heavy brows jerked upward. Strip from him forty years, and he could be his son. 'Truth?'

'Truth.' Liam pointed at my ring. 'The lion, my lord. The one in my grandmother's tapestry.'

'Bring him in!' Shea bellowed. 'See he is given food and drink!'

Fatuously, I smiled. Liam merely grinned. 'The royal welcome, puppy. Shea himself has spoken!'

Food: rare beef, hot bread, sweet cheese. Drink: a powerful smoky liquor, as much as I could swallow. I ate as much as I could keep down on my brutalized belly, and drank too much of the liquor.

Shea sat in an iron-bound chair in the center of the hall. Liam paced silently, head bent as he turned the cap over and over in his callused hands. I watched him closely, wondering – uneasily – why the Prince of Erinn was not at home in his father's hall.

'Are you done?' Shea growled. 'Have you slain the hunger and slaked your thirst?'

His speech, at times, was almost archaic. In my muddled mind, I had trouble deciphering the dialect. 'For the moment,' I answered at last. 'My lord—'

'A shipwreck, you say. That I believe; what could survive that accursed witch's meddling?' He swore in a language I did not know. 'If you were not coming here, where *were* you going, lad?'

'I was on my way to Atvia.' I glanced sidelong at Liam.

Shea frowned, fingering the hilt of the massive knife at his belt. 'What business have you with my enemy?'

Again, I said, 'I thought there was a truce.'

Briefly, Liam paused in his pacing. He looked intently at his father.

Shea buried bearded chin in the heel of his hand as he leaned upon one arm. He watched me silently, green eyes mostly hidden in lowered brows. I waited uneasily for his answer.

'Why were you Atvia-bound?' the Lord of Erinn inquired, and I realized that *was* my answer.

'I am to wed Alaric's daughter.'

Shea's eyebrows shot up again. 'The Cheysuli lass?'

Guardedly, I watched him. 'She is my cousin, my lord. Her mother was my aunt.'

Shea shifted in his chair. 'I saw Bronwyn, once, before she died. The lass, I am told, resembles her mother, not her father. Yet you resemble neither.'

Liam was pacing again. 'No,' I agreed. 'The heritage is mixed. If Gisella resembles her mother, she shows her Cheysuli blood. I – do not.'

'Why do you wed the lass?'

The liquor was making me sleepy on top of all the food. 'Alliance,' I said succinctly, because it was all I could manage.

Liam strode between his father and me and faced me

104

directly. 'Alaric of Atvia calls my father usurper and outlaw. He claims the title Lord of the Isles for himself, when he has no right to it at all. Why is Homana desiring an alliance with the jackal of Atvia?'

After a moment, I nodded. 'There *is* no truce, I see.'

'Alaric believes there is.' Shea displayed yellowed teeth. 'Betimes a lie or two will help to win a war.'

I stared at Shea a long moment. Then I looked at Liam. Neither man was a fool. Neither man was a friend.

My fingers and toes were numb. I rubbed distractedly at salt residue in my hair. Weariness made me dangerously frank. 'Truce or no, it does not matter. It makes no difference to Homana *who* claims this island title. We have our own concerns.'

Shea sat upright in his chair. 'A petty feud between petty kingdoms. Is that what you are saying?'

'No.' It was all I could do to mouth it.

'Then what *are* ye saying, pup?'

Liam gets it from his father. I licked my lips and tasted the smoky liquor. 'My father defeated Alaric in battle nearly twenty years ago. Since then, Alaric has paid Homana tribute twice a year. Atvia is our *vassal*.' I struggled to speak sensibly. 'My lord, outside of accepting tribute, we hardly know what Atvia does. Your battles are your own.'

'I have seen the tribute ships,' Shea mused. 'Twice yearly, as you say.' His eyes glittered shrewdly. 'As vassal to Homana, Alaric has the right to request Homanan aid.'

'He would never get it.' I tried to sit upright in my chair. 'My lord – my father loathes the man. It was Alaric's brother, Osric, who slew Carillon – my grandsire – and made my father Mujhar.'

'He was not wanting the title?'

'Not at the cost of Carillon's life.'

Shea nodded benignly. 'Then why does he wed his son to Alaric's daughter?'

My good eye insisted on closing. My wits were failing too quickly. 'My lord—?'

'Why does Donal wed Niall to Gisella of Atvia?'

105

The deceptively gentle tone woke me as nothing else had done. I looked at Shea more clearly. 'For the alliance,' I said. 'We need no trouble with Atvia. We have enough with Solinde and Strahan.'

'Ihlini,' Liam said. 'Kin to Alaric's witch.'

Shea rubbed his beard. 'Alaric desires this marriage?'

'I think he does, my lord. I am proxy-wed to—' I stopped. I could not bear to say her name: my brother's murderer.

'Alaric desires the marriage.' Shea nodded. 'Good.'

I drew in an unsteady breath and tried to clear my head. 'What will you do with me, my lord? Will you send me to Atvia?'

Erinn's gruff lord rose and walked to me. He stopped. Smiled down on me warmly, kindly; in infinite empathy. 'You are weary, lad, and injured. You are requiring rest. I will ask my son to help you to your room.'

Shea wavered before my eyes. 'You have not answered my question.' I waited. 'My lord,' I appended faintly.

Shea and Liam shared contented smiles. But it was the older man who spoke. 'If Alaric's wanting this wedding so badly, then, he will pay for it, will he not?'

'Pay for it?' I asked dully.

'Aye,' Shea said in satisfaction. 'One way or the other, I'll be getting the concessions I want from him. In exchange for his daughter's betrothed.'

The weariness washed out of me on a wave of comprehension. 'And if he is unwilling to grant those concessions?'

Shea gestured eloquently. 'You are heir to the throne of Homana, lad. We'll be treating you accordingly. You need not fear for your life.' He smiled. 'You will be honored as our guest . . . for as long as Alaric insists.'

CHAPTER NINE

The Aerie of Erinn, Kilore is called. Apropos, I thought. *Surely Shea raises eagles in place of sons and daughters.*

Kilore perched atop a chalk-white, rocky headland at one nubby corner of Erinn. It afforded any long-sighted man a glimpse of Atvia, to the north across the channel the Erinnish call the Dragon's Tail. It was only a shadowed view, distorted by sea spray and distance; distorted also by tears of grief and the bitterness of frustration.

I stood on the windy battlements and glared out at the choppy channel, cursing the dragon whose capriciousness had stolen away my brother. An Erinnish wind blew in my ears, singing a lament I knew too well. Each night it kept me awake. Each night it made me dream; dream of my brother.

Grief dulls the pain of physical wounds and ailments. My ribs knitted, my eye opened, the scrapes and bruises healed. I was whole again because of Erinnish care, but I found I regretted it. It gave me time to think of Ian again.

'Longing for your Atvian bride?'

I turned. The wind dried the remains of my tears. I saw Liam had exchanged plain soldier's garb for finer garments of blue-dyed wool, fastened with hammered gold platelets. His shining curls were brushed smooth, but the wind already whipped them into brassy disarray.

'No,' I said flatly. 'It is difficult to long for a woman when you have never seen her.'

Like me, Liam pressed his belly against the wall and hooked elbows over the top of the crenel, boundaried on either side by taller merlons. 'A striking girl, she is. I saw

107

her once, when she sailed the Dragon's Tail to get a better look at Shea's unruly children.' He grinned. 'Atvia is so close, she might as well have shouted.'

I did not wish to talk with him, no more than I ever did. But Liam was blind to my sullen silences . . . or else he did what he did to ease them. 'You want her for yourself.' It was something to say; I said it.

Liam laughed long and loud. 'Easy explanation, is it? Another thing to resent me for? *Hah!* I am already married, lad; I am wanting nothing of that girl. You may have her.' He looked at me closely out of speculative green eyes. 'But you should not be placing such trust in alliances made in the wedding bed, my lad. They do not always hold.'

'What would *you* know of that?'

Liam nodded a little, staring out at the distant island. 'More than you might be thinking. My mother was Atvian.'

That snapped my head around. 'Your *mother?*'

Liam picked at mortar with a blunt finger. The nail was already blackened; this would peel it back. 'Aye, Atvian she was. Shea married her to settle this accursed feud between the realms. For a while, it did. Then I was born, and Shea desired a title for his son. So he took back his claim as Lord of the Idrian Isles.' He glanced at me levelly. 'Alaric is my uncle.'

In disgust, I looked away. 'My marriage will make us kinsmen, you and I.'

'*If* you wed the girl.'

'And what would keep me from it?' I turned to face him squarely. 'Do you intend to do it?'

Liam smiled. Then he laughed. 'The puppy growls. Then be growling as loudly as you wish; I know better than to judge a dog by the sound of his voice.'

Inwardly, I swore. Outwardly, I showed him an expressionless face. 'I am proxy-wed to Gisella. The marriage will be made.'

'Proxy-wed to that *witch*.' Liam swore, spat over the wall and made the ward-sign against Ihlini evil. 'But at least you did not bed with her, or surely your loins would be cursed.'

I grunted. 'If I had bedded her, *that* marriage would be real.'

Liam went back to picking at the mortar. 'Lad, you *must* see it. Alaric is unlikely to succumb to Shea's latest raft of demands. He never has before; they are two old hounds baring rotten teeth over a bitch who does not care.' Sunlight gilded beard and curls. 'No insult to ye, lad, but he can get a man for his daughter anywhere. Homana is hardly the only kingdom in the world, nor you the only prince.'

I reached impotently for the knife that did not rest in my sheath. Not to harm Liam, whom I judged the better fighter, but out of an almost insane wish to cut at *someone* just to ease the bitter frustration. 'Alaric sends no word?'

'None yet, save for that first one of calculated outrage.' Liam's grin was crooked. 'Methinks the value of his daughter's prince declines.'

My teeth clicked closed. I forced the sentence through them. 'Then let me send word to my father, and you will *see* what value I have.'

Liam, laughing, lolled against the wall. 'I am having no doubts Donal values his heir. But 'twould bring the entire Homanan army down upon our heads, when 'tis only a dogfight betwen Erinn and Atvia.'

With great effort, I kept myself from kicking the wall with my boot toe. 'How do you know *Alaric* has not sent word to my father? He would like nothing better than to have Donal of Homana needing something from him.'

'Because I know Alaric's pride,' Liam answered. 'I have a measure of my own, lad; are you forgetting?' He rubbed distractedly at a sea-filmed clasp. 'Alaric will wait. Alaric will play out the game. For now, Homana is not involved. There is no need for it.'

'How is there no need?' I cried. 'My father does not even know his other son is dead!'

Liam released the clasp at once and looked at me in shock. 'You had a *brother* on that ship?'

'Had,' I echoed numbly. *Gods, why did it have to be Ian?*

109

'Aye. He went down, like all the others, swallowed by the dragon.'

The levity was scrubbed clean from Liam's face. 'You are certain he died?'

I shrugged listlessly and turned away; turned to stare out at the white-capped Dragon's Tail. 'How could he survive?'

'*You* survived, lad. 'Tis possible he washed ashore as you did.'

'Dead,' I said. 'Without Tasha . . .'

Liam pushed hair from his eyes. ''Tis hard on a man to lose a woman, but it does not always kill him, Niall. There is still a chance—' He broke off as I stared at him incredulously. 'Why are ye gaping at me, lad? 'Tis not foolishness I spout, but truth!'

Slowly I shook my head. 'Tasha was not his wife, Liam, nor even his light woman. Tasha was his *lir*. Without her, he is a dead man.'

'How can you be so certain of that? Was he a sickling, then? A weakling?' The wind tugged at beard and hair. 'Looking at *you*, Niall, I think he must be a tougher man than you think.'

'It has nothing to do with toughness.' *And everything to do with it*. I reached out and caught his wrist, baring the sinewy underside to the sky. 'If I took a knife and cut deeply enough to spill all your blood onto the stone, would you die?'

'Are ye daft, lad? Of *course* the bleeding would kill me!'

'Because you require the blood to live.' I let go of his wrist. 'Think of a *lir* as that blood. Without Tasha, Ian dies.'

Liam stared down at his wrist. Heavy blond brows knotted; he resembled his father more than usual. But when he looked at me, I saw compassion in his eyes. ''Tis that, then? The price? The cost of being Cheysuli?'

I met his gaze squarely. 'For every warrior – except, of course, myself.'

Green eyes narrowed as he studied me. 'Would ye be wanting it, then? This cost? If ye knew the animal, taken

110

from ye, would result in your death though you be *healthy*
– would ye still be wanting it?'

'Aye,' I said. 'If a god came to me and offered a *lir* in
exchange for an eye, I would give him both of them.'

'I am sorry,' he said abruptly. 'Prince or no, you are an
honorable man – and due better treatment than this.'

Hope rose. 'Then you will let me send word to my father?'

'No.'

I reached for his throat; closed my fists on air and shook
them in his face. '*Gods*, Erinnish, do you do this to torture
me? You are worse than the Ihlini!'

''Twould not serve my father,' Liam declared, but I saw
the glint of anger in his eyes.

'Your father!' I spat. 'That old fool? You yourself call
him an old hound with rotten teeth.'

Liam caught my left arm in an iron grasp and shut off
all the bloodflow. 'In my place, would you be allowing me
to send to mine? Would you risk bringing an army of
shapechangers into your land? I think not, puppy – I think
not at all!' Liam shook me. It was a measure of his strength.
It was a measure of his anger. 'Shea cannot be sending to
Donal, or he leaves us open to the arts you shapechangers
claim!'

'Gods, I wish I *had* them!' I shouted back. 'I would break
you like a rotten piece of bone!'

A quiet voice intruded. But it was not Shea's familiar
growl. 'Sometimes I'm wishing someone *would* break my
brother. His arrogance knows no bounds.'

Liam thrust me against the wall as he released my arm.
I winced as spine met stone, but stood upright almost
immediately. I tried to ignore the numbness in my arm.

Liam laughed aloud as he turned back to me and slumped
against the wall, all his anger banished. 'She is back, lad.
We'll be knowing no peace at all.' The laughter died away.
'She is Deirdre of Erinn, Niall. My sister.'

She was a feminine version of Liam, but lacking all the
rough edges. Like him she was tall, but in her his bulk was
slenderness. The hair was the same brilliant, brassy gold;

unbound, the wind blew it away from her face. She wore green to match her eyes and no jewelry at all. She did not require it.

'Deirdre comes and goes as she pleases,' Liam said casually. 'Shea gives her inordinate freedom.'

'For a woman?' she demanded. 'He gives as much to you; *more*, being a man.' Her features were more masculine than feminine, bearing the father's prominent stamp, but it did not lessen her striking looks. It merely gave them a different quality. 'Why should I remain in this drafty pile of bricks and mortar when there is a world to see?'

'The world being Erinn,' Liam retorted. 'Give it up, lass; while the war lasts, you'll not be leaving the island.'

'This war will last forever.' She pulled hair away from her eyes and clasped it, forming a single thick plume. Her nose bore two golden freckles. Her cheekbones were sharply angled – as much as Liam's, I thought, but his were mostly hidden in his beard – and the wind whipped color into her cream-fair Erinnish skin. She smiled a warm, conspiratorial smile, as if we were boon companions embarked on a reckless childhood scheme. 'Can you really break Liam for me?' she asked. 'Like a piece of rotten bone?'

'Given the opportunity.' And yet I knew I could not.

Defined brows rose consideringly. 'Then I shall be seeing you get it.' She glanced at Liam. 'This is the hostage prince?'

Liam winced. '*Guest*, Deirdre . . . Niall is our *guest*.'

She shrugged. 'Hostage, guest, captive . . .' Deirdre looked at me. 'You are Niall of Homana. My father told me you were here.'

'Against my wishes, aye.'

She folded her arms beneath her breasts, tucking hair out of the wind's insistent fingers. 'He did not tell me why. Will you?'

Liam reached out a booted foot and gently tapped the toe of her slipper. 'If he was not telling you, lass, there is a reason for it.'

'I am a *woman*. Shea forgets I am his daughter with as

many wits as you.' Her teasing smile was fleet and fading; she reserved most of it for me. 'Why are you here, Niall of Homana?'

I wanted to answer sharply, bitterly; to strike out at another of Shea's proud eagles. But I did not. This one was not deserving of it.

'I was shipwrecked. Shea keeps me because of my value to his enemy.'

Her brows quirked. 'To Alaric? What value would *you* be having?'

In her the lilting cadence was softer, more attractive, though I did not doubt women longed to hear Liam's as well. 'I am to wed his daughter.'

'Ah,' she said softly, as if in discovery. And then she laughed aloud, turning into the wall to stare out at Atvia. 'So, my kinswoman will precede me into the marriage bed after all.'

'Were you expecting otherwise?' Liam asked in affected irritation. 'You send all the suitors away.'

'Are you formally betrothed?' Deirdre asked me, plainly ignoring her brother.

'I am proxy-wed.'

She nodded thoughtfully. 'I was betrothed, once. When I was very young.'

Liam growled deep in his throat. 'You should have let me kill him, lass, for breaking the betrothal.'

'I *wanted* him to break it. His heart was lost to another.' She shrugged. 'He went home to Ellas perfectly happy to leave me far behind.'

'*Ellas!*' I looked at her sharply. 'He was Ellasian?'

'Evan,' she said. 'Brother to High King Lachlan. He came here because his brother sent him, hoping to make an alliance. But there was another woman for Evan. He wanted none of me.'

'Evan wed a kinswoman of mine!' I told her. 'Meghan. Daughter to Finn, my father's uncle.'

Deirdre watched me over an angled shoulder. She frowned a little, then shrugged. 'I'm not knowing the names.

113

Someday you will have to tell me a little of Homanan history.'

I laughed. 'Lady, there will *be* no "someday" if I have any say. I intend to go to Atvia.'

Deirdre smiled sympathetically. 'A futile intention, I'm thinking. Shea will never allow it.'

'There is an alternative.' Liam turned to face me squarely with the wall at his back. 'Make a *new* alliance, lad. One with Erinn instead.'

I sighed. 'I am proxy-wed, Liam. In Homanan law, it is the same as being truly married . . . and we do not end proper marriages. If I did not wed Gisella now, having already been proxy-wed to her representative, it would be justification for Alaric to cry war and sail to Homana with every soldier he can muster.' I shook my head. 'I am not a fool, Erinnish.'

Besides, there is the prophecy . . . if I were not to wed Gisella, what would become of my tahlmorra? Would I forego the afterworld?

Liam squinted in consideration and scratched at his brassy beard. 'Neither is Alaric. He would be thinking more than once about sailing to Homana while Erinn sits on his flank.' Nodding a little, he smiled. 'If he goes to Homana, lad, it will be with no more than half his army. The rest he would leave behind. Because if he were foolish enough to take *everyone*, Atvia would be mine.'

I shook my head. 'Half a warhost or not, there is no reason to plunge Homana back into war. Even with victory guaranteed.'

Liam shrugged. 'An idea, lad, and worth the trouble to think it. I only meant there are other princesses in the world besides Gisella of Atvia.'

As he meant me to, I looked immediately at Deirdre. Her back was to me. But she spun around to face us both. 'I am not a piece in one of your foolish games!' she cried. 'D'ye think I never wed because I waited for *him?*'

'Deirdre, I'm wanting less noise from you.' He smiled winningly. ' 'Twas only an idea.'

114

'Put it back in the acorn you call your head,' she told him crossly. 'Leave my marriage to me.'

'Then you'll never be wed at all.'

'Perhaps 'tis what I prefer.' She smiled, curtsied, gathered up her skirts. 'I'll be leaving you now, *my lord*, if you'll be having no objection.'

He sighed. 'Go, Deirdre. Take your babble to our father.'

She went, green skirts swinging, and Liam shook his head. 'Wild, too wild, my father's lass. But our mother died ten years ago, when Deirdre was only eight. Shea took a second wife – and a good woman, she is, but too timid in the ways of raising children. Even I can make no headway, no matter how hard I try.'

I thought of Isolde, wild in her own way. Ian knew – *had known* – her better than I, being full-born brother instead of half, yet even he had muttered about her recklessness. But 'Solde, I knew, was harmless. I thought Deirdre was as well.

'She is not beautiful,' Liam said bluntly, 'but she has a way about her. Your visit will be more comfortable now that Deirdre is home.'

'Why?' My tone was equally blunt. 'Will she be sharing my bed?'

Fast, so fast, he caught me by both arms and lifted me off my feet, pressing me up and over the crenel. Parting the veil of beard and mustache were taut lips and gritted teeth.

'Say it again,' he invited softly, 'and I promise you the *rocks below* will be your bed.'

I did not have to look. I did not have to speak. I merely nodded at him.

Liam let me go. I slumped back against the crenel, clutching one of the merlons next to it. 'You chafe,' he said, 'I know. It would drive me mad as well. But do not make my sister the target of your anger.'

Slowly, I rearranged my clothing. I could think of nothing to say.

Liam shook his head. 'Do as you wish. If you choose to

make an enemy of my sister, you make one of my father. As for myself, I care little for what becomes of Donal's yapping puppy.'

He left me alone on Kilore's windy battlements. As he went, I was aware of genuine regret.

On his part as well as my own.

CHAPTER TEN

Liam's anger did not last. He was too fair a man, too content with life to allow darkness to possess his soul for long. His empathy for my plight surprised me with its depth; he seemed to understand what I felt better than I did myself. And so we made our peace without passing a word between us, and life became infinitely easier.

As the days passed, the shackles were loosened a bit. I was given a horse out of the royal Erinnish stables, a pale gray gelding, and told I might ride whenever I chose. I chose to often, galloping across the endless heights and headlands. Liam assigned a six-man contingent to ride with me when he himself could not, and so I learned what it was to be a hostage to hospitality; on my honor as a prince – with no complaints to voice concerning my treatment – I could not attempt escape.

Often I sought refuge in solitude on the windy headlands overlooking the Dragon's Tail. This morning I watched what I always watched: fisherfolk, Atvian and Erinnish alike, sailing out with the tide into the Idrian to work the waters until the tide brought them back again.

The morning mist had lifted, but the brassy sun could not quite dispel the chill of approaching fall. I pulled my fur-lined cloak more tightly about my shoulders and halted my horse, staring bleakly at the beaches below.

Nearly fall. It has been months since I sailed from Hondarth. Three, they say, from Homana to Atvia. I swear it has been twice that, and my father in ignorance.

The distant jangle of trappings gave away an approaching rider. In irritation I looked up, prepared to order my human

117

watchdogs farther away; they knew better than to bother me with close surveillance. But the words died in my mouth when I saw Deirdre, crimson cloak whipping as she came riding across the headland. A single braid slapped her back as she rode, all bent over in the saddle to let the dark gray gelding gallop on unhindered.

She rode straight at me, straight at the end of the headland, at the edge of Erinn itself. She was laughing. I saw crimson-dyed doeskin boots shoved into iron stirrups and the cloak went flapping, flapping as she galloped, laughing in joyous exultation. I had known the feeling myself, but not since my imprisonment.

Not since Ian's death.

She bobbed upright in the saddle and set the reins, calling something to the gelding. I watched him tuck dark haunches and slide, plowing through damp turf so that it flew up behind him like muddy rain. But he stopped. At the edge of the world, he stopped.

Deirdre was laughing breathlessly. The wind and the ride had pulled tendrils free of the single braid; they curled around her flushed face in gilded disarray. Her green eyes were alight as she turned the gelding to fall in next to my own. The horses nosed one another, grays dark and light, blowing, then picked with greedy teeth at succulent turf in perfect companionship. Bits and bridles clattered a counterpoint to the shrieking of the gulls.

'So,' she said, 'you have discovered the peace in turbulence.'

I looked from her to the wind-whipped Dragon's Tail. 'Are they not enemies to one another?'

Doeskin gloves matched the crimson boots. She made a sweeping gesture. 'You see below us the turbulence of the wild sea, and feel the cold breath of the dragon whistling through his teeth. Wind and water have a peace of their own, and balm for a troubled soul.' Her gaze was very green, very clear as she looked at me. 'And are you not seeking that peace?'

'Why should *you* seek it?' I countered. '*You* are not a prisoner.'

Beneath the crimson cloak she wore a fine white tunicked gown, belted with gold-plated leather. The colors became her as well as the wild wind that stripped hair from her braid and whipped it into her face. 'Is a woman not prisoner first to her father, and later to her husband?'

I smiled. 'If *you* are a prisoner to your father, it is the most unbalanced captivity I have ever witnessed. As for a *husband* – you have only to tame your tongue, and doubtless you would be wed within a six-month.'

Deirdre laughed aloud, unoffended. 'But what would my father do without me?' Abruptly, her laughter died. 'He has wed two daughters into foreign lands and lost a third to childbed fever. I am his youngest, his favorite . . . of all his girls. He would rather keep me by him if I choose to stay.'

'And do you choose to stay?'

She lifted one shoulder in a half-hearted shrug. 'I would like to see the world. But not at the price of taking a husband I do not want.'

'Shea would never force you into a political marriage.'

'No,' she agreed. 'He is a loving man, my father, for all his gruff words and ways. He is not a harsh lord, no matter what *you* believe.'

'He keeps me against my will.'

She did not smile. 'You could escape. Down there.' She did not so much as glance down. 'You could.'

I could. Here the chalky cliff face was broken, crumbling downward toward the sea like a spill of riverbank. It was not impossible.

And yet it was. 'I have given your father my parole. To break it is to break the honor of my House. That I would never do.' A gull screamed overhead. 'I do have *some* pride, Deirdre.'

'Near as much as Liam,' she said softly. 'And as deadly, too, I think.' She stared down at scarlet leather as she replaited her gelding's mane. 'He said your brother went down with the ship.'

'He did.'

She looked straight at me, hiding none of her empathy. ''Tis sorry I am, Niall. I lost a brother when I was very little. To fever, but death is one and the same, whatever face he shows.' She looked at me a moment longer, then twisted her neck to peer fixedly out to sea. Gazing westward. 'Were you in Homana now, what would you be doing?'

I almost told her it was possible I might be bedding my Atvian wife, but I did not say it. Somehow, before Shea's gilded, green-eyed daughter, I could not speak of Gisella.

'I would be in Homana-Mujhar – my father's palace – learning statecraft from my father's councillors. The gods know I have need of such training.' Like Deirdre, I stared westward toward Homana. 'Or I would be in Clankeep . . . wishing myself whole.'

She looked back at me quickly. 'Whole? Are you missing a part of you, then?'

I smiled, but it faded soon enough. 'No. Not in flesh and bone. I speak of spirit, of soul . . . of the thing that makes a man worthy of the world. It is a Cheysuli thing.' I waited for the familiar gnawing pain to rise in my belly; when it came, it lacked its normal intensity. Regret, as always, was present – the longing of a man in need of security, but the lack was not as painful. 'A warrior without a *lir* is not accounted whole,' I told her. 'Such men do not stay with the clan, but seek death among the forests as soulless men, until the death is given to them.'

I fully expected her to recoil in horror, remarking on the barbaric beliefs of the savage Cheysuli, but she did not. She studied me silently, as if she considered the implications of my words.

'You are here before me, alive,' she said at last. 'Why are you still alive?'

I looked away from her. 'Because, never having had a *lir*, I did not lose one. I am not expected to perform the ritual. But – also because I am two men.' Bitterly I defined them. 'Prince and warrior. Homanan and Cheysuli. I am not wholly one or the other.'

'And neither accepts you fully.'

'No.' The breath of the dragon whistled. I felt the touch of his icy teeth.

'What are you, Niall?' she asked. 'Tell me who you are.'

'What I am . . .' I looked up into the skies. 'I am a vessel the gods would make use of to shape a prophecy.'

' 'Tis the fate of all men, that. To be part of their *own* prophecy, regardless of origin.'

After a moment I reached out and touched her gloved hand. 'I see why your father has no desire to lose you. Were I Shea, I would never let you go.'

The wind whipped hair into her eyes and made them tear. Smiling sadly, she withdrew her hand from mine and turned her horse from me.

I watched her go at a gallop. Then I turned back to seek the peace in turbulence.

And to curse my *tahlmorra* in silence.

I dreamed. In my dream I was a raptor, circling in the sky. Below me, in a castle garden, two girls played with a doll wearing a gilt brooch-crown. Each was the antithesis of the other: blue-black hair/thick gold hair. Young skin the color of copper-bronze/young skin the color of cream.

And as the seams split and spilled dried-bean blood onto the ground, I saw Deirdre's tear-streaked face framed by bright gold hair.

But the other girl's face I did not know.

A sound awakened me. I could not put a name to it, knowing only it had intruded upon my dreams rudely, leaving me sitting upright in bed in a somewhat befuddled state. A glance at the candle with the hours marked in it told me I had only barely slept at all; perhaps half an hour, a little more. Enough only to lose myself so completely that it was difficult to recover all my senses.

There. Again. A voice. Muffled by the wood of my heavy door, but clear enough for me to identify.

Deirdre's.

The tone was urgent, both pleading and exasperated all

at once. I heard her call out her brother's name, and then I could make no more sense of the words at all.

I considered trying to go back to sleep. It was none of it my business. But my curiosity was roused; I slid out of bed; pulled on trews, shirt, boots, and went to open my door.

The hinges creaked. I put my head into the corridor and saw the guard standing at one end, as he always did, by the spiral stairway, set there to keep an eye on me. At the other end, as I turned, stood Deirdre, half in a nightrail, half in woolen trews. She had stuffed the ends of the nightrail into the waist of the trews, but some of the linen still trailed over her rump to the backs of her knees. And over the linen trailed her brass-bright hair, unbound, unkempt, infinitely provocative.

'Ye *skilfin*,' she told the closed door directly in front of her face. 'Why, when I'm needing you, d'ye drink yourself insensible?'

The door was opened. I saw only a portion of the face in the crack between door and jamb, but it was definitely not Liam's bearded features.

Ierne's. Liam's wife.

'Aye, he's drunk,' Ierne told Deirdre. 'Have mercy on his poor head, Deirdre, and hush your shouting.'

'But I *need* him!'

'Are we under attack?' Ierne asked calmly. 'Has Alaric come raiding again across the Dragon's Tail?'

'No, but—'

'Then be letting the poor man sleep, Deirdre. He doesn't do it often, now, does he?'

'No, but—'

Firmly, Ierne said: ''Tis a wife's prerogative to keep her husband in bed, Deirdre. One day, you'll be exercising your *own*.' And, as firmly, Ierne closed the door in Deirdre's face.

'*Skilfin*,' Deirdre muttered, threatening the door with a fist. Then, sighing, she turned away and saw me. Her head came up. Her face brightened. 'Well, come on, then. You'll do.'

'*I'll* do? I'll do what?'

She tossed heavy hair back, strode down the corridor in muddy boots and shut her hand upon my wrist. 'You'll do because I have no better, Liam so lost in drink. 'Tis Brenna, you see. Come along.'

She did not wait to let me close my door. 'Brenna?' I asked as I went with her, wrist still trapped in her hand.

'Brenna,' she said firmly. 'She's needing a man's help.'

'A – man's?'

'Aye. I always get Liam to help, but he's lost for the night. Brenna doesn't know you, but once I introduce you she'll be fine. She doesn't like the others.'

Deirdre led me past the guard and released my wrist as she started down the twisting stair. Behind her, I saw hair turned to molten gold in the torchlight; a slender hand sliding against rough stone as she went down and down and down, never hesitating. Gone was the prince's sister I had seen on the battlements of Kilore, green-clad against the gray of the skies and the gray of the Aerie walls. Gone was the elegant princess of Erinn in white wool, crimson and hammered gold, atop the chalk cliffs on a storm-gray horse. It was a different woman I saw now: rumpled, half-dressed, all intent upon a thing. And as she turned her head to look over a shoulder at me as she reached the bottom of the stair, I found I wanted – suddenly, irrationally – to kiss her.

'Do ye know horses?' Deirdre asked.

With great care I removed myself from her immediate presence, taking two steps back up the stairs. 'Horses?' Horses were the last thing on my mind.

'Aye. Why – were ye thinking Brenna was a woman?' *Her* mind, clearly, was only half on me; she frowned, then laughed. 'No, no, a *mare*. And one about to foal. Come on, then, or she'll be done before we get there.'

'Would that be so bad?' I thought surely a mare knew best how to bring her young into the world.

'D'ye know nothing of horses, then?' she asked impatiently. 'Agh, go back to bed. I'll do it myself.'

Obviously, Brenna was a favorite. Well, I'd had them myself. And at the moment, I had no desire to leave. 'I'll come.'

Deirdre took me out of the castle proper to the stable inside the curtain wall. There was almost no moon, so that I stumbled over the uneven cobbles like a child just learning to walk. Deirdre, knowing the bailey, cast me an impatient glance and hastened onward with only a single torch in her hand. It smoked and flared in her wake.

A man met us at the stable. He looked at me in mild surprise, then turned his full attention to Deirdre. He seemed unconcerned by his lord's daughter arriving at the stable in the dead of night in nightrail, boots, and man's trews. He simply took the torch from Deirdre's hand and told us to go on.

'She'll be having naught of me,' he said quietly. 'At least until the foal is born. 'Tis always Brenna's way.'

'Aye.' Distracted, Deirdre went by him into the stable and I followed.

'Oh, *breagha, breagha*,' Deirdre said softly as she slipped into a stall. 'Oh, my Brenna *breagha*, 'tis a fine foal you'll be showing us.'

The stables were thickly shadowed, illuminated only by a few lanterns. Looking into the stall Deirdre entered I could only see blackness, and then the blackness moved.

I saw the glint of eyes. Heard the flaring snort from velvet nostrils. Smelled the faint acrid tang of a horse in extremity.

The mare lay on her side. She heaved her head up, touched Deirdre's hands softly with muzzle, stiffened with exertion. I saw the contractions roll through the mound of glossy belly.

Deirdre moved away at once, stepping closer to me as she gave the mare room. Black Brenna grunted, strained, lay back again.

'There,' Deirdre breathed. 'See the hooves just under Brenna's tail? There's the sac. The foal will follow soon enough.'

She spoke softly, so softly to the mare, soothing her with

infinite care and affection. Brenna seemed calmer with Deirdre talking her through the labor; she gave a great heave and the foal slid out into the clean straw of the stable floor.

'Now,' Deirdre breathed, and knelt down to tear the wet sac from the newborn foal. Brenna aided her, catching what she could with her teeth, then began to lick.

And stopped, almost as abruptly.

'Brenna *breagha*,' Deirdre soothed. 'A bit of a stud-colt for us, is it?'

She was soaked in birthing fluids, the ends of her bright hair stiffening into sticky curls. I saw the damp shine on her forearms as she shoved the sleeves of her nightrail above elbows, reaching down to free the colt's nose of residue.

'Ah, no,' she said abruptly. 'Ah, *no*.' Hair whipped as she jerked her head around. 'Seamus? Seamus – are you there? Quickly, man. The colt's not breathing!'

He was with us in an instant, hanging the lantern onto a nail. Now I could see clearly how still the colt was, how limp he was in Deirdre's arms and in the soiled straw.

He bent even as the mare lurched to her feet. Brenna turned her back on the colt. Her exhaustion was plain to see; so was her rejection of the stillborn colt.

'Hold her,' Seamus told me plainly. I did as was told, taking hold of Brenna's halter and keeping her in a corner of the stall as they ministered to the colt.

The mare was too weary to resent my presence. She shut her eyes as I stroked her face, marveling at the purity of her coloring. Black, all black, with not a single spot of white anywhere. Priceless.

'*Breagha*,' Seamus said, and I knew he did not speak to the mare, '*breagha*, 'tis nothing left to do. He's gone from us.'

'Ye *skilfin*, you've not tried hard enough.'

'I have,' he said solemnly. ''Tis nothing left but to give him to the *cileann*.'

'Nothing.' Deirdre echoed. 'Eleven months spent a-waiting for this birth, and now there is *nothing—*'

'You've got the mare, *breagha*.'

125

'Aye,' she said finally, and rose. She came to me, to Brenna, and clasped the mare's neck in her arms. 'Oh Brenna, Brenna, such a fine little colt he was, so *fine* . . . fitting, I think, for the *cileann*. They'll give him honor and all the freedom of his days.'

'I'll be bringing him, then,' Seamus said.

'No.' Deirdre swung around, but not before I saw the sudden kindling in her eyes. 'No, 'tis for Niall to do, if he'll do it.'

There was no need to ask me. And I think she knew it as well as I, though we dared not look at one another.

Seamus's face closed up. 'Homanan,' he said only. And then he added: 'shapechanger.'

'Surely the *cileann* won't begrudge him *his* fair share of magic,' Deirdre chided. 'They are honorable folk, and generous. They'll be giving him welcome, Seamus, as much as Shea himself.'

Subtle reprimand, I thought, reminding the loyal servant that the woman he served was the daughter of a king. Reminding him also that what respect I was given by that king was owed by Seamus as well.

'Then I'll be tending the mare. She'll have me by her, now.'

Deirdre looked at me. 'Can you lift him?'

Silently, I did so, gathering the wet, still body into my arms. He weighed substantially less than one of Liam's wolfhounds.

She nodded. 'Bring him, then. We've a thing to do.'

Deirdre took me out of Kilore and into the hills of Erinn. With no moon to speak of it was difficult to see, and yet Deirdre seemed to know the way. I followed the pale luminescence of her linen nightrail and the faint gleam of burnished hair. She did not stop, did not speak, did not even turn as if to see how I fared with the weight of the colt. She simply walked on, intent upon her thoughts, and I left her to her silence.

At last, upon a crumbled hilltop, she stopped. Over the colt I saw the stone cairn and low altar beside it, also of

126

stone, all carved with alien runes. I knew, without Deirdre's instruction, what I was to do, and so I lay the colt down upon the altar. Then Deirdre motioned me back, and I saw there was a thin circle carved into the turf. Chalk white, it glowed faintly in the darkness.

'The tor,' she said, 'belongs to the *cileann*, the oldfolk. They were in Erinn long before we were. Many have forgotten them, but not all. And none of the House of Eagles.' Her eyes were black in the darkness, though I knew by day they were green. 'We will wait the night through until dawn, so we know he is safely taken.'

'Taken—?' I looked at the cairn and altar. 'I mean no disrespect, but what would the oldfolk do with Brenna's stillborn colt?'

'What they do with anything born without breath in its body – give it welcome, give it life, give it the freedom of the *cileann*.' She sighed a little. 'I have seen women leave stillborn babies here, and children murdered kittens, all with equal grief. But also equal certainty that the death is only of the earth, and not real in the land of the oldfolk.'

She sounded so certain, so absolute in her conviction. 'And have *you* waited before?' I asked.

'Twice,' she answered calmly. 'There was Callum, my brother. And Orna, the sister who died in childbed.'

'And did the oldfolk take them away?'

'That is a question best answered at dawn,' she told me quietly. 'And by the *cileann* themselves.'

It was cold upon the tor, and windy, and heavy with ancient magic. *Lirless* I was, but neither blind nor deaf to power when it is so strong. I tried to sleep and could not; Deirdre did not even bother to close her eyes. We lay on our backs on the cool turf with the cairn and altar behind us and stared up at the stars, talking of dreams and aspirations, sharing portions of ourselves we had never thought to share, holding them too precious, and waiting for dawn to come.

And when it came, just as I put out a hand to touch her, Deirdre scrambled up and spun to look at the altar.

I was forgotten. She was lost in the rite of welcome given to a new day.

Sunlight gilded the cairn. The world was born again. And the altar was perfectly empty.

I moved, slowly, toward the cairn. Now I could see her face, where the sun touched it even as I longed to touch it; as the light set her hair afire. I saw a smile of blissful satisfaction. She murmured something in a tongue I did not know, and then she looked at me.

She wore a soiled, dirty nightrail and a pair of men's nubby wool trews. She had spent the night upon the sacred tor with a man she hardly knew, and yet knew better now than he himself. We had thrown open the corners of our hearts that men and women kept secret from one another, too afraid to set light into those corners for fear the other would laugh or, worse, find the secrets not worth the hiding.

And I had waited for her to grieve, speaking of the colt. But she had not. Like a Cheysuli, she locked it away. But I thought she waited for something.

I looked at her. At her smudged, proud face with the look of an eaglet in it, waiting to leave the aerie. Knowing the day will come when she will ride the air and lay claim to all the world.

Deirdre looked at the empty altar. She sighed a little, and turned her face back to me. 'Now,' she said. '*Now* I can cry.'

And as the tears ran down her face, I shut my arms around her.

My captivity continued. I was well-treated, honored for my rank, assigned warm, comfortable chambers. I was allowed to hunt and hawk with Liam and his hounds. Shea taught me of ships and war.

But it was Deirdre who taught me what it was to love a woman.

Evenings were spent with the family: Shea, his wife; his son and daughter; Liam's wife and their two-year-old son. Sean was Liam's only child as yet, but Ierne had conceived again and was due in seven months' time. The boy was brown-eyed like his mother, but his hair, like Liam's, was brassy gold. Shea's stamp was on all of them; Kilore, the Aerie of Erinn, was home to magnificent eaglets.

And Deirdre. Present always, serving me even as her stepmother served Shea; as Ierne served Liam. Making no promises she could not keep, saying nothing of the future. But wanting as much as I did.

I sat before the cavernous fireplace after dinner and stared silently into the flames. Servants moved softly, removing platters and empty wine jugs. Shea and his clutch gathered some distance away; I was treated as part of the family until politics intervened. Then I was a hostage who must be kept in ignorance of his future.

Sean, defying his elders, came running across the floor to fall against my legs. He hugged one knee and grinned at me, saying something in what I believed was the ancient Erinnish language, until I realized it was only his childish mumblings. Obligingly I lifted him into my lap and settled him there. He squirmed around until he sat against my chest, head slumped on my collarbone and one fist thrust into my woolen jerkin. Like me, he stared into the flames in deep, thoughtful silence.

I realized I had never held a child before. I felt distinctly discomfited; did I have the arms and legs settled comfortably? Sean did not seem to notice my concern, so I assumed he fared well enough. But I was not certain I liked the responsibility. Children, I had always believed, were crying, petulant things when they were not shouting and shrieking in play, and yet Sean was quiet enough. Slowly my unease abated and left me feeling tentatively contented.

I felt her presence before she spoke, as always. 'You are good with him.' Deirdre stood behind me. 'He does not always please himself so easily.'

Having no wish to disturb the boy, I did not try to turn. 'I am a stranger. He will lose interest soon enough.'

'Sean is not one for losing interest in a thing. 'Tis independent he is, like his father.'

'Like you.'

Laughing softly, she moved around the chair and sat down on a stool at my feet. Pale yellow skirts of softest wool settled around her like a cloud. ''Tis a good father you'll be making one day.' Intently, she watched me, waiting; absently, one slender hand touched the fabric of my breeches.

Deliberately, I said: 'If I am ever given leave to wed my betrothed.'

Her eyes flickered in response to the wry challenge in my tone. She took her hand away. 'Then 'tis still *Gisella* you desire.'

'I do not desire *her*, Deirdre . . . only my freedom so I may wed her. There is a difference.'

The firelight behind her set her bright hair aglow. Her face was in shadow, but I saw her clearly. I knew her too well by now. 'What of me?' she asked evenly.

I looked away. I had to. 'What *of* you?'

Her tone hardened. ''Tis so easy for you, then, this thing between us? This thing that has the binding on us both?'

I drew in a careful breath. *Ah gods, forgive me for hurting her* – 'There is a prophecy, Deirdre, to which I am bound more firmly than any woman.'

'Even Gisella?' The barb was sharp. 'Is she not a *part* of that prophecy?'

'She is a part of my *tahlmorra*, my fate, as you would call it. She is half Atvian. It is her blood we need, for the prophecy of the Firstborn.'

'Are you forgetting, then? *I* am half Atvian, too.'

She and Gisella are cousins even as Gisella and I are. Gods, what a tangled tapestry—

Sean squirmed, sensing the tension between Deirdre and me. I set him down and watched him make his way to his father, still talking with Shea near the door.

'But you have no Cheysuli blood,' I said finally. 'Deirdre, I have told you what I lack. No *lir*, no gifts, no strength as the warriors know it. I lack even the *color*—' I stopped. It would do no good to expose my insecurities and

130

resentments. '*One day a man of all blood shall unite, in peace, four warring realms and two magic races,*' I quoted. '*All blood,* Deirdre. If I cannot hand on the proper gifts to my children, the prophecy will not be properly served.' I drew in a breath through a painfully constricted throat. 'Gisella is half Cheysuli. What *I* do not have, she does. I need her, Deirdre, for that.'

She sat before me, rigidly upright; rigidly proud. 'And I need *you*.'

I reached out and touched her glowing hair. Beneath my hand she trembled with the strength of her conviction; with the strength of her desire. Even as I myself did.

Dry-mouthed, I said: 'There is nothing I can do.'

And hated the man who said it.

The old lord called me into his personal chamber weeks later. I went with foreboding in my soul, for hope had been banished months before. I found Liam present as well.

Shea waved me to a chair. 'Sit, sit, lad . . . what I have to say is better heard in private.'

I watched Liam's face for some hint of what was to come. He gave nothing away, nothing at all, save the gravity of the matter.

Shea sat down also. ''Tis word from Donal, your father.' His mouth behind the beard, twisted in a grimace. 'Alaric at last sent word of your presence with me, saying other messengers must have gone astray.' He grunted. 'I think Donal is no fool, lad. He'll not be believing *that*.'

I felt light-headed with relief. 'What does my father say?'

'He inquires after your health. I told the Homanan messenger it was excellent. He'll be taking that back to the Mujhar already.'

All the relief fell away. '*You have sent him away?*'

'The messenger? Aye. I saw no reason to have you trade words with him, lad. I was not wanting you disturbed.'

'*Disturbed!*' I overturned the chair as I jumped up unsteadily. 'By the gods, you pen me up for five months and then send away a man who bears word from my father?'

131

Shea's thicket of eyebrows jerked up into his hair. 'Has it been that long? I'd be saying three months, I think, not five.' Frowning, he turned to Liam. 'Five months, he says. Truth?'

'Truth,' Liam answered.

Shea glanced back at me. '*Sit down!*' he roared. I righted the chair and sat down. Appeased, he rubbed thoughtfully at his beard. 'I let him see ye, lad, to know how you fared.' His faded green eyes were oddly watchful. 'You were with my daughter, lad . . . Liam says you looked well content.'

I felt heat and color spill into my face. I shut my mouth on a curse, but sent Liam an angry glance. He smiled crookedly and shrugged.

'He's wishing to send a personal envoy to Kilore,' Shea said. 'To negotiate for your release.'

My hands closed over the arms of the chair. 'Well?'

'I have agreed.'

'To my *release?*'

'To his coming. No more than that, lad – 'tis all I can give you, for now.'

I pushed myself out of the chair and faced the old man. 'My lord—'

'You'll be staying here till I see fit to let you go.'

I drew in a careful breath. 'And if the Mujhar sends forces with that envoy?'

'I'm thinking he will not,' Shea remarked. 'He is well occupied with Solinde at the moment.'

'Solinde,' I echoed blankly.

'The Ihlini have risen, lad.'

Oh gods – it is Strahan – 'My lord,' I begged, 'let me go home to my father.'

'Until Alaric gives in, you go nowhere.' Shea glared at me and shifted in his chair. 'There's a thing I must ask you, lad. Will you give me honest answer?'

'Ask me.' I was too overcome to dissemble.

'Would you be in mind of breaking your pledge to Gisella?'

I stared at him in shock. 'I could not.'

'And if I offered you your freedom?'

I looked at Liam. I saw compassion in his eyes; he knew

what the answer cost me. 'No,' I said again. 'I – cannot.' But I would not cite the reasons. I thought Shea would not understand. And I thought *I* might not, if I ever spoke them aloud.

The old man nodded slowly, as if the answer was precisely what he expected. 'Well,' he said, 'Deirdre told me what you would say. But 'tis sorry I am you cannot be my son.'

I could not speak. Obscurely touched, I could only stare at the man.

Liam shrugged broad shoulders. 'You'll be doing what you must. 'Tis what makes you the man you are.'

I turned my back on them both, intending to walk from the room. And then I turned back again to face them. 'Wait. *Wait* – perhaps there is something.' I drew in a breath. 'I cannot be a son or brother, but I *can* be a kinsman.'

Shea glared. He tapped the arm of his chair. 'Set it out here, lad, where grown men can see it plain.'

'I will wed Gisella,' I declared, 'and when we have a daughter, I will offer that daughter to Sean. He will be lord of this island one day – and Lord of the Isles, no doubt – but my daughter will be a princess of Homana. Would that be enough for you?'

Shea grunted. 'For myself, aye, 'twould. But I'll not be here to see it. 'Tis for Liam to say whom his son will be taking for a wife.'

Expectantly I looked at the Prince of Erinn. His smile was crooked, half-hidden in his gilded beard. 'I'm thinking Sean is a bit young, yet, to have his marriage settled for him, but I'll be considering it.' He nodded. '*If* you get a daughter on the lass.'

'Gisella and I were cradle-betrothed,' I pointed out. 'At least Sean is *walking*.'

Liam laughed. 'But Gisella is not even *bedded*.'

'She will be. Once I am free of here.'

Shea grunted. I saw affection and amusement in his eyes. 'Take yourself away, lad, and leave me to my son.'

I took myself away feeling oddly liberated.

CHAPTER ELEVEN

Liam sent word for me to meet him in one of Kilore's audience chambers, but when I went I found myself alone. No doubt *important* business kept him: one of his wolfhounds was due to whelp, or a mare to foal, or perhaps even Sean demanded his attention. Wryly, I reflected that the Prince of Erinn's priorities were different from those of most men.

The chamber was cold. The fire had been allowed to die, or else a servant had neglected to light it. The sunlight coming in one of the deep, crudely-cut casements hardly reached the center of the room. Kilore was not a luxurious aerie for the Erinnish eagles, being more fortress than palace, but it served well enough. It did not matter to me that the rush-strewn floors were uneven, the tapestries faded and threadbare, the furniture but crudely made of knotty greenish wood. It was here Deirdre had been reared; that was all that counted.

I slumped against the edge of the casement sill and stared out. From here I could see neither the Dragon's Tail nor Atvia. All I could see was the green Erinnish turf stretching forever and ever to the edge of the world, where the wheel of life continued turning for everyone save myself.

The door creaked open (none of Kilore's heavy leather-hinged doors were silent) and I heard Liam's bootstep. 'Niall.'

Not Liam – I turned, then thrust myself off the wall. A stranger faced me, except he was no stranger at all. He had been a part of my life since birth. 'Rowan!'

My father's closest companion – and Cheysuli general

134

of all the Homanan armies – stared at me as if he distrusted his eyes. I did not doubt he *did*, after nearly a year. And then he smiled a smile I feared would break his face, so broad and transparent he was in his relief, and I met him halfway across the chamber in a bearhug that required neither apology nor explanation.

The rampant black lion on Rowan's crimson tunic clawed silk impotently as I stepped back from the embrace. In the months of my absence the general had aged. Cheysuli do not show the years as easily as Homanans, but Rowan was no longer young. I could not number his years precisely, but he claimed several more than fifty, I knew. And it had begun to show.

'The gods have been kinder than we expected,' Rowan said on a sigh of relief. 'I thought to find you weak and wan as an albino calf.'

'No.' Emotion welled into my chest with such intensity I feared I might shame myself. It is rare for a Cheysuli to show precisely what he feels. Oddly, I saw the same struggle in Rowan's careworn face.

Why not? He and I share the same capricious gods.

Lirless, both of us. Cheysuli born and bred, and yet we neither of us claimed a *lir*. Rowan's explanation was straightforward enough: orphaned in Shaine's purge of shapechangers some forty-five years before, he had been taken in as a foster son by immigrant Ellasian crofters who did not know he was Cheysuli. In those dangerous days no shapechanger was safe; he did not dare divulge his heritage, or he would give himself over into certain death. And so he had been reared Homanan, growing into Homanan habits and traditions; when the time came for him to go out and make a bond with the *lir* intended for him, he did not. *Lirless* he was and would remain so, until the day he died.

And I? Perhaps it is time I learned to live with it, even as Rowan has.

I motioned with my head. 'What you see has been my prison. Kilore is not an unpleasant one.'

Though the black hair was graying to a decided silver,

135

his yellow eyes were sharp and steady as Ian's or my father's. The netting of sunlines and silvering scars in his face only underscored the years he had spent at the side of Homana's Mujhars, insuring domestic and personal security.

He frowned, just a little; enough to crinkle eyelids and pull at the weatherburned flesh over angular cheekbones. I thought he listened to my tone more than he did to my words.

'Have they suborned you with this?' In *his* tone I heard tremendous restraint, and yet I also heard a multitude of emotions. Traces only, but enough to emphasize what my disappearance had meant to my father and mother. And, perhaps, to Rowan.

I wanted to laugh at him and clasp a shoulder and lead him to a chair, to pour the smoky Erinnish liquor and laugh *with* him, that he could ask such a thing of me. But I did none of those things. I looked at him steadily as I had looked at no man before and told him the truth.

'No. But I will not lie and tell you Shea has been a harsh lord or inhumane when he has offered me honor and affection.'

'Eight months of it? – assuming, of course, the voyage took *you* the three months it took me.' Rowan's posture was the rigid stance of a longtime soldier and officer at rest, which is to say he was not precisely resting. And his elaborately casual tone was as inflexible as his spine. 'I think perhaps we misjudged your reaction to my coming; Aislinn said Carillon's grandson would devise an immediate means of departure. Donal said it was more likely you would leave the devising to me.' The general did not smile. 'Yet you say *nothing at all* of departure.'

Carillon's grandson. Even now she does not refer to me as her son, only heir of her legendary father, one generation removed.

'There is no need to *say* anything,' I told him curtly. 'Shea will not let me go. Not until Alaric grants the concessions he demands.'

'And what are those concessions?'

I shrugged. 'He does not tell me such things.'

Rowan looked away from me briefly, toward the casement. Then he turned and went to it, staring out even as I had before his entrance. 'It is unlikely Alaric will grant Shea anything. He is too concerned with mustering men to aid Strahan against Homana.'

I started. 'But – the alliance—?'

'Contingent upon you making his daughter Princess of Homana.' Rowan's tone was distant. 'Oh, aye, the proxy ceremony makes you husband and wife in Homanan law, but until she is properly wed and acclaimed Princess of Homana, the alliance does not exist. And now it seems impossible that it ever *will* exist, does it not? At least, while Shea keeps you here.' He turned to face me and the lion rippled, clawing at his right shoulder. 'Eleven months ago you left Homana to fetch Gisella home to a Homanan wedding. Circumstances aside, Alaric has every right in the world to declare the proxy wedding invalid and the cradle-betrothal broken.' His face was a mask; his tone was not so well-schooled. 'A broken betrothal and an invalid proxy wedding taints a woman as well as a man, Niall. A father would be justified in levying war in his despoiled daughter's name. And as for you, who would you find to wed? Who would have you?'

Deirdre would—

'Who would bring the proper blood to the prophecy?'

Deirdre would not— Angrily, I glared at him. 'I did not *put* myself here!'

'No.' Frowning, Rowan stared down at his boot toes. 'No, you did not. Alaric is aware of that; no doubt more aware than *we* are, being so close to Erinn, but . . . regardless—' He looked at me again, and I saw a weariness of spirit so totally alien that it brought me striding across the room to him.

'Rowan—'

His raised hand stopped me short. More intensely aware of the man and his feelings than I ever had been before, I marked the callused palms and battered knuckles, ruined nails and crooked fingers, all badges of his profession. His life. And I saw the bleakness in his eyes.

'Niall, there is trouble at home. Serious trouble.'

Fear flared. 'My father? *Mother?* Rowan—'

'Both well,' he said at once. 'No, it has nothing to do with their welfare. It is—'

'Strahan,' I finished, 'is it not?'

'Not – entirely.' He straightened and thrust himself away from the wall, pacing away from me toward the cold fireplace. I noticed for the first time he limped, though only a little, as if his aging bones and muscles reminded him he had fought in too many battles. Most of them with Carillon, whom he had served for nearly twenty-five years. The last twenty had been with my father, but I knew the bond was not the same.

And now he must fight another.

He turned. I saw him muster the dry factuality necessary to a competent, effective general. Necessary to a ruler, for that matter. One day, I would have to find the same within myself. 'It concerns you,' he said flatly. 'And – Carillon.'

'Carillon!' I stared at him blankly. 'How can this concern a man who has been dead for twenty years?'

'Because while he lived he sired children,' Rowan answered in the same even tone.

Baffled, I nodded agreement with the obvious. 'How else would I be his grandson?'

'I did not say *child*, Niall.'

No. He had not. He had said *children*.

Suddenly, I was very cold. The chamber darkened around me. 'A son,' I said distantly. 'A *son*.'

'A bastard.' Rowan's voice was very quiet. 'We know very little. His age: thirty-five. His mother: a Homanan woman who followed Carillon's rebel army as he made his way from Ellas to Mujhara.' He shrugged. 'I remember her myself. Carillon was not the sort of man who wanted or needed a woman with every meal, and when he took one, he kept her. Sarne was – worth keeping.'

'But he did *not* keep her, did he?' I was detached from

the man who asked the questions. 'No. Once she carried a *bastard*—'

'No.' The word cut through my rising bitterness. 'Once Electra came.'

Of course. *Electra*. The witch who had bound even Carillon the Great into a web of deceit and encorcellment until he had nearly fallen victim to Tynstar himself. Electra the witch.

Electra: my mother's mother.

I looked for a chair. Found one; collapsed into it. Rubbed absently at my scalp; it itched from the sudden prickling of trepidation. 'Well,' I said at last, 'he must have sent her away.'

'She asked to leave. She came to me and said she had conceived. She no longer wished to remain with the army; she would go home.'

'With Carillon's bastard in her belly.'

'I gave her money. A horse. A soldier went with her.' Rowan's smile was very faint. 'A crofter-turned-soldier, who discovered he was much better at wielding scythe than sword. He married her.'

I looked at him sharply, frowning. 'Then how do you *know* it is Carillon's son? If she married the crofter—'

'He is the image of an older *you*, Niall. Or a younger Carillon, before the disease aged him. As testified by a Homanan priest and a Cheysuli *shar tahl*.'

Like Shea, he stamps his get— 'They have *seen* him? Is he so bold as to press his claim based on bastardy when I am legitimate?'

Rowan did not avoid my eyes. 'There are Homanans in the world who would prefer a descendant of Carillon on the throne who is *not* Cheysuli.'

My laugh was a bark of sound. 'How can they call me Cheysuli? I have no *lir*, no magic, no shapechange . . . I am more Homanan than anything else.'

'It is said you hide your magic, so as to *trick* the Homanans into believing you are wholly Homanan, and less of a threat than a man who assumes the shape of beast or bird.' A

139

muscle jumped in his jaw. 'I repeat what is said by the zealots.'

Under my breath, I swore. 'I wish I had magic to *hide*.'

'I know it, Niall.' The tone altered; I heard a trace of empathy for the first time. 'They claim you will unveil your true self only after you hold the throne.'

'So, they want to replace me with Carillon's bastard, who *is* wholly Homanan.'

'Aye.'

'I am tainted by the Solindish witch's blood.'

'Aye.'

I sat forward and rubbed my eyes with rigid fingers. 'What would they say if they knew there are some Cheysuli who feel the same?' I asked wearily. 'Gods, I think I was never meant to inherit the Lion.'

'You were. You will.'

'Have *you* seen him?' I raised my head. 'Have you seen this misbegotten image of myself?'

'No. He is too well-guarded by Homanans dedicated to his cause. They say if his location were divulged, Donal would have him slain. They wait to gather men to his cause.' He spread his hands in a futile gesture. 'They allowed the priest and the *shar tahl* to see him, to prove he exists. That is all. Neither spoke with him.'

I slumped back in the chair again. 'A pretty coil, Rowan. How do we get free of it?'

'By having you leave Erinn for Atvia, where you will settle things with Alaric and bring Gisella home to Homana,' Rowan said flatly. 'Your absence has strengthened the bastard's cause. When we feared you *dead*—' He shrugged. 'We need you home. As soon as possible. With Gisella and Ian . . . I think only Ian can settle this thing with the *a'saii*, since he is the one *they* wish to put upon the throne.'

'You knew,' I mused, thinking of the *a'saii*. Then I was on my feet. 'You do *not* know! Gods, Rowan, there *is* no Ian! He died in the storm.'

All the color ran out of his face, leaving it a stark, empty mask of shock that only slowly was refilled by a comprehension and grief so intense it made me want to run from the man, the room, the castle.

To find my brother in the belly of the dragon.

'*Rujho*,' I said; no more. The pain was new again.

After a moment, Rowan cleared his throat. 'I must send word to Donal.'

'*Take* it to him,' I said at last. 'I think – it would be better if you told him.'

'And what do I tell him of *you?*'

'That I live.' I drew in a breath that cleared my head. 'That I will be home with Gisella as soon as possible.'

'And if Shea does not let you go?'

'Then I will have to break my parole.'

Looking at me steadily, Rowan shook his head. Just a little. 'Whatever else this captivity has done, it has also tempered the sword.'

'What is left to hone the edge?' I asked. 'War?'

'Assuredly,' he answered softly, and then came forward to hug me again. 'The gods be with you, Niall.'

'With them, without them – what does it matter?' I asked. 'They are the ones who fashioned this *tahlmorra*.'

I could not sleep. In the darkness of my room, my bed, my spirit, I stared sightlessly up at the woven curtains forming my Erinnish womb and tried to think of things other than war, *a'saii*, bastards. I tried to think of everything, and nothing at all made sense.

Until Deirdre came to me.

In the darkness, all unknowing, I thought of enemies. I rolled and reached through the slit in the curtain for my knife and remembered I did not have one.

'You'd be needing no weapon against *me*, Niall.'

'Deirdre—'

'I heard you speak to your father's man. Is that what a true Cheysuli looks like? So fierce, so solemn . . . so *dangerous*. I'm thinking I like you better as a Homanan.'

'Deirdre – you *heard?*'

'There are secrets in Kilore even Shea does not know,

141

or has forgotten already. Do not worry. No one else was there when you spoke of breaking your parole.'

'Deirdre—'

'Have we driven you from us, Niall? Have we kenneled you too closely, like one of Liam's hounds?'

The blackness of the room was not so all-encompassing as my eyes adjusted to it. I could just see Deirdre in my bed, and put out a hand to draw her to me. As she came, she shed linen shift and I realized she was naked.

'Gods, you drive me only to madness . . .' I groaned against her throat. 'Deirdre—'

Her hand covered my mouth as I moved to cover hers. 'Do not speak. I have not come here for speech. There is something more than that, I'm thinking, between us, you and me.'

I locked my fingers in her hair. Its color was muted in the darkness, but I gloried in its texture. 'I am not one for gainsaying you in this, the gods know—' fervently '—but do you know what you are about?'

She pressed herself against me, winding heavy locks of hair around my neck as if she sought to set iron there. 'Only rarely am I *not* knowing what I am about, my lord.' Her breath was warm against my ear. Low-voiced, she said, 'Don't be worrying about what I heard today. I have no intention of telling my father or brother. We'll be keeping it between us.'

I bore her down with me, shivering with pleasure at the sensual touch of her hair and skin. '*Meijha*—' Then purposely, I used the Erinnish inflection '—you will have me thinking you are not jealous of Gisella . . . and I am knowing better.'

Laughing softly, she stroked my naked shoulder, tracing shapes of her own devising in a languid, sensuous fashion, then set lips and tongue against it. ''Tis a jealous woman I am, but I know when I have lost. What was that word you called me?'

'*Meijha*,' I breathed, 'Cheysuli . . .'

'That much I was thinking myself.' A trembling forefinger traced the line of my mouth. 'What does it mean?'

I kissed the fingertip, then reached for the hand, the arm, the breast. 'Do not judge too hastily a people you cannot know,' I whispered. 'In the clans, warriors may have both wife and light woman – *cheysula* and *meijha*. There is no dishonor, none at all, for the woman who is not a wife. I swear by all the gods of Erinn and Homana—'

'Don't be swearing by gods you're knowing nothing about.' Her breath came faster still. ''Tis disastrous when they take note of it.'

'Gisella is Cheysuli. I think she would understand the custom, once I have explained it.'

She drew back a little. 'Are you telling me 'tis what *I* would be? Your – *meijha?*'

Her accent twisted the word. I did not correct her. 'If you wish it, Deirdre.' *I wish it, I wish it.*

In the shadows I could not see her expression. 'I might prefer to be a wife.'

I set my forehead against her shoulder in defeat. 'Deirdre—'

'But if I cannot be taking you *that* way, I'll be taking you the other. Now enough of this babble, Niall, and let us be making our *own* alliance between Erinn and Homana.'

Laughing exultantly into her untamed hair, I covered her body with my own.

CHAPTER TWELVE

It was three days before I could pursue my intention to escape, and even then it was coincidence that gave me the opportunity. Liam, riding out to hawk with me along the cliffs, was called back by a servant from the castle. And because Liam himself had come with me, the six human hounds had been dismissed.

I did not hesitate. I spurred the gray gelding toward the broken clifftop and rode off the edge of the world.

The gray plunged down the chalky slope, jarring my spine until I felt at least a handspan shorter. I cursed raggedly, not daring to shout my discomfort aloud, and hooked stirrups forward to brace against the jolting downward momentum.

Below me, fishing boats were scattered like pebbles along the shoreline, most of them untended as the fishermen dragged bulging nets onto the sandy beach. I must steal one quickly and, using the knowledge Shea had divulged, somehow sail it across the Dragon's Tail to the rocky coast of Atvia.

Almost down—

The horse stumbled beneath me, lurching forward onto his knees. I could not wait to see if he had injured himself or had the heart to go on. I threw the reins free and scrambled out of the saddle—

—sliding, sliding, scrabbling at the chalky escarpment of the tumbled base of the cliffs—

Gods, get me down from here with both legs and arms left whole.

—sliding, churning up clouds of white chalk dust to coat

my face, my clothing; to settle on my tongue and make me mouth my distaste. I wanted to spit; it would have to wait until I was down.

On my buttocks I went down, down, *down*, one hand thrust back to brace myself against the broken cliff. The chalk crumbled away, spilling me over like a round rock in a storm-fed stream. I fell; falling, I rolled—

—came up into a crouch at the bottom of the cliff; spitting, I thrust myself upward and ran.

I heard an outcry from the top of the cliff and knew the voice was Liam's. What he shouted I could not decipher, hearing only anger and epithets. I did not look around, intent only on reaching the boats before Liam could form a proper pursuit. I did not blame him for his rage, no more than I blamed myself for causing it.

And yet I *did* blame myself; a broken oath is no simple thing. I thought of how I had proclaimed myself incapable of ending the betrothal to Gisella because I could not break an oath. Now I broke an oath equally important.

For the sake of Homana— And I knew it was. As much as wedding Gisella was for the sake of the prophecy.

Chalk dust filled my lungs. I coughed, spat, wheezed, still running for the boats. Almost. *Almost.*

Netting tripped me up, throwing me sprawling to the wet sand. I scrambled up, trying to run again, but the net was tangled around my spurs. Cursing aloud I ripped frenziedly at the strands, then stopped yanking, still cursing, and carefully picked them free. I ran again.

The first boat was too far, bobbing in the waves at the end of its tether. I went on to the next one, reaching for the line that anchored it to the shore. Waves slapped at my boots as I bent to jerk it free.

I heard the pounding of hooves echoing against the cliffs. Closer, coming *closer*.

Oh gods, it is Liam!

I saw his furious face as he urged his horse on faster, riding directly at me. *At* me, as if he would ride me down.

Forgoing the boat, I dropped the line and ran.

145

The horse's chest caught me high on the left hip. A hoof ripped the heel off my boot entirely, clipped my heel, drove me headlong to the ground. I curled, sucking air as another hoof came down on the side of my thigh. The horse squealed, flailing thick legs desperately, trying to avoid me even as I tried to roll away. I tasted sand and salt and seawater. And blood from a bitten lip.

The hooves were gone. I tried to rise, to run again, but Liam leaned down from the saddle and buffeted me on the temple with a gloved, powerful fist. 'False prince!' he cried. 'False friend!'

I fell. I spat blood. Saw two of everything. Tried to clear my vision. By the time I did, Liam was off his horse and hauling me to my feet.

'I should slay you here, even unarmed as you are!'

I am tall, I am heavy, but Liam himself is not small. And in his rage he was larger than any man ever born. By my tunic, he lifted me almost completely clear of the sand. 'Liam—'

'I should *slay* you! D'ye hear, ye faithless cur of a faithless bitch? By the gods, I swear I *will!*'

But he did not. He released me with a shove, as if he could no longer bear to touch me, and stood staring at me with chalk and spittle fouling his gilded beard. His chest heaved; like me, he panted.

'Liam—' Breathless, I could hardly manage a word. 'Liam — I had to — I *had* to . . . for the war, for the realm.' I tried to catch my breath. 'Alaric — *Alaric* intends to join Strahan — there is domestic dissension at home!'

'I care *nothing at all* for your incestuous domestic wars!' Liam roared. 'Not when you're in *Erinn* seducing my sister!'

Prepared to defend our incestuous domestic wars, I discovered we were at odds over something else. Something I could not defend at all. And so I shut my mouth.

'False prince,' Liam said hoarsely, 'you have betrayed my father's trust, and mine. When we have honored you with our favor!'

'Liam—'

'Were you armed—'

'Then give me a knife!' I shouted. 'I am not shirking the fight!'

Liam spat blood and chalk. His green eyes were hard as glass. 'I'll not be giving *you* the honor of a fight! I'll be letting you taste the hospitality you should have known *before.*'

No protest. I could not. Because before I could summon a word, Liam loosed a blow that felled me to the ground as easily as if I were a stalk of wheat.

The dungeons of Kilore are damp and smelly. Sore and more than a little sullen, I sat against a clammy wall because I had no other choice. Someone – Liam, no doubt – had ordered me chained in place, though there was no place I could go.

The stone beneath my buttocks was cold and damp. What straw existed was musty, stale, undoubtedly filled with vermin. Seawater dripped from the ceiling. I was cold and lonely and afraid, and also filled with guilt.

Deirdre came to me willingly, but how can I say that to her father and brother? What sense is there in besmirching her reputation?

None. What honor remained to me (little enough, after breaking my parole) kept me from being able to make the admission, regardless of the truth.

My ears rang. My head ached. Liam's blow had caught me solidly along the jaw, loosening teeth. I tongued them gently, afraid to push too hard for shoving them out entirely. Even my cheekbone hurt.

Footsteps. I turned my face toward the door and listened, trying to determine if the footsteps brought a man to me or to another prisoner, if there was one. I had no candle by which to see. There was no light in the cell save for what came in under the wooden door. And the gods knew *that* was little enough.

The footsteps stopped. Iron rattled: keys. Finally one was

fitted into the lock. I waited, and at last the door was shoved open. It scraped along the slimy floor.

Shea himself. Not Liam, come to gloat. The old lord instead, holding a fat candle in one hand. It guttered, danced, flared up again as it took life from the corridor air.

Skin was stretched too taut across age-defined cheekbones. His jaw worked impotently beneath the thinning beard. I saw the glitter of anger restrained in the cat-green, grieving eyes.

Gods, forgive me for what I have done to this man.

''Tis how Donal rears a son to be Mujhar, is it? To be breaking parole and pledge when he has been honorably treated?' Tears shone briefly in his eyes. 'To be taking a lass's virtue beneath her father's roof?'

I looked away and stared blindly down at my manacled hands. 'No.'

'No? *No?* 'Tis all ye have to say?'

I swallowed thickly. 'Do not judge the father by the son.'

The candleflame guttered violently. I did not look at Shea.

'Well,' he said hoarsely, 'come up. I'll say what I say above.' He glanced into the corridor and jerked his head in my direction. 'Loose the iron and bring him up. I'll be seeing him in the hall.'

The old lord stood in the doorway as the guardsman slipped by and knelt to unlock my shackles. Limping from a badly bruised thigh – the horse had struck me squarely – I followed Shea up winding stairs to the audience hall. I had half expected Liam to be present. He was not. Neither was Deirdre. It was for Shea alone to pass judgment.

He gestured to the guardsman to leave us alone. I heard the door thud closed. Then I turned and faced the old man.

His nostrils flared. 'Ye stink,' he said, plainly offended by my dungeon stench.

I felt inordinately ashamed.

'Have ye an explanation?'

'No.'

'Were ye for it merely because 'twas *offered*, or did ye truly want it – much as a dying man cries for water?'

I had thought him diminished by what I had done to his daughter. Now I realized he was not, it was just that I saw a man instead of a king. A father instead of a man.

I drew in a breath and released it very slowly. 'I needed it,' I told him clearly. 'I *was* that dying man.'

Shea hooked thumbs in his wide belt and considered me. And then he spoke, and his tone held all the gruff affection I had come to expect from him. 'She was not meaning to betray ye, lad. 'Twas her unhappy manner that gave ye away. 'Twas the lack of her wildness and gaiety.'

'My lord?'

'Oh, she was happy enough for having despoiled herself with you. She *told* me that. No. 'Twas knowing you must leave. But by the time I was realizing what she meant, you had ridden out with Liam.' He paused. 'She said she was willing, lad.'

I was silent. Even now, I would say nothing that might reflect poorly on his daughter, who was a princess. That much of rank I knew too well.

'By Erinnish law I am in my rights to have you slain.'

'By any man's law, my lord.'

'Yet you are the Mujhar of Homana's son. His heir. As much as Liam is mine.'

'Aye, my lord.'

Shea sighed. 'Lad, lad, 'tis all bound up I am. I'd be seeing the two of you wed, but for that pledge to Alaric's daughter. That you cannot be breaking, for all you broke the one to me.' There was no bitterness in his tone. 'Deirdre told me what the Cheysuli general said to you. About war, and bastards, and a throne in jeopardy. Those things I understand. And so I will not be blaming ye for breaking your parole. There are pledges taking precedence over other pledges given.' Through the beard, I saw the hint of a weary smile. 'I will not keep ye here when your father needs ye so. I'll be seeing you sent to Atvia before the day is out.'

'My lord?' I stared.

'Homana is not my enemy. I'm not wishing to see your father broken by that Ihlini demon or even Alaric's spite.

149

Go wed your Atvian cousin, and take yourself home to your father.'

Hope sprang up. 'And – Deirdre?'

'She stays,' he told me flatly. 'My daughter will be no man's mistress, no matter how much *honor* it claims before the Cheysuli.' He sighed. 'But I will be asking something of ye, lad. A pledge. And this one ye'll not be breaking; Liam will see to that.'

I touched my aching face. 'Aye, my lord. I give it willingly.'

'Ierne is due to bear the child soon. Be that child a girl, let her wed your firstborn son. Or the next one for *your* next one, if this one is not a girl and that one not a boy. But I want it, lad. I want a granddaughter of Shea of Erinn to be queen in Homana one day.'

I smiled. 'A fair enough exchange, my lord. A daughter of mine for Sean, a granddaughter of yours for my heir. I think it will please the gods.'

''Twill be pleasing *me*,' Shea growled. 'And 'twill be enough, I'm thinking.'

I put out my filthy hand to the man. He did not seem to notice as he folded it in his. 'Deirdre—' I began.

'No,' he said. 'I'll be giving her your farewell.'

After a moment, I nodded. But I knew it would not be the same.

I had been bathed, shaved, garbed in fresh clothing. No longer did I stink. But it did not wash away the sorrow I felt at leaving Deirdre behind.

It was Liam himself who came to escort me to the ship. He was sternness itself with his hard, stark face; he said nothing at all as he preceded me down the twisting stairway to the entryway. We were met by the eleven men who had accompanied him the day I was rescued. Rescued and taken captive.

There was little enough sunlight. Liam's brassy curls were dulled by the gray of the day, as much as by his unusual solemnity. His mouth, in the beard, worked a little; the words at last issued forth.

150

'Where would you go, lad, before we send you to your bride?'

Where would I go? To Deirdre, of course . . . and yet I knew if I asked it, he would deny me the thing I most wanted.

I looked out into the muted sunlight. 'To the tor,' I said. 'To the altar of the *cileann*.'

Liam's green eyes flickered. Still, he did not smile. He nodded, once, and gave the order for us to mount. Eleven prince's men; one heir to Shea's wild aerie; one hostage foreigner. Together, we rode out to the tor.

In daylight, with the sun well up, the place was different. Much different. I tasted no magic; smelled no hint of ancient power. And all I saw was an altar full of memories.

Deirdre. Deirdre and her colt. And the *lirless* man who loved her.

Liam's eleven men remained on horseback some distance away. Liam came closer, but even he gave me what distance he could. Privacy enough, for the moment. And so I used it. I used it to stand on the tor outside the old chalk circle and give Deirdre my good-bye.

'Time to go,' Liam said, when he saw me lift an arm to scrub briefly at my face.

Aye . . . time to go. I turned. The Prince of Erinn held the reins of my horse. I walked down from the tor, took them out of his gloved hand and mounted the pale gray gelding. And thought of Deirdre's wild laughter as she rode headlong at the edge of the chalky headlands overlooking the Dragon's Tail.

'Lad,' Liam said; all I could do was nod.

The escort stopped short of the dock. I boarded slowly, so slowly, then swung back to grip the rail. Liam stood on the deck. The wind whipped his brassy curls and reddened his high, sharp cheekbones, tugging at his beard. His cat-green eyes were cool. 'So, puppy, you leave Erinn a wealthy man.'

'Wealthy?'

151

'You've gained my father's trust, won my sister's love, and have pledged children neither of us yet have, saving Sean. Ye leave with a *little* pinch more than ye came with.'

The wind stripped freshly-washed hair out of my face. 'Perhaps you should have thrown me back into the sea the day you found me . . .' I squinted against the wind. 'Perhaps you should have let the dragon have me.'

'No,' he said. 'You were too sickly, too battered. Not worth the trouble to feed an Erinnish dragon. I'm thinking there would have been little pleasure in it.'

'The pledge we made together, and the one I made with your father—' I shrugged. 'You will be king after Shea. It is for you to break them, if it is truly what you desire.'

Liam bent and spat off the dock into the Dragon's Tail. He folded his arms across a broad chest. 'I'm thinking not. I'm thinking I'm not much of a man for breaking pledges. Unlike *you*.'

I clutched the rail. 'I can sail to Atvia later. We can settle this matter now. With knives or swords or fists.' I grinned. 'I leave it to you, *my lord*.'

Reluctantly, Liam grinned. The green cloak fastened to his wide shoulders curled and cracked in the wind. 'We are of a like size, I'm thinking, lad. I have spent nearly fifteen of my twenty-nine years fighting Atvians, and *you* are Cheysuli – even without the *lir*. I'm thinking 'twould not be so wise to strip Donal and Shea of their sons in a silly, boyish battle that could get either – *or both* – of us slain.' He shrugged. 'Besides, my sister loves you. Where's the sense in beating a man for that?'

I laughed. 'But it would have been something to see.'

Liam, sighing, nodded. 'Aye, 'twould. Well – perhaps another day, puppy. Now get you to Atvia.'

I leaned over the rail as he gave the signal for the boat to be cast off. 'Liam – a message for Deirdre?'

He squinted into the wind. 'What would you be saying to her *now*?'

'That if she wants me – if she *needs* me – do not hesitate to send word. Even to Homana! I promise I will come.'

'I'll be caring for her here.'

'*Liam—*'

'No, lad. She needs no more of you.' He stared hard at me. Then his bearded face softened. 'But I'll be telling her what you said.'

I clung to the rail as the ship moved out into the channel. Wind-whipped swells crashed against the prow. But I hardly noticed. I watched the dark bulwark of the Aerie silhouetted against the sky and then I watched the Erinnish shore. Until all I could see was the green speck of Liam's cloak. And then I turned my face to Atvia.

And to my Cheysuli bride.

Part II

CHAPTER ONE

Rondule, like Shea's city of Kilore, was a fishing port. Except for minor differences in architecture, I saw no real distinction between Rondule and Kilore, or between Rondule and Homana's own Hondarth, for that matter. I had sailed hundreds of leagues westward, and yet I saw little that made this part of the world any different from my own.

Until I heard the language. In eight months with Shea and his folk, I had grown accustomed to the lyrical lilt of the Erinnish tongue, which was little different from Homanan except for nuances and a few words held over from the old days of Erinn. I did not doubt that I had acquired a trace of the accent myself, after so many months. But I knew I would never acquire the sound of Atvia, no matter *how* long I stayed on the island.

I thought it an ugly language, choked with consonants rather than vowels, and those spoken harshly. It was a sibilant tongue that put me in mind of a serpent hissing in the darkness. I did not much like the imagery. More than ever wished I could avoid Atvia altogether.

The boat docked. In Erinnish finery borrowed from Liam (though we were both big men, the clothing did not fit well; the gods had put us together differently) I disembarked into a maelstrom of activity. The tide was turning; time for the fisherfolk to return home with the day's catch. And I in the middle of it.

I heard the hissing chatter of the men as they hauled in the nets; the women as they hastened down to help their men. I smelled fish everywhere. It clogged my nose and insinuated itself in my mouth, my clothing, my hair. A fleeting thought told me it had been no different in Kilore, but I chose to see Rondule in a harsher light.

'My lord.' A boy's voice, speaking accented Homanan. The familiar words were almost throttled in his throat, but I could decipher them. Just.

He was half my height, clothed in a bright blue tunic. An intricate border in white yarn drew my eyes; it was very nearly Erinnish knotwork. But there was a difference. Just as there was in the boy's attitude toward me. He was not rude, not precisely, but neither was he as warm as the Erinnish.

'Aye,' I said shortly. 'Has Alaric sent you to fetch me?'

He did not smile. I judged him ten, twelve; his brown eyes were older. 'If you are Niall of Homana.'

'Oh, I think so. And you, boy?'

'Belen,' he answered. He pointed at two horses tied nearby, waiting patiently. 'Come.'

I came. Belen led me through the twisting cobbled streets toward the center of the city. And when we had reached it, I found myself having to close my mouth because I did not wish the boy to see my awe.

Like Kilore, Alaric's fortress perched atop a rocky cliff. But his did not have the headlands and heaths stretching in all directions. Instead, the castle capped a palisade that jutted up from the center of the city. The promontory was cone-shaped but lacked a smooth, uniform roundness, displaying craggy flanks full of crevices and treacherous faults in the stone itself. I saw no road or path at all winding its way up to the castle on top of the world. And I began to understand why Shea had told me, again and again, that a frontal assault on Alaric's castle was the strategy of a madman – or a fool.

Being neither, he never tried. They fight their own wars on the seas and beaches.

'Come.' Belen set heels to his spotted horse.

There was a path after all. It followed the natural grain of the stone, rising, twisting, zigzagging through faults and square-cut protrusions. Here and there pockets of turf carpeted the terraced face, but most of it was rock. Hard, cold rock.

The wind beat at my face, threading tiny fingers through the weave of my borrowed garb. I shivered. Belen, ahead, did not seem to notice the chilly breath of the dragon. He rode steadily onward, always ascending, never looking back. I heard the familiar wailing song of the dragon as its exhalations curled around the rocks and buffeted me front and back. I thought of Deirdre. I thought of the chalky, wind-whipped heights of Erinn, so close I could nearly touch them. I had only to put out my hand and reach across the Dragon's Tail, and Deirdre would be mine.

'Dragon's Teeth.' The boy had turned in his saddle. He jerked his head a little, indicating the rocky ramparts of the cliffs. 'The castle is beyond.'

Higher still, and then atop the promontory. The wind spat into my face.

'Castle,' Belen said.

A boy of few words. But I paid no mind to him. I looked instead at Alaric's fortress.

Unassailable, aye; no man foolish enough to risk himself against certain death would ever try to take the castle. Perhaps Rondule, or other cities. But never the actual fortress. Like Homana-Mujhar, it was invulnerable.

But once, Homana-Mujhar had fallen.

Belen led me through a barbican gate warded by six massive portcullises and into the outer bailey beyond. Guards hedged the sentry-walks and battlements. Colored pennons snapped in the wind. I heard the echoes of iron on cobbles as we entered the inner bailey.

Boys came running for the horses. I dismounted, hissed a bit as the landing jarred my bruised thigh, nodded irritably as Belen motioned me to follow. One might think I was the prisoner here, instead of Gisella's betrothed.

The boy took me through candlelit corridors and into a private chamber. Here the stone floor was carpeted with rugs I recognized as Caledonese; we had similar in Homana-Mujhar, including my bedchamber. Lighted braziers

159

warmed the room. There were no casements; I could not stare out and search for Erinn from the top of the dragon's head.

'Someone will come,' the boy announced, and then he shut the door.

Alone, I looked around the room. Chairs, a table, a chest, a jug of wine and silver goblets. Having nothing better to do, I poured myself a cup.

Not wine. It was a clear, pungent liquor. I lifted the goblet, recognized the powerful contents and set it down again. '*Usca*,' I said in surprise.

'Trade routes,' a voice commented equably. 'All the way from the Steppes to Atvia.' As I turned the man smiled and shut the door. '*I* am not Ihlini, Niall; did you think I conjured it?'

Alaric. I knew him at once, though I had never seen him. Once, my mother had described him to me, telling me how he had come to Homana seeking the Mujhar's sister as a wife. Then, she said, he had been tall, slender, brown-haired, brown-eyed. Handsome, she had added, if you liked men with silken manners and silver tongues. Bronwyn had not, but she had wed him anyway. My father had given her no choice.

Nineteen years had passed since then. I thought he was a year or two older than my father. He looked younger than his years, though time and wars had roughened the too-smooth edges. He had not thickened, maintaining a tensile slenderness, and he moved with an awareness of a subtle but acknowledged strength. In body as well as spirit.

In understated black, he put me in mind of Strahan. He reminded me of Lillith.

He smiled. His Homanan was quite good. His accent was very slight. 'You are well come to Atvia. Although – for a moment – I thought it was a dead man standing before me.'

'Carillon.' I forced a smile, as always. 'No.'

Alaric moved to the table and poured *usca* for us both. Out of courtesy I accepted the goblet; I have no taste for *usca*. 'I met Carillon once,' he said reminiscently. 'I was but a boy, no older than Belen, but I knew enough to be impressed. It was not long after Tynstar had stolen twenty years of his life. Already the disease ate away at his bones.' Still smiling, he drank. I did not.

'My lord—' I began.

'I never saw him again.' Clearly, Alaric was not finished. Until he was, he had no intention of allowing me to speak. 'When my brother slew him, I was here. Beating back Erinnish wolfhounds from my shores.' Alaric continued to smile.

I set down my goblet with a thud. *Usca* slopped over the rim. 'It was for *you* to end my captivity.'

If my curtness surprised him, Alaric did not show it. Politely he set down his own cup — he would not drink if I did not — and motioned calmly for me to be seated. I considered refusing. But my stiffening thigh ached and my head still rang from Liam's blow. I sat down.

'It was for me to end your captivity.' Alaric sat down and crossed his legs. His boots, I saw, bore massive spurs of rune-worked gold. 'And did you curse me for not doing it while you bedded Deirdre of Erinn?'

The breath ran out of my chest. There were no words in my mouth; no aborted explanation. Not before *this* man; he was Gisella's father.

Alaric rubbed idly at his clean-shaven chin. His manner was calm, too calm; he put me in mind of a cat waiting for the mouse to jump. 'Well?'

'You ally yourself with Strahan and the Ihlini. Against my father.'

A corner of his mouth twitched in amusement. He knew very well why I altered the subject. 'What I do is my own concern.' He shifted minutely in the chair. The golden spurs glinted. Oddly, they reminded me of *lir*-bands. 'I have no intention of filling your head with Atvian history, Niall. Suffice it to say it was never my wish to give my fealty to Donal.' He shrugged a little, dismissing it. 'We are uneasy bedmates at best. He takes — I give. And I am weary of it.'

161

I stood up. 'My lord, if you have no intention of honoring the alliance, I have no intention of listening to you.'

'Sit down,' he told me coolly. 'If I have ruffled your feathers, accept my apology. But I am being frank with you, Niall. You are not a boy any longer.'

No, I was not. The quick anger and affrontedness spilled away almost at once; I sat down. It would harm nothing to listen to the man.

'Think of what I would gain if the alliance were ended,' he suggested.

'War,' I answered promptly. 'And my father has beaten you once.'

Brown eyes narrowed a little. He studied me a moment. And then he smiled. 'War. But even Homana grows weaker when the wars drag on for decades.' Politeness forgone, he reached out and took up his goblet, swallowing *usca* again. 'You *are* here,' he said. 'A trifle tardy, perhaps, but that is no fault of yours. I see no reason for invalidating the proxy wedding. Gisella would be – disturbed.'

He spoke so calmly of his daughter and the wedding when he knew about Deirdre and me. I wondered uneasily how he had gotten his information. If he had a loyal Atvian servant somewhere in Kilore – or, for that matter, a *dis*loyal Erinnish one – Shea and everyone else could be in danger.

'My lord, if you truly wish to let this marriage go forth, why did you not give in to Shea's demands?'

'Because I give in to no one.'

It was my turn to smile. 'But you gave in to my father. I know all about it. You knelt on the floor and kissed his sword and swore fealty to him.'

'And in return I got his sister for my wife. Gisella for a daughter.' He raised dark brows. 'Who gained, who lost? Surely *I* benefited more than Donal did.'

Surely he had. And he knew I knew it. 'Is a title so important? Worth so many wars?'

'This one is.' A signet ring glinted on Alaric's hand: silver set with jet. 'It has belonged to the Atvian lord since before I was born. My grandsire, Keough, won it from Ryan of

Erinn. Shea did not contest it until his heir was born.'

'Your sister was wed to Shea. Does it mean nothing to you?'

He uncrossed his legs and leaned forward, elbows on his knees. 'Boy, you must learn the practicalities of alliances and wars. When one is broken, the other invariably follows.' A warning, perhaps? He rose. 'For more than two hundred years Erinn and Atvia have been at war. Intermittently, of course – we cannot *always* fight. But it is as much a part of the Atvian and Erinnish way of life as shapechanging is of yours.' His movement was arrested. 'Ah, but of course – you cannot. I had heard you lack a *lir*.'

I thrust myself out of the chair. Impotent rage welled up as Alaric continued smiling.

Gods, if only I could close that mouth forever—

'Niall,' he said gently. 'Did you expect us to be friends?'

With effort, I said, 'I expected us to be civil.'

He put his emptied goblet on the table. 'This *is* civil, boy. I am not Shea of Erinn.'

'Shea of Erinn possesses more integrity, honor, and manners than you could ever *hope* for!'

'No doubt,' he said easily. 'Nonetheless, he is a fool.' He looked past my shoulder and smiled, gesturing a welcome. 'Niall, there is someone who wishes to see you.'

Gisella. I turned, trying to arrange my face into a mask of civility – Gisella was due it even if her father was not – and saw Lillith instead of Gisella.

Again, she wore crimson. She was cloaked in the weight of her hair. 'I offered you a choice,' she said calmly. 'You refused to accept my help. But I see you had other alternatives.'

No more would I look away from the woman. I stared intently back at her. 'The gods look after their own.'

After an arrested moment, Lillith began to smile. 'The months have done you good,' she said obscurely. And then she laughed.

I watched as she went to Alaric and kissed him intimately, ignoring my presence entirely. He locked one hand in the

163

curtain of her hair. The other pressed her against his loins. Because they wanted to make me uncomfortable, I did not look away.

Lillith broke from Alaric and turned to me. Her black eyes seemed blacker yet. 'I have come to escort you to proper chambers. Tonight we honor you with a feast; you will need to rest until then.'

Her hand was on my arm. She waited. But before I went, I looked over my shoulder at Alaric.

The Lord of Atvia was smiling.

My assigned chambers, as I shut the door in Lillith's lovely face, were deeply shadowed. Again, there were no casements to let in the sunlight. Only candles, and most were not lighted. Though it was only afternoon, the room was gloomy. I wanted nothing to do with it.

Lillith had remarked on my lack of clothing, saying those lost in the shipwreck would be replaced with others. Now, made aware I had nothing of my own save the ruby signet ring and my silver-plated belt, I found myself longing for Cheysuli leathers.

'Niall.' A shape moved out of the shadows of the room. I spun, reaching for the knife I still did not have, and then I stopped moving altogether.

The face was thin, too thin, so *gaunt*, fined down to flesh stretched nearly to splitting over the prominent bones of the skull. I saw hollowed pockets beneath high, angular cheekbones; circles like bruises beneath eyes, the yellow eyes, filled with a dozen haunted memories of what it was like to lose a brother. What it was like to lose a soul. He was a stranger to me, my brother, and yet I knew him so very well.

'Ian!' And almost instantly: *Oh, gods, what have they done to my brother?*

He was thin. His clothes were of Atvian cut; no Cheysuli leathers here. When Ian had worn nothing else. His thick hair was dull, though clean, and had been cut much shorter than normal. It did not quite cover his ears; I saw the

nakedness of his left lobe and realized what he had done.
Or what they had made him do.

What have they made of my brother?

'*Rujho?*' he asked tentatively, and I saw the apprehension
in his eyes.

I took a single step toward him. 'Gods! Ian, I thought
you were dead! I thought you had drowned in the storm!'
I stopped. I wanted to go to him, to embrace him even as
Rowan and I had embraced; to give him welcome as I could
give no other man. But I did not. Something in his manner
held me back.

'Niall,' he said. 'Oh – gods – I thought she lied – I
thought she told me *lies*—' He shut his eyes so I would not
see the tears. 'But you are *here*—'

'Here,' I echoed numbly. *Oh*, rujho, *what have they done
to you?* 'Ian . . .' At last I stretched out a hand to touch
his shoulder. But as I touched him he moved rigidly away.
Like a hound afraid of his master.

'She said you were coming,' he told me. 'She *said* so, but
I did not believe her. She tells me so many things.' His
heavy swallow was visible, even in the shadows. 'When
there is one truth in twenty lies, I cannot always choose
which one to believe in.'

'Ian, what is *wrong?* What is wrong with you?'

He flinched. Visibly. As if the master had struck the
hound. 'I know, now. I know what it is, now. The pain.
The emptiness. The void within a heart.' He drew in an
unsteady breath. 'I have seen how it is, how it has been with
you all these years—'

'Ian.'

'—and now I know myself—'

'Ian.'

'—what a *lirless* man goes through—'

'*Ian!*'

'—when his *lir* is taken from him.' The sinews knotted
even as his jaw muscles did. 'I *know* what I must do. *But
she will not let me do it!*'

I did not hold back. I crossed to him in a single stride

165

and took him into my arms. And I thought how odd it was that I, the younger, the *lirless* Prince of Homana, now comforted a *lirless* warrior of the clan who had always comforted me.

With words and without.

Beneath the woolen Atvian doublet and linen shirt, I felt the nakedness of his arms. In shock I drew back. 'Where is your *lir*-gold?'

'Gone. I put it off.' He pulled away, turning away; turning his back on me.

As if he cannot face me. 'Ian—'

'A *lirless* warrior has no right to wear the gold.' And then he turned. '*You* should know that, Niall.'

Niall. No more *rujho*. Had Tasha's loss also made him forget other bonds?

Or is it what they have done to him?

I wanted to shout at him. I did not. I drew in a steadying breath and told him, very quietly, 'You have more right to wear the *lir*-gold than any warrior I know.'

Ian laughed. There was no humor in it. Only the vast emptiness of a man who has lost himself. 'It is what a warrior does,' he told me bitterly, 'this putting off of the gold. A true warrior. One who conducts himself according to the Cheysuli tradition—'

'—and seeks the death-ritual?' I finished. 'In Homana I would never question it. But we are in Atvia, and—'

Interrupting rudely, another sign he was not himself, Ian spat out an oath in the Old Tongue. 'Do you think *that* matters? – what kingdom I am in? Oh, Niall, our customs are not determined by *where* we are but by *who*. I am Cheysuli. My *lir* is lost. There is only one thing left to do.'

'Then why are you here?' I wanted to shout it, knowing the question was the only way to trick an explanation from a man who so patently did not want to give me one. 'If you are willing to stand before me and prate about Cheysuli tradition and *lirlessness*, then why not complete the ritual? Live up to your heritage, shapechanger. Go out and seek your death.'

He twitched. Suddenly he was not Ian before me, not my brother; not the boy to whom I had looked for guidance nor the man to whom I had looked for companionship and protection in the court of the Lion Throne. Somehow, he was – *diminished*.

'Oh *rujho*,' I said in despair, 'what have they done to you?'

'Not they,' said a female voice distinctly. 'What *she* has done to him.'

This time it *was* Gisella. I had only to look at her as she shouldered shut the door. 'You do not deny it, then?'

She did not answer. She came forward into the wash of candlelight and I saw her eyes: yellow as my brother's. No, Alaric had not stamped Gisella as Shea had stamped Liam and Deirdre. Nor as Carillon, through his daughter, had come back to live in me. In flesh and bone and spirit, Gisella was more Cheysuli than I.

Ian said nothing. Nor did I; I could think of nothing succinct that would express what I was feeling.

She wore a gown the color of blood. Not the bright crimson red of Lillith's velvet skirts, but the color of day-old blood. Dull, a man might say; ugly, a woman would, but on Gisella the color was right.

She smiled. Ignoring Ian, Gisella smiled at me. 'I was not to let you see me before tonight's feast. But I could not wait.' Her black hair was worn Cheysuli-fashion: braided, looped, twisted, fastened in place with golden combs that glittered with ice-white diamonds. She had a widow's peak. It gave her a look of elegance, of maturity, and yet I knew she lacked both. She was oddly childish. Or was it child*like*? 'My father wanted you to be pleased with me. *Are* you pleased with me?'

It is as if Ian is not even in the room. 'I think I might be more pleased if I knew what Lillith has done to my brother.'

Gisella shrugged. The gown was cut wide of her shoulders, displaying smooth dark skin, elegant neck, a rope of gold and diamonds. 'Only what she has done before. Though they were not Cheysuli.' She looked at Ian and smiled. Her eyes lit up and she laughed. 'Because she

167

wanted to do it. Because he hated her. Because he lacked a *lir*.'

'*I* lack a *lir*.'

Her lips parted in surprise. 'Lillith would never ensorcell *you*!'

I turned to Ian. 'We will discover what she has done, *rujho*, I promise. And then we will—'

'—do *what*?' Gisella came closer, skirts swinging. 'He is *lirless*, Niall. Without a *lir* he will go mad. But Lillith will keep him from it. She *said* so . . . she said she *wants* him.'

I stared. Her tone was utterly unconcerned, as if it mattered not one whit to her that the witch had ensorcelled my brother. 'Gisella—'

She spun and spun in place, holding out blood-colored skirts. 'Did Lillith not make me pretty?'

'Gisella!' I cried. 'By the gods, girl, are you blind? The woman is Ihlini!'

She stopped spinning. The skirts settled. The diamonds stopped blinding me with their brilliant glitter. 'The woman is my mother.'

'Your *mother*!' Aghast, I gaped openly. 'Has she driven the sense from your head? Lillith is not your mother. Your mother was Bronwyn, sister to Donal of Homana. My aunt – *su'fala* in the Old Tongue. You are my kinswoman, Gisella . . . my cousin. No matter what she has told you, Lillith is *not* your mother.'

Gisella frowned. Lifted a hand. Her nails, like Lillith's, were silver-tipped. And they ripped a hole in the air to replace it with living flame.

Cold, *cold* flame . . . and a lurid Ihlini purple.

CHAPTER TWO

Gods!

She ripped the air apart but a handspan from my face. I lurched back awkwardly, trying to escape the flame. Off-balance, I fetched up against a chair, overset it, went over myself, rolling, trying to get up before she could send loose another blast of icy, encompassing flame.

'Gisella – *no!*' I heard my brother shout.

'But I *want* to,' she said simply, and I wrenched sideways, thrusting up an arm to shield my blinded eyes.

Flame licked out, caressed shrinking flesh, charred wool and linen . . . singed the reddish hairs upon my forearm. Backward I scrabbled, gulping air; came up against the stone wall and was stopped. 'Gisella,' I gasped, '*no!*'

Sparks hissed from silvered fingertips, winking out even as they fell. A crackling aureole of livid lavender gloved her slender fingers. '*Godfire*,' she said, 'do you see?'

Ian took a step toward her. Stopped. I did not blame him. No man, facing a girl as irrational as Gisella, would want to go closer to her.

What has Lillith done to her? What has that witch done to both of them?

'Ian,' I began, 'wait—'

He thrust out a silencing hand.

Gisella's eyes were fixed on me in an opaque, unwavering stare. Diamonds glittered. 'Lillith said you would be *mine*.'

Gods . . . do they expect me to wed this girl? Do they really expect me to bed her?

Ian's hand motioned for me to stay precisely where I was. Decisively; he was Ian again. And for the first time since

169

Gisella's attack, I looked at my brother instead of my cousin.

He stood rigidly before her, in three-quarter profile to me. He was intent only on Gisella, marking her posture, her position in relation to me, to the rest of the room, to him. Like me, he was unarmed, but I knew, looking at him, even lacking knife or bow he was as lethal as he was with them.

An odd juxtaposition. They were very like one another, Ian and Gisella, reflecting kinship as well as racial heritage. Again, it was *I* who was so different. *Lirless* I was even as Ian was, but still so very different.

Slowly, Ian stretched out a hand to Gisella. Their fingertips nearly touched. Gisella gazed at him fixedly, as if she sought to judge his intentions. Still the *godfire* clung to her hand.

And then his, as he touched his fingers to hers.

Ian?

'No,' he told her gently. 'Loose no magic at him, or you will surely anger the gods.'

'Gods?' she whispered. '*Gods?*' Like a striking viper, her other hand shot out and clawed at his face. In its wake I saw the afterglow of flame slicing the air apart as easily as steel.

Ian caught her striking hand. The other he claimed as well. By the wrists he held her, nearly suspending her. She cried out angry curses I did not know, fearing them Atvian or, worse, Ihlini invective. Such curses could summon demons.

From rigid fingertips ran blood, raisin black. Or fire; I could not say. It ran down fingers to wrists and spilled onto Ian's hands. Gisella laughed even as he cursed.

I scrambled up, thrusting myself from the floor. Against both of us, surely, she could not persevere; I moved toward them both, intending to aid Ian however I could.

Gisella saw me. Her eyes, swollen black in the muted candlelight, shrank suddenly down to pinpricks. Yellow, so *yellow*, filled with the ferocity of a beast.

And so she was. Even as Ian cried out against it, I saw

the precursor to the shapechange. A ripple. A blurring. The sense of a shattered equilibrium. And then the void, so all-encompassing, as it swallowed the woman whole and spat out the mountain cat.

She struck out, clawing, ripping the air where Ian had been only a moment before. She was black, black as pitch, with tufted ears pinned against wedge-shaped head. Yellow eyes glared at us with a feral intensity.

I have seen housecats, enraged, huddle back as if in fear. And I have seen the subtle sideways twisting of their heads; heard the eerie wailing of their song; sensed the awesome magnificence of their rage. In Gisella, that rage was manifested as clearly as was her madness.

She struck out twice more, slashing with curving claws. Had Ian not been quicker, she would have shredded wool and flesh. She did not try for me. Ian was her target.

He moved as only a Cheysuli can move, with a grace and fluency of motion echoing that of the cat herself. I wondered if it was born in the blood or came with the *lir*-bond. I thought the latter. I had none of my brother's grace. But then, *he* had none of my size.

She screamed. It lifted the hairs on the back of my neck. It was the cry of a hunting mountain cat who has decided on her prey.

I can slay her, I thought dazedly, leaping behind the overturned chair even as Ian lunged back against the wall. *I can slay her and* end *this madness*.

But to do that would end the prophecy before its final fulfillment.

One man of all blood shall unite, in peace, four warring realms and two magic races.

But how does a man get children on a woman such as Gisella?

'*Gisella!*' shouted Alaric from the doorway.

Almost instantly, she was back in human form. She twisted hands in heavy skirts, backing away even as her father advanced. 'No,' she said, 'no. Please? No.' The yellow eyes, once so filled with a virulent anger, now reflected the fear of a disobedient child discovered. 'It is so hard *not* to—'

Alaric caught slender shoulders in slender hands. Gisella's hands splayed across her cheeks as she tried to look away from his angry face. 'Again,' he said curtly, 'again. Will you never learn, Gisella? There are *reasons* for what I forbid.'

'I will learn,' she promised, 'I will. But – sometimes I *have* to do it!'

'Even against your father's wishes?'

She threw back her head and laughed. *Laughed*. And then she wrenched out of his hands and faced him as defiantly as she had faced us. 'You are only angry because *you* cannot shapechange! Oh, no. Not *you!* Not even *Lillith* can.' Throwing out her arms, Gisella let her head fall back against her spine. She spun in place. How she spun, my poor, mad cousin. 'I can,' she sang, 'I can . . . and nobody else can do it!' Spinning, spinning, she crossed the floor. Gold and diamonds spun with her, all aglow in the candlelight. And then she stopped short, so short; so close to Ian her skirts tangled on his boot tops. 'Not even *you* can,' she told him cruelly. 'Not since Lillith took your *lir*.'

I looked at the Lord of Atvia. 'She is mad,' I told him. 'Quite mad.'

He smiled calmly. 'But you will wed her anyway.'

'Wed me!' his daughter cried. 'Niall is to *wed* me!' She left Ian behind and came at once to me, locking hands into the fabric of my doublet. 'They have told me I must wed you and be Queen of Homana. Will you make me Queen of Homana?'

Gods. One day I *would*.

'Gisella.' Gently, I tried to unlock her fingers. 'Gisella, I think there is something I must discuss with your father.'

'Why?' she cried. 'He will only say *you* should not shapechange, either. He is always telling me that.' She jerked her hands from my grasp, locked arms around my neck. 'Niall,' she said, 'when will we be wed?'

'As soon as he takes you to Homana,' Alaric told her smoothly. 'Once all the celebrations here are finished.'

I peeled Gisella away and set her aside, confronting Alaric squarely. 'There will be none,' I said briefly. 'By the gods, you fool, why were we never told? Why was this travesty allowed to continue? Do you think I wish to wed *that*?'

'Does it matter?' he asked. 'You will. Because your prophecy demands it.' Even as I started to speak he silenced me with a gesture. 'Turn your back on my daughter, *child of the prophecy*, and you twist that prophecy. Perhaps even end it precipitately.' He smiled. 'In addition, your father will discover me on his doorstep. Armed. With at least five thousand men-at-arms. Is that what you wish to see?'

'Twenty-five hundred,' I countered bitterly. 'Liam has promised me *that* much.'

Alaric's brows rose. 'The truce already broken? Ah well, I have other plans. I doubt Liam would be so willing to levy war against Atvia when all of his kin are slain . . . including his wanton sister.' He smiled. 'I thought that might get your attention.'

'You *do* have an informant in Kilore—'

'*Informants*,' he corrected. 'Assassins, more like. A word from me – or a beacon fire on the cliff – and the royal Erinnish eagles are dashed to the rocks below.' Alaric smiled. 'I might even have it done tonight.'

Gods – I bared my teeth. 'Why not?' I asked. 'What good do they do you alive?'

'I have been advised it might be best to play this game carefully.' Alaric shrugged. 'I am not so proud that I cannot accept assistance from someone more – patient – than myself.'

'Lillith?' I demanded. 'Aye, patient! And what *else* is she, my lord?'

'My mother,' Gisella said promptly. Almost instantly a hand flew to cover her mouth; she looked at her father fearfully. 'But – that is not *really* true . . . is it? *You* told me—'

'I told you the truth,' Alaric answered evenly. 'Bronwyn bore you, Lillith raised you.' He smiled. 'How else could you combine Ihlini illusion with the Cheysuli shapechange?'

173

'Illusion,' I said, startled. 'None of it was real?'

Gisella thrust out a hand. Fingers snapped open. Even Alaric squinted in the glare of the blinding flame. 'Real,' she said flatly. '*Real!*'

'Real,' he agreed patiently. 'Of course it is, Gisella.' He looked at my brother and smiled. 'Lillith wants you, Ian. Had you not better go?'

Before my eyes I saw my brother diminished. He said nothing; indicated nothing by posture or movement, but he could not hide the revulsion in his eyes.

For himself. Not for Lillith.

'*Rujho—*' I began.

Ian did not even look at me. He walked past me and out of the room.

Alaric laughed. 'Interesting, is it not? To see a Cheysuli humbled?'

'Not Ian.' But even in my ears the declaration sounded hollow. 'Do you intend to humble me?'

Alaric glanced at his daughter. 'Gisella. The game.'

She smiled delightedly. Eyes alight, she put out fisted hands. To me. 'Choose.'

'Not *too* quickly,' Alaric cautioned. 'Wait a moment.' He moved behind her, resting hands on the bared flesh of her shoulders. Then he smiled at me, and I saw the game was on. 'Should we humble you, Niall, as Lillith has humbled Ian? *Could* we? You are very different. Half-brothers, perhaps, but very different. Like two pearls from the same oyster: one black—' Gisella opened her right hand and displayed a pearl, a perfect pearl, blue-black in copper-toned flesh '— the other white. Do you see?' I saw. In the other palm was displayed the other pearl. White. Aglow against her hand.

'Very pretty.' I granted it because I knew they would demand it.

Alaric moved around his daughter and took the pearls from her hands. Inspected them. 'Aye,' he agreed, 'very pretty. But at their best only when given into a *woman's* keeping.' His brown eyes were very steady as he looked at me. 'Do you understand?'

174

'What does she want with him?' I ignored the implications in Alaric's game of pearls and men. 'What does she *do* to him?'

Alaric, shrugging, smiled. 'Some men keep hounds, some women cats. Lillith keeps men.'

'You?' I thought it an odd arrangement: light woman to a king, yet collector of other men.

Alaric's eyes glinted. 'She came to Atvia twenty years ago from Solinde. She had grown bored, she said, with her young half-brother's machinations; she wished to try her own. I saw her. I wanted her. And when I learned precisely what she was, I gave in gracefully.' His smile grew. 'She said she always wanted a tame Cheysuli.'

'He will die,' I said hoarsely, 'or give himself over to death.'

'Because he lacks a *lir?*' Alaric laughed. 'I do not think so.' He dropped the pearls to the floor. As they struck, they splashed. And I saw they were only tears.

'I must go,' Alaric said brusquely. 'There is a feast to oversee – in *your* honor, my lord Prince of Homana. Will we see you there?'

'Have I a choice?'

'Of course,' he said politely. 'You may come or not, as you wish.' He looked at his daughter as he put his hand upon the door. 'Gisella . . . you know what to do.'

'I know what to do,' she said brightly. '*I* know what to do!'

Alaric shut the door.

I stood very still in the center of the room. And then slowly, so slowly, hardly realizing what I did, I righted the overturned chair and sat down awkwardly, like a man with too little sleep. My eyes burned as I stared at Gisella.

Arms outstretched, she began to spin in place. 'Did Lillith not make me *pretty?*'

I shut my eyes. *Oh gods—*

'Niall!'

Oh gods—

'*Ni*-allll!'

175

'Pretty,' I mumbled. 'Aye.'

'But you are not *looking* at me!' Hands were suddenly on my face, peeling my eyelids back. 'How can you see me when your eyes are closed?'

I caught her wrists and threw her hands away from me. I rose even as she protested. 'Bronwyn's daughter, are you? By all the gods of Homana, girl, how could you turn out like this? Because of Lillith? Because of Alaric? Because you know no better?'

She tried to twist free of my grasp, but I held her too tightly. Still, I could not help thinking of how she had reacted to Ian's touch; how she had assumed the shape of a mountain cat as if to mock his loss of Tasha.

'Bronwyn's daughter,' I said again. 'You claim the Old Blood, do you? And take on any form at will?'

'When he *lets* me,' she said, pouting. 'He does not let me very often.'

'Why not? Does Lillith then lose control?'

'Because of what happened to my mother. My *real* mother.' She tried to twist free again. This time I let her go.

'What happened to your mother?' I was assailed by sudden suspicion as well as apprehension. 'What happened to Bronwyn, Gisella?'

'She died.' Bronwyn's daughter rubbed sore wrists and glared at me from beneath lowered brows. 'She shape-changed, and she died.'

'Shapechanged! Why? And *how* did she die?' Suspicion flared more brightly. 'Was it Lillith?'

'No. My father.' Gisella shrugged. 'He did not mean it. He *told* me he did not mean it. Because he had no wish to slay *me*.'

'Gisella!' I caught her upper arms. '*Tell me how she died!*'

'He *shot* her!' she cried. 'With an arrow! He thought she was a raven!'

'A *raven*?'

'In Atvia they mean death,' she told me. 'Ravens are death-omens.' She shrugged. '*Everybody* shoots them.'

So Bronwyn tried to flee her Atvian husband. 'Gisella!'

176

I tightened my hands. 'What did he tell you happened?'

She twisted to and fro, protesting ineffectively even as she answered. 'He said — he said he only meant to slay a raven. But it was *her* . . . it was her . . .' She stopped moving. Her eyes were very clear. 'He slew my mother, Niall. While she was carrying me.'

'And she fell . . .'

'I was born that day,' Gisella told me, 'before my mother died.'

I looked into her eyes and saw no pain, no grief. Only a calm matter-of-factness; only the innocence of a child repeating what she has been told. What Alaric meant his daughter *never* to tell.

'Gisella,' I said gently, 'I am sorry.'

Her smooth brow creased. 'Do you think it hurt?' she asked. 'The fall? I cannot remember any pain.'

'No pain,' I said, 'not now.' I let go of her arms. But Gisella moved in against me, like a child seeking comfort, so I enfolded her in my arms and gave the child the comfort she craved. 'No pain ever again.'

Her face was against my neck. 'Sometimes I am afraid.'

'I will take away the fear.'

She murmured something against my throat. And then she pulled away, laughing, and reached up to clasp my jaw in both her hands.

'Gisella—'

'She said you would be *mine*—'

—and I was falling, *falling*, even as I stood there; even as I tried to speak and could not; tried to reach out; tried to wrench away; tried to break free of the woman who held me trapped within her hands.

Something is in me, something in *me — something*—

—something indefinable — something reaching into my mind, my soul, my *self*—

—until there was nothing left—

—*nothing left*—

—of Niall at all.

'Niall,' she whispered, 'we have to go to *bed*.'

CHAPTER THREE

A torch was put into my hand. 'Light the beacon-fire, Niall. We must warn ships of the dragon's presence.'

The dragon. Aye, the dragon, with his cold breath and endless appetite, swallowing helpless ships.

'Light the fire, Niall.'

The wind gusted. The torch flared, roared; streamers of flame were snatched from the pitch-soaked rag and shredded in the air, the *cold* air; the breath of Alaric's dragon.

Or was it Lillith's dragon?

'*Light the fire, Niall.*'

I stretched out my arm toward the cone-shaped stand of faggots. Flame snapped, whipped; *yellow* flame, pure, clean *yellow*, with not the faintest trace of purple.

The flames drew my eyes. Transfixed, I stared. I could not look away.

'*—or a beacon-fire on the cliff—*' Alaric had said. But I could not remember why.

We stood on the dome of the dragon's skull, wrapped in the dragon's breath. Visible yet intangible, it rose to cloak us like a mantle, all five of us: Ian, Gisella, Lillith, Alaric, and myself. At sundown, as daylight spilled out of the sky to be replaced by moonlight. Even now the platinum plate was visible scudding above the ragged chalky headlands of the island across the Tail.

Erinn. So close. So *far*.

Aerie of the Eagles.

'Light the fire, Niall,' Alaric told me gently.

I twitched. Blinked. My eyes were filled with fire. I could see nothing but the fire.

Hands were on my right arm, tugging me toward the pyre. Slender, feminine hands, but almost masculine in their demand. '*Do* it,' she said plaintively. 'I want to see the fire.'

And for her I would do anything.

I plunged the torch deep into the heart of the stack. Kindling snapped, caught, blazed up. I fell back, shielding my face against the flame.

'Fire,' she whispered. 'So pretty—'

Alaric removed the torch from my hand. He was smiling, but it was an odd, thoughtful smile, full of secret knowledge. He stepped to the edge of the promontory and was silhouetted against the rising moon; laughing, he threw the torch as far as he could into the darkness beyond.

I watched it fall, spinning, *spinning*, shedding light and smoke and flame.

'*That* for Shea of Erinn.' His words were thick with a joyous satisfaction.

'And *Deirdre*,' Gisella said sharply. 'Deirdre, *too*.'

Alaric turned. For a frozen moment he looked only at his daughter, seeing the fixed, feral stare of her yellow eyes, and then he stepped away from the edge to wrap her in his arms. He embraced her tightly, cradling her head against his shoulder. In the light of the blazing beacon-fire I saw the glint of tears in his eyes. 'No more,' he told her softly, rocking her in his arms. 'No more Deirdre, my lovely girl; my beautiful, fragile sparrow. No more threat to your happiness. That I promise you.'

'When will the baby come?' she asked. 'When will my baby come?'

'Six months,' he told her gently. 'In six months you will hold your baby.'

Her hands slipped down to touch her belly, splaying across heavy skirts. And then she broke away from her father and threw out her arms. Spinning, *spinning*, she tipped back her head and let the black hair spill out into the wind, whipping, *whipping*, as she whirled atop the dome of the dragon's skull.

'A baby!' she cried. 'A baby of my own . . .'

179

'Niall.' Above the howl of the wind, I heard the other woman. 'It is time for you to go home.'

In the bright light of the roaring flames, I saw Lillith with my brother. She did not touch him; she did not have to. She had only to be near him, and he was lost.

Lost.

But in his grieving eyes I saw a reflection of myself.

The man came to me as I stood on the dock, prepared to board the ship. He looked familiar, but I did not know him at once. 'My lord,' he said, in a smooth, cultured baritone, 'I am to sail with you. As envoy to your father's court, and as companion to the princess.' When I said nothing, he smiled. 'My name is Varien. Do you not remember me?'

And then, of course, I did. 'I thought you drowned,' I told him. 'I thought you swallowed by the dragon.'

'No, my lord.' So polite, so sincere, so much in control of his emotions; I envied him. 'The Lady Lillith saw to it I survived.'

'She is generous,' I said simply. 'She kept my brother from drowning, as well.'

'And you?'

'No.' I shook my head. 'No. I washed ashore . . . I think it was near Rondule. That is where they found me.'

'Of course, my lord. I recall.' He gestured gracefully toward the ramp. 'Shall you board? Everything is prepared. Even your brother waits.'

'Ian?' I looked at Varien sharply. 'I thought Lillith was keeping him.'

'No, my lord. She has what she wants from your brother. Ian goes home with you.'

Alaric stood on the dock and hugged his grieving daughter. 'Do not cry,' he told her. 'Do not fret, Gisella. You go to become a queen.'

'But I want to stay here with you!'

'I know. But now your place is with your husband, not your father.'

'But I will miss you so!'

'No more than I will miss you.'

She clung to him a moment longer as if she would never let him go, then abruptly pulled back to look up at him expectantly. 'Will he give me other babies?'

Alaric smiled and stroked her windblown raven hair. 'He will give you all you want.'

She reached up to kiss him. And then she boarded the ship.

'A gift,' Lillith told me, 'to see you safely home.' And she put something in my hands.

I looked. A tooth. A smooth white tooth, thick at one end, narrow and curved at the other. A dog's tooth, or a wolf's. It was set into a cap and hook of gold, which depended from a thong.

'Wear it,' she said, smiling. 'Wear it and think of me.'

I put the thong around my neck.

The sea is an endless place, a place in the world where time nearly stops and all a man knows is patience. I had found what little I had of it, rationed it well, and managed to keep myself whole. But for Ian, I could not say the same.

He stood at the rail near the prow of the ship, staring eastward, ever eastward, toward Homana. In two months I had watched him dwindle to a shadow, hardly a man at all. Physically he was present, but elsewhere he was not.

Homana, for me, is home. For Ian it is his death.

Waves slapped the sides of the ship. Timbers creaked. Canvas billowed, cracked taut. I heard the song of a ship under sail.

Midsummer, nearly. But it would be another month before we were home. I thought we would miss the Summer-fair in Mujhara. It would be the first time since I could remember. The first time for either of us.

Us.

Slowly I crossed the deck. Though I knew he heard me, he did not turn. He stood at the rail and clutched it, dark hands locked around the wood. Two months since we had set sail. His hair had grown to cover his ears; to cover the mark of his shame. To hide the naked ear. Even now, free of Lillith, he left off Cheysuli leathers and wore Atvian garb instead, much as I did; low boots, snug trews and a full-sleeved linen shirt, billowing in the salt-breeze.

I settled a hand on his shoulder. 'Ian—'

'No.'

'*Rujho*—'

'*No*.'

'At *least* do me the courtesy of allowing me to share your company while you yet live,' I snapped. 'Gods, *rujho*, you will be gone from me soon enough. Why do you already leave?'

He turned so sharply I fell back a step. '*I* did not leave – it was *you!*' He clamped a hand around my arm. His eyes were filled with despair. 'Gods, Niall – do you even *know* what you have done? What they have done to you? Or should I say: what *she* has done to you, since it takes a Cheysuli to do what the girl has done.'

'It was to *you*.' I was precise in my amazement. 'It was Lillith—'

'*Aye*,' he said harshly. 'Lillith. And who was it for you?'

'I,' she said. 'It was I.'

I turned. 'Gisella!'

'It was,' she said. 'Lillith told me I could do it. She said I *should*. Otherwise you would never lie down with me.' Hands cupped belly protectively. 'And then there would be no baby.'

Already the child showed. Gisella was slender, *too* slender; she did not carry the baby well. Though only five months along, she was huge. Ungainly. Wearied of the weight. The summer warmth was crueler to her than to others; though she wore a thin linen gown with sleeves cut off. I saw the dampness of perspiration soiling the fabric. A fine sheen filmed face and arms, already burned darker by the sun. She had tied her heavy hair back, but strands of it crept loose to straggle down the sides of her face.

She looked at Ian. 'I am Cheysuli. I know a few Cheysuli

182

customs – those they have let me learn.' Much of her intensity had vanished, replaced with a weary vacancy. She seemed to have tired of what they had told her she must say and do. 'Without a *lir*, you die.'

'There is a ritual involved,' he said; roundabout agreement.

'But you *die*.' Yellow eyes met yellow eyes. 'I think Niall would not like that. I think I will give you your *lir*.'

Ian laughed. I could not.

Quick tears filled Gisella's eyes. 'Do you think I *lie*? Do you think I would lie to you?'

He opened his mouth to answer at once. I knew what he would tell her. *Aye, Gisella, you lie. I think you would lie to me.* But he shut his mouth and said nothing, because we both knew she could not help it. She was incapable of knowing the difference.

The tears spilled over. A low moan issued from a trembling mouth, and then she spun and ran away. Thinking of the baby, I started to follow; Ian jerked me back.

'Let her go. Like a child, she means to cry. And then she will fall asleep, and the world will be right when she wakes.'

I wrenched free of his hand. 'How can you be so cold? There was a time *you* might have been the one to offer comfort.'

'To Gisella?' he asked. 'No. She has a *taint* about her. The smell of an Ihlini.'

'Tricks,' I said. 'Lillith only taught her tricks. She has no Ihlini powers.'

'Tricks,' Ian mocked. 'Aye. The sort of tricks Tynstar taught Electra.' He looked at me intently and shook his head. 'But what does it matter if she knows a few Ihlini tricks? She has done enough damage to you with the gifts the gods gave *us*.'

And then Gisella was back, still crying. In her hands was the glint of gold. 'Do I lie?' she asked. '*Do I lie?*'

She threw down the gold. It rang and thudded against the decking; a cat-shaped earring and two massive spurs. Alaric's rune-worked spurs.

183

Ian did not move. *I* did; I knelt. Picked up the earrings and then the heavy spurs with their leather straps dyed black. Looked up at Gisella in amazement.

She rubbed the back of her hand across a sweat-sheened brow. 'He melted them,' she explained. 'The bracelets. He wanted them for himself.'

'Not bracelets,' I said numbly. '*Lir*-bands. The mark of a boy become man.' *Gods, what I would give for gold of my own—* I rose, turning to Ian. In shaking hands I held them out. '*Rujho—?*'

He did not move. 'That is gold. That is not my *lir*.'

'I could not carry *her*,' Gisella said tearfully. 'Not while I carry the child.'

Ian's head snapped up. '*Her?*'

She scrubbed tears from sunburned cheeks. 'Below,' she said. 'Below.'

I hooked the straps over my wrist and grabbed her arm before Ian could. 'Where?' I asked. '*Show us where.*'

Gisella showed us. She took us below to the hold where the cargo was carried, where we had no cause to go. To the back, near the bilges.

'*Wait,*' she said sharply, pushing through the chests and other gear. At last she bent over a canvas-shrouded crate. She plucked something from the crate and turned, hiding it behind her back. 'You may come now.'

Spurs clinking, I caught Gisella and dragged her hand into the open. 'Gisella, let me see.'

She resisted. Gave in. Opened her hand as I told her to. In the palm was the withered foot of a predator bird, curved talons spread as if to strike.

Gisella shrugged, twisting shoulders defensively. 'She told me it was from a *lir*. A hawk, she said. She said she needed it for the spell.' She glanced sidelong at Ian. 'So you would not know the cat was in Rondule.'

'Rondule!' I cried. 'All this time Tasha has been in Rondule?'

'Lillith wanted to keep her. So she could keep *him*.' Again, she looked at Ian. 'But then – she said she did not care to keep him any more; that he had given her what she wanted. She said now it would be sweeter to know he gave himself over to death while his *lir* was so close at hand.'

I looked at the thing in her hand. But even as she spoke, the withered foot and curving talons fell away into grayish dust.

Gisella sucked in her breath. 'No more spell!' she cried in despair. And then, singing softly, 'All gone away . . .' She turned her hand palm down and poured out the grayish dust. 'All – gone – away . . .'

Ian tore open the crate as I stared at the girl who was my wife. My poor, fragile-witted wife.

Whispering, '*All – gone – away* . . .'

'Gisella—'

'Gods, it is *Tasha*. It *is!*' Ian was almost incoherent. '*Rujho*, help me—'

He had not asked it for so long. I turned from Gisella to Ian and helped him lift the slack body from the bottom of the crate. We dragged Tasha free of the crate entirely and settled her on the flooring. She was alive, but only just. Still, her eyes knew us both. One paw reached out weakly and patted Ian's foot.

He sat down awkwardly, as if he could no longer stand, and pulled what he could of the cat into his lap. I could tell by the look in his eyes that he spoke with her in the link. Once more, I was shut out. But this time I did not care.

'Whole,' he whispered. '*No more a lirless man—*'

This time – this time only – it did not seem to matter to me that I still was.

When he had assured himself, or been assured by Tasha, that the mountain cat would survive, Ian looked up at Gisella. In his eyes I saw the tears. '*Leijhana tu'sai,*' he said unevenly. '*Leijhana tu'sai,* Gisella.'

I rose. I caught her shoulders in my hands. 'Those words are Cheysuli thanks,' I told her, when I could. 'You have made him whole again.'

'But not *you*,' she said obscurely.

And then she sat down and drew pictures in the dust of a murdered *lir*.

185

CHAPTER FOUR

She sang a song I did not know and hardly heard. It was not meant for me, but intended only for herself. And perhaps for the child.

'Gisella,' I said gently, 'there is nothing to harm you here. This is Homana-Mujhar.'

She stood in a corner of the antechamber, hugging herself. Hugging herself, rocking herself, singing to herself. Softly, so very softly; she meant to disturb no one. She meant only to lock herself away from the fear of what must come.

I stroked the hair from her eyes. She had gone away from me to that very private place she had sought more and more the closer we came to Mujhara. I had lost her somewhere on the road from Hondarth. Physically she was with me, but otherwise she was not.

She sang. She hugged. She rocked.

I shut her up in my arms and tried to still the rocking. Her swollen belly pressed against me, intrusive and unyielding. She was bigger still than before, having two months less to wait for the birth of the child. Only two, now, before I would be a father.

'Niall? Are you here? I was told you would be here!' It was my mother hastening into the adjoining room; I felt Gisella stiffen in my arms.

'Wait,' I called, perhaps a trifle curtly. No doubt it was the last word she had expected to hear from me. 'Gisella,' I said gently, 'Gisella, I promise you. No one here will harm you.'

She sang on, rocking herself within the circle of my arms. And so I left her to herself and went into the chamber to greet my mother.

I said nothing. What she felt was manifest in her face. I crossed to her and let her put her arms around me, acutely conscious of how large I was in comparison to her. 'Mother—'

'Say nothing.' Her words were muffled; most of her face was pressed against my chest. 'Just – let me *hold* you.'

And so I let her hold me, even as I held her. It was odd to think of her as the woman who had borne me nineteen years ago, even as Gisella would bear *my* child. Somehow it was impossible to think of the Queen of Homana as ever being little more than a woman in travail, trying to give Homana an heir for the Lion Throne.

'Fourteen months,' she whispered. 'Oh Niall, I feared I would never see you again! Even after Alaric sent word that Shea of Erinn held you. Even after *Rowan* came home and said you fared quite well in Erinnish captivity.' She pulled away and stared up into my face. 'How much was the truth?'

'All of it,' I told her. 'Never once was I treated with anything less than my rank was due.'

She sighed in relief. 'Thank the gods!' She hugged me again, then stepped away. 'There. Enough. I have no wish to embarrass you with tears or clinging ways.' Laughing a little, she pressed one hand against her mouth. 'You see? Already I cry again.'

I smiled. 'Embarrass *me?* No more than I might embarrass you. Gods, it is good to be home again!' And I pulled her back into my arms and hugged her one more time.

'Then the messenger had the right of it concerning your arrival,' said my father as he came into the chamber. 'His words were worth the gold I spent.'

I released my mother and went at once to him, to clasp his arms Cheysuli-fashion and then pull him into an embrace. In all the years of my life I had wanted to do it, and yet somehow I never had. He had seemed closed to me, somehow; closed to demonstrations of affection.

'*Leijhana tu'sai*,' he murmured fervently. 'All those

187

months I had to be strong for your *jehana* . . . yet there was no one to be strong for the *jehan*.'

I could not imagine my father needing anyone but himself. And yet, once I might have said the same about my brother. 'You know about Ian?' I stepped back out of the embrace. 'The messenger *did* tell you he is alive?'

'Aye,' my mother said dryly. 'Your father made him repeat it four times, just to be certain.'

I searched for resentment and found none; she was genuinely relieved. But I was not certain how much was for my father's sake rather than my brother's.

'Where is he?' my father asked. 'I expected him to be with you.'

'Ian is – at Clankeep.' I saw the minute twitch of surprise in his face. 'He said he required – *cleansing* . . . and that you would understand.'

'*I'toshaa-ni*.' My father turned away from me as if to hide his thoughts and feelings. But when he turned again I saw a residue of a fear I could not comprehend. 'Is he all right?'

'Well enough,' I answered. 'Tasha is mostly recovered and so Ian is more himself, but—' I could not avoid the truth any longer, and so I would not '—he is not the warrior I knew before we left for Atvia.'

'No. Not if he is in need of *i'toshaa-ni*.' Troubled, my father looked more grim than I could expect of a man who knew both of his sons were alive when he had believed them lost.

'What *is* it?' my mother asked. 'I know so little of Cheysuli customs . . . but what could keep Ian away from his father when he has only just returned?'

'A ritual of cleansing,' my father said, patently reluctant to speak of it at all. 'It – is a private thing . . . when a warrior feels his spirit soiled by something he has done – or by what others have done *to* him – he seeks to cleanse himself through *i'toshaa-ni*.' He made a gesture of subtle finality and I knew the subject was closed.

It was obvious my mother knew it as well. She wanted to speak but did not, having learned his moods so well.

I wondered if Gisella would ever know mine.

Or if any *man can know hers.*

'Niall,' my mother said. 'Niall, is this *Gisella?*'

I turned abruptly. It was. She stood in the doorway to the antechamber. The curtain was caught over one shoulder so that half of her was hidden. But not enough. It was obvious she was weary, too weary; overburdened by the child. I had thought to give her time to rest, bathe, change . . . but now that time was taken from us both.

I went to her at once. She was quiet, very quiet; no more singing, hugging, rocking. Under my hands she trembled. 'Gisella, I promise you, there is no need to be afraid.' I pushed the curtain off her shoulder and brought her into the room.

'By the *gods!*' My mother's tone was couched, all unintended, in the brutal honesty of shock. 'The girl has already conceived!'

My father was less forceful than my mother, but his surprise was no less obvious. 'Niall—'

'She is very weary,' I told them quietly. 'The sea voyage was hard on her, the journey from Hondarth harder. Once she has rested, you will see another Gisella.'

'Niall,' my mother said helplessly, 'what am I to *say?*'

'Say she is well come,' I told her. 'Or – is she not?'

'Niall.' There was no hesitation on my father's part, no careful search for diplomacy. 'She is as well come as your *cheysula* ever could be . . . but what your *jehana* means to say is that the Homanans will claim the child is not your own.'

'Does it matter what they claim?' Beneath my hands, Gisella trembled. 'When have *you* ever cared?'

He did not smile, my father, being less than pleased with me. 'On the day when I at last understood what my *tahlmorra* truly entailed, I was *made* to care. But you may not have that chance.' He did not so much as look at Gisella, being too intent on me. 'Even now there are growing numbers of Homanans who rally around a faceless, nameless bastard, known only as Carillon's son. Not his grandson,

189

Niall – his *son*. And as those numbers grow, so does the threat to you. So does the threat to the Lion. And, by the gods! – *so does the threat of the prophecy of the Firstborn!*'

'Donal.' My mother, as ever, seeking to turn his anger from her beloved son.

'No, Aislinn. He will have to know the truth.' He moved closer to me, confronting me squarely, still ignoring Gisella. 'On the day our kinsman has you slain in the name of *Homanan* rule, will you ask then if it matters what the Homanans claim?' His face, like his voice, was taut with suppressed emotion. And now he did look at Gisella. 'Will you ask it when they have slain *her* as well, because she bears a child who might become a threat to them? Think of *that*, Niall, if not of yourself.' He smiled, but there was no humor in it. 'And now – ask me again.'

'No.' Chastened I was, but I did not look away. 'No, there is no need. I spoke too hastily.' I took a deep breath and started over again. 'This is Gisella. And aye, she bears my child.' I glanced briefly at my mother, still silent in her shock, then looked back at my father. 'I do not doubt but that the wedding should be very soon. Not just because of the child, but because of Carillon's bastard.' I shrugged. 'How better to secure the Lion for *our* line instead of his?'

My mother turned away. The line of her spine was rigid; no doubt it troubled her deeply to know her father had sired a bastard. No doubt it troubled her more to know that bastard offered a very real threat to me.

'Niall.' She turned, skirts swinging. 'Niall – will you forgive him?'

Gods, how she needed me to say it; to say *aye, of course I forgive him.* As if it might absolve her of her guilt for believing in him so. So she could believe in him again.

'Carillon was not a god,' I said clearly. 'He was a man. A *man*. And so is his bastard son. *So is his daughter's son.*'

'Niall?' Gisella, breaking her silence. 'Niall, is he the Mujhar?'

I laughed aloud, relieved to hear her voice after she had been so long silent. 'More than that,' I said. 'He is your

190

mother's brother. Your *su'fali*, in the Old Tongue.'

Color came into her waxen face. Some of the weariness dropped away. 'Donal of Homana! My father speaks of you.'

My father's smile was wry. 'Aye, no doubt he does. And does he speak of me with kindness?'

He did not expect her to answer honestly. He expected embarrassed prevarication. But then, he did not know Gisella.

'No,' she said, with all the guilelessness of a child. 'He says you are a leech upon the treasury of Atvia, and that one day he will squash you.'

Before my mother could express her shock, my father laughed out loud. 'Aye, well, I imagine he might well say so. In his position, I might say much the same. But then, it is a position *Alaric himself* brought about.' No tact from him, not when she gave *him* none. 'When you see him again, Gisella, you may tell him that for me.'

'But I will never see him again,' she told him seriously. 'I must stay with Niall. Niall will be Mujhar. Niall will need me *here*.'

'Surely he will allow you to *visit* your father.' My mother hid much of her growing dislike, but I heard it plainly in her tone. 'He will not keep you chained to Homana.'

'But he will *need* me,' Gisella insisted. 'They said he would always need me.'

I saw my mother begin to frown.

'Gisella,' I said hastily, 'this is my lady mother, Aislinn, the Queen of Homana.'

But Gisella was uninterested in my mother. Her attention was on my father. 'I forgot,' she told him. 'There is a thing I am to do.' Giggling, she tried to curtsy deeply, offering him what awkward homage she could manage.

Immediately he stepped forward. 'Gisella, there is no need for *that*—'

—and she was up, clawing *godfire* from the air with her left hand while her right hand clawed for his face.

No. Not *clawed*. Her hand was filled with a knife.

191

'Gisella – *no!*' I caught her from behind even as she lunged for my father. I clamped her arms against her body, hugging her with all my force, while she struggled impotently to twist free of me to strike at him again.

'Dead – dead – dead—' she chanted. '*Dead – dead – dead—*'

'Gisella – *no—*'

The air was choked with lilac smoke. The *godfire* was gone, but its aftereffects were not. My mother coughed, pressing an arm against nose and mouth. My father, having fallen back from Gisella's attack, now reached for the knife still clutched in her hand.

'*Dead – dead – dead—*'

'No,' I told him, 'let her be.'

'Niall—'

'*Let her be!*' I shouted. 'She is weary, so weary of the child. She is *not* herself – *not* Gisella – not Gisella at all.' Still I held her, clamping her arms against her sides. 'You do not understand her.'

'I understand she has just tried to murder me,' my father said angrily. 'Am I not to question it?'

'*I* question it!' my mother cried. 'By the gods, *I* will!'

'No,' I told her flatly. 'Let Gisella be. She will be better when she has rested.'

'Better!' My mother stood by my father now, buttressing his side as if she were a soldier. 'You speak as if this were only a momentary aberration, Niall.'

'She is *weary.*'

'She is *mad!*' my mother interrupted coldly. 'Do you think you will marry *that?*'

'I have every intention of it.'

'Mad?' my father asked. 'Or is it something Lillith has done?'

Gisella stopped struggling. 'Lillith,' she said. 'Lillith is my mother.'

'No, no . . .' Already I could see the shock forming in their faces. 'No, *Lillith* is not your mother, Gisella. Bronwyn was your mother.'

'She died,' Gisella told them earnestly. 'He shot her out of the sky.'

My father recoiled as if she had struck out at him again, but this time the blade went home.

'Out of the sky,' Gisella repeated. 'And she fell . . . and she *fell* . . . and she crashed against the ground . . .' She sighed. 'After I was born, she died. She died of her broken body—'

'No more,' I told her softly. 'Gisella, say no more.' Because I could not bear to see the look in my father's eyes.

'My father slew my mother,' she said brightly, and sucked on a piece of hair.

'Gods,' my father choked. 'That *ku'reshtin* murdered Bronwyn, but it was *I* who sent her there.'

'Donal, *do*, do not blame yourself!' My mother's hands were on his arm. 'I beg you; do not do this to yourself—'

'*I* gave her in marriage to that man . . . *I* made her wed him when she wanted nothing of it!'

'Donal, you had no choice,' she told him firmly. 'You told me yourself — there was the prophecy to think of.'

'*Prophecy*.' He said it like a curse. 'Gods, Aislinn — when I think of the things I have done in the name of that thing . . . all the lives I have altered—'

'Donal.'

'Even *yours*,' he said. 'Even yours.'

There was the tone of bittersweet acknowledgment in her voice. 'Aye,' she said, 'even mine. But do you hear me curse you for it?'

'No,' he said at last, 'though the gods know I deserve it.'

'She died,' Gisella said. 'He shot her out of the sky.'

'Hush.' I pulled the hair out of her mouth. 'Hush, Gisella . . . *please*.'

My mother looked at Gisella. 'You cannot marry *that*.'

'He has to,' my father said wearily. 'The prophecy requires it.'

'She just tried to *slay* you!'

'And once, *you* tried to do the same.'

It was clear she had made herself forget that once she had

been no less a tool for murder than Gisella. That once Tynstar, through Electra, had set a compulsion within her mind: to slay the man she was meant to wed. I knew the story. My father had told me once.

'Oh *gods*,' she said brokenly, and tried to turn away.

But my father did not let her. '*Shansu*,' he said, 'it is over. A long time over.'

She turned back. She did not bother to wipe the tears away. They – and her anguish – remained. 'And if Gisella tries again?'

'*You* did not,' he told her.

'Because you had Finn go in and find the trap-link,' she said impatiently. 'Donal, have sense! Gisella has spent her life with an Ihlini witch as well as with a father who despises you. Do you think she will not try again?'

'Not if I defuse the trap-link . . . *if* there is a trap-link.' He looked at me. 'Niall, you know what I must do.'

I shook my head. 'You see how weary she is.'

'All the better. There will be less resistance.' He looked at Gisella, who still held the glittering knife. 'I will risk neither my son nor myself to the chance she may be ruled by an Ihlini.'

'My lord—'

'Prepare her, Niall. I have already summoned my *lir*.'

I did my best to prepare Gisella, telling her what to expect though I hardly knew myself. All my life I had known Cheysuli magic existed, gifts from the gods themselves, but never had I seen my father use it past taking on the shape of wolf or falcon. Even Ian, who had as much power as any warrior, had shown me nothing other than the shapechange. Though father and brother also claimed the ability to heal, my childhood hurts had been allowed to heal naturally, without recourse to magic. Nothing had been serious enough to require it.

Now, I knew, there was. But I wanted no part of it.

I put Gisella to bed, covering the mound of her belly with a silken coverlet as she leaned back against the bolsters. She needed food, rest, sleep. She needed to be rid of the weight of the child.

'Two more months,' I said aloud, splaying my hand across her belly. 'Two more, Gisella, and you will be free of this burden.'

Her own hand covered mine. 'A baby, Niall. Something that will not drown as my puppies drowned, or break as my kitten broke.'

Someone touched a cold fingertip against the base of my spine. But there was no one in the room. 'Gisella – a baby is nothing like an animal. Nothing like a *pet*.' I stroked black hair away from her weary face. 'A baby is more important than anything in the world.'

'More important than the Lion?'

Her tone was earnest. So was her expression. But there was opacity in her eyes, as if she hid from me the other side of her question.

I drew in a careful breath. 'Gisella, if this baby is a boy, he will *become* the Lion.'

She giggled. 'How can a man become a lion? There *are* no lions, Niall. They have all gone out of the world. Not even *I* can become a lion!'

'He will be the Lion of Homana,' I told her. 'Mujhar.' I put out my hand and let her see the ruby ring. 'See the stone, Gisella? See the rampant lion?'

One finger touched the stone. I saw her pensive face as she traced the tiny etching in the flat ruby signet. 'The Lion,' she murmured. 'The Lion of Homana . . .' Abruptly she looked up at my face. 'Are *you* the lion, Niall?'

I shook my head. 'Not yet. Not for a long time to come.'

She sighed. 'But I want to be a queen.'

A step sounded in the room. 'Aislinn has no intention of relinquishing her title for a long time to come,' my father told her bluntly. 'Your pride will have to be satisfied by a lesser title.'

'Father,' I reproved, 'she hardly knows what she says.'

'Do you?'

'Do *I*? Of course!'

'*Do* you?' he asked again. 'Is that why you almost never refer to me as *jehan?*' He was unsmiling. 'Is the Cheysuli word so hard for you to say?'

It hurt. I felt the twist in the pit of my belly. 'You have *Ian* to use the Old Tongue.'

'And you for something else?' He shook his head as he moved to Gisella's bedside. Taj perched himself upon the casement sill as Lorn lay down on the floor at the foot of the bed. 'No, now is not the time; my *lir* reminds me of it plainly. You are just home after more than a year away, and reprimands can wait. I apologize.'

An apology from my father. I stared as he sat down across from me on the edge of Gisella's bed. I could not recall if he had ever offered me an apology before.

Or if I had ever deserved one.

Or if I deserved one *now*.

'I will not harm you,' he told her gently. 'I promise you that, Gisella. You are Cheysuli yourself; you know of all the gifts.'

'*I* know.' She was a petulant, impatient child, suddenly, claiming superior knowledge. 'I know many things.'

My father did not smile. 'Aye. I imagine you do. How *much*, I will find out.'

He did not touch her. He merely looked at her, even as I did. And then I looked at him.

His eyes matched hers in expression as well as color: pinpointed pupils, opacity, a look of total detachment. Though my father sat on the bed at Gisella's side, I knew he had gone *elsewhere*, seeking her. And I sensed Gisella's retreat.

Still I held her hand. I could feel the tension in it; the rigidity of flesh and tendons. She did not try to hold mine. I think she was unable. I think she was enmeshed in a battle of wills with my father, and had no time for me.

Suddenly, I was alone in the chamber. Gisella was in the bed, my father on its edge, his *lir* present as well. And yet, I was alone. So *alone* . . . because I was a shadow-man, a shell of nothingness. *Lirless*, I lacked even the slightest hint of the power that was manifest in my father. Manifest in Gisella.

Is this irony? I asked the gods. *That certain* Homanans *desire to replace me because they believe I hide my magic, while certain* Cheysuli *desire the same because I have no magic at all?*

Irony, aye. Or my downfall.

Gisella's hand clenched itself within the palm of mine. I felt the fragile, rounded knucklebones rise up to test the flesh, as if they might break through. And I heard her moan of pain.

There was an expression of grim determination on my father's face, though the eyes retained the blank, detached stare. It was as if he were the hungry hunter running down terrified prey: unflagging flight and an unremitting pursuit.

Gisella writhed in the bed, though no one touched her – but me. She cried out.

'Wait—' I blurted. 'Father.' No. *Jehan.* But I could not say the word. 'Wait you—'

But his fingers locked around the wrist of her other hand – she screamed—

—*Gods, how she screamed—*

'*Jehan* – no!' Now the word came easily as I tried to break the grip. I tried to break it – but the sudden burst of fire within my skull hurled me back, *back,* away from the bed, until I crashed into the tapestried wall.

The world was upside down. Or was it me? I could not tell. I crawled on hands and knees to the bed, leaving a trail of blood behind. My nose was numb; I could not feel the blood, only taste it. My ears buzzed, rang, hummed. My vision was obscured by broken images.

—*my father – Gisella – Taj and Lorn—*

Bleeding, I sprawled face down across the bed and tried to touch my father, to tell him no, *no* – to somehow gainsay the power he leveled against her. Images blurred, twisted, revolved. The movement made me retch.

'Niall? *Niall!*'

My father's voice? *My* name? I could be certain of neither; my ears made too much noise.

'Niall – oh *gods*, let the boy be all right!' Hands caught me, pulled me up from the bed and then settled me on the floor with the side of the bed serving as backrest. 'Niall?'

His face was split into sixths; I could make no order of the pieces.

'Niall, can you hear me?'

Blood ran down my chin. 'Why? Why – harm – *her*—?'

One of his hands slipped behind my neck and cradled my wobbly head. 'Never, *never*, touch a Cheysuli in mind-link, Niall. Have you not been warned against it?'

His face was in thirds, now. An improvement. And I could hear him better. 'What did you do to Gisella?'

'Nothing,' he said firmly. 'Better to ask: what did she do to *me*?'

'You?' My eyes shut of their own accord. I put the back of my hand to my face and tried to stanch the blood.

'What you felt did not come from me, Niall. It was all Gisella's doing.' His tone was grim. 'Later, we will discuss it. Not now. Not in front of her.'

'She will be my wife,' I protested weakly. 'It should all be in front of her.'

'Look at me.' I did as told. 'Aye, you are better. Can you rise?'

Only with his help, and even then I nearly fell down again. I grasped the closest tester with one shaking hand; the other I locked under my nose. But the river was slowing to a stream. 'What happened?'

'You broke the link,' he said; now, looking at him with normal vision again, I saw the traces of blood in his own nostrils. 'But it is just as well. Gisella was preparing to throw me out, which would have been more painful yet.' He smiled a little and rubbed at bloodshot eyes. 'For all she was raised far from any clan – and by an Ihlini, at *that* – she knows many of our tricks. And has many of our strengths.' The smile fell away. 'But none of our sense, I fear. When Alaric slew Bronwyn, he slew the girl's wits as well.' He shook his head. 'What happened to her cannot

198

be healed, even by a Cheysuli — even by *several* Cheysuli. The damage was too severe.'

I raised a silencing hand and turned to see if Gisella had heard. But she slept. She slept deeply; she slept smiling, as if pleased by what she had wrought.

I shivered. And then I looked at my father. 'There was no trap-link, then?'

'No. There was no hint of Ihlini meddling — at least, not *within* her mind.' His tone was level, unyielding; he would play no games with me. 'Perhaps only *to* it, from things the others told her.'

Others. Lillith, no doubt. And Alaric.

I nodded. 'How soon can we have the wedding?'

I thought he meant to protest; to make some comment regarding *my* witlessness. But he did not. Bleakly, he said, 'As soon as arrangements are made.'

Again, I nodded. 'Things will be better, then.'

My father looked at Gisella. But he said nothing at all.

CHAPTER FIVE

Arrangements were made in an almost obscene haste. I knew
it was Homanan custom, particularly *royal* custom, to invite
neighboring aristocracy as well as royalty, as a means of
sealing the ceremony. In this way no one could claim the
throne was unsecured, and make plans to invade Homana.
I had no doubts the Homanan Council, as well as my mother
– and possibly even my father – would have preferred the
custom adhered to, for the sake of displaying the Lion's
successor and his Cheysuli bride to as many people as
possible. But because of Gisella's advanced state and the
domestic threat promised by Carillon's bastard, as well
as Strahan himself, we could not afford to wait.

I put on the finest clothes I had for the wedding, since
we could not even delay in order to have new ones made.
And so Torvald made certain I was fit to appear before the
guests, laying out the silks and velvets Homanans preferred,
while also selecting Cheysuli ornamentation from my jewel
chest. I wore garments of amber, sienna and russet, set off
with gold and garnets; a braided torque, hammered flat,
with matching plated wristlets, and a belt studded with
unfaceted garnets, glowing in the sunset.

As Torvald finished, my mother came into the chamber.
At her nod he bowed and took his leave. And then she came
to me. 'You look well. Very well.' But she did not smile.
'Niall, there is still a little time.'

I nodded absently, bending to adjust the droop of my
amber-dyed boots.

'Niall, do you understand what I am saying? You do not
have to go through with this.'

200

Sighing, I straightened. In yellow, she was lovely. It made her gold-netted hair more vivid than ever. 'I have said it before: I have every intention of marrying Gisella.'

'Why?' she demanded. 'That erratic, addled girl is a poor choice for Donal's heir!'

'And for Carillon's grandson?' I turned from her and paced to my jewel chest, studying the remaining contents idly. I approved Torvald's choices, but it gave me something to do. 'We were cradle-betrothed, mother. Such a thing is not broken lightly, even if I *wished* to have it broken. And I do not.' I picked through the brooches, wristlets, rings, then turned to face her. 'She is mad. Aye. I will not deny it. But it does not mean she cannot be my wife.'

'She will be *queen*.'

'One day,' I agreed. 'By then, perhaps she will be better.'

She stared at me in obvious perplexity. Slowly she shook her head. 'I do not understand. You are not – the same. Not since you went away.'

'In fourteen months, I was bound to become a different man.' I shrugged. 'Perhaps I have grown up.'

Again she shook her head. 'There is something—' But she broke it off. 'Niall, do you truly love her?'

'I think, as much as I am able.' I shrugged. 'I say that because you ask. My father would know better, being Cheysuli. So perhaps it is that the Homanan portion of me loves her, while what little Cheysuli is in me will not admit the feeling.'

'Then you *do* have reservations.' She came close, resting a hand upon my arm. 'Niall, if you are not completely reconciled to this match, I will have it broken.'

'And give Alaric cause to march against Homana?' I shook my head. 'You are Queen, and undoubtedly you have the power to sway most if not all of the Homanan Council . . . but I doubt you would sway my father. I doubt you would sway the Cheysuli.'

Her hand tightened. 'I *know* there is the prophecy! How could I *not*, being wife and mother to men fully caught in its demands? But it does not name Gisella! It does not *say*

201

she is the one you must wed, merely that you must wed to gain another bloodline. What of Erinn, Niall? Shaine himself wed an Erinnish princess before he wed Lorsilla. Save the Atvian line until later . . . the Erinnish might serve as well. We could speak with Shea.'

'*No*.' Quite suddenly, I felt ill. A hasty swallow steadied my belly again, but I could feel it threatening, waiting.

A beacon-fire on the cliff.

And I had lighted the fire.

'Niall?' A hand, tugging gently at my arm. 'Niall?'

All I could see was the fire in my eyes, and the blackness of the night as I stood upon the top of the dragon's skull.

'*Niall!*'

The vision faded, but it left me with the bitter taste of guilt. An immense, abiding guilt, made worse because I could not say *why* I should feel guilty.

'No,' I said. 'I wish to wed Gisella.'

'And so you shall.' Ian's voice; he stood in the doorway, ablaze with Cheysuli gold: his *lir*-bands were whole again, unblemished by Alaric's hand. His leathers were pure, unsullied white edged with scarlet silk. 'Everyone waits below.'

'Then we shall go.' I put out my arm to my mother. Reluctantly, she took it.

To match the preparations, the ceremony itself was brief in the extreme. The Homanan priest said the same words he had said more than a year before when he had performed the proxy wedding. The *shar tahl*, summoned from Clankeep, echoed the other's sentiments, but in the Old Tongue. I understood all of it well enough, having learned the language in childhood, but Gisella, listening closely, merely looked left out. It made the bond between us stronger, I thought; I was left out of all the magic, while she lacked the language.

When it was done and Gisella and I were truly wed, my father announced the celebration would begin in an adjoining audience hall. But those who had cause to give

the Prince and Princess formal greeting were to stay behind
and do so. And so I was able to watch and name to myself
those Homanans who had no wish to greet me formally, and
I realized that was precisely why my father had arranged
it that way.

Gisella was seated in a chair upon the dais, near the Lion
itself. I stood beside her, noting with concern the weariness
in her face. There was no hiding her pregnancy and no one
had bothered to try; she wore loose, full robes that swathed
most of her body, billowing over the mound that was my
child.

My father and mother themselves went into the adjoining
chamber, to give us this time alone. I knew why. There are
men in the world who do things only when their lord's eye
is on them, to curry favor, no matter what they think. And
so by leaving, the Mujhar made certain those who stayed
to greet me were doing so for reasons other than those. No
doubt he would expect me to mark who said what, and
report it to him later.

Enough Homanans came by with a word or two of
congratulations that soon enough I could not name them
all. I did not bother to keep track of each one, no more
than I did with the Cheysuli. But when Isolde and Ceinn
came through at the end of the line, I forgot my detachment entirely.

'So handsome!' But 'Solde's bright eyes mocked me as
they had even in childhood. 'I would have welcomed you
to *my* wedding, *rujho*, had you not been gone so long.'

'You have already wed?' I looked sharply at Ceinn,
whose expression was once again blandly cordial and utterly
closed to me.

'Aye,' she answered. 'About a sixth-month after you and
Ian sailed for Atvia.' One hand went out to briefly touch
Ceinn's hand; for a Cheysuli, a broad display of emotion.
But I saw nothing in his eyes that indicated he wished she
had not done it.

*Does he truly care for her? Or is she so valuable to his cause
he will let her do as she wishes?*

'Solde slanted a sidelong glance at Gisella, who was staring blankly into the emptied hall. 'Is she – all right?'

I turned. 'Gisella,' I said. Then, more forcefully, 'Gisella!'

Her black hair had been braided Cheysuli fashion and looped against her head, pinned with silver combs hung about with tiny silver bells. As I called her name, she started, and all the bells rang out.

'Solde, never one for hanging back, reached out and caught Gisella's hand. 'I am Niall's *rujholla*,' she said, 'so now I am yours as well.'

'*Rujholla*?' Gisella echoed.

'Solde frowned only briefly. And then she laughed. 'I forget. You have been reared in Atvia, so why should you know our language? It is only that you look more Cheysuli than anything else, and so I expect you to know the customs as well as the language.' She glanced at me and laughed. 'Niall will teach you *everything*, I am sure.'

'Isolde is my sister,' I told Gisella. '*Rujholla*, in the Old Tongue.'

'Niall's sister?' Gisella stared at her. 'Oh, of course, my father told me. You are the Mujhar's bastard daughter.'

All the gaiety died out of 'Solde. White-faced, she stared blindly at Gisella. Then, abruptly, she let go of Gisella's hand at once and turned to leave the nearly empty hall.

''Solde – *'Solde . . . wait!*' I caught up to her, leaving the dais and my blunt-speaking wife behind. ''Solde, she does not understand our ways. And she is weary, *so* weary of the child. I beg you, try to understand.'

'Solde's arm was rigid beneath my delaying fingers. 'I understand,' she said clearly. 'I understand very well, Niall. I should have expected it.' I had anticipated anger from her, and harsh words – 'Solde is not a silent sort – but not the magnitude of her pain. She shrugged. 'She was reared by the enemy.'

'Gods, 'Solde, do not judge her so harshly. You do not understand.'

Suddenly, Ceinn was at my side. 'She understands as well as I do, *my lord*.' His pupils had shrunk so that I saw mostly yellow, an intense, *intent* yellow. 'Forgive my plain speech, my lord, but you have worsened your position with the clans by taking Gisella as your *cheysula*.'

'She is half Cheysuli,' I pointed out evenly, trying not to lose my temper. 'She is the Mujhar's niece.'

'She may be his *harana*—' the Cheysuli word was emphasized, as if to point out my use of Homanan in its place '—but she is also Atvian. Daughter to Alaric, who is no friend of ours.'

'Atvian, *aye*.' I was through with diplomacy. 'And *necessary to the prophecy*.' I caught his arm as he reached out to turn Isolde away, as if he intended to leave my presence and take my sister with him. 'No,' I told him plainly, 'I am not finished with you.'

His bare arm slid out of my grasping fingers as he jerked it sharply away. My nails scraped across the bear-shape worked into the gold of his *lir*-band. 'Finished with *me?*' he echoed, though he knew precisely what I had said. 'Oh, *no*, my lord. I think we are finished with *you.*'

'Ceinn!' 'Solde was clearly shocked by the virulence in his tone.

'I think the time *has* come for plain speech.' Somehow I managed to summon an even tone, though I wanted to shout at him. 'Well enough, hear what I have to say.' I moved a step closer to him and was pleased to see that *this* time, he fell back a single step. 'I am fully aware of the existence of the *a'saii*, and the preferences for my replacement in the line of succession. But I challenge you to tell me how *that* would serve the prophecy you claim to know better than other warriors.' I made a beckoning gesture. 'Well? I wait.'

'Niall.' Isolde, again, trying to turn my rising anger before it could burst its banks. 'How can you say that to Ceinn? Of *course* he serves the prophecy.'

'By seeing to it I am slain?' Though I watched Ceinn, I saw her twitch of shock. 'What did you think he wanted from me, 'Solde – a peaceful retirement into the country?'

'Niall—'

''Solde – *enough*.' That from Ceinn, as if he had no more time for verbal maneuverings even from his wife. 'Plain speech, aye; and *aye*, I serve the prophecy! So do the rest of us.' He turned a bit closer to me, edging Isolde out entirely. We confronted one another squarely. 'You have some of the blood, it is true, but you also bear *other* blood—'

'*So does Ian*,' I said clearly. 'If it is true the *a'saii* desire a return to the days of purebred clans, how does it serve the prophecy? The prophecy *demands* a mixture – it *points* us to other realms.'

'Other realms, aye,' he agreed. 'I do not contest the need for the blood of other realms; it can only strengthen us. But I do contest your absolute *lirlessness*, your lack of Cheysuli gifts, your lack of Cheysuli *customs*.' He drew in a breath made uneven by the intensity of his anger; by the depth of fanaticism. 'There are so few of us left now, those with untainted blood, and if it were possible I would prefer one of the *a'saii* to take the Lion on Donal's death. But we are not so blind as to turn our backs on a warrior who has more right than most—'

'—that warrior being Ian,' I finished. I thrust out a hand and pointed at Gisella, still huddled in her chair. 'In her body lies the *seed* of that prophecy, Ceinn – a child born of Homana, Solinde, Atvia and the Cheysuli. How can you tell me *that child* should be replaced?'

'Because it should be. And *will* be.' He reached out and caught Isolde's elbow. 'Come, 'Solde. My business with him is finished. Let us go to the other hall.'

'Ceinn – *wait*.' She pulled free of him even as he had pulled free of me. 'Is it the truth? You want Ian to take Niall's place?' She thrust up a silencing hand even as he began to answer her question. 'You know Ian would never do it. He is Niall's liege man as well as his *rujholli*. Do you think he would break that service merely to accept *yours?*'

Ceinn's mouth was grimly set, lips pressed tight against one another. 'If he will not, we will simply find another with similar heritage.'

'*Similar heritage*—' Isolde fell back a step. Then she stood

206

very still. 'Would *identical* be better?' she inquired bitterly. 'Augmented by *yours*, no doubt . . . do you think a child from us would do?' Isolde smiled, but it was the smile of a predator. 'My *jehan* is likely to live for at least another twenty years, perhaps more. By *then*, no doubt a son of ours would be old enough to accept the Lion. Is that it? Is that it, Ceinn?'

''Solde—'

'Just answer!' she cried. 'Just *answer*. I do not want an explanation. Tell me aye or nay!'

Whatever else he was, Ceinn was not a liar. 'Aye,' he told her evenly. 'I want our son to rule.'

Isolde shook visibly, she was so angry; so shocked, so bound up in what she had learned. I saw tears welling into her eyes but they were not solely the tears of sorrow, though that was present also. They were the tears of rage and discovery; of a discovery so devastating it breaks the world into pieces.

'Solde's world, at least. I have shown her the man she has married.

'Well,' she said, and I was amazed at her self-possession. 'I think there will be no son.'

' *'Solde!*'

'No.' She did not shout it, scream it, cry it. She merely *said* it; I saw my father in my sister. 'No.' She pulled the bear-torque from her throat and dropped it to the stone at Ceinn's feet. 'No.'

Crimson skirts swirled as she turned. Ceinn reached out to catch an arm, but I caught his and jerked him back. 'You heard what my sister said.'

'*Ku'reshtin*!' he swore. 'Do you think I only wanted her for the child? I wanted her – still *want* her – for herself!'

I laughed aloud. 'Then tell me you love her, Cheysuli. Say the *Homanan* words to me, since there are none of the Old Tongue.'

As I released his arm, Ceinn bent and scooped up the gleaming *lir*-torque, the mark of Cheysuli marriage. When he faced me again, I saw how tightly he clutched the torque;

how tightly he clenched his jaw. But in clear, fluent Homanan, lacking Cheysuli accent or hesitation, he told me he loved my sister.

I had no answer for him. And he had none for me.

I watched the proud, angry warrior stride away from me, going after Isolde. And I began to think he was more of an enemy than at first I had believed. Because a man, so dedicated to a certain thing that there is no room for anything other than zealotry in his life, does not consider how or why he slays. But a man who loves, a man able to express that love, will think of what he does even as he does it, because he has something – some*one* – he believes is *worth* the thing he does. Even if it is assassination.

'Niall?' It was Gisella, at my side. 'Niall . . . can we go see the dancing?'

I did not want to go. 'You look weary,' I told her truthfully. 'It might be better if you went to bed instead.'

'I want to see the *dancing*.'

And so I took her to see the dancing.

CHAPTER SIX

I saw to it Gisella was settled comfortably in a cushioned chair on the dais with three other chairs. Two were for the Mujhar and his queen, the other for me. But all three remained empty.

As I stood solicitously by Gisella, she reached out and caught my hand. The motion reminded me of 'Solde and how she had reached for Ceinn. It reminded me of the conflict in her face as she had removed the *lir*-torque from her throat and told Ceinn there would be no child.

Holding Gisella's hand, I looked down upon my wife and the child who swelled her body. Fruit of a man's labors, and a sign of fertility so necessary to the House of Homana. And yet — it seemed I could hardly recall the first time we had lain together. Only the faintest flicker of a fleeting memory that told me once I had known someone other than Gisella.

Inwardly, I grimaced. I had hardly kept myself celibate before sailing to Atvia. No doubt what I recalled so dimly were the women who did not matter, being more interested in *who* I was rather than in what I could do to pleasure them.

I thought suddenly of the children born of such unions, the fruit of a man's labors in fields that had already been well-tilled. I thought it likely I had no bastards because surely a woman who conceived of a prince would tell him in hopes of winning coin or jewel or favor. But I knew also it was entirely possible I *had* sired a child or two before the one in Gisella's belly. And it made me think of Carillon, who had gotten a woman with child, and how that child now threatened my very existence, let alone my right to inherit the Lion.

The Lion of Homana. Gisella had asked if I were the Lion myself. And now I looked at the man who *was*.

He wore Cheysuli leathers dyed a rich, deep crimson, hem and collar set with narrow gold plates stitched into the leather. On his brow he wore a simple circlet of hammered gold and uncut rubies. And at his left side, scabbarded in rune-worked leather, hung the sword others claimed was ensorcelled.

My father did not move about the room; he let the room come to him. Quietly he stood near one of the groined archways and received those who wished to have word with him. He might have done it from the chair upon the dais, next to me. But it was a mark of his nature that he did not, preferring to stay away from such trappings as thrones and trumpeted announcements of his arrival. That he wore the sword surprised me; only rarely did he clasp the belt around his hips. Only rarely did he ever put hand to hilt, as if reluctant to display his absolute mastery of it.

Of course, he would never admit to being the master; rather, the servant. He had told me how once the brilliant ruby, the Mujhar's Eye, had been perverted by Ihlini magic into a thing of ugliness. A dead black stone, dull and lusterless, had sat within the golden pommel prongs. For nearly all of the years of Carillon's rule the stone had remained dull black.

Until the day Donal put his hand upon it, and it came blazing back to life.

There is a legend within the clans that a sword made of Cheysuli craftsmanship bears Cheysuli magic, and knows the hand of its master even when the master is unknowing, he had told me. *The gods know I was aware my grandsire had made that sword, but it was for Shaine, I thought; for the Mujhar who began the qu'mahlin that nearly destroyed our race. Shaine gave it to Carillon, who bore the blade for all the years of his exile and all the years of his rule. Only when he was dead did it come into my keeping.*

And only at the cost of a warrior's life: Finn, my father's uncle. Strahan had sheathed the sword in Finn's body, and in so doing had unintentionally bequeathed the magic unto my father.

The magic that slew Osric of Atvia, Gisella's uncle, and put Alaric on the throne. I glanced down at her pensively. *So many people dead . . . and all in the name of the prophecy.*

I saw my mother moving among the guests, speaking quietly with countless members of the aristocracy, Homanan and otherwise. The gold netting enveloping rich red hair shone in the light of the setting sun as it slanted through stained glass casements. The rose-red floor was awash with brilliant color.

And then I saw Isolde.

I turned to Gisella. 'Forgive me if I leave you, but I must speak with my sister.'

Her fingers tightened on my own. 'Niall?'

'You will be well, I promise.' Carefully I detached myself from her and stepped off the dais, moving through the throngs of people surrounding the dancers in the center of the hall. I answered greetings absently, too intent upon reaching 'Solde; when at last I did, I saw the desolation in her posture. She stood by one of the casements, back to the hall, as if by ignoring the people she could also ignore her loss.

She turned as I placed a hand on her shoulder, and then she tried to turn again; to turn her back on me.

''Solde—'

'Leave me be.'

''Solde, *please.*'

'Niall—' She broke off the beginning of her plea and swung back to face me squarely. I saw bitter grief in her ravaged face. 'I would be the last person in the world to wish you in peril, Niall . . . but surely you will not blame me if, for the moment, I wish also to have nothing to do with you.'

A flicker of grief; a larger one of defensiveness. 'I did not *ask* you to renounce him.'

'What *else* could I do?' Impatiently she brushed tears away, as if their presence was anathema. And in a way, they

211

were; Cheysuli do not grieve in public. 'Am I to renounce *you?*'

Sighing deeply, I took her into my arms and crushed her against my chest. She was rigid, denying herself comfort, until I rested my cheek on her hair and told her I would forgive her if she went back to Ceinn.

'Go *back!*' She pulled away to stare up at me. 'How can you say that after what *he* has said?'

'Because I know what *else* he has said.' And I told her.

I thought it would help. I thought it would make her happy to know her *cheysul* genuinely cared, not intending to use her merely because of who she was. But I misjudged her. I misjudged her badly.

'Do you value your life so little?' she asked angrily. 'Do you value *me* so little? How can you expect me to go back to a man who wishes to see you stripped of your rank, your title – your *life?*'

'I think it will not come to that,' I told her. 'The *a'saii* are no longer secret, and I have no intention of allowing them to succeed. They are only a tiny portion of the Cheysuli, 'Solde, I doubt they have *that* much power.'

She shook her head. 'I will not take the chance.'

''Solde—'

'No.' She nearly choked on the word. 'How *can* I, *rujho?* I already bear his child!'

Pain rose up in my belly, the old familiar pain I associated with *lirlessness*. Yet now it came as I thought of what 'Solde must face, bearing alone the child of the man she loved.

'Gods,' I said, 'does he know?'

'No. I planned to tell him after your wedding. But now,' she shook her head. 'Now I will say nothing.'

''Solde, he is the child's *father*.' I thought of Gisella. I thought of myself in Ceinn's place, not knowing my wife carried my child in her body. For all I hated the man for his zealotry, I could not hate him for desiring a child.

Even one he would use against me.

'Solde drew in a deep breath. 'Aye. And right now, not knowing, he plots to put Ian on the throne. You are safe so long as he and the others work toward that goal, *rujho*, because Ian will never agree. But once he knows I have conceived, they will have a new candidate. A candidate they can control.' Through her tears, she smiled. 'I am a child of the prophecy as much as you; do you think I will allow my *cheysul* to destroy it?'

I was touched by her resolve, deeply touched, but could not ignore the brutal truth of the undeniable transience of that resolve. ''Solde, in a month – two, three – the child will begin to show. What will you say to him then?'

She stood very straight before me. 'In a month or two or three, perhaps you will have cut out this canker in our midst.'

I wanted to speak, to say something that might dilute her pain, if only a little. But 'Solde's pride and resolve took all the words from my mouth; took even the pride from *me*, because she was far stronger than I could ever be.

She gives her husband over to death.

And knew *exactly* what she did even as she did it.

I tried to swallow down the painful lump in my throat. '*Cheysuli i'halla shansu,*' I said thickly. I could think of nothing more fitting than wishing upon my Cheysuli sister the peace of the race she served so faithfully.

'Solde smiled a little. And then she put out her hand – palm-up, fingers spread – and made the eloquent gesture that had the ordering of an entire race. '*Tahlmorra,*' she said quietly, and then she walked out of the hall.

I watched her go, then swung around abruptly to return to Gisella. And I stopped just as abruptly, because Varien stood in my path.

The Atvian envoy smiled and inclined his head. 'My lord, please accept my congratulations on your marriage to the Princess of Atvia.' The smile, so smooth, widened only a fraction, not enough to offer offense. 'And now the Princess of Homana.'

'My thanks.' I was brusque, but it was difficult to be polite after witnessing 'Solde's grief.

'My lord.' He detained me easily with merely an

intonation. 'Here, my lord. I have brought you wine.'

Each hand held a silver cup. I took the cup he offered because indeed I *did* desire wine . . . *anything* to ease the ache in my spirit. I felt bruised from 'Solde's decision. I could not argue that it was the right one, but neither was I the sort of man who would be pleased to see his sister in such pain.

Varien, unctuous as always, lifted his cup in a brief salute. 'Your fortune, my lord.'

I drank deeply. So deeply I drained the cup too quickly; Varien instantly motioned a servant to refill it. And then, as I drank again, the Atvian stepped closer. So close, a velvet-clad shoulder brushed my own.

'May I speak freely, my lord?'

My mind was not on Varien at all. 'Of course.' I looked past him toward the dais, and saw Gisella picking half-heartedly at her silken robes.

'My lord, I will be frank with you; your wife is not entirely like other women.'

Looking at her, I recalled how changeable were her moods; how violent the swings. 'No,' I agreed.

'This is a delicate subject, my lord, but I am certain you would prefer it discussed. It has bearing on your future.'

I frowned a little, looking at him more attentively. 'If it concerns my wife, of course it has bearing on my future.'

Teeth showed briefly, so briefly, as he laughed silently. And then the laughter was gone, leaving in its wake a cool, quiet amusement. 'My lord, let us agree the lady is – of divergent humors. Because of these humors, it is entirely possible she will not always be a willing partner.' He paused delicately and lifted the cup to his lips. But he did not drink. '*Bed*partner, my lord.'

I looked at my wife. 'That is something between Gisella and me, envoy.'

'My lord, of course.' He bowed just enough to emphasize his subservience. 'But with you I feel I must be completely frank.' Smiling, he said, 'If Gisella ceases to please you, I can show you another way.'

214

In distaste, I frowned at him. 'Do I hear you aright? On the day of my wedding you offer other women to me?'

'Not – entirely.' The smile did not fade. 'My lord, let us say I have admired you greatly since first we met. Admired, respected – *desired*, my lord.'

My fingers slipped on the cup; I nearly dropped it. But I recovered my grasp and clenched it tightly, so tightly my hand shook, and wine slopped over the rim to splatter against the floor. '*What did you say?*'

'I said I desired you, my lord.' He made no indication of shame, regret, embarrassment. His tone was perfectly controlled, as if every day he said such to a man.

As perhaps he does. Incredulously, I stared at him. I was too shocked to be angry.

Varien sipped wine and smiled, infinitely patient.

I became aware that a hand had reached out and caught Varien's wrist in a crushing grasp. The hand dragged the silver wine cup away from Varien's smiling mouth. Sharply. So sharply it caused the cup to fall; falling, it rang, silver on stone; spilled blood-red wine across rose-red floor.

And I realized the hand was mine.

Around us, there was silence. A falling wine cup, even spilling its contents, is not so uncommon as to silence so many people. But the sight of the Prince of Homana confronting an Atvian envoy *is*; eyes watched avidly.

Sweat beaded on Varien's upper lip. His face was pale from the pain. But still, he managed to smile.

I wanted to shout at him that what he offered was worthy of execution, but I did not. Not before so many people; before Gisella, my father, my mother. I wanted to tell him that what he offered was worth his ostracism; at the very least I could send him home. But something held me back. Something shut up my mouth and chased the words back down my throat to my belly, where they twisted and tangled and bound up my guts with bile.

And *still* Varien smiled.

I let go of his wrist. 'You are here at Alaric's behest.'

'Alaric's – and Lillith's.'

I frowned a little. My toe touched the cup; it rolled. 'Lillith's?'

'Of course, my lord.' Varien fingered the collar of his indigo doublet. I saw a hint of silver: a chain. He drew it forth, and from the links dangled a single curving tooth, capped with shining silver. 'Lillith.'

Lillith's gift. My hand went at once to my own collar. Beneath the wedding finery was a matching tooth, hanging from its thong. I had nearly forgotten.

Varien bowed. 'Forgive me, my lord; I intended no offense.'

I stared after him, bewildered by the sudden upsurge of emotions. Sorrow, anguish, emptiness . . . a horrible emptiness, as if someone had stolen from me a thing I had always desired, demanded, *needed* – before I could say what it was.

I was lost. Amid the throng of guests who had witnessed my marriage to Gisella, I was lost: an eye of emptiness in the middle of the maelstrom.

A shadow of a man.

And when the servant filled my cup, I drank.

I drank.

I drank—

—and when I could stand the confinement no more, I went out of the hall and out of the palace proper, climbing narrow stairs to the sentry-walks along the curtain wall. Night had fallen with the sunset, but Homana-Mujhar is never in total darkness. There are torches along the walls and tripod braziers in the baileys. There is always a pall of yellow light, flickering in fickle winds. Preying on the shadows.

Now I *sought* the shadows, seeking escape from the light, the noise, the *emptiness*. Except even here, atop the narrow sentry-walk along the parapet, I found solace in nothing; no answer to emptiness. Only redoubled sorrow, and an anguish born of nothing I could name.

In my hand was a cup of wine. A deep cup, and filled to brimming; tipping it slightly, albeit unintentionally, I heard the wine spill out to splatter against the stone. Even as I righted the cup I did not care; I had drunk so much already that stopping now would serve nothing at all.

I caught hold of the wall and leaned between the merlons of the parapet to hang over a crenel, pressing my belly against it. Lights from the city flared and danced and melted together, until I blinked away the dazzle from my eyes. My fingers dug into the stone. Digging, *digging*; I felt the protest of abraded flesh. But still I dug, as if the pain might give me surcease from the demon in my soul.

'An easy target, for an enemy.'

I pushed myself up raggedly, still hanging onto the merlon. The torchlight from below set his gold to gleaming. All his gold; suddenly, I found I hated him for it. 'I came out here to be alone.'

'I know.' Ian's tone was even, unperturbed even by the belligerence in my own. 'That is why I followed.'

'Why? Did you think I would throw myself from the wall?'

'You look as though the thought had crossed your mind.' Like me, he bore a cup of wine. But he did not drink from his. 'Niall, what did Varien say to you?'

I tasted something in my mouth that made me want to spit. Instead, I gulped more wine. 'He said he desired me,' I said flatly, when all the wine was gone. 'Perhaps he thinks I will share his bed when I cannot share Gisella's.'

The torchlight polished Ian's angular face. He was so much like Isolde. So much like our father. 'There was a time I could have told you the truth of Varien. I grew to know him well in Atvia because I had no choice.' He paused. 'Not in the way he wishes to share with you, but because we spent time together. But as for telling you, I was not certain you would listen. I was not certain you could.' He looked straight at me. 'Can you, *rujho*? Can you hear the truth?'

'What truth?' I demanded. 'I think I have heard it all.'

He took the empty cup from my hand. 'No. You have heard nothing.' Smoothly, he threw the cup over the crenel.

I saw a flash of silver in the torchlight; it was gone. 'Do you hear it?' he asked, and I heard the dull clang of the cup striking stones below.

'Ian—'

'Gisella has addled *your* mind as much as her own is addled,' he said plainly. 'I know you cannot see it, but *I* can; I can see precisely what she has done to you, and I do not like it. It is time something was done to destroy the taint.'

'*I'toshaa-ni?*' I asked rudely. 'Or does that lie solely within *your* province?'

'It lies within the province of every Cheysuli warrior,' he answered quietly. 'Even within that of a *lirless* Cheysuli.'

He might as well have taken a knife and thrust it into my belly. I felt the invisible blade go home, twisting, *twisting*, until I nearly cried out with the pain. As it was, I clutched at the merlon. Sweat broke out on my face.

'*Ku'reshtin*—' I cursed him raggedly. 'Look to *yourself* when you speak of taint. It was *you* Lillith kept.'

'Aye. *You* she gave away.' The silver cup glittered against the darkness of his hands. 'You she gave to Gisella.'

I swore again, very softly; I was nearly doubled over from the pain. 'Gisella is my *wife*.'

'Gisella is your bane . . . and *will* be, until we do something to prevent it.'

'We?' I asked bitterly, leaning against the merlon. 'Do you speak of the *a'saii?*' I laughed in the face of his sudden shock: 'Perhaps you *do* desire the Lion; perhaps Ceinn and the others *have* found a willing substitute for me.'

'The gods forgive you for that,' he whispered. 'How can you think it of me? I am your *liege man*—'

'You leave out *brother*,' I said harshly. 'Is it because we only share a father that you discount the kinship? Is it because I am Homanan and Solindish that you brush aside the other blood between us?' I laughed. 'Why not? *Ceinn* is willing to let that be reason enough to drag me out of a throne I cannot yet claim as my own. Do you abet him? Do you abet the *a'saii?*'

218

'No,' he said softly, when he could speak again. 'I abet only the gods.'

'In what? Your march to the throne?' I thrust out a rigid arm and pointed toward the massive palace proper. 'It waits, Ian. In the Great Hall. All crouched down upon its wooden haunches with its wooden eyes gleaming even as the mouth spills out its wooden tongue. The Lion *waits*, Ian – why not claim it for yourself?'

His posture was so rigid I thought he might break. 'Because I do – not – *want* – it.' He thrust the words out between clenched teeth. 'And one day, you will understand why. One day, I think you will beg me to take the Lion from you.' He put his cup into my hand. 'But even when you *beg*, I will not take it. Because I am the Lion's shadow . . . not the Lion himself. I leave that title to you.'

'Ian—' But he had turned, going back into the shadows until I could not see *him*, only the glinting of his gold. All his Cheysuli gold.

Gods, why can I not have my own – 'Ian! Ian, *wait!*' Unsteadily I ran along the narrow sentry-walk, still clutching the cup in my hand. Wine slopped over the rim and splashed against thigh, boot, stone. 'Ian – come back! I need you, *rujho*. I *need* you . . . I need you to take away the *pain*—'

But he was gone. He did not hear, or else he did not care to answer.

I stopped running. I fell against the parapet and gasped for breath, trying to still the roiling in my belly. I wanted to spew all the wine over the crenel onto the stones below. I wanted to start over again, to tear up the spoiled parchment and begin again with a fresh one. I wanted to shout and scream and cry, because I was so empty, so gods-cursed *empty*.

And a man cannot live when he is made up of emptiness.

The cup in my hand was also empty. And so I threw it over the crenel to join its fellow far below, wishing I could be rid of *myself* as easily.

How can a man be rid of himself when he has no wish to die?

He leaves. He *leaves*.

CHAPTER SEVEN

I fled Homana-Mujhar on fleet horse and fleeter need to escape the blackness in my soul. That I had a demon in me I did not doubt; I could feel it within me, clawing, gnawing, shredding the interior of my belly. I shouted orders to the guard and clattered out of the cobbled outer bailey and through the wide front gates even as they were shoved open. Free of the outer curtain wall, I spurred through winding alleys and streets, ignoring the shouts of passers-by. Never an indifferent horseman, I took negligent care to avoid trampling anyone, and therefore no one went down beneath my stallion's iron-shod hooves.

Sparks flew; I bent low in the saddle and urged the horse on faster, past the watch and through the massive barbican gate, portcullis raised: the East Gate of Mujhara. Onward through the clustered spillage of outer dwellings; I recalled the night I had met Strahan. So long ago − had he really warned me not to wed Gisella?

Aye, he had. As well as promising to take my sons. Now the promise was more dangerous than ever; Gisella could bear me my first son soon, and set Strahan's plans into motion.

Through the winding footpaths of the outskirts; out of dirt onto heath, digging divots of tight-packed turf and clods of soil. I shut my eyes and trusted my horsemanship to keep me in the saddle as I battled the emptiness.

It is difficult to describe how overwhelming emptiness can be, how utterly encompassing, until even the thought of death becomes less important than the driving need to be *filled*. It is worse than melancholy; worse than the depths of despair. It is a complete cessation of functioning. A man simply ceases to *be*, and yet he knows that physically he still exists. It is only his spirit that has been torn asunder.

The need burned away the liquor in my blood. I was not drunk, though a part of me longed to be. Nor was I made ill by the poison I had poured so liberally into my body. I was simply *empty*.

Under the quarter moon the horse and I went on, galloping across the open plains until we could gallop no more, and then we slowed. I heard the whistle in the stallion's wind and knew I had come close to slaying him outright; I might even have ruined him permanently. He carried his head very low, dangling on the end of his shaven neck. His ears lolled back loosely, flopping as he walked. He staggered, stumbling repeatedly; at last I dismounted and led him. But I did not turn back. I led him ever eastward, into the deepwood that swallowed the eastern plains.

Spittle from the stallion had soiled my velvet doublet. It was past midsummer, moving into fall, but the night was not cold, only cool.

Ahead of me, hidden by leagues of deepwood, lay Clankeep. But I did not intend to go there; could not, in my need. I knew Ceinn and the other *a'saii* would mock me, denigrating me before the clan, using my emptiness and *lirlessness* to turn other warriors against me. And then there would be more than just a few; more, even, than twenty or thirty. There would be enough to pull me out of the Lion's presence and put Ian in my place.

At last, weary as the stallion, I stopped stumbling eastward and searched for shelter. In a copse of close-grown beeches I unsaddled the stallion, unpacked the few things I had brought with me – bow, full quiver, waterskin, a pouch of dried meat, one of grain, cloak – and made a bed of leaves. I threw myself upon it and rolled up in my cloak once I had tethered and grained the horse. I knew he would not try to break the rein and wander. Like me, he wanted nothing more than the forgetfulness of sleep.

I burrowed into the leaves, reflecting the Homanans would not believe it of their prince, and let the darkness overwhelm me. I heard the night sounds; smelled the sap, the soil, the fragrance of the forest. I stared up at the arching fretwork of limbs against stars and thought of the gods who had decreed there be a people put onto the land, and so they had put the Firstborn upon the Crystal Isle. I thought of the Firstborn who had watched their children become so blood-bred their very existence was threatened; until even the Firstborn knew they themselves could not recover. And I thought of the prophecy that bound the Cheysuli so tightly; that bound *me* so tightly, like the pillory that imprisons thief and liar.

The stallion grunted. I turned to look and saw him go down, shifting sideways, until he lay on his side; until, on his back, he twisted and hunched, flailing long legs as he rolled against deadfall and dirt. He shed dried sweat and discomfort in the age-old equine rite; I wished I could do the same.

He lay still a moment, blinking; the quarter moon set his eye afire with light. And then he was up, awkward in the attempt as horses always are; he stood, shook violently – shedding hair and debris – then locked his knees and shut his eyes. He would sleep standing, perfectly comfortable, while I tried to sleep lying down in leaves against a ground that would be damp by morning.

The night was colder than I had expected. When dawn chased away the morning mists I awoke shivering with a bone-deep chill. I tried to wrap the cloak more tightly, but it was only a summer cloak of fine-combed wool, not a heavier winter cloak lined with fur. And so I gave up on sleep altogether and rose, aware of a sourness in my throat that bespoke a belly gone bad on too much wine. I had thought the effects purged by the flight from Mujhara; they were not. The condition of my head told me that.

I drank water sparingly, ate dried meat, sat hunched on a cold log wishing myself a man who did not imbibe;

knowing one day, and probably too soon, I would do the same again.

Finally I rose and went to the horse. With both hands I brushed his back free of the debris remaining from the night before, placed blankets across his spine and prepared to hoist the saddle up and settle it on top of the blankets. I had every intention of going back to Homana-Mujhar. *Every* intention: no doubt my brother and father worried – I *knew* my mother worried – and I had left Gisella as well. Poor, sad Gisella, deprived of the ordering in her wits that would have made her worthy of any man.

And yet, I thought she was worthy of me.

Grimly I reached for the Homanan saddle. But even as I caught hold and hoisted it, I realized the emptiness was not gone. Only a bit laggard in renewing itself in my soul.

Gods, what am I to do? Tell me what I am to do!

But the only answer was the snort of my chestnut stallion and the chatter of a jay in the tree.

Do I go back? Has anything changed from last night, except the condition of head and belly? No. I am still empty, still naked, still bound up in the need for the thing I need so badly.

And so I did not go back. I tended the stallion more carefully than the night before, pulling the blankets from his back, once again, and found him mostly recovered from my irresponsibility. I grained him, watered him as best I could by tucking the skin beneath an arm and pressing water into cupped palms. He drank, but I did not doubt he would prefer a stream or river.

'Later. First, we – *I* – need fresh meat. This pouch will not last long.' I patted him, left him rein enough to graze around the tree, took bow and quiver and set out to hunt on foot.

After half a day spent tracking, I slew a roebuck and carried it back to the campsite slung over my shoulders. There I hung it up and butchered it, enjoying the messy task not because I enjoyed butchering, but because I took satisfaction in doing the thing myself. So often there were others to do it for me. Even Ian. And I thought of the red king stag.

I built a fire and roasted the meat, knowing most of it would spoil before I could eat it all. The stallion cropped contentedly at forest grasses and the grain I gave him, untroubled by his sojourn away from luxury into the depths of the shadowed forest. And even though I was empty still, I began to know a little peace.

We moved on, the horse and I, after another day. He had stripped the copse bare of grazing and I wanted to find a proper stream. So I saddled him, packed him, mounted him, intending to head back.

But instead, we went deeper into the woods. And, as the days passed, more deeply still, until I left behind all thoughts of Homana-Mujhar and contented myself with doing for myself, as I had never done before.

I let my beard grow, since I had only a knife with which to shave it, and no polished plate at all. I slew a deer and fashioned a set of boots, since my others – intended only for ceremonial wear – were nearly destroyed. The fur was lush against my legs. The remaining pelt I made into a rough jerkin – hair-in, hide-out, no sleeves – and belted it with a strip of leather. Beneath it all I still wore the soiled silks and velvets of my wedding finery, as well as the garnets and gold.

The horse began to grow his winter coat, losing the sheen of summertime and gaining the blurry outline of colder months. His mane, no longer shaved, grew straight up to a height the width of my hand before it began to fall. At Homana-Mujhar, he was stabled, closely tended, knowing shelter against the seasons. Here he knew only the honesty of the forest.

We moved on twice more, because the emptiness increased. Each day I awoke prepared to go back, to go *home*, and yet each day I felt myself emptier than ever. The only surcease I knew was to busy myself with living as I had never lived, learning the forest as I had never really known it. I thought of Gisella, growing larger with my child. I thought of Ian, whom I had sent from me with cruel temper and crueler tongue. I thought also of my father, deprived yet again of his legitimate son and heir so soon after he had finally gotten him back; needing him more than ever. And, of course, my mother, who no doubt worried every hour of every day and night. But this was *my* time, *my* freedom . . . my final chance to learn precisely who I was before I must become the man they *desired* me to be, and not the man I might have become on my own.

I did not go back. Because I *could* not, yet.

And then early one morning, just before dawn, a bear came into camp. I knew it at once by the smell, even as the stallion awakened me with the noise of his fear; his attempts to break free of the rein tying him to the sapling. He broke it, but as he spun to run the bear was on him, and in the bright light of a full moon I saw the hunter clearly: a cinnamon-colored rock bear.

There was nothing to do for the horse. By the time I caught up my bow, the bear had slain him. And so I took what I could reach of my belongings, silently, and left at once, not wishing to contest anything so deadly as a rock bear for campsite *or* gear.

I went away as far as I could and slept the rest of the night beneath the spreading limbs of a huge old oak, rolled in my summer cloak. And when at dawn I awakened, I found the rock bear sitting beside me.

I was up before I could speak, running before I could walk, caught before I could pray. I felt the spread paw slap at my ankle, catch, jerk, and then I was down, rolling, trying to yank my knife free of its sheath even as the bear slapped my hand. The knife went flying. With unexpected precision, the bear used only one claw against the back of my hand. The stripe turned white, pink, red; opening, it spilled blood down through my fingers.

I sprawled on my buttocks, braced against one rigid elbow even as my booted feet scraped rotting leaves, searching for

225

purchase in drifting debris. The bear sat back on his haunches. I saw the yellow eyes; the eyes of a Cheysuli.

And then, of course, I *knew*.

'*Ku'reshtin*!' I shouted hoarsely. 'Is *this* how you mean to do it?'

The bear blurred before me. I squinted as the void swallowed the bear and spat out a man, a Cheysuli: Ceinn. Still he squatted before me, close enough to touch; I did not move. I knew better than to move.

'My lord,' he said calmly, 'there is a thing we must discuss.'

'The two of us have *nothing* to discuss!'

'Oh, aye – we all of us *do*, my lord.'

As he spoke the others came out of the thinning darkness, gliding from trees and shadowed pockets, all in human form, except for the *lir*. That hurt most of all, more than anything I had expected; that there were *lir* in the world who would join the *a'saii* in attempting to replace me.

I could not count them all, warriors or *lir*. I knew only there were more than I had expected. More than I had dreamed possible.

Ceinn smiled. It made the scar by his eye crease. It made him look like a man who would be a good friend. A man whose companionship would be valued.

As no doubt the *a'saii* valued him.

'My good fortune amazes me,' he said. 'We have been so patient, expecting to wait a very long time. *Prepared* to wait a very long time. Yet now you are here, and *we* are here, and this thing can be settled at last.'

I still sprawled on my back, one knee thrust up. The claw mark continued to bleed. 'How many?' I asked.

'Of the *a'saii*?' Ceinn shrugged. 'Enough. I have not counted lately. At least two or three from every clan.'

'*Every* clan?'

'Even those from the Northern Wastes, across the Bluetooth River.'

I tried not to show my dismay openly. But I was stunned by the magnitude of the Cheysuli rebellion. There were, at

226

last count, at least thirty clans in Homana, some large, some small, some smaller, but all invaluable to the completion of the prophecy. And now, in their misguided zealotry, they desired to destroy it.

I did not bother to look at the others, though I addressed them as well. I looked only at Ceinn. 'How much of this is personal?'

'None of it,' he answered instantly, so sincerely that I believed him even as I desired not to. 'There were *a'saii* in Homana before Isolde and I ever lay down together.'

It was a shock as well as an unpleasant realization. 'And now?'

'Now?' He nodded thoughtfully. 'I admit I enjoy the idea more.'

Apprehension knotted my belly. I could not help it; I winced against the familiar pain. 'Would it do any good if I told you there are *Homanans* who feel much as you do? That they also desire to replace me with another?'

'The bastard.' Ceinn nodded. 'We know.'

I had hoped to buy my way free. I should have known better. 'Ian will never agree,' I told him. 'And 'Solde has renounced you . . . who will you choose to hold the Lion now? You?' I thought perhaps to breed dissension among the others; Ceinn's personal ambitions might disturb them enough to delay their immediate plans.

'Ian may not agree while you are alive,' Ceinn told me, 'but what happens when you are dead? The Queen is barren. Donal has no other sons. Who else will succeed him?'

'Carillon's bastard.'

Something flickered in his eyes.

I smiled, albeit was unamused. 'If I am dead, it gives the Homanan *a'saii* more chance than ever to put the bastard on the throne. They are every bit as loyal and fanatical as you are; do you think they will suffer *Ian* to hold the Lion? You are a fool, Ceinn – you and the others. You will bring domestic rebellion to Homana again, and destroy all hope of fulfilling the prophecy.'

227

'Eloquent,' he said, 'but our decision has been made.'

Slowly I sat up all the way, forgoing my unintentional posture of submissiveness. In the muted light of early dawn, I looked at as many faces as I could. 'How will it be? Will it be the *lir*? Or all of you in *lir*-shape, leaving only scraps of clothing and broken bone – with perhaps the ring remaining on my hand to make certain my identity is known?'

'That may well be your fate,' he agreed, 'but it will not be our doing. It will be your own.'

'*Mine*—' I laughed. 'I hardly think—'

'*I* do.' He interrupted smoothly. 'You are a *lirless* man, Niall. Cheysuli, for all you sublimate it beneath Homanan looks and customs.' He glanced in distaste at my thickening beard. 'And a *lirless* Cheysuli gives himself over to the death-ritual.'

'I never *had* a *lir*.' It took all my determination not to show my fear. 'I am not constrained to the ritual.'

'No,' he agreed, 'but when we are done with you, you will *believe* you had a *lir* – and you will believe you lost one.'

Gods, they can do it. I tried to scramble up, to lunge away from Ceinn, but it did not matter. The others closed in even as he rose and brushed off his leathers.

'*Rujho*,' —how he mocked me, in his expressibly gentle tone— 'for Isolde's sake, I promise we will not hurt you.'

Gods—

I tried to scream it. But by the time I opened my mouth, I had lost the means to speak.

Or even the desire.

CHAPTER EIGHT

Oh gods – my lir—
—my lir is dead—
—my lir—
I knelt on the ground, hunched upon my knees so that
my heels cut into my buttocks. My forehead was pressed
against the layer of brittle fallen leaves; I shut my eyes so
tightly all I could see were the pallid colors of my death:
smutty blue, muddy black, an edge of maggot white in the
ashen darkness of my grief.
—my lir – my lir is dead—
Fists dug holes in the crumbling leaves; digging, *digging*,
until they touched the cool dampness of soil beneath; the
humid, sweaty soil; of the consistency of clay; the clay that
is used to seal the eyes of a dead man closed.
—my lir—
I have known grief in my life, much grief; I recalled how
it was when I had believed my brother dead, but I have
never known, have never *imagined* what it would be like
to lose a *lir*. It was as if a man had thrust a hand through
flesh and gristle and bone to grasp my heart; grasping it,
he wrenches it from my chest and throws it aside, leaving
me both alive and dead. Alive because I do not die; dead
because everything within the fragile shell of human flesh
is dead, so infinitely *dead*. How does a man *live* like this?
How can a man survive?
He does not.
And then I knew what I must do.
I wrenched myself up from the ground and ran, *ran*;
running, I felt the grief rise up from my belly to clog my

229

chest, my throat, my mouth, until I could hear it rising from my lips to kite upon the wind made of my own passing; a keening deathsong, a wailing griefsong; a song composed of all the pain in my heart and soul and mind: *my lir is dead, my lir is dead; why can I not be dead as well?*

I ran. *I ran.*

So hard. *So hard.*

—gods – how is it you can gift a man with such a miracle as a lir, and then take him away from that man—?

I ran.

Vines slashed down across my face. A tree limb scraped across my cheek, lifting skin and beard. A thorny creeper looped my throat; tugged, tore.

I ran.

Bracken fouled my legs, slapping at my thighs. Deadfall limbs cracked and rolled beneath my feet; I stumbled, caught myself; ran on.

Gods – how I ran—

There is pain in my belly, in my chest, in my throat. I can hear my breathing wheezing, hissing, whistling, like that of a wind-broken horse. There is dryness in my throat, such gods-awful dryness; it burns, it *burns* . . . I think it will burn me alive—

Gods – why did you take my lir?

I trip. I fall. I rise.

—run—

Something is running behind me. I can hear it. I can hear it coming; hear it slipping through the path I break as I run; running more quickly than *I* can run as I try to leave it behind.

I can hear it. I can hear it tearing through the vines and creepers and bracken, unhindered by the thorns, the roots, the traps that plants will lay for a man, seeking to bring him down.

I can hear it. I can hear it breathing, *breathing*; I can hear its heavy panting.

I can *hear* it—

—and then I realize it is *myself* I hear; there is nothing behind me, nothing at all, except grief and pain and the awful weight of knowledge: *my lir is dead, my lir – my lir is gone from me—*

Oh gods. Will you not lift this weight from my soul?

Aye, they tell me. *Aye. You have only to trust in us; trust yourself to us; give yourself over to us.*

Aye. It is best. For the best. It cannot be so hard.

—I give myself over to you—

No! A new voice I do not recognize. Not myself. The gods?

—I give myself—

No!

—I give—

And more urgently yet: *No!*

No? Who – or what – is that which tells me *no?*

I slow. I stop. I turn. But all I can see is the grayness of finality; the grayness turning black, so *black,* it promises relief. It promises an end to all the pain and grief and wretched *emptiness—*

No, the new voice tells me. Firmly, as if I am a child.

And I think: *perhaps I am one.*

Not a child. No. But a man. A man. A warrior. A Cheysuli.

And I laugh. Aloud, I shout: 'How can I be a Cheysuli when I have no *lir?*'

And then I realize what they have done to me, Ceinn and the others; what they have tried to do.

And failed.

I fell. I fell down, painfully, and felt thorns clawing at my face, catching the corner of my eye; tearing. A stone was beneath my temple, pressing inexorably. I moved a little, seeking relief; found it.

Gods – I would have given myself over to death.

I lay face down in dirt and leaves and fern, nearly blind from overexertion. I had tried so hard to run both *from* my end and *to* it; to give myself over to the beast that would take my life, to relieve the pain of my loss.

231

Except there had been no loss. None at all: I had no *lir.*
You do now.

My breath stirred the crackling skeletons of leaves that
were no longer leaves. Motes rose, danced, insinuated
themselves beneath my lids. I felt sweat run down my nose,
my brow, my jaw; the tears run down my cheeks.

Lir, you would do better to get up.

I felt stones beneath my hip. But I had no strength to
move.

Lir.

Something cool, something damp, something impossible
to ignore; it reached beneath my neck and nudged, nudged
again; *pushed—*

*I cannot lift you, lir . . . I am a wolf, not a man; not a
warrior.*

Am I?

It pushed. It *shoved.*

I rolled. Opened my eyes. Saw black nose, silver muzzle,
green-gold eyes.

And *teeth.*

I lunged upward, away, *away*; then, kneeling, hunching,
bent to spew the contents of my belly onto the ground.

You ran too hard. Lir, you should not have run so hard.

My belly was empty, but still it cramped. How it cramped,
knotting itself like yarn from a woman's fallen spindle.

I will wait.

I clawed for my knife and found the sheath empty. I faced
the wolf bare-handed.

Slay me and you slay yourself. The tone, unaccountably,
gentle. *Lir – be not so witless. Have they made you deaf as
well as blind?*

A wolf. Male. Silver-gray, with green-gold eyes, and a
mask of deepest charcoal.

He sat down. He *sat.* And his tongue lolled out of his
mouth.

'You are a – *lir?*' I croaked aloud.

I am Serri. I am yours. I have been empty so long, so long—
Suddenly he rose, approached, butted his head into my

shoulder before I could scramble away. *I am filled — I am filled — my spirit and soul are complete—*

I nearly fell over. My arms were full of wolf; my *lap* was full of wolf. So – much – *wolf—*

I am Serri, he said. *I am yours. And I am no longer empty—*

And I realized, neither was I.

'Serri?' I whispered. '*Serri?*'

There is no need to speak aloud, unless you wish it. We share the lir-bond, lir.

I laughed. Once only; I was too shocked, too utterly overcome, to blurt out anything more.

Serri?

You see? You may speak, or you may not – it no longer matters, lir.

'Serri?' This time, aloud; it was a croak, not a word, but the sound brought tears to my eyes.

Tears of joy, of disbelief; of relief and exultation. But also tears of an absolute *completion* I had known before only in a woman.

Sul'harai, Serri said. *That is what the Cheysuli call it. But do not judge it too soon.*

Apprehension lifted the hairs on the back of my neck. 'Too soon?'

Too soon. You will see. It is often better than this.

'Better than this?'

Better. When you trade your shape for mine.

I laughed. And then I cried. And then I pulled the wolf into my arms and hugged him, *hugged* him, as I had hugged no one before.

Serri! I cried. *Oh gods – why did it take so long?*

Because it was your tahlmorra.

I hugged him harder. I hugged him until he sneezed; I laughed until he grunted.

'I am *nineteen*, Serri – am I not a bit too old?'

Your jehan was too young, they say. You are too old, you say. But age has nothing to do with it, lir; it has to do with being ready.

'And I am ready?'

233

For me, and for your tahlmorra.

I fell back against the ground, still hugging the wolf against my chest. I felt paws and nails digging into flesh as Serri tried to right himself; tried to regain some semblance of dignity. But I did not let him. I wrapped him more tightly yet in my arms and buried my face against the thick ruff warding throat and neck against attackers.

'Serri—'

Ihlini! The word rang a tocsin in my head. *Lir – on you – Ihlini—*

On – *me?* 'Serri—'

Ihlini – Ihlini! And then he was grasping at my throat, lips peeling back from his teeth.

I thrust myself away at once, trying to ward my throat with a shaking hand. 'Did Ceinn send you?' I asked. 'Is this another trick?'

Ihlini – lir – Ihlini— Even as I tried to scramble away, the wolf was leaping for my throat.

My fingers caught the leather thong, and suddenly I knew.

Lillith's gift – Lillith's tooth—

I pulled the dangling tooth from beneath my clothing. 'This?'

Be rid of it – be rid of it – lir, be rid of it at once!

I scraped the thong over my head. In my palm lay the curving tooth: thick at one end, capped by gold; pointed at the other. A dog's tooth, or a wolf's.

A wolf's.

'Such an insignificant thing . . .' I said aloud.

Be rid of it, lir – at once—

I stared at the tooth. 'Lillith,' I said aloud. 'Lillith, Alaric – *Gisella*—' And I knew what they had done.

What they had made *me* do.

My hand spasmed. Fingers shut over the tooth. Tightly, so tightly; the tooth bit into my flesh. 'Oh gods – *Deirdre . . . they have made me slay them all!*'

Lir, be rid of the charm!

I thrust an arm against the ground and pushed, rising

234

unsteadily. And then I hurled Lillith's gift as far as I could into the forest depths.

They have made me slay them all. Deirdre, Liam, Shea – even Ierne and the unborn child—

Oh *gods*.

I began to run again.

Lir! Serri came running behind me; running, *running*, even as I went running. *Lir – wait—*

Dead. All of them *dead*.

All the proud eagles of Erinn, proud, fierce Erinn, with its aerie upon the white chalk cliffs overlooking the Dragon's Tail.

Deirdre.

Oh – gods – *Deirdre—*

I stopped running. I stood in the sun-gilded clearing and felt the warmth upon my face as I turned it toward the sun. *Gods*, I said, *how is it that in the moment you give me the greatest gift of all, you take away another? You give me the knowledge of what I can do . . . and the knowledge of what I have done.*

Serri, beside me, lifted his head and licked my hand. *Lir, be not so bitter. What is done is done; look not to lay blame upon your platter when it was another who had the fashioning of that platter.*

The fashioning of that platter . . . 'Gisella?' I asked aloud. 'No. It was Alaric who put the torch into my hand; Lillith who stood by him even as he did it.'

I recalled it so well, that night upon the dome of the dragon's skull. And all the light in my eyes as I set torch to beacon-fire.

Gods. All dead.

Gisella: who had spun a web within my mind and bound me to her will.

At her own instigation? Perhaps not. Perhaps she as much as I was a puppet caught in the tangle of strings pulled by Lillith and Alaric. I thought she lacked the wits and concentration to make or carry out such plans.

And yet it had been Gisella who had ensorcelled a *lirless* man.

235

A man who was *lirless* no longer.

'Serri,' I said aloud, 'there are things that I must learn, and I must learn them well. Things such as taking *lir*-shape. Things such as healing.' I paused. 'And the gift of compelling a person to do as I wish him to do.'

Lir—

'And then we will go to Clankeep. And then to Homana-Mujhar.'

Lir—

I looked down at the wolf, my *lir*, and knew myself complete even while I felt the emptiness of grief; the hollowness of despair. 'Serri,' I begged, 'teach me what I must know.'

Serri seemed to sigh. *It begins*, he said, *with the shape-change* . . .

CHAPTER NINE

Gods – but I cannot begin to say what it is to trade human form for animal. There are no words to describe the melding of heart and mind and spirit, the perfect bonding of a man and animal. I knew only that I could not comprehend how I had lived before, so empty, so insubstantial, so *unwhole*; so vague a shadow of what a man can be when he is a Cheysuli warrior.

It is a trade, the ability to put off one form and wear another. A transience unlimited by beginning and end, simply a time of *being*; when I was a wolf I was a wolf, not a man, not Niall; not even the Prince of Homana. Not even a Cheysuli. Just – a wolf, and bound by such freedom as an unblessed man cannot possibly comprehend. Not even a Cheysuli. Because even a warrior, in human form, lacks the perfection of the animal he becomes when he trades one shape for the other. Even a *Cheysuli* is less than he can be.

I began to understand. And I began to see why my race is so arrogant, so insular, so certain of their place within the tapestry of the gods. Our colors are brighter. We are the warp and weft of Homana, and all the patterns besides. Pick us from that pattern and the shape of the dream collapses. The shape of *life* collapses.

As Homana herself would collapse.

Gods, but what responsibility. And I began to understand what my father faced, trying to merge Homana and the Cheysuli. Trying to blend recalcitrant yarns into a harmonious tapestry.

I learned to think as a wolf, feel as a wolf, act as a wolf.

I learned how vulnerable is a man's naked flesh; how much stronger are hide and fur. I learned sounds I had never heard, scents I had never smelled, flavors I had never tasted. I learned what it meant to be alive, *alive*, as no man can ever be until he claims a *lir*.

I learned that to be *lirless* and trapped forever in the shape of a man is a torture of the kind no Cheysuli should ever experience.

I thought of myself as I had been; *lirless*, unblessed, a shadow of a man, lacking a soul altogether.

And I thought of Rowan. And began to respect him as I had never fully respected him, knowing only I had resented him as I had resented myself, because we neither of us claimed a lir.

O gods, I thank you for this lir.

Serri taught me the shapechange and the responsibilities inherent in the ability. There was, he said, a matter of balance, a matter of retaining the comprehension of *self*. Without it, a man in *lir*-shape who grows too angry can also grow too careless, and he can tip the delicate balance. Tipping it, he loses himself, and slides over the edge into the madness of permanent *lir*-shape.

Because a man, he said, is a man; locked in *lir*-shape forever, he loses the thing that makes him human and becomes a beast instead.

I wondered aloud: would it be so bad to be an animal forever?

And Serri had answered that a man, born a man, was *intended* to be a man; the gods, seeing how unbalanced the scale had become, and why, would take their retribution.

And I had said: Our gods are not retributive; that is a thing of Asar-Suti, the Seker, the god of the netherworld.

And he had answered: *It is a thing of all gods, high and low, when their children go astray.*

Aye, a trade. The putting off of human form and the replacement with animal flesh and blood and bone. But where does the man-shape go when the man desires the guise

238

of an animal? Into the earth. We vouchsafe our human forms to the power of the earth, whose magic gives us the ability to borrow the animal shape for as long as need be. We are so rooted in the earth, we Cheysuli; so intricately *rooted*.

And I wondered what it was like to be Firstborn; to know myself foremost of all the children to come. To have power in abundance, more so than Ihlini or Cheysuli, and yet also to carry the seeds of self-destruction.

I thought of Ceinn and his fellow *a'saii*, harking back to the days of the Firstborn and desiring the power again. Their desire was not *wrong*, precisely – the prophecy, fulfilled, would give us that power again, with added stability gained from the bloodlines merged – but their method of attaining the power was. Could they not see they valued the Old Blood too much?

But zealots are too often blinded by the magnificence of their vision; while dedication can be an admirable, awesome thing, it can also be incredibly deadly. As it might have been for me.

Enough. The time for contemplation is done. 'You have taught me,' I told Serri, 'and I have learned. Now it is time to go.'

I have taught you a little, lir, and you have learned a little less. Be not so drunk upon the wine of accomplishment.

I laughed. 'Drunk, am I? No, I think not. I think I am afraid . . . and I think I am angry, too. But not so angry as to forget what *little* I have learned; I have no intention of challenging all the *a'saii*. Only to ask for what is owed.'

Nothing is owed a man, lir. Unless it is the service the man himself owes to the gods and the prophecy.

'Serri, you are sounding pompous. As for things owed – aye, a man owes service to the gods. But a man also owes respect to another man when that man has earned it.'

As you have earned it?

'I have. I have gained my *lir*.'

Serri sighed. *Not so much, I think, most of the time. But, then again, sometimes I think perhaps it is.*

'And *sometimes* we are in accord.' I bent, tugged a

239

charcoal-tipped ear, suggested silently we go on. It was time to go to Clankeep.

A long walk.

'Who speaks of walking when I can run?' I asked, and blurred into my *lir*-shape.

What joy it is to slip the bonds of human flesh and wear the shape of a wolf instead.

Gods, how we ran!

The guardsmen burst through the underbrush in a blaze of black and crimson. Horses beat the deadfall and brush aside, trampling it down even as the riders urged them forward. I saw the glitter of bared steel as the Mujharan Guard hacked their way through the forest.

Serri?

Taken by surprise — responding with the instincts of a wolf — I leaped over a fallen tree to hide behind a screen of limbs even as Serri leaped beside me.

Serri—

I am here. I am always here.

'*There!*' one of the guardsmen cried. 'Did you see him? *There* — the white wolf—'

'And a second wolf as well,' claimed another.

'But not white,' said a third. 'Gray or silver — I could not tell.'

And then Ian, with Tasha leaping beside him, rode out of the trees to join the others. 'We are not tracking *wolves*, captain. We are tracking the Prince of Homana.'

Screened behind a veil of leaves and heavy fern, I saw my brother rein in by the man who had spoken first; an older man, brown-haired, with a coif of mail shrouding most of his head.

'Aye,' the solder agreed grimly, 'but are we to ignore a white wolf when we see one? The plague—'

'We are not certain the plague is carried by wolves,' my brother said mildly. 'After all, how many white wolves can there be?'

White wolves? I *myself* was white when in *lir*-shape; it

240

had concerned me greatly at first, for albino coloring is undesirable, signifying weakness. Albino stock is always slain; I had seen it done to an entire litter of puppies born to one of the captains' hunting bitches when I was just a child. But Serri had assured me I was *white*, not albino. My eyes were blue, not red; my hearing was unaffected. There was nothing in me of weakness.

But – plague?

I heard one of the men mutter: 'There is a bounty on white wolves.'

'And would you risk the plague to bring one in for a copper penny?' the nearest rider asked.

'Silver,' the first retorted. 'For silver, I might do it.'

'Ride on,' my brother said. 'We are hunting a man, not a wolf; I think the Mujhar would pay more than a silver penny to the man who finds his heir.'

I heard someone mutter something about a body, and realized they thought me dead. I am not a man much taken with jokes of death, real or not; at once I took back my human form and stepped out in front of them all. 'But what coin for the heir if he finds himself?'

Hands went to swords and knives, then fell away. I heard startled exclamations, curses, murmurings of relief.

'*Rujho!* Gods, *rujho*, you are *alive!*' Ian swung a leg across his horse's neck and leaped out of the saddle, beating his way through the ferns and dangling creepers.

I met him half way and clasped his bare arms, grinning as I felt the gold beneath my fingers. 'Alive,' I agreed. 'Ian – truly I did not mean to worry everyone. But—'

'It is enough that you are alive,' he interrupted. 'I am not our *jehan* – let *him* give you the reprimands.'

I grimaced. Aye. No doubt he had more than one for me. 'Ian—'

'Gods, we thought you were dead! We found the remains of your horse – the gear—' He shook his head. '*Rujho.*'

'There was reason,' I told him. 'In a moment, I promise you will understand . . .' I went from him to the captain, still mounted, and caught his horse's rein. 'Captain, take

241

word at once to the Mujhar and the Queen that I am well – *quite* well – and tell them I will be home in a few more days. There is something else I must do first.'

'My lord.' He stared. As if I were a spirit risen from the dead; perhaps, in a way, I was. But I had no time for such speculation when my father and mother believed I was dead.

I frowned. 'Go at once, captain. Do not tarry any longer.'

He tightened his reins to turn, signaling to the others. But even as *they* turned, he hung back and drew in a deep breath. 'My lord – forgive me, but . . . for a moment, I thought you were Carillon.'

He was deadly serious. And he was old enough to be.

'You served him, did you not?' I pushed the horse's nose away from my face. 'You knew him, then.'

'I did not *know* him – not as General Rowan or others of higher rank; I was not a captain then. But aye, I served him.' He smiled. He was older than I had thought, but career soldiers are often an ageless lot, become old before their youth is spent. 'My lord, it has always been said of you; that you resemble the late Mujhar. But now it is doubly striking. Now that you wear a beard.'

I had forgotten the beard entirely. I would have to shave it off. But – not yet. For the moment, I found I did not mind the comparison.

Carillon never had a lir. I smiled. 'Go back, captain, and carry word the heir is alive. And I will be home soon.'

'My lord.' He spun his horse and was gone, leaving broken vines and bracken in his wake.

I turned to Ian. 'I swear, I intended no one to worry.'

'They did. We *all* did. Gods, *rujho*, what do you *expect*? I saw what your temper was before you disappeared; for all I knew, you had sought the death-ritual.'

I shrugged. 'I did.'

Ian's face was taut. 'Once we found the horse, I thought a beast had taken you.'

'One did,' I said grimly. 'A Cheysuli beast called Ceinn.'

'*Ceinn!*' Ian stared. 'What has Ceinn to do with this?'

'What has Ceinn to do with *anything*?' I asked bitterly.

'He very nearly had his heart's desire, *rujho* – Niall dead, and only Ian left to accept the Lion Throne.'

'*Rujho—*'

'It is the truth,' I told him gently. 'And when we see him, you may ask him.'

The first shock of my appearance had worn off. Now Ian looked more closely than he had before. I saw him begin to frown.

'The beard,' I told him.

'No – well, aye, but not *only* the beard. There is more. You are – harder.'

'Grown up,' I told him. 'Aye, a little.' I bent down on one knee to greet Tasha as she glided through the trampled fern. She purred, butting her head beneath my jaw in her customary greeting. 'Still the lovely girl,' I told her warmly. 'If Ian ever grows weary of you, you may come to me.'

Ian grunted eloquent dissent.

'Oh, aye, I know. You would not weary of her anymore than I would weary of Serri.' I grinned. 'Would you care to meet my *lir.*'

Before he could answer, I summoned Serri through the link. And when the wolf came, eyes slitted against the sunlight, I turned to watch my brother's reaction.

He stood incredibly still for a long moment. And then, slowly, he knelt down amidst the tangle of deadfall, brush and bracken. 'Oh wolf,' he whispered, '*leijhana tu'sai – leijhana tu'sai* for making my *rujholli* whole . . .' And put a shaking hand against Serri's lovely head.

A moment later, almost awkwardly, he rose and turned to face me squarely. 'How could I not have seen it? How could I not have known?'

'How *could* you have known, Ian? I did not know myself.'

He shook his head. 'I myself have been *lir*-sick. I know what the craving is, the emptiness that drives a boy out into the forest to find his *lir*. I have seen it before; I have *felt* it before . . . *rujho*, I should have known.'

'Well enough, I curse you for it.' I spoke the weakest one I could think of. 'Now, shall we go on to Clankeep?

243

I have business there with Ceinn and the other *a'saii*.'

He looked troubled. 'Perhaps the *a'saii* might wait.'

'Perhaps not,' I suggested. 'I would prefer to settle the question of my worthiness once and for all. I think now the clans might accept me willingly.'

'*They* might,' Ian agreed grimly, 'but what of the Homanan zealots? Your blood at last asserts itself; your magic is no longer "hidden." It will give them further cause for alarm and outcry.'

'But it will not give them the Lion.'

He caught my arm as I turned to go. 'It *might*,' he said flatly. 'Niall, have you forgotten how to count? You were in Erinn and Atvia for more than a year. And then, barely home again, you disappear for another month. You have given the Homanan rebels every opportunity to gain a foothold in this battle for the Lion.'

'Carillon's bastard,' I said grimly.

'*Aye*, Carillon's bastard.' He glared. 'Niall, he has begun to gather an army.'

'The *bastard?*' It was my turn to stare in disbelief. 'How can he do that?'

Ian shrugged. 'How not? He wants to take the throne.'

'But – our father is Mujhar.'

My brother sighed a little. 'The cost of growing up in a realm at peace is complacency, I see – or, perhaps, ignorance. Have you no comprehension of politics?'

'Do you?'

'Some,' he said shortly. 'Cheysuli or no, I understand what this means. As *you* should . . .' He shook his head. 'Even now he gathers an army as well as public opinion in his favor—'

'—and when he has enough of both, he can petition the Homanan Council for a change in the succession.' I nodded, pleased to see the surprise in Ian's eyes; he had expected me to understand nothing at all. 'And, of course, the Council, led by our father, will decline the petition—'

'—which will open the road to civil war,' Ian finished. 'It is no idle threat, Niall; no unlikely happenstance. And

244

you forget something else: the Council is made up of Homanans. All of them served under Carillon; our *jehan* has appointed no one, except for Rowan, and even *he* might prefer Carillon's son as opposed to Carillon's grandson.'

'*Rowan?*'

Ian shrugged. 'Perhaps. Who can say for certain? When you look at the petition closely, you will see there are possibilities for its approval. He *is* Carillon's son, and therefore a part of the prophecy.'

'But he is not Cheysuli.'

Ian did not smile. 'Let us say the Homanans are less impressed with the need to fulfill the prophecy than the Cheysuli are, Niall. But let us say also there are those on the Council who *do* desire to see the prophecy fulfilled . . . how better to lay proper claim to the Lion than to wed the claimant to a woman with the necessary bloodlines?'

'Cheysuli,' I blurted. 'But who would agree to such a thing? *I* am the rightful heir!'

'Gisella might,' he said evenly. 'With you dead, why should she decline the chance to be Queen of Homana? The title was promised her at birth the moment her gender was known.'

It shook me, as he intended it to. Aye, Gisella might. And the gods knew she had the proper blood; it was why *I* had had to wed her.

'Gisella!' I said bitterly. 'Gods, but I wish she had *died* in her mother's fall!'

'Niall!' Again, Ian caught my arm. 'Niall – by the gods, you *know*—'

'That she ensorcelled me? Aye, I know – I knew the moment I gained my *lir*. Whatever spell she wove must have had Ihlini origins, not Cheysuli. I remembered it all once I had linked with Serri.' And then all the pain and grief welled up again. 'Oh gods – Ian . . . *what they made me do*—'

'I know.' He caught me in a compassionate embrace. 'Oh *rujho*, I know . . . they made me watch as you lit the fire.'

'*All* of them,' I cried. 'All the eagles in the aerie—' I

245

hugged him as I never had before, never having required it so badly before. 'Gods, they made me give the order to slay Liam – Shea – *Deirdre*–'

He heard the change in my tone as I said her name; the pain, the anguish, the grief. 'Deirdre,' he echoed, mostly to himself, and it intensified the pain to hear him say her name.

Oh – gods – Deirdre—

I sank down to kneel in the trampled grass and ferns. 'They made me murder *Deirdre*.'

Silently he knelt down on one knee and caught the back of my neck with a single hand, forcing me to look into his face. '*Rujho*,' he said, 'if you loved her that much, I am truly sorry.'

It shocked me, even in my grief. '*You* speak of love?'

'Why not? It exists, no matter what the customs say. Do you think there is no love between our *jehan* and his *cheysula*?'

'*Is* there?'

'Of course. I see them differently, *rujho*, because they allow me to. Or–' smiling a little, he shrugged '—perhaps they do *not* allow it, and yet I see it. But be certain it exists.'

'There was Sorcha first. *Your* mother.'

'Aye. But she died many years ago, and there is no law that says a warrior may not love another woman.'

I saw Deirdre in the distance. 'Not I,' I said remotely. 'By the *gods*, not I . . . I will never love Gisella.'

After a moment, he sighed. 'No,' he agreed. 'No, I think not. I think no man will ever love Gisella . . . except, perhaps, her *jehan*.'

'Alaric?'

'Aye. You were too bedazzled by what the girl had done to you – but aye, Alaric loves her. And I think he does not forgive himself for being the man who made her the way she is.'

'Compassion for the enemy?'

'Compassion for the *jehan*.' He clasped my neck briefly and pulled my head against one shoulder in a brotherly

246

gesture of affection, then tousled my hair as he rose. 'Perhaps you have the right of it *rujho*. I think we should go to Clankeep.'

I stood up. 'After telling me we should not?'

'There is something left for you to do.' He grinned, and then he laughed aloud. 'After all these years, have you forgotten the *lir*-gold? It is your right to wear it, now.'

My right. I looked down at Serri, waiting beside my left leg. *Lir-gold, Serri!*

It is *your right to wear it.*

I laughed. 'Aye! It is!' I caught Ian's neck and hugged him awkwardly, nearly jerking him off his feet. 'Aye, *rujho*, let us go and get my gold!'

Frowning a little, he felt at the lobe that bore the cat-shaped earring. 'We have only one mount, and you are too heavy for my horse to carry both of us. There are times he wants nothing to do with *me*.'

'Who speaks of riding, *rujho*?' And as he watched bemusedly, I blurred into my *lir*-shape.

As I ran, I heard him curse, because he had a horse. Because, like me, he wanted to go in *lir*-shape.

And I laughed, because there is not a Cheysuli alive who prefers a horse when he has another form to serve him.

Gods – what freedom there is in lir-shape—

CHAPTER TEN

I took back my human form at the gates of Clankeep and turned to watch Ian come up on his stallion. Beside him ran Tasha, sleek and sinuous in the sunlight, chestnut coat burnished bronze. Serri warded my left leg, pressing a shoulder against my knee; through the *lir*-link, I sensed his insecurity.

A lir? I asked in surprise.

In my place, how would you *feel?* he returned. *Clankeep is a place of many people, many lir . . . and I have known none of them.*

It was amazing insight into how a *lir* felt about things. All too often it was easier simply to believe them above us all, closer to the gods, and yet Serri's defensive tone reminded me of myself when faced with a thing I could not fully understand.

Was it the same for Tasha?

Serri peered around my knee as the mountain cat came to join us. *The same for us all, when the link is first made. We are not so different from men.*

I would have disagreed, verbally or otherwise, but Ian jumped off his horse and called out in the Old Tongue for the warriors guarding the entrance to open the gates for us.

I waved away drifting dust, then stepped back as the wooden gates swung open. Once, I had been told, there was no need for gates to shut the Cheysuli in. But the time had come to shut the enemy *out*, and the gates had become traditional. More and more, Clankeep reminded me of Mujhara.

Ian, leading his fractious stallion, fell into step beside me.

'We will go to the *shar tahl*. It is for him to make the arrangements for the Ceremony of Honors.'

I felt a shiver of pride and excitement lift the flesh on my bones. *Ceremony of Honors* . . . and at last I would wear the gold.

But even as we walked away from the gates, one of the warriors called us back. 'The *shar tahl* is not at his pavilion, Ian. He is with Rylan, and the Mujhar is with them both.'

'*Jehan?*' Frowning, Ian glanced at me sharply. 'Something serious, I think . . . what else would bring him out of Mujhara *now?*'

I thought the emphasis strange, and said so. But Ian, walking fast enough to pull the stallion into a trot, merely shook his head. 'I will let him explain . . . no doubt he has much to say to you. *Rujho* – hurry.'

And so I stretched out my longer legs and moved ahead of him entirely, which afforded me the chance to tell *him* to hurry. But Ian was too preoccupied to be amused.

Serri?

I cannot say, lir. I am new to the politics of Homana.

Then what does Tasha tell you?

Only that her lir is very worried. It has to do with Ihlini, the plague, the bastard . . . there is much he concerns himself with. Much.

Grimly, I agreed. *Ian is better suited to politics than I. He understands them better.*

We wound our way through clustered pavilions, dodging the black-haired children who played some game in the trees and knee-high bracken, spilling out into the beaten earth of the walkways. Woodsmoke smudged the skyline; I smelled oak, ash, a hint of fresh-cut cedar. But mostly I smelled the meat. Bear, I thought; someone roasted a bear. And it made me think of Ceinn.

'Ian.' I intended to address the problem of the *a'saii*, but he was calling out to one of the running children; a boy, who swerved away from the game and trotted over.

'Blaine, will you do me the favor of taking my horse to my pavilion? I have business with the clan-leader.'

'Aye.' Blaine reached out for the reins. 'Did you know the Mujhar is here?'

'Aye. *Leijhana tu'sai.*' Relieved of his horse, Ian nearly ran.

Worried, Serri told me.

That I can see for myself.

'Here,' Ian stopped before a green pavilion bearing a silver-painted fox half hidden in its folds, hardly noticing as Tasha threw herself down on a rug beside the doorflap. Lorn was there as well, blinking sleepily in the sunlight. Golden Taj perched upon the ridgepole. And the brown fox curling next to Lorn moved over to offer Tasha room. I did not know his name, only that he was Rylan's *lir.*

So little time have I spent here that I know too little of my clan, I reflected guiltily. *It is no wonder there are warriors who prefer to see Ian in my place. I think Ian knows everyone.*

My brother scratched at the doorflap and identified himself. A moment later the clan-leader himself pulled the folds aside; when he saw me he opened his mouth to speak, then shut it sharply. I saw the flicker of surprise in his eyes; I was the last man he had expected to see, and in such a guise as this.

And then he smiled. 'You had best go straight to the Mujhar, Niall. He is with Isolde, walking the wall path.'

'Go,' Ian told me. 'It is important he knows you are alive. I will stay here with Rylan and the *shar tahl* to speak of the arrangements.'

'Wait!' I swung down the pouch from my shoulder and pulled wide the thong-snugged mouth. Reaching inside, I caught the heavy belt I had worn at the wedding and pulled most of it free of the pouch. 'Gold,' I told the clan-leader. 'Cheysuli gold, made by a master's hands. I would wear it again, but in the proper shapes.'

Rylan looked at the wolf who stood so close to my side. I saw him begin to smile.

Ian took the pouch and stuffed the belt inside it once again. '*Rujho,* go. I will see to the gold.' But even as I turned, he caught my upper arm. 'There is also *i'toshaa-*

250

ni,' he said seriously. 'All will be explained, but you must prepare yourself.'

'Will *you* be the one to explain it?'

He grinned, suddenly young again in the time before he had learned so much of responsibility, and the concern in his face was banished. 'If that is what you wish.'

'I wish.' And then I was gone, running after my father, with Serri running at my side.

The wall path . . . Rylan meant the footpath that edged the green-gray wall surrounding Clankeep. It reminded me a little of the sentry-walks atop the battlements of a castle, ringing the parapets, but there was nothing of castles about a Cheysuli Keep. Only a wall, curving through the trees like a granite serpent, lacking merlons and crenels, showing only an undulating line of piled stone, unmortared, but sealed with moss and ivy. The vines threaded their way up lichened flanks and clung tenaciously, setting roots and questing fingers into cracks and crevices. Trees from the other side sent reconnaissance patrols across over the wall and down, breathing Cheysuli security. Mistletoe clustered in crotches. Columbine twined the boughs and mantled the top of the wall.

I saw them ahead of me. Isolde sat on a shattered tree stump with head bowed and all her thick hair hanging around her face. I could not see her expression. Then she cried, I knew; one hand was pressed to her face and I could see how her shoulders trembled.

My father stood over her, one hand placed upon the crown of her head. And then the other; he squatted down so he could look into her face, and I saw how gently he smoothed the hair back behind her ears.

I could not hear what he said. But I saw 'Solde lean forward, hug him awkwardly, then rise and hasten away. My father remained squatting by the stump a moment, head bowed, as if he felt a measure of his daughter's pain. And then, as I slowed from a run to a walk, he rose and turned toward me.

And *recoiled*. 'Carillon—' he blurted.

I stopped walking. I stood in the middle of the footpath quite alone; Serri had paused along the way to make the acquaintance of a coney too far from his burrow. My first instinct was to resent the mistaken identity; once, I would have, but now I could not. I was too shocked. Though others often did, never had my father even remarked upon the resemblance. Never had he so much as likened me to my grandsire. *Certainly* he had never looked at me and called me by Carillon's name. Not even by mistake.

And it was not a mistake now. Because, for that instant, he believed I *was*.

It passed. It passed quickly. I saw the shock turn to startled recognition, and then the color was back in his face. But he did not move at once. We faced each other, my father and I, across an acre of ground that was only the length of a man.

'No,' I said finally. 'Niall.'

'I know.' His tone was odd. 'I – know. Forgive me.'

I shrugged. 'It is nothing.'

'It is *something*. Do you think I do not know?'

I started to answer, to dismiss the common mistake, but his raised hand silenced me. 'There are many things to be said, not the least of which is to note you are alive when everyone else believes you are *dead*, but even that will wait. There is something else. Something I should have told you long ago.'

He sighed. And then he sat down on the stump Isolde had vacated and sighed again, as if searching for the proper words. 'He was an incredibly courageous man. An incredibly *strong* man, and I do not speak of the physical, though there was that as well. No. I speak of spirit, of dedication, of the willingness to shoulder burdens far beyond the ken of most men.' He reached down, plucked a jointed blade of grass from the ground, began to tear it apart. 'After Tynstar stole his youth and gave him the disease, he lost much of his remarkable strength. But none of the dedication. None of the willingness to take on so many burdens. Because it was his duty. Because it was his *tahlmorra*.'

252

He looked up at me; I nodded and he went on. 'Every day I looked at him, seeing how he drove himself to make Homana whole — seeing how he drove himself to serve a prophecy not even of his people, and I wondered. I wondered: *how will I ever be able to take the Lion from this man? How will I ever be able to carry on the things he has begun?*

I stared at his hands. I watched him shred the stalk of grass, and then I saw him spill the pieces through his fingers as easily as now he spilled the self-doubts of his youth.

'He told me: *be Donal.* He told me: *you should not judge yourself by others.* But, of course, I did. Even as you do now.'

'I hate him,' I said hollowly. 'I hate a dead man, *jehan*.'

'But mostly you hate yourself.'

I sat down awkwardly in the middle of the footpath because I could no longer stand in the face of the realization. 'Aye,' I said on rushing breath. 'Oh, *jehan* . . . I have.'

'Be Niall,' he said gently. 'Do not judge yourself by others.'

I laughed. I heard the sound cut through arching boughs like a scythe through summer grass. 'And when Carillon told you that, *jehan*, did it mean anything to you?'

My father did not smile. 'It meant something that he said it.'

Abashed, I looked at the dirt between my deerhide boots. 'Aye. Aye, *jehan*, it does.'

'He left me a legacy. He left me the knowledge I had nothing to be ashamed of; that I would do the best I could do, no matter what the odds. And I have.' He smiled a little. 'Oh, aye. There are people who will disagree; people who claim I serve only my own self-interests, but I try to serve Homana. Homana and the Cheysuli.' I saw the smile begin to widen. 'I think only as I watch my own children wrestle with the power of adulthood do I come to understand that I am not a failure. That I am not a bad Mujhar. And the day will dawn when *you* come to know the same about the Mujhar who follows Donal.'

253

'The Lion of Homana.' I shook my head. 'I think what disturbs me most, now that I begin to see it more clearly, is that they have been so unfair to you. Always it is Carillon. Even from my *jehana*. It is so easy for everyone to see *him* when they look at me. And yet − they overlook that it was *you* who sired me. It is thoughts and memories of *you* I should invoke.'

He laughed a little, showing the face I knew better as Ian's, albeit older than my brother's. 'Aye. It brightens a man's pride to hear the son compared to him − when the comparison is *favorable*.' He nodded. 'But I think the dye has been set, Niall. It is Ian who reminds them of me, and you who reminds them of Carillon.'

I grimaced wryly. 'Well, I think it no longer matters. I think—'

'—*I* think it is time we spoke of business and set aside self-examinations.' He rose, stepped to me and caught my arm as I raised it. 'I will not belabor it, Niall. You should never have left as you did.'

I was up, brushing at my breeches. 'No, but—'

'I want no excuses; what is done is done. But I expect you to accept more responsibility in the future.'

'*Jehan*—'

'We are at war, Niall,' he said plainly, as if I could not understand. 'Strahan raises an army in Solinde. And so does the bastard here.' He sighed and scraped the hair back from his face, leaving it bare and bleak. 'Everyone thought you dead. And so I had to contend with a Homanan Council who bestirred themselves to consider the possibility of naming the bastard to your place − they would sooner have *Carillon's* bastard in place of mine − and a *Cheysuli* Clan Council who spoke of Ian as your successor, citing the prophecy.' He shut his eyes a moment. 'Gods, I feel like I have been juggling unbalanced knives . . . Aislinn sick to death with worry − this plague that begins to spread − trying to placate hostile councils − and, of course, there is Strahan. Gods, there is always Strahan.'

Abruptly he turned away, showing only his back to me.

His hands were on his hips, head bowed; he looked more disgusted than anything else, but I thought perhaps he was only weary. Weary of all the burdens Carillon had bequeathed to him.

And that he will bequeath to me.

'Niall.' He turned back. 'There is yet another thing. Perhaps the *most* important – the gods know it turned the councils upside down.' He smiled. 'Suddenly they could no longer speak of which bastard would inherit, but who to name as regent for the Prince of Homana's heir.'

'The Prince of Homana's – *heir?*' I stared. 'Gisella bore the *child?* A *son?*'

'Two,' he said succinctly.

'*Two?*'

'Both boys.' He grinned. 'And so I am made a grandsire.'

'Both boys,' I echoed in a whisper. 'By the gods, I have an *heir*.' And then I looked at him more sharply. 'Gisella?'

His grin faded. 'She is well . . . but no different from before.'

'No,' I agreed grimly, 'it is a permanent affliction.' And then, unable to dwell on Gisella in the face of such news, I began to smile again. 'Two boys! How will I ever tell them apart?'

'It is possible even now. But I will let you see for yourself.' He reached out and clasped my arm. 'No more delays, Niall. We must go back to Homana-Mujhar.'

'No – *jehan* . . .' I thought of the two boys at Homana-Mujhar, and the choice suddenly became much harder. *Gods, what do I do?*

'No?' my father asked in amazement. '*No?*'

Torn, I tried to pull away. 'I – cannot. Not yet.'

'*Cannot.*' He swung me around to face him. 'Niall, my patience is wearing thin.'

'*So was mine!*' I cried. 'Why do you think I left Mujhara? Because I *could not wait* any longer!'

'Niall, I cannot express to you how precarious is our position at the moment . . . nor my surprise that you can so easily dismiss two newborn sons.'

255

'I do not *dismiss*,' I said curtly. 'Gods, *jehan*, I could not. But – I need to stay. I must. There is a thing I have to do—'

'What *thing* is more important than the security of your claim to the Lion Throne?' He was angry, very angry; I wanted to look away and could not. 'Do you understand what I have told you, Niall? As Strahan assembles another army in Solinde, the bastard assembles one *here*. There is plague all through the north, creeping down even now from the Wastes into the rest of Homana. And you have the audacity to tell me you *cannot come to Homana-Mujhar?*'

My answer was to summon Serri to me. I heard his response within the link, and even as I turned the wolf came running, *running* to meet me. His ears lay back along his skull and his mouth gaped open, allowing the tongue to loll. The black-smudged tail stood out behind him like a pennon in the wind. How he ran, my magnificent *lir*; how he ran to answer my call.

I dropped to one knee and caught him in my arms. He snugged his muzzle against my neck and muttered into my flesh and beard, forgoing the link to express his feelings aloud. And then I twisted my head to look up at my astonished father. 'I left because I had to. I had to find my *lir*. And now I stay because I have to, so I can be fully acknowledged a warrior – a *Cheysuli* – before my clan.'

He said nothing. He did not have to. All the world was in his eyes.

'*Jehan*—'

'Three days,' he said quietly. '*I'toshaa-ni*, for the cleansing, and then the Ceremony of Honors.' He swallowed heavily. 'For this, I can give you three days. I wish I could give you three years.'

And then he walked away.

But not before I saw the tears of pride and thankfulness in his eyes.

CHAPTER ELEVEN

I'toshaa-ni.

It is a mystery to most men because the Cheysuli keep it that way, desiring no profanation. It has always been a mystery to me, not because I am not Cheysuli, but because it is a highly personal thing, an expression of the intense need for the cleansing of flesh, spirit, mind, heart and soul.

For Ian, the need had come upon him twice: once, during the rituals associated with the Ceremony of Honors; again, when he had been so soiled by Lillith's Ihlini sorcery. He did not speak of his experiences to me, saying only that I would be born out of smoke and sweat and pain to be a man again, new-made, as no other man can be. Certainly not a Homanan.

At dawn, I went out of Clankeep into the forest. There I painstakingly built a shelter out of saplings, binding them with vines and sealing the cracks with leaves until the shelter was a hummock against the ground, closed to the world save for the tiny entrance.

I took stones from the ground and built a firecairn in the center of the shelter. And when it was made I lighted a fire and fed it with herbs the *shar tahl* had given me. The smoke made me cough. The stench made my eyes water.

I shaved. Bare-faced, I stripped. My clothing I left in a pile outside the door; naked, *lirless*, alone, I sat down beside the fire and let the smoke form a shroud around my body.

I waited.

When at last the sweat ran down my flesh and the tears ran out of my eyes, I began to see a reason for the ritual of cleansing. For three days I would fast, until there was nothing left in my body; until the sweat cleansed the impurities from my flesh; until I was a new-made man, lacking the soil of the former life.

I dreamed of Carillon. Though I remained in the shelter I had built, a part of me broke free. It left behind the shelter and the fasting and the smoke and went elsewhere, to Homana-Mujhar; to the Great Hall, where I sat in the Lion Throne. I stared down the length of the empty hall and saw it was not empty at all; that a man approached, and I knew him.

Carillon.

I knew it was him, though I had never seen him. Because he looked like me.

He was — old. Though he stood rigidly straight, I saw how his shoulders hunched a little; how his spine seemed to pain him. And I saw the hands, so twisted, so wracked, so ruined. But mostly I saw the spirit of the man, because its intensity was such that it set the hall ablaze.

'Grandsire,' I said. 'You are dead. How can you come to me?'

'I come to you because I am a part of you, as I am a part of your mother, your sons, the children yet to come. I am in them as much as I am in you, and so it will ever be. You can rid yourself of me no more than you can shed your flesh and become another man.'

'Not another man,' I agreed, 'but an animal. I am Cheysuli, grandsire.'

'And in animal form, do you become someone who is not Niall?'

I frowned at him. 'No, grandsire — of course not. I am still myself.'

He smiled. And then the shadows swallowed him, and I was back in my smoky shelter.

On the second day, naked, *lirless*, alone, with only a snare and a knife to my name, I caught and slew a young ruddy-colored wolf. He fought his death. He fought me. He left weals upon my flesh and anguish in my heart, thinking of

258

Serri, but I slew him. And then I bathed in the blood and ate the still-warm heart, to vanquish that portion of myself that might be suborned by the freedom of the *lir*-shape.

I dreamed of Ceinn. He stood before me as I sat upon the Lion Throne of Homana and told me to get out of it; that I was unworthy because I lacked the lir-gifts; because I was not a proper Cheysuli. He told me I was forgotten by the gods and therefore no part of the prophecy; my abdication would be a blessing to all the folk of Homana, Cheysuli and Homanan alike.

I listened. I waited. And when he was done reciting the things the shar tahls had told him since birth, even as they had told me, I rose and stepped away from the Lion, relinquishing the throne. I gave it over to Ceinn willingly. And as he stepped forward, intent on climbing it himself, I saw the wooden lion's head move.

The jaws widened, waiting. I tried to cry out, to tell him no; to say the Lion would swallow him – but he did not hear; he did not choose to hear. And so as Ceinn sat down upon the Lion Throne of Homana, the gaping jaws closed over his skull and crushed it.

On the third day I bathed in an isolated pool and washed the blood from my flesh. With handfuls of sand I scoured the grime and smoke-stench from my body, raising blood into the wolf-wounds, and then I washed it off with clean, cool water. And at last, clean within and without, I put on the fresh leathers someone had left outside the shelter and went back to Clankeep a new-made man, born again of *i'toshaa-ni*.

In the center of the clan pavilion, I knelt on the hide of a spotted mountain cat. Around me sat ranks of warriors and their women – not all of them, because the pavilion was no longer large enough – but those members of Clan Council, the ruling body of the Cheysuli.

Once, it was believed there was only a single clan

remaining in all of Homana, because of Shaine's *qu'mahlin*. My royal Homanan ancestor had done his best to rid the realm of every Cheysuli by ordering all of them slain. The *qu'mahlin* had failed, thank the gods, but only after thirty years of methodical elimination. And mostly because Carillon had stopped it once he had reclaimed the Lion Throne from Bellam of Solinde. In those days an entire clan would have filled only half of the pavilion; now most of the people had to remain outside.

It was evening. Only the fire in the cairn before me lighted the pavilion, throwing odd illumination over the faces of the warriors and the women. Looking at them, I thought of the days of the Firstborn, when all men and women of the clans claimed the ability to assume *lir*-shape. But because we had become so blood-bred, so isolated in our insularity and arrogance, the gifts had begun to weaken. Only through the fulfillment of the prophecy would we reclaim the power that we once took for granted.

So many faces. Nearly all of them characteristically dark, angular, polished bronze by the sun of Homana. Black hair, yellow eyes, so much gold in ears, at throats, on arms and hips and wrists. So much *strength*; why was it the people of other realms desired to break that strength?

Why did the *Homanans* desire it?

Not all, Serri said. *Many, still, because it is natural for the earth magic to frighten those who do not claim it, do not know it . . . but not all. Carillon began the change in common opinion. Donal furthers it. And you will further it even more.*

He lay beside me on the edges of the pelt. I moved hand from lap and buried it in Serri's lush pelt. In so short a time he had become my world, my other *self*; I wondered how I had managed to live before we had found one another. How I had functioned without my *lir*.

Much of the ceremony had already been concluded. But there remained the most important part: the bestowing of the *lir*-gold to signify I was a warrior of the clan, a man grown, a Cheysuli in place of a *lirless*, soulless body.

Rylan himself sat before me on the other side of the cairn.

The firelight made his face a mask of black and bronze, stark in the harsh shadows, but smiling. And as he smiled, he spoke.

'*Before all the old gods of the Cheysuli, I as clan-leader bear witness that you have sought and found a lir according to the customs of our people. That you and the lir have linked as a lir and warrior must link, to make the magic whole. And I bear witness that through this link the lir has accepted you in heart and soul and mind as well as spirit, as you have accepted him.*'

He waited. I inclined my head in affirmation.

'*The lir-bond is for life. While you live, the lir lives. But should your life be taken from you within the natural lifespan of the lir, regardless of the manner, the lir shall be released from the bond to return to the freedom of the forests, no longer bound to the body that once was a Cheysuli warrior.*'

Again, I nodded.

'*Should the lir die in battle or in sickness or by other unknown causes, you will be made soulless, empty, unwhole, and you will give up your name as a Cheysuli warrior to seek an ending however you may find it, in the death-ritual of the clan, unarmed and alone among the beasts of the forests.*'

I had tasted *lirlessness* once already. I did not hesitate to accept the consequences.

Rylan's eyes held mine steadily. 'For you, I must be very clear: the *lir*-bond requires payment, even from those who rule. You will be two men, warrior and Mujhar, but the bond will constrain you still. Should Serri die, my lord, you will be required to renounce the Lion and go alone among the beasts.'

I thought suddenly of Duncan, my other grandsire, who had not ruled because he had helped to win Carillon the Lion. He had been clan-leader even as Rylan was, required to perform the rituals of the Ceremony of Honors as Rylan did now for me. Aye, I thought of Duncan, my long-dead grandsire, who had lost a *lir* and lost his life, giving it over willingly even though he also gave up the leadership of the Cheysuli.

And I thought of my father, who, too young, had accepted

261

the responsibilities of the *lir*-bond before he had known he would be Mujhar.

And I thought: *It is not a thing done lightly.*

No, Serri agreed, *and no man will force you to it.*

I drew in a deep breath and nodded to Rylan, '*y'Ja'hai,* clan-leader. *Ja'hai-na.*' I nodded again. 'I accept. The price is willingly accepted.'

'*Ru'shalla-tu,*' he said quietly. *May it be so.* Quietly he moved aside and made way for the *shar tahl*, who carried a roll of bleached-white deerskin in his arms. He was Arlen; not young, not old, but the most high of all the clan members, being a man totally dedicated to serving the prophecy and the histories of the Cheysuli.

Arlen knelt before the cairn and carefully unrolled the deerskin, making certain it did not wrinkle or tangle itself. Hands smoothed it efficiently; he must have done this so many times, *too* many times, and yet he made no indication he was weary of the task. He merely did it. And by doing it, he made me a place in my clan.

'*One day a man of all blood shall unite, in peace, four warring realms and two magic races.*' A finger touched the rune-signs painted on the supple hide. 'Already we begin to approach completion, the fulfillment of the prophecy of the Firstborn, *so:*' He touched a faded green rune. 'Here is *Hale,* liege man to Shaine the Mujhar, and *jehan* to a daughter got on Shaine's Homanan daughter.'

Arlen glanced briefly at me, as if to be certain I followed him; I did. I could not take my eyes from the finger that so carefully showed me my heritage.

He touched another rune, this one red, of a different shape. 'Here is *Duncan,* born of the line of the Old Mujhars, in the days before we gave the Lion to the Homanans. Here is *Carillon,* born of Shaine's brother, *harani* to the Mujhar, and who took back the Lion from the enemy.' The finger moved yet again. 'And here is *Alix,* daughter of Hale and Lindir, who bore a son to Duncan: *Donal,* who accepted the Lion from Carillon, and who sired a son on Carillon's half-Solindish daughter.'

The finger stopped on a bright blue rune. There were none under it, only a blank space waiting for the name of my newborn sons.

But Arlen looked at me. 'And here is *Niall*, son of Aislinn and Donal, who shall inherit the Lion from his *jehan* and name a son to inherit it from him.'

I smiled. 'Brennan,' I told the *shar tahl*. 'There is a son already born; I shall call him Brennan. And behind him, Hart. Liege man if he chooses; *rujholli*, companion, *kinspirit* – they were born in a single labor of Gisella of Atvia, daughter to Alaric and Donal's *rujholla*, Bronwyn.'

Arlen inclined his head briefly to acknowledge the furthering of the succession, then re-rolled the deerskin and moved back to his place in the front ranking of warriors and women.

It was Rylan's turn once more. 'There is now the bestowing of the *lir*-gold upon the newborn warrior. It is customary for the warrior to choose a *shu'maii*, a sponsor, from among his fellow warriors. It is the task of the *shu'maii* to pierce the lobe and place the earring in it, as well as placing the bands upon the arms. It is a mark of respect from warrior to *shu'maii* to ask; it is acknowledgment from *shu'maii* to warrior before Clan Council and others of the clan that he accepts the responsibilities of a bond almost as binding as that of the *lir* or a liege man. That he honors the newborn warrior with all the honor of his heritage as a Cheysuli born of the clan and all its traditions.'

He said nothing more, having explained the final task that faced me. Like the others, he waited for my decision.

I looked at the empty place in the ranks ringing me. Empty because my father had returned to Homana-Mujhar, unable to remain even for my Ceremony of Honors. I would have named him as my *shu'maii*, naming his name with great pride, but he had gone, and I could not say the name of a man who did not exist in the moment of my birth.

I looked at my brother, sitting beside the empty place, and saw how he waited with eyes downcast. He was the

263

natural choice, I knew, and certainly the most appropriate. But Ian was already pledged to me.

And so I looked at Rylan. 'I name the name of Ceinn.'

I heard a woman gasp: Isolde. And I heard the low-voiced murmurings of the men.

It was to my brother I looked first, to see if I had hurt him. Perhaps I had, but he did not show it to me. He merely smiled a tiny smile, as if I had done a thing that surprised him with its shrewdness but also met with belated understanding. He smiled, did my brother, and I knew I had chosen well.

'Ceinn,' Rylan said. 'Do you accept the honor offered?'

His face was a mask to me, but his eyes were not. From out of the mask they stared, hard and cold and *yellow*, and in their depths blazed the flame of fanaticism. Oh, aye, he would accept. In the face of his dedication to clan and custom, he could not do otherwise.

'*Ja'hai-na*,' he said only, and rose to make his way through the others to the cairn. He sat down on my right side, Serri was at my left.

Rylan accepted the leather pouch offered him by another warrior. From it he took a silver awl and handed it to Ceinn. Firelight glinted off the silver. The point was ground quite fine, but I knew it would hurt regardless.

I pushed the hair behind my ear and faced Ceinn, kneeling. Saying nothing, he pinched and pulled down my left earlobe, stretching it thin, then pressed the awl against the flesh. I set my teeth; the point slid in, beyond . . . I felt Ceinn twist it into my flesh, until I heard the pop of completion. He withdrew the awl and put out his hand; into his palm Rylan set the golden earring.

Wolf-shaped, of course; a small wolf born of incredible skill, showing face and paws and tail. From its back rose the curving prong. Ceinn shut his fingers on the wolf and pushed the prong through the hole he had made; hooked the tip into the loop with a deft twist. I heard the tiny snap and knew the thing was done.

My earlobe stung. The weight of the gold set up an ache

I found bearable regardless of its irritation: I was very nearly a warrior.

Rylan set the heavy armbands into Ceinn's waiting hands. The mask was shown me again; such a hard, cold mask, expressing bleak acknowledgment that what he did made a pledge that could not be broken; his time with the *a'saii* was done, even if he preferred otherwise. He would not, *could* not break the bond, or forswear the traditions that bound him of all men so very tightly.

The armbands clinked together as Ceinn brought them closer to me. Such massive, magnificent things, full of runes braided one into the other, tangling cheek-by-jowl all the way around at top and bottom edge. And in the center of each, flowing around the curves, was the shape of a running wolf, fluid in the metal, as if he would leap out of the gold and into the midst of us all.

Gods – how beautiful is my lir—

Ceinn slipped one over my left wrist and slid it up until it went over my elbow and snugged against muscles. Then the other on my right, holding my wrist as he settled the band into place. Again, he snugged it, and I saw the rich flash of his own gold in the firelight as he made me a man before the others.

'*Leijhana tu'sai*,' I said quietly. And I meant it.

His lips thinned. '*Cheysuli i'halla shansu.*' But I knew the *last* thing he intended me was Cheysuli peace.

And yet he could do nothing about it.

I swallowed heavily. I had no wish to show what I felt to the others. And yet I could not help but show it to Ceinn; he was too close, too intent. He could not help but see how moved I was. And I saw him begin to frown.

Rylan's voice broke the moment, and then made it more poignant yet. '*Ja'hai-na*,' he said simply. 'By the clan, by the gods, by the *lir*, the warrior is accepted.'

It was for Ceinn, the *shu'maii*, to begin the welcomings. I waited, and when he rose he also pulled me up, clasping my arms above the *lir*-bands to give me Cheysuli welcome.

At my right he stood, keeping himself in silence as the

others filed by. Rylan. Arlen. Others I could not name. And Isolde, reaching up to kiss my cheek even as I bent down to hug her in a blatant display of affection. A sidelong look at Ceinn showed a rigid, unyielding face as my sister went by him without a word, and then I saw the blaze of grief in his eyes.

Lastly, Ian, who forgot proprieties as quickly as our sister; who embraced me twice and said very little because he could not manage it. '*Rujho,*' he said only, 'you make a man proud to be Cheysuli.'

And then he and the others were gone, save for Serri, Ceinn and a handful of the *a'saii.*

They did not come to me. I knew I had taken their weapon from them because my *lirlessness* was banished, and yet they did not come to me. As one they looked at Ceinn, and as one they turned their backs on him and exited through the back flap. In their silence was eloquence.

He took a single step forward, as if he meant to go after them, to say a word or two; to ask them what they meant. But he knew very well what they meant. He of all people.

He stopped. He did not go after them. He did not ask. He stared blindly into the emptiness of the pavilion.

'*Shu'maii,*' I said quietly, 'when a man cannot make a friend of an enemy, he takes the enemy from his friends.'

After a moment, he shrugged. 'Why not?' he asked dully. 'You have already taken his *cheysula.*'

''Solde does as 'Solde chooses; surely *you* understand that better than most. But I would not have it said she cannot change her mind.'

He looked at me sharply. 'Would she?'

I shrugged. 'I cannot speak for her – not now; not anymore than I did when she publicly renounced you. But she renounced you because you were *a'saii* . . . and now you are *shu'maii.*'

He expelled a ragged breath of realization. 'Gods – do you think—?' But he did not finish. He stared at me in rigid silence, unable to voice his hope for the intensity of his

266

emotion; the magnitude of his fear that, once spoken, the hope would be taken away.

'I think I took an enemy from his friends, and gave a friend back to his *cheysula*.'

As well as saving him from the Lion.

A muscle leaped in his cheek. 'Do you think it is so easy to fashion friends out of enemies? I *believed* in what I did. And if you were *still* a *lirless* man, I would do it all again!'

'I know that,' I said gently. 'A man can also be measured by the dedication of his spirit. Aye, you believed. Too much, perhaps, in the old traditions, but it was a true belief. I cannot condone it. You tried to slay me, but I can comprehend it. Can you not see it, Ceinn? It takes men like you to restore a blighted race. Men like you . . . Carillon . . . my *jehan*. And I will need every one I can find.'

'For what?' he asked sharply. 'What do you intend to do?'

'Rule Homana,' I told him. 'Hold the Lion, once my *jehan* is dead.'

He looked at Serri. He looked at the gold he himself had given me in my Ceremony of Honors. And then he turned sharply as if to go; to leave me alone in the tent with my *lir* and my memories.

But he swung back. '*Ru'shalla-tu*,' he said flatly, and then he was gone from the pavilion.

I smiled. And then I laughed aloud.

May it be so? Serri's tone told me he did not understand my amusement.

'Aye,' I agreed, still laughing. 'But – from *Ceinn*.'

CHAPTER TWELVE

My sons, I said to Serri in amazement. Slowly I shook my head. *Of this imperfect vessel are magnificent children made.*

Given time. Serri agreed as he leaned against my knee; the posture was becoming habitual whenever I stood still. *At this age, there is not much magnificent about them except a magnificent odor.* His lips peeled back from his teeth; Serri sneezed. And then he went away from me to flop down upon a rug near the fireplace.

Laughing softly, I hooked hands over the side of the big oak-and-ivory cradle and leaned down to look more closely at the contents. Two babies, swaddled in costly linens and mostly hidden beneath a white silken coverlet stitched with crimson rampant lions. That I had fathered *one* was a miracle in itself; two was utterly incomprehensible to me.

Carefully I smoothed the coverlet and felt the lumpy bodies beneath. 'You will be warriors of the clan,' I told them quietly, 'as well as princes of Homana. And one of you will be Mujhar.'

That one, Serri told me, even from the rug. *I can feel it in him as you touch him . . . he is firstborn – he will be Mujhar.*

'And the other?'

Prince of Solinde?

I grunted. 'Solinde prepares for war yet *again* . . . I begin to think no Mujhar of Homana will ever hold that realm in peace. At least – not a long-lasting peace.'

Prince of Atvia?

I nodded thoughtfully. 'Possibly. With no male heirs, Alaric has only Gisella's son to look to for a man to succeed him as Lord of Atvia.'

Then again, there is Erinn.

I felt the old pain flare up in my belly. The grief renewed itself. 'No, *lir* . . . not Erinn. I think the Erinn I knew is gone forever.'

Again I smoothed the silken coverlet, trying not to recall how *I* had lighted the beacon-fire that signaled Alaric's assassins to begin. Two small heads I touched, very close together. Both soft with fine black fuzz; black-haired were my sons, my half-Cheysuli sons.

One of them stirred beneath my hand. And almost instantly, the other one did as well. Some form of communication? They were children of the same birth . . . who could say what the strength of their link would be?

'Mujhar,' I whispered to the one Serri had named the firstborn. 'Such a heavy title for such a little boy.'

Face down, he turned his head even as his brother did. They opened their eyes and peered at one another uncertainly, as if to make sure the other one was present. And I saw, looking at their eyes, why my father had said one could tell them apart already. The older, Brennan, had the brass-brown eyes that would turn Cheysuli yellow. Hart, the younger, had eyes the color of the sky on a summer day. Very like my own.

I smiled and cupped a palm over each of the black-fuzzed heads. '*Cheysuli i'halla shansu*, little warriors. And may your lives be long and full.'

Lir— Serri said sharply, and I swung around with a hand to my borrowed knife.

But it was only Gisella – no, not *only*. Never would I attach that word to her name again.

She stood in the open doorway and stared at me sorrowfully. 'You went away from me,' she accused. 'On our wedding night.'

I felt a vague sense of guilt; aye, I had left her on our wedding night, when a man and woman should spend the time together. Even heavy with the babies, she was due common courtesy from her husband.

And then the guilt evaporated; what I felt was anger.

Anger and *helplessness*, because she was no more responsible for her actions than were our two small sons, soiling nightwrappings in their sleep.

'I went away,' I told her, 'because I had to go.'

She trailed a wine-red bedrobe across the floor as she wandered into the chamber. Beneath the robe, which hung mostly off her shoulders, was a linen nightshift. Her feet were bare upon the cold stone floor.

'You went away from me.' She was a heartbroken child, repeating the thing that had hurt her. 'You left me all *alone*.'

'Gisella—'

But her face brightened abruptly. 'Have you seen my babies? Have you seen my sons?'

'*Our* sons, Gisella,' I said gently, even as she hastened across the floor to bend over the cradle. 'They are mine as well as yours.'

'*Babies*,' she whispered, and reached down to tuck the coverlet more closely around their bodies.

'Gisella.' I caught a shoulder and pulled her around to face me. 'Gisella – do you recall the night upon the cliffs, when your father told me to light the beacon-fire?'

She stared at me blankly. Her hair was bound back from her face in a single loosely woven braid. It hung over a shoulder and dangled against her hips. Gone was the bulk and weight of pregnancy. Her face was reminiscent of Isolde's, I thought, but that was not unusual as many Cheysuli resemble one another. She had regained her grace and allure. In sheer cream linen and wine-colored velvet she was a woman who would make another man think of bed, but *I* could not think of bedding her without also thinking of Deirdre.

'Gisella, do you remember?'

'You mean – in Atvia.'

'Aye. In Atvia.'

Abruptly she twisted away from me, pulling out from under my hand. Her back was to me, but I saw her drag the bedrobe up to cover her shoulders. She pulled the velvet very tight around her body, nails scraping rigidly at the nap, and I saw the silver tips. They reminded me of Lillith.

'Gisella—'

'You think of *her* instead of me.' I saw how the nails dug into the velvet, as if she meant to hurt herself. 'You think of her instead of *me*.'

I shut my eyes a moment; when I opened them, Gisella was facing me. I saw the tears in her eyes. I saw how the slender fingers worked their way into the weave of her braid, tugging, *tugging*, as if she intended to jerk the hair out of her scalp.

'Did you know?' I asked her. 'Did you know what lighting the fire would begin?'

'I wanted you for *me!*'

'By the gods, Gisella, *did you know what it would begin?*'

She pressed the braid against her mouth and I saw the white teeth bite in. Gods, how she trembled. 'It was so pretty,' she whispered over the shining hair. 'The fire was so bright . . . it lit up the dragon's smile and I could see all his teeth.'

'Do you know what you have done?'

'But it was *pretty*, Niall!' Suddenly she was angry. She jerked the braid from her mouth. 'I like to see pretty things. I *want* to see pretty things.'

I caught her arms before she could finish. '*Do you know what you have done?*'

'Aye!' she shouted back. 'I have borne you *boys* – the Lion is secure!'

I heard the rising wail issuing from the cradle. In a moment another joined it; we had disturbed their sleep.

I have borne you boys – the Lion is secure.

That much of things she understood well enough. She had secured her *own* place as well as the future of Homana. What manner of man would I be if I set aside the woman who had borne me two healthy sons at a single lying-in?

In that moment, looking at her, I knew a futile anger of the sort that might drive me to murder. What would it take to place my hands around her throat and squeeze, shutting off her breath forever? She was responsible for altering my

consciousness, for making me a man with no wits or will
. . . a man capable of giving the woman he loves over to
the hands of an assassin. And yet I knew Gisella could not
be held accountable. Not – entirely.

All the anger spilled out of my body. Deep despair was
left in its place. 'Oh – gods – *Gisella* . . . will you never
understand?' I turned from her and locked my hands onto
the side of the cradle, staring blindly at my sons. 'You will
never understand.'

'The babies are *crying*, Niall. We have made the babies
cry—' And she was instantly at my side, bending over the
side of the cradle to make certain of their welfare.

She sang. Some little atonal melody I had never heard,
and which I found utterly unbearable. How carefully she
tended the babies. How solicitous she was. How concerned
she was for their welfare, even as she ignored – or forgot
– how she had made it possible for Deirdre to be slain.

She sang. And as she sang I backed away. And when I
reached the door I turned and lurched out of the chamber
even as Serri lunged up from the rug.

I did not get far. Even as I shut the door with a solid bang,
I fell against the wall, pressing my brow against it. Gods,
if I could only shut away the memories and guilt as easily
as I shut away the sound of crying babies; the sight of their
half-witted mother. *If only* . . .

If only I could go back to Erinn and repeat my captivity
there, because then all the eagles would be alive.

'Niall.'

I spun, feeling Serri's warmth pressed against my leg. And
saw my mother approaching from a turn in the corridor.

'Oh, Niall,' she said in sudden concern, 'what has put
you in such pain?'

'Need you ask? The woman I have married.' I shook my
head. 'I wish I might have listened to you when you gave
me the chance to gainsay the wedding.'

'Well, you did not, but it was not within your power.' Her
eyes were on the wolf. 'Donal told me of your *lir* . . . and
how it was Gisella's sorcery that blinded you to the truth.'

272

'*Jehana*,' I saw the minute twitch of surprise as I addressed her in the Old Tongue. '*Jehana*, I think there is a thing we must discuss, you and I . . . will you give me the time?'

'Gladly,' she said. 'We have had so little of it to share this past year.' She placed a cool hand upon my wrist. 'You know I would give you anything that you desire.'

Inwardly I grimaced; *but will you give me my freedom when I ask you for it now?*

I escorted her to her favorite private solar, a round room in one of the corner towers of the palace, with wide, glassy casements and whitewashed walls. She had six women to attend her whenever she desired it; three were in the solar now, but before I could request privacy my mother asked them to leave. And so we were left alone, save for Serri, and I found myself suddenly reticent to speak of the thing at all.

My mother smiled. She turned from me and went to one of the casements, staring out as if to give me time to assemble the words I wished to say. I looked at her back and saw the firm arch of her spine beneath the tight-fitting glove of the green-dyed linen gown. The sleeves also were very fitted, snugged against her arms from shoulders to midway down her hands. All the glorious red-gold hair was bound up in a green-wrapped loop of braid at the back of her slender neck.

Still so slim, my mother; still so youthful looking.

I drew in a deep breath, held it a moment, let it out carefully. 'I am not Carillon.'

The spine was rigid. She spun, bracing herself with hands thrust against the casement sill. '*What?*'

'I am not Carillon.'

I saw a mixture of emotions in her face: astonishment, perplexity, a trace of apprehension. As if she began to understand precisely what I meant to say. 'Niall—'

'And if you mean to tell me so emphatically that of *course* I am not, I wish you would gainsay it. Mother—' I stopped. '*Jehana*, too many times in the past you have made me to

273

feel inferior. You did not *mean* it, I know. If anything, you meant to bolster what manhood I claim by comparing me to *him*, but it has always made me feel the reverse. Incapable. Incompetent. A shadow of the man your father was.' I spread my hands. 'I have his height, his weight, his color – certainly a legacy I might respect . . . were I allowed to respect myself.'

Still she braced herself against the sill, head held rigidly upon a slender neck. Garnets glittered in her ears; I saw a flash of the gold chain around her throat. The links dipped down beneath the bodice of her gown, caught between flesh and fabric. I thought she might speak; she did not. She did not even move.

'He was not perfect,' I told her. 'He was flawed, as any man is flawed. It does not make him less than the legend he has become. It merely makes him a *man* . . . as his grandson is a man.' I felt the weight of the gold upon my arms. The ache in my left earlobe. *At last, I am Cheysuli.* 'I need to be myself. I need to know my own name. I need to walk unhindered by the weight of my grandsire's legend.' I paused. 'I need to be allowed to respect the memory of the man, instead of resenting it.'

I saw the pain in her eyes. 'Have I done that to you?'

'You did not *intend* it.'

'*Have I done that to you?*'

I swallowed tightly, loath to hurt her any more. 'I think – perhaps . . .' I stopped short; why avoid the truth in the name of tact when I had already made the wound? 'Aye.'

She flinched. Only a little, but there was no doubting the blade had gone cleanly home.

'Oh – gods—' she said, and covered her face with her hands.

I went to her at once, wrapping her up in my arms. She did not sob aloud, merely cried silently into my leathers. Such dignity, has my mother . . . such rigid awareness of self.

When she was done with tears she lifted her head and looked up into my face. 'I loved him so much. He was everything to me. I had no mother for most of my life . . . he had already banished her. And when at last I *did* come to know my mother, it was to know also that she intended to use me against him.' The anguish laid bare her soul; she had carried her own weight of guilt. 'He was my world for so many years of my life . . . and then he was taken from it.'

'Men die, *jehana*.'

'Not Carillon of Homana.' Her tone was very grim. 'Men such as he are kept alive in lays and sagas; we have the harpers to thank for that.'

'Then *let* him live,' I agreed. 'Let the truth of his deeds live on in the magic of the music.'

'But not in the life of his grandson?' She nodded a little, though mostly to herself. 'I know . . . he became what he was because he *had* to, to make Homana whole. I cannot – and *should* not – expect you to mimic him. The times are different now . . . the requirements different also. It is not fair to ask you to be someone other than yourself.' She sighed. Fingers traced the shapes in the gold on my arm. 'For so long you have been Homana's *Homanan* prince, when you are also Cheysuli. But it was so much easier to follow the mold already made, than to trouble myself with fashioning another.'

I shrugged. 'I am whatever I am: Cheysuli, Homanan, Solindish. The rest is up to me.'

'The rest is up to the gods.' She smiled even as I bent to kiss her brow, before I took my arms away. 'It is difficult for a woman with only one child *not* to try to shape the clay precisely as she wishes. And more difficult yet to realize the clay may prefer to shape itself.'

'Well, I think the clay is unfired.' I smiled, shrugging. 'Who can say what I will become?'

'All of *them*,' she said seriously. '*All* of them will say. The councils, the races – the loyalists and the rebels. And certainly the enemy.' Pensively, she smoothed the silk of her shining hair. 'Be wary, Niall . . . be wary of everyone. Friend and foe alike.'

And into the room on the tail of her words came the echo of Strahan's voice: '*Look to your friends . . . your enemies . . . your kin – lest they form an alliance against you.*'

CHAPTER THIRTEEN

I lost my freedom almost as soon as I had won it. It was nothing my mother, my father, the Cheysuli or even the Homanans had done. It was a combination of factors: imminent war, the plague, civil turmoil. Although the *a'saii* were, for the moment, disarmed, I knew it was possible the Cheysuli fanatics might seek other avenues to replace me. No one could say I lacked the gifts of my race, not with Serri and our link so blatantly obvious, but they *could* say they preferred someone with a different strain of the required blood. And perhaps they would.

The plague began to prey upon Homana in earnest. What had initially begun as a vague illness defined mostly as fever in Homanan herders and crofters spread down from the north to invade central Homana, and Mujhara lay in its path. Reports of deaths were brought to the Mujhar, and, too soon, the vague illness was diagnosed as something far graver. From Homanan crofters and herders, isolated in the Northern Wastes and the greater distances between towns and villages, the sickness reached out to touch even the Keeps, and word came of Cheysuli deaths.

The bounty on white wolves rose. A trip to the furrier in the Market Square showed me a man whose purse was fattened almost daily by trappers coming in with pelts. Some were ruddy, others silver, some a charcoal gray, as if the trappers took no chances and slew all the wolves they could catch. But there were white pelts as well . . . pelts as white as my own, when I wore my *lir*-shape.

And so, when I went into the city, I made the greatest sacrifice of all: I left Serri in Homana-Mujhar. I would not risk losing my *lir* to an overzealous citizen intent on ridding

276

Homana of the plague, or – more likely – intent on putting a silver piece in the palm of his bloodied hand.

I did not like leaving Serri behind. Not at all. But certainly no more or less than my father liked leaving Lorn behind when *he* went into the city.

Or even to Clankeep.

My sons thrived, though I learned all too quickly demands upon my time by governmental matters stole away the hours I had meant to spend with them. I saw them infrequently at best; mostly I toiled with my father in sessions of strategy and hypothetical situations, learning how men plotted the course of war. Lessons in my youth had taught me Homana's history of wars and civil turmoil; I began to see why they had been required of me. All too often one of the councillors tossed the name of this battle or that into the discussions to cite an example of proper procedure, thoughtful initiative, even dismal failure. All too often I heard the name of Carillon invoked . . . and then one day, in listening to yet another discourse on what the late Mujhar had done as well as why, I began to see the reasons for the invocations. My grandsire, flawed man that he was, as I had taken care to point out to my mother, had known instinctively what might win the battle, and so the war as well.

Or *was* it instinct? Perhaps it was simply *experience*, won from out of the midst of carnage and put to use in later confrontations.

If it was instinct, perhaps I had inherited a portion of it. And if it was experience, I had little doubt I would soon know that as well.

Relations with Gisella continued much as before. She was quixotic, unreliable, unpredictable. Servants disliked serving her and argued among themselves as to who would take her trays, for she only rarely came down to meals in the dining hall, preferring, she said, to eat with the babies. Quietly I made certain there were always two or more women with her and the children; I did not wish to risk my sons to the whims and odd fancies of a woman such as Gisella.

We spent little time together because of the demands of the planning sessions. More and more my father asked me for my opinions in an attempt, I thought, to familiarize me with the idea of conducting a war as much as familiarizing the others with the idea of my contribution. Ian, also present, said less than I and was asked less, even by my father; his place was at my side, not in the line of succession for the Lion or even in orchestrating wars. But I did not doubt that when the time came, his responsibilities would be as great as mine. Simply drawn from a different background.

Gisella did not appear to miss my company, although she was always glad to see me. I thought surely she would stifle, ever keeping herself within the confines of Homana-Mujhar, but she said no. She did not wish to go to Clankeep or into Mujhara or even outside the walls of Homana-Mujhar. She wished only to stay with the babies.

I could not forbid it, any more than I could force her to leave the palace. And I was not certain I *wanted* her to leave Homana-Mujhar; there was no telling what she might do or say in the city or at Clankeep. The gods knew *I* could never predict it.

Any more than I could have predicted her desire.

I had not sought her bed since the birth of Brennan and Hart, even though enough time had passed to make it physically possible for her. It was repugnant to me. *She* was not − it was just that I could recall so little of the time before Serri had freed me from Gisella's ensorcellment. The idea that I had been little more than a toy to her, performing at her whim, disturbed me deeply. I had no desire to learn how malleable I had been in her bed.

And yet it seemed I would.

She came into my bedchamber as I prepared to blow out the candle. Naked, I glanced up as the latch lifted (I did not sleep with it locked) and started in surprise as Gisella slipped through and shut it with scarcely a sound. She wore only a nightshift and the black cloak of her shining hair.

As she turned toward the bed, seeking me, I heard the whisper of the linen; saw the cloak swing against breasts and thighs.

She saw me through the filmy screen of the gauzy hangings. She stopped. Stood very still. Then, slowly, a spread hand caressed her breasts, sliding diagonally from the left shoulder to stop eventually at the dimple of her navel. The hand trapped a portion of the linen and pulled the fabric tight against her loins.

Even against my will, I felt myself respond.

She said nothing. She crossed the room, came to me, placed her hands upon my shoulders. Her palms were warm as she kneaded my warming flesh.

She smiled. There was no doubt I wanted her, even when I thought I could say I did not. Her nails scraped down and caught in the gold on my arms; I heard a metallic scratching as she dragged tips across the flowing shapes.

'Wolf,' she whispered, 'I, *too*, can be a wolf . . .'

She pressed herself against me. I caught handfuls of her hair. I thought suddenly of Serri, curled at the foot of the bed. Serri, who shared my life through the link.

And then I did not care.

'Wolves,' she whispered. 'Let it be as *wolves*.'

'Niall? *Rujho*, the council has called an emergency meeting.' Ian unlatched and pushed open the door, speaking even as he did it. And then he stopped short, silenced abruptly; he had not expected to find Gisella in my bed.

Well, no more than *I* had – at least, initially.

Light spilled through the casements. Early morning, *too* early; I rubbed a hand across my face and tried to wipe the dullness from my mind. 'Emergency?'

Ian hovered between divulging an answer and leaving at once. Beside me, Gisella pulled the coverlet over her nakedness.

'Ian—' I began, frowning.

'Just – get dressed. I will wait outside.' As he backed out he pulled the door shut with a thump.

I got up and dragged on leggings, jerkin, hooked a belt around my waist. Boots were last; I tugged them on, then turned and bent down to kiss Gisella briefly, but the brevity was replaced by elaboration. She smiled, stretched languorously, promised me the world with her half-lidded, sleepy eyes.

Gods — who can say what is ensorcellment or lust? I wondered vaguely, and went out the door with Serri at my heels.

Ian's face was conspicuously blank as I joined him in the corridor. Tasha sat beside him, cleaning a spotless paw. Wryly, I smiled; my brother would say it was not his place to comment, but it would not be necessary to say anything at all. By his very blankness I knew what he was thinking.

He gestured down the corridor and we matched our strides as we walked even as our *lir* trailed us. 'I know little more than you,' he told me. 'Some word of the bastard.'

I swore. 'With this war becoming more and more imminent, the *last* thing we need is trouble with the bastard.'

'Until he is dead, he will make it.' Ian shook his head as I looked at him sharply. 'No, I do not speak of assassination, but no doubt others do.'

Assassination. It was a political reality, a tool kings and others used to remove potential rivals as well as very real ones. Alaric himself had used it against the House of Erinn.

And for that very reason, I could not imagine myself condoning its use against the bastard. Even to lessen the threat to me. Surely somewhere there would be someone who grieved. His mother. His foster-father. Perhaps even a wife.

We descended spiraling staircases one behind the other; the steps were too narrow to support more than one man at a time. Down and down, around and around, with only a rope for a guide on the inner column. The twisting staircase with its narrow confines was designed for ease of defense: it was easier to defend the palace against the enemy one man at a time, instead of one against many.

On the bottom floor we passed by guards in the corridor

and nodded greeting to those just outside the wooden door. One reached in, unlatched, pushed the door open for us; we entered, had the door pulled closed almost at once— —and walked into the eye of a storm.

No one took note of us. Where ordinarily men stopped speaking to acknowledge me with bows and murmured greetings, now none even knew I was present. The ranks of benches along the walls and just before us were filled; more men, standing, lined the walls and filled the aisles. Sitting, standing, they were shoulder to shoulder, blocking our view of the dais and its table where our father customarily sat. Over the low-voiced mumble of constant comments, I could hear someone haranguing the Mujhar.

Ian and I exchanged startled glances. Then he shrugged and began pushing a way through the standing men, murmuring apologies even as the others swore, shifted, glared. Many of them, as I followed, were unknown to me; no doubt they were annoyed by the audacity of two much younger men.

I stepped upon a boot toe, apologized, nearly tripped over another. The irritation was mutual as the owner of the toes and I exchanged scowls. Behind me, Serri grumbled aloud; within the link I felt his disgust with mannerless Homanans. But I also heard the murmuring arise in our wake; Ian and I were named by those who knew us, and by the time we reached the center of the hall, where room was left for speakers and petitioners, the men moved aside willingly. But by then we no longer needed the courtesy; our father, rising, was summoning us to the dais.

We went at once, crossing the open space in the center of the hall. A man stood before the dais in a posture that bordered on defiance. He turned as Ian and I approached; I saw his expression of outrage, as if he intensely resented the interruption. But as he saw me, following in Ian's wake, the expression changed. He stared. And I saw him murmur something silently to himself. A prayer. Or a curse.

The men on the benches rose. The sudden silence was loud and very brief; I heard the murmuring begin again almost at once. There was a note of anticipation in most of the low-voiced comments. Apprehension in others.

And even hostility.

Ian hesitated only a moment before he stepped up behind the table. Tasha was a shadow behind him, tail whipping as she paced silently onto the dais. Like Serri, she sensed the tension in the hall.

There were three chairs on the dais. The middle was obviously my father's: Taj perched upon the back. Lorn lay beside it, eyes slitted. Ian went by him to the left and waited behind it even as I took my place at the right. Into the hush my father spoke quietly, presenting both of us to those assembled. I saw faces I knew and faces I did not. The council members ringed the floor in the curving front row. I knew none of them well, save Rowan; I looked to his face for some indication of the gravity of the session, but it was a mask to me.

We sat down as my father did. Still there was silence. The men in the middle of the floor continued to stare at me.

'Be seated,' my father announced, and the silence was replaced by the sound of benches scraping, the ring of spurs, the clatter of sheaths and scabbards striking wood.

The stranger in the center waited in tense silence.

'This is Elek,' my father said. 'From the north, across the Bluetooth. He represents that faction of Homanans who support the right of Carillon's son to inherit the throne when I am dead.'

Every man in the hall looked at me, to judge my reaction. No doubt they expected shock, anger . . . perhaps even hostility. And a few, probably, fear. But I gave them none of those things. Instead, I looked at Elek.

He did not look like a rebel, a fanatic, a madman. He looked like a *man*, and not so much older than myself. He was brown-haired, brown-eyed, clean-shaven with an open, earnest face. His clothes were plain homespun: tunic and breeches, without embellishment. His knee-boots were muddied, but otherwise the leather was good. Not a nobleman, Elek, but neither was he a poor man.

No doubt his wealth lay in his convictions.

I rose, scraping my chair against the dais. Silently I bade Serri stay by the chair; slowly I stepped off the dais and crossed the open center of the floor. In silence I stopped before Elek, marking how he wet his lips; how he had to look up to meet my eyes. And marking also the faintest tang of perspiration. Elek was nervous, now that I stood before him. And so I knew he had been exceedingly eloquent, championing the bastard's right to usurp my place in the line of succession.

'Why?' I asked. That only.

He swallowed. His gaze flicked between me and the Mujhar. Clearly, he did not know how to answer.

I waited. So did all the others.

After a moment, Elek cleared his throat. 'He is Carillon's son.'

'He is Carillon's *bastard*.'

His chin rose minutely. 'It is customary for the *son* to inherit from the father.'

'Rather than the grandson?' I nodded. 'Aye, I grant you that. But the circumstances were different.'

'We maintain that had he known, Carillon would have named his son as his successor, rather than Donal of the Cheysuli.'

'I am his daughter's son,' I said quietly. 'If, in Homana, women could rule in their own right, Aislinn, my mother, would have inherited the Lion Throne. As it was, her husband did. Do you really think Carillon would have disinherited his daughter to make way for a bastard son?'

'Had he known—'

'How do you know he did not?' I looked past Elek to Rowan. 'My lord general, you are the best man to answer my question. Did Carillon know the woman had conceived?'

Elek wrenched his head around to stare in disbelief at Rowan; had he thought to make his case uncontested?

Rowan's smile was very faint. As always, he wore the crimson silk tunic with the black rampant lion sprawled across its folds. With his Cheysuli looks, the colors were good on him. 'Aye, my lord. He knew she had conceived.'

Elek turned sharply to refute Rowan's statement, but my raised hand stopped him. 'Before you ask it, Elek, let me answer your question: that is General Rowan himself, who served Carillon for nearly twenty-five years. Do you intend to question his veracity?'

'I question his prejudice,' Elek answered curtly. 'He is Cheysuli. Do you think he would prefer to have a Homanan replace a fellow Cheysuli in the succession?'

'There speaks ignorance,' I retorted. 'Were you never taught the histories? In your zeal to champion Carillon's son, did you never learn the names of those who served the father so faithfully?' I shook my head. 'No, you did not. Else you would know that General Rowan is a *lirless* Cheysuli. He was raised Homanan, Elek . . . he has no *lir*-gifts, owes no loyalty to his race, does not claim a clan. What benefit would he gain from lying to you?'

Elek did not respond.

I looked again at Rowan. 'He knew she had conceived, and yet he let her go.'

'She requested it my lord.' Rowan was so calm, and yet I sensed a trace of amusement beneath the surface of his tone. Did he have so much faith in me?

'She requested his leave to go.'

'Aye, my lord. She wished to have the baby elsewhere, away from the brutalities of war. The Mujhar made no attempt to dissuade her.'

He did not notice his slip. *The Mujhar.* To him, no doubt, Carillon would always be the Mujhar. But I thought in this instance the mistake was a good one; Elek, turning again to look at Rowan, frowned a little, as if disturbed by the reference. A man who was so dedicated to Carillon that he still referred to him as Mujhar unconsciously emphasized where the depth of his loyalty lay.

'Were you present when he gave her that leave to go?'

'Aye, my lord. He gave her coin and his best wishes for the birth of a healthy child.'

'And did he say nothing about bringing the child to

him? That if it was a son, he would want the child given into his keeping?'

'He said nothing of it, my lord.'

'Why do you think he would not? A son is a son.'

'A bastard is a bastard.' Rowan did not smile. 'He intended to wed Electra of Solinde.'

'And expected a son of *her*.'

'It – was hoped. Certainly.' Rowan's faint smile was gone. No doubt the questioning aroused old memories. Painful memories of earlier days, when Carillon's youth precluded the thought of illness and accelerated age.

'Aye!' Elek shouted triumphantly. 'But he *got* no son of her – only a daughter.' He swung to face me again. 'Only a daughter, my lord . . . who could not inherit the throne.'

Still I looked at Rowan. 'You knew him better than most, general. Do you recall at any time that Carillon considered – or *wished* to consider – sending for his bastard?'

'No, my lord. He said nothing of it.'

'To *him!*' Elek cried. 'But does a man – a *Mujhar* – confide everything to another, even his general? I say *no*, he does not. I say he divulges what he wishes, and keeps some things private, as every man does. Even a Mujhar.'

I laughed. 'And do you seek now to tell me my grandsire's private thoughts?'

'No. There is no need for me to do it. I will let the woman do it instead.' It was Elek's turn to laugh even as I stared at him. 'Aye, my lord – the woman. The *bastard's* mother. Why not ask *her* these questions? She is just outside the door.'

I did not dare show him my concern. It had become quite obvious many of the strangers in the hall were companions of Elek's, fellow supporters of the bastard. And I could not be certain how many of the men supposedly loyal to my father intended to remain so. It was possible Elek and those present with him hoped to gather more supporters even within the walls of Homana-Mujhar.

'By all means,' I said quietly. 'Have the woman brought in.'

285

There was no sense in confronting her as I confronted Elek. And so as a man was sent to fetch the woman, I returned to my seat upon the dais.

My father's face was grim. 'He did not say the woman was here.'

I glanced at him sharply. 'Do you think *that* will change anything?'

'He is making a formal petition of the Homanan Council,' my father answered. 'It is possible a majority of the members might agree with his claim in the name of Carillon's bastard.'

'But you could *overrule* it.'

'And I would immediately do so. But it would have serious repercussions. It could split the council entirely, which would more or less split Homana. And the gods know I do not need a hostile, divided council, going into war.'

'What of the Cheysuli? Have *they* no stake in this?'

He did not appreciate my tone. 'And will *you* speak of the *a'saii*? Or will Elek?'

I did not answer because the woman had arrived. I watched pensively as the men made way for her as they had not for Ian and me.

At first I was surprised. She was short, too heavy, at least ten years older than my father. Her graying brown hair was pulled back from a sallow, puffy face into a knot at the back of her head. She wore, like Elek, simple homespun, but the quality was not as good.

A gray woman, I thought. Gray of dress, gray of hair, gray of spirit. Nothing in manner or appearance spoke of the young woman who had captured a Mujhar's interest.

She stopped beside Elek. She curtsied awkwardly, as if she had forgotten how. Her eyes were downcast, yet as she raised her lids and looked at my father, I saw they were also gray. But a large, lovely gray, clear as glass and brilliant. No matter what else she was, she was not a stupid woman.

Carillon bedded this woman and got a son upon her.

Rowan rose. 'My lord?'

My father nodded.

The woman turned toward him as he approached. I saw the look they exchanged; an agreement to disagree. He knew her, she him, and yet their loyalties were spent on different men.

He nodded. Silently he returned to his bench. 'My lord.' Again, Rowan looked to my father. 'It is the woman, my lord. Her name is Sarne.'

'Sarne.' My father leaned forward in his chair. 'You bore Carillon a son.'

'Nearly thirty-six years ago, my lord. When I was twenty.' Her voice was as cool as her eyes; whore she might be, but she was also bound to the man they called the bastard.

'And now you come to us claiming he should be Prince of Homana in place of *my* son.'

'My lord – he is *Carillon's* son.'

'*Illegitimate* son.' I knew how much the emphasis cost my father, with Ian seated beside him. It is not a Cheysuli custom to curse a bastard for his birth, and yet for my sake he had to.

'Bastard-born, aye,' she answered forthrightly. 'But acknowledged by his father.'

The Mujhar nodded. 'By his father. Which one? Carillon – or the crofter you married?'

Her sallow face was suffused with angry color. Her eyes glittered. I was put in mind, oddly, of my own mother, when I had seen her angry. The eyes were similar.

And I wondered, suddenly, if that had been the attraction. My mother's eyes were her mother's, and Electra was notorious for the power of her gaze. If Carillon were susceptible to the color, it became more understandable how Sarne had appealed to him.

'He was acknowledged by his *father*, my lord, when I brought him to Homana-Mujhar.'

I heard the gasp go up from the assemblage. No one had expected that; no, perhaps some of them *had*. Not everyone looked surprised.

A sidelong glance at my father's face showed the faintest trace of consternation in his expression. Beyond him, Ian

287

frowned blackly at the tabletop. Almost idly, he picked at a blemish with his thumbnail. But I knew my brother too well; he was also deeply concerned.

'And when did you come to Homana-Mujhar?' my father inquired calmly.

Sarne nodded a little, as if she had anticipated the question. 'You weren't here, my lord. You'd gone to the Crystal Isle to fetch home the Princess of Homana.' She nodded again. 'It was before you wed her. When the only son you claimed was also a bastard, like mine.'

I was on my feet at once. 'You go too far,' I told her plainly, over the murmurs of the throng. 'Give my brother no insult *here*.'

Her dignity manifested itself subtly, and yet I was aware of its presence. 'Then give *my* son no insult here, my lord.' She took two steps forward; a short, heavy woman, yet powerful in her pride. 'Do you think I don't know Cheysuli custom? Do you think we put forward my son out of some perverse desire to *steal* the throne from you? *No*, my lord – we only want what's right for him – what's *his* right, because he is Carillon's son! Bastard, is he? *Aye*, he is! And so is that man there!' She thrust a hand toward Ian. 'So is that man who sits at the Mujhar's *side* bastard-born, and suffering none because of it. Cheysuli he is, and therefore not pushed aside because his father never married his mother. And I say to you – what right have you to push aside *my* son? What right have you to refuse him his proper place? *Carillon* never did!'

'What place did Carillon *give* him?' my father demanded. 'By the gods, woman, nothing was ever said! Not to me, not to Rowan . . . if Carillon promised you a place for your son – a title or otherwise – no one ever knew it!'

'Why would he say so to *you*?' she countered. 'He had already promised you the throne. Everyone in Homana knows how the shapechangers serve their prophecy. Perhaps he thought you or the other Cheysuli would try to harm my son.'

My father nearly gaped. 'You are mad,' he told her,

288

shaking his head slowly from side to side. 'You are *mad.*'

'Am I?' she retorted. 'As mad as the Princess Gisella?'

'*Enough!*' I shouted. 'Woman, you go *too far!*'

'Everyone knows it!' she cried. 'You are wed to a mad-woman, my lord. Who can say what manner of children you will get?'

Even my father was on his feet. 'No more,' he said. 'By the gods, woman, *no more!*'

'Why? Because I speak the truth? Because I *dare* speak the truth before all the others?' She whirled, facing the gathered men. 'It's true! *All* of it! My son was acknowledged by Carillon, who intended to give him a place. And now when we *ask* for that place, the Mujhar denies it to us.' Her body vibrated with the intensity of her emotions. 'He fears my son. He *fears* what it means for the prophecy. But I say we are *Homanan* – we need no prophecy. Why not make Homana *Homanan* again?'

Men were on their feet, trying to shout her down. Others shouted over them declaring their support of the woman's son. And all the while I watched in astonishment.

Ian pushed back his chair. 'I will fetch the guard.'

'No.' My father caught his arm as he moved to rise. 'Remain here. I do not want you going near that crowd.'

'*Jehan—*'

'I said *no.*'

'She is mad,' I said dazedly. 'Madder than Gisella.'

'*What sort of man do you want on the Lion Throne?*' the woman was shouting. 'A Cheysuli? A Homanan? The child of Carillon's son? Or the child of mad Gisella?'

I looked at Elek. He was smiling. He watched the woman and smiled, as if he waited for something.

Beyond him, Rowan had turned to the men. I saw his mouth move, but his shout was lost in the tumult. Like Ian, I wanted to fetch the guard. But I did not move to try it.

'It was a *Cheysuli* who slew Carillon!' I heard the woman shout. 'A *shapechanger* slew the Mujhar. He gave him shapechanger poison!'

'Oh *gods,*' I heard my father exclaim. 'How can she

289

know about the *tetsu* root that he wanted for his pain?'

'*Carillon's son should be Mujhar — Carillon's* Homanan *son — let the Lion remain Homanan.*'

I saw men draw steel in the midst of the shouting throng. I heard shouts, curses, threats; I heard the woman's voice rising over it all like the shrill cry of a hunting hawk.

'*Let the Lion remain Homanan!*'

And then, abruptly, a man broke free of the throng. He darted forward even as I leaped over the table and onto the floor, trying to turn him aside. But I was late, hobbled by a poor landing; he thrust, left his knife in the woman's body, and looked directly at my father. 'My lord — that was for *you* — to prove my loyalty.'

And almost at once he was dead. Elek, rising up from Sarne's crumpled body, thrust with his own knife and drove the man down to the floor.

I heard the ring and hiss of steel from more than a hundred swords and knives. I caught a glimpse of Rowan battering back an attacker. *Gods — they will not slay* Rowan—

And yet I knew they might.

They advanced: a wall of human flesh. Elek was a target; so, I thought, was I.

'Niall, *get back!*' My father's voice, shouting over the others.

Elek twisted, mouthing obscenities at me. Others held him, knocking the bloodied knife from his hand. I did not think he wished to slay me, only to curse me for Sarne's murder. And yet clearly the others thought he did. En masse, at least twelve bore him to the ground.

'Do not slay him!' I shouted. 'By the gods, *do not slay him!*'

'*Rujho* — get back!'

And then I felt Serri go by me into the mass of men, snapping at a throat. 'Serri! Serri *no*—' *Gods — they will say he has gone mad — they will say he must be slain — and then I will be slain as well*— 'Serri *no!*'

I dove after the wolf, trying to catch him in my arms.

290

All I caught was the tip of his bristled tail, and then I was down, sprawled on the floor, with stomping boots too close to my face.

Serri—

'My lord, get you *up*.' Someone caught the back of my jerkin and yanked me to my feet, steadying me even as I staggered. I felt a knife pressed into my hand. 'My lord, *arm* yourself!'

Serri—

There was no answer in the link.

Hands were on me. I felt something sharp slice through my jerkin. My belly stung.

Someone is trying to gut me like a fish—

'My lord!' I was turned, shoved, the knife in my hand sank deeply into flesh.

'No!' I cried in horror.

Elek's face, mouth gaping in shock and horror. Blood flowed over my hand. And then he sank down slowly to his knees until he was lost in the crowd.

Gods – say I did not do it—

And yet I knew I had.

'Serri!' I shouted. 'Serri!'

'*The prince has slain him!*' someone shouted. '*The prince has murdered Elek!*'

Hands were on me, dragging me back from the throng. I twisted frenziedly, trying to free myself, until I heard my brother's voice. 'Stop fighting me, *rujho*, and let me save your life.'

'Serri,' I said dazedly. 'Oh gods – *where is Serri?*'

Here, came the familiar tone. *Lir, I am well. You need have no fear for me.*

Ian jerked me down behind the table, thumping my head into the chair. 'Stay down,' he said. 'Let the guard do their job.'

'The guard—?' I sat up even as Ian tried to shove me back down. And then Serri was in my face. 'Oh gods – *lir—*'

I am well. I am well. Lir, do not fear for me.

His nose was pressed into my throat. I latched an arm

around his neck and hugged as hard as I could. *Lir, where did you go?*

There was a man who was trying to slay you. I had to stop him, lir.

I heard the ring and clash of steel on steel, the shouts of the Mujharan Guard. Benches overturned, men cried out, cursed, petitioned the gods for deliverance even as I had myself.

I tried to thrust myself up to peer over the table, but Ian jerked me down again. 'You fool,' he said, glaring. 'You did precisely what they wanted, so they could claim you murdered Elek. Do not give them more satisfaction. *Stay down!*'

'Where is our *jehan*?'

'Here,' he said from behind me. 'I was fetching Rowan out of that mess.' He knelt even as I twisted my head to look. 'Are you harmed?'

I looked down at myself. Blood stained my leathers, but none of it was mine. 'No. This is all Elek's, I fear.'

Behind the Mujhar stood the general. His fine silk tunic had been torn. But the ringmail beneath was whole. 'Almost clear,' he reported. 'I think the madness is over.'

'But for how long?' I asked in disgust. 'Gods, what an ugly thing.'

'As it was meant to be,' Rowan agreed. 'It was elaborately planned.'

'Planned?' I stared up at him as I reached out to touch Serri for reassurance. 'Some of it, aye, I can see it easily enough. But – Sarne's murder? Elek's?'

'How better to divide loyalties as yet unsecured than by inflaming them with murder?' Rowan shook his head grimly. 'My lord, she was murdered by a man claiming his loyalty to the Mujhar . . . it was made to look as though Donal desired it. But Elek was not quite careful enough. I saw him speaking to the man in the corridor just before the audience began.'

I recalled how he had looked, as if he waited for something. 'So she was sacrificed.'

292

'Aye,' my father said grimly. 'And so was Elek, though he did not expect it. It makes these people doubly dangerous. They will slay their own to lay the blame on us.'

'Gods! Will it work?'

'It might,' Rowan answered. 'Word of it will get out: that *Niall* slew Elek, and it will draw more people to the bastard. The rebels will use it against us all.'

'How do we stop it?'

'We do not,' my father said. 'Not physically. We do not dare, on the heels of what has happened today. All we can do is deny it.'

I shook my head. 'Not a powerful weapon.'

'But the only one we have. We cannot afford another. All we can do is let this rivalry sort itself out – with what subtle aid we can give the sorting – until the Homanans will listen to reason.' He offered his arm and pulled me up.

I blew out my breath in shock even as Serri pressed against my knee. Men littered the floor. Some were dead. Some were near it. Others were merely wounded. Much of the Mujharan Guard still filled the hall, though others remained in the corridor enforcing the Mujhar's peace.

'Gods,' I said in despair, 'what madness infects this realm?'

'Not madness,' Rowan said. 'Rather, call it ambition. The desire for a throne.'

'And Carillon's bastard is behind it.'

Rowan's expression was horribly bleak. 'How the father would hate the son . . .'

'Would he? Could he really?'

'For this?' Rowan nodded. 'If he could rise up from out of his tomb, he would put an end to this. He would put an end to his son. But he cannot . . . and so we must do it for him.'

'*You* would do it?' I asked. 'Could you slay Carillon's son?'

Rowan smiled a little. 'I am pledged to the Mujhar of Homana, and after that to his son. Carillon's time is done; Donal is Mujhar. And the son I will serve is you.'

293

I grinned. 'You will be an old, old man.'

My father grimaced. 'And I will be a *dead* one. Let us speak of something else.' He turned as if to step out from behind the table and off the dais, but one of his guard approached.

'My lord, a message has arrived.' He held out the sealed parchment. 'It was to be given to you at once.'

'My thanks.' He broke the wax and unfolded the creased parchment. And then he looked at Rowan. 'Ships,' he said. 'Solindish ships, sighted off the Crystal Isle. Hondarth is in danger.'

'And so it begins again.' Rowan wiped and sheathed his bloodied sword. 'My lord, how shall you deploy us?'

'I will do it as Carillon once did, when he was endangered on two fronts. You and I will go to Hondarth. My sons I will send to Solinde.'

Rowan smiled a little. 'And I will say of *them* what once I said of *you*: they are unschooled in warfare and the leading of men.'

'Aye, but they will learn. I send the Cheysuli with them.'

Gods, I thought, *Solinde*.

My father looked at his sons. 'I cannot put it more plainly: in the morning you go to war.'

Gods, I thought, *Solinde*.

Part III

CHAPTER ONE

'*Rujho* – get *down*!'

Even as I lunged out of the saddle I felt the nip of arrow at shoulder, plucking at the leather of my jerkin. My foot was half-caught in the stirrup; the horse, shying a single step from the wail and whistle of arrows, dragged me off-balance. I fell, twisting awkwardly as I tried to free my foot before my knee was wrenched out of its proper alignment. Heard hum and hiss of additional feathered shafts; jerked my head aside as fletching dragged at a lock of tawny hair.

'Get *down*,' Ian repeated.

'I *am* down.' Irritably, I jerked my boot from the stirrup and rolled, flattening on my belly, scowling at my brother. Like me, he lay belly-down in the thin dry grass of the Solindish plain, barren in the first gray days of winter. 'Where are they? How many?'

Ian, peering westward through the screen of grass, shook his head. He pulled his warbow out from under a hip, rolled sideways to take an arrow from his quiver, nocked it. Slowly he rose, hunching behind the thigh-high grass. He blended perfectly with the stalks and scrubby vegetation: amber, ivory, sienna; no greens, no browns, no richness, only the dull saffron of banished fall. The land was made bland in brassy sunlight as it burned through the flat light of a winter's day.

Just beyond Ian, at his left, crouched Tasha, chestnut indistinctness dissected by slanting stalks. Nothing moved to indicate she lived, not even the tip of her tail. She was stillness itself; I was reminded, oddly, of the wooden lion in Homana-Mujhar, crouching on the dais.

297

Serri?

He came, even as I thought of him, dropped low in the slouching walk of a wolf who skulks, avoiding contact with the enemy. His tail was clamped at hocks, curving inward to brush tip against loins, protecting genitals. Tipped ears lay back against his skull. He was hackled from ruff to rump.

Beside me, he crouched, much as Tasha crouched. He stared at the distances. *Ihlini, lir. Ahead.*

I looked at once at Ian, intending to tell him; saw the grim set of his mouth and realized there was no need for me to speak. Tasha had already relayed the information.

Ihlini. At last. After two months in Solinde, entangled in skirmishes that did little but waste our time – as well as wasting lives – we were to meet the true enemy in this war. Not the Solindish, though they fought with fierce determination. No. *Ihlini.* Strahan's minions, who served Asar-Suti.

Ihlini. And it meant Ian and I were summarily stripped of our Cheysuli gifts.

Even now I could feel the interference in the link with Serri. A numbing, tingling sensation, faint but decidedly present, lifting the hair on my arms, my neck, my legs. Irritability: something insinuated itself within the link I shared with Serri, shunting the power aside. It was as if someone had split a candleflame in two, snuffing one half entirely . . . spilling the other half into a darkness so deep even the *light* was swallowed up. I could feel the power draining away into the earth, leaving me, going back into its mother. And I was not certain it would return.

I shivered. *How eerie that the gods give us the gifts of the earth magic, then take them away when we are faced by the Ihlini . . .*

How *disconcerting* that we are stripped of our greatest weapon when confronting our greatest enemy.

'More than Ihlini,' Ian muttered. 'They do not use the bow. They leave that to others.'

'Atvians?'

298

'Atvian bowmen are perhaps the most dangerous in existence.'

'Except for the Cheysuli.'

Ian cast me a glance. 'Do you forget? There are only two of us. I am the last to decry our warrior skills, *rujho*, but I am also the first to face realities. Judging by the number of arrows loosed, we are badly outnumbered.'

'Only for the moment. The camp is not far from here – I will send Serri for reinforcements.'

Ian nodded grimly. The link no longer functioned normally, but I trusted Serri's instincts better than my own. As I put my hand on his shoulder, the wolf rose, turned, loped away, heading eastward. Toward the Homanan encampment.

For two incredibly long months we had been in Solinde, breaching the borders and advancing steadily until we were easily three weeks from the Homanan border. From Mujhara, farther yet. And from Hondarth, where our father remained, we were at least a two-months' ride.

We had come in with mostly Cheysuli, but Homanan troops had followed on our heels. It was not war such as I had expected, being comprised primarily of border skirmishes and raids by quick-striking Solindish rebels, but I soon learned that death was death, regardless of its manifestation.

Carillon's methods, one of the captains had told me. *It was what defeated Bellam when Carillon came home from exile. If nothing else, the Solindish have learned in the intervening years.*

Oh, aye, they had learned. They knew that if you cannot raise a warhost of thousands, you raise what you can of hundreds. And use them carefully.

How many times? I wondered. *How many more times will Solinde levy war against Homana?*

'They come,' Ian whispered.

Aye, they came. As I crouched in the thin Solindish grass, I watched the Solindish come. So carefully. So *very* carefully; like locusts methodically consuming the life of every stalk, they trampled down the grass even as they used it for a shield. I could see no men, no shapes; hear no words or weapons. Only the soft and subtle sibilance of an approach through winter grass.

There was no question the enemy knew where we were. Though we were screened by the grass even as they were, our horses marked our presence. Grimly I looked at them: Ian's gray stallion and my own red roan, browsing idly in the grass. Bits clinked, trappings clattered; Ian's stallion snorted.

And then, abruptly, the horses no longer grazed. They stared. Westward. Toward the enemy.

Serri, I said, *hurry*. Though I knew he could not hear me.

Ian darted upward, loosed an arrow, crouched down almost at once. I heard a shout from the enemy – it was of discovery, not of pain – and realized what Ian had meant to do. They marked our position very well now . . . and it was time we left it.

Ian caught my eye, pointed toward the horses. It was unlikely we could mount and escape without detection, but we could use the stallions for a distraction. Also a living screen. Much as I disliked the thought of sacrificing my horse, I disliked more the thought of sacrificing myself.

I nodded. Flattened. Tried to belly-crawl toward the horses without disturbing so much of the grass as to give our purpose away.

But we reached neither of the horses. Without warning, the grass in front of us burst into smoke and flame.

It was an acrid, oily smoke that filmed our faces, our eyes; tried to breach our mouths and make its way down our throats. I coughed, gagged, spat. My eyes burned. Teared. I could see nothing but smoke and flame.

The horses snorted, squealed, ran. Westward, away from the enemy.

Gods, but how I wished Ian and I could do the same. But we could not see to do it. We could not even *breathe*.

Out of the smoke there came a man, and then another. Solindish, with swords in their hands and determination in their eyes.

300

Another. Another. But I could not see to count the others.

Beside me, Ian lurched to his feet. I wanted to jerk him down again, to catch an arm and *jerk*, but I did not. I could only cough, wheeze, spit – and watch as he loosed arrows from a bow that trembled from the trembling of his hand upon it. He could not see, and yet he fought.

Two of the Solindish went down at once; Ian's skill was such that even half-blinded, even choked by acrid smoke, he could find the target. In this case, two. And in silence he nocked yet another arrow.

More men stepped out of the billowing smoke. And behind them came the Ihlini.

I knew him at once. Somehow, I *knew* him, though I had never seen him.

Blood calling to blood? No. That was Strahan's weapon, to make me think we were linked through blood and heritage.

And yet, it made me wonder.

Much as my brother had, I lurched upward to my feet. I jerked my sword from the sheath at my hip. The first man came in with his rusted blade – *rusted blade* – and swung at my head. It surprised me; not that he would strike, but that he left himself so open. No swordsman, this. Just a man. A man with an old, old sword. And a man about to die.

A single step forward, even as I ducked beneath the blow. A single thrust with my own blade. I felt the tip cut through the leather of his belt, scrape momentarily against a soft brass buckle, continue onward into belly, parting flesh, muscle, the vessels thick with blood. And how it spilled, the blood. How it ran out of the man to stain the fabric of his tunic, the silver of my steel; to splash, drop by rubescent drop, against the thirsty stalks of saffron Solindish grass and dye it lurid crimson.

I unsheathed the blade yet again, pulling it from the human scabbard, and turned to face the enemy once more.

This time it was the Ihlini.

Smoke peeled back from his shoulders as he crossed the

ground to me. He wore gray, a pale lilac gray, twin to the smoke billowing at his bidding. His hair was black, his eyes blue; I thought at once of Hart, my second son.

'My lord,' he said, 'a message from Strahan.' The Ihlini was calm, quiet-spoken. And he smiled. I judged him only a year or two older than myself. Young, strong, powerful. Filled with the confidence of his mission. Consumed by his dedication. 'He says: *"Tell Donal's cub he should never have wed Gisella. Tell Donal's cub one day he will come to me."* '

The sword hung from my hand. I had only to lift it—

But I did not. He had taken the intention from me. 'No doubt,' I answered. 'No doubt I should not have, because it will be Strahan's undoing. I have children of the woman, Ihlini — sons. *Sons.* And so the new links are forged.'

The smoke was a nimbus around him, clinging to his shoulders, hands, boots, like seasalt to a spar. It rose, billowed, built a wall, swallowing those around us until we were two men alone, confronting one another across generations of hatred, distrust . . . *fear?*

Could it be the Ihlini feared us?

Honesty undermines the falsehoods of arrogance: I knew I feared the Ihlini. And I was not afraid to admit it.

Silence lay around us. Within the walls of smoke there was no sound. The world had surely stopped. And without? Perhaps the wheel had warped; I thought he had made the time to stand quite still.

I faced him. 'Strahan has said Ihlini and Cheysuli are kin. Children of the Firstborn.'

He smiled a little. 'It is said we are.'

'Do you believe it?'

'I know better than to *dis*believe a thing that may be true.' He shrugged; ash spilled down his shoulders.

'Is it repugnant to you?'

His black brows rose a little. 'That the races may be linked? No. Not repugnant. Perhaps – *unappreciated*.' Again, he smiled. 'Why do you ask, my lord?'

He gave me my rank, even as Strahan had. And without

302

irony; a simple statement of address. Moment by moment, he peeled away the preconceptions I had built out of ugly stories.

Prejudice? No doubt. But I was not certain the Ihlini did not deserve it.

'I ask because if it is true the races are linked, you and I are kin.'

He laughed. 'The beginnings of a plea for leniency? You require mercy of me, my lord? Well, do not waste your breath. I intend to do to you what you desire to do to me.' He tilted his head a little, as if he listened to a thing I could not hear. 'Even were we *brothers*, it would not alter the melody.' He began to smile even as I began to frown. 'Can you not hear it? It is played, my lord, for us; because we will dance the dance of death.'

He lifted a hand in a gracefully eloquent motion. In his fingers I saw the glint of silver, polished bright. Brilliant, blinding silver. But it was not, I saw, a knife.

He inclined his head in a gesture of subtle deference. Or was it in farewell? 'My lord.'

The hand was thrust skyward. I saw how the smoke parted, making way for the thing in his hand. It glimmered, flashed, streaked upward into the sky.

I watched it. I tipped my head back, watching the silver fly; I saw it arc upward, slicing through lilac smoke, and then I knew what he intended.

I snapped my head down. 'Oh, no,' I told him, 'you do not divert me with childish tricks of misdirection.'

He did not even attempt to avoid my blade. I spitted him cleanly, front to back, and heard the scrape of bone against blade. And as he lay in a spreading pool of brackish, blackened blood, he laughed.

He *laughed*.

'My lord,' he said, still smiling, 'say to me *which* diversion was misdirec—'

—and he was dead. I stared down at the face gone suddenly slack in death, the abrupt cessation of *life*, leaving him empty, *spent* . . . so devoid of that which had made

303

him a man. Ihlini, Solindish, even Homanan or Cheysuli. He was a man. And he was dead.

And then the silver lanced out of the sky and buried itself in the top of my left shoulder, and I understood his words at last.

Misdirection, aye. And now it might prove lethal.

The pain drove me to one knee. Of its own accord my right hand loosed the hilt of the sword and flew to clasp my shoulder. I felt steel, sharp, deadly steel, wafer-thin, deeply imbedded; a flat, curving spike was all that protruded above the surface of my flesh, my jerkin; the rest was firmly sheathed in muscle and bone. My left arm dangled helplessly at my side.

I caught the elbow, dragged the forearm around so I could cradle the limb against my abdomen.

—oh – gods – the *pain*—

'Serri—' I gasped. 'Ian—?'

The smoke was gone. I saw the last wisps of it sucked back into the Ihlini's body as if it were a part of his soul; now that he was dead, so was the power dead. Crushed grass was his shroud; bloodied soil became his bier.

My fingers twitched. Again. All the muscles in my arm tautened, from shoulder to fingertips. My fingers curled up, tucked beneath my folded thumb. The rigidity was absolute.

'*Ian*—'

I vomited. Shuddered. Retched. Sweat ran down my flesh beneath the clothing. I twitched. I smelled the tang of fear. The stink of helplessness.

Oh – gods – Ian—

I put out my hand and touched the face of death.

CHAPTER TWO

I heard someone cry out. The sound hurt my ears. It set my head to throbbing. Inwardly, I cursed the man who made the noise . . . and then I realized he was myself.

'Gods!' I blurted aloud. 'What are you *doing* to me?'

Lir, be still. That from Serri, seated next to the cot.

'Pulling a tooth.' Ian's voice, and very near.

'Tooth?' Dazed from pain I might be, but I knew well enough that what resided in my shoulder was not anything like a *tooth*.

'Sorcerer's Tooth,' Ian answered. 'An Ihlini weapon . . . the name suits, I think.'

I lurched nearly upright as the pain renewed itself. Hands pressed me back down upon the cot. Ian's. Another's. And yet a third dug at the tooth in my shoulder. 'Gods, Ian — can you not do this yourself? Save me some pain — use the earth magic on this wound!'

Lir, be still. Do not bestir yourself.

'I cannot. The Tooth is an Ihlini thing. It will have to heal of its own.'

'Give him wine,' someone suggested. 'Let him drink himself into a stupor.'

'No.' A third voice, also unknown to me. 'I know little enough of the Ihlini, but I *do* know they resort to poison much of the time. I think the Tooth was not tampered with — but I will not take the chance. Give him no wine, or we may kindle the poison.'

I gritted my teeth so hard I thought they might fall into dust in my mouth. 'Just — pull it out. *Cut* it out . . . will you rid me of this thing?'

'My lord, we are trying.'

'Try harder.' Sweat ran down my face and dampened the pillow beneath my head. Poisoned or not, the Tooth was setting my body afire.

'*Rujho—*' Ian again '—one more moment—'

Hands tightened on me. I felt the sharp pain slice into my flesh, and then abruptly the thing was wrenched free.

'There,' someone said; fatuous satisfaction.

'Let it bleed,' the other suggested. 'If there is a poison, the blood will carry it out.'

'And if there is not, the blood will carry out his *life*.' Ian had never been impressed with the sometimes questionable skill of Homanan physicians; being Cheysuli, he had alternatives. But at the moment, I did not. 'Pack it, bind up the wound,' he said calmly, but I heard the note of command in his tone. 'Then let him sleep.'

They did as he told them, and so did I. I slept.

Something landed on my chest. A small weight only, but it awakened me. I opened my eyes, saw Ian standing by me, shut them again.

'The Tooth,' he said. 'You are lucky; it carried no poison. You will survive, *rujho*.'

I did not feel like it. I felt wretched. My mouth was filmed with sourness; I licked my lips, wanted to spit. Wanted to swallow wine or water, hoping to wash away the bitter tang.

I opened my eyes and looked up at Ian. The light in the field pavilion was thin, hardly enough to illuminate the interior, but the fabric was unbleached ivory and lent meager strength to the dim winter light. Still, Ian was mostly clothed in shadow; his eyes, lids lowered, were black instead of yellow.

'Tooth,' I muttered. I scraped my good hand across the rough army blanket and found the thing my brother had dropped. Picked it up; felt the cool kiss of the shining steel. Ice in my hand, I thought. And yet the wound in my shoulder burned.

It was a thin, circular wafer of steel, perfectly flat, edged with curving spikes honed to invisible points. Star-shaped, in a way, except the shape was too refined, too fluid; the spikes flowed out of the steel to form a subtle vanguard at the wafer's edge. There were runes etched in the metal.

I grimaced. This thing, thrown from the sorcerer's hand, had lanced out of the sky to imbed itself in flesh and bone. As if it had a life of its own. As if it knew its target.

Abruptly, I held it out to my brother. 'Take it. The Tooth is out of the jaw; now you may dispose of it.'

Ian, accepting Ihlini steel, smiled a little. He tucked it into his belt-pouch.

Serri?

Here, lir. I felt a nose, cool and damp, pressed against my hand. I opened my fingers and stroked the place between his eyes, in the center of his charcoal mask. His eyes watched me avidly. *You will recover, lir.*

I did not really doubt it. I looked at Ian again. 'How many slain?'

'Ten Solindish; there were only twelve of them. The reinforcements arrived directly after you went down.'

I nodded. 'How many of us were slain?'

'Two Homanans. Two wounded.'

I frowned. 'What is it they mean to do? Here we are in Solinde, where we have been for two months, and yet we hardly fight. Occasionally, aye — I do not discount the men we have already lost . . . but I am perplexed by the enemy's intentions. We have Cheysuli with us as well as Homanans, and yet we hardly see more than twenty Solindish at a time.'

'Gnats nipping at horses.' Ian nodded. 'As Sayre says, it was Carillon's way. But I think there may be an explanation.' He shrugged a little. 'A thought, only — but what if the enemy's numbers have been vastly over-estimated? What if the rebellion itself is far smaller than we have been told?'

'But the intelligence comes out of Lestra, from the regent.' I frowned. 'You cannot mean Wycliff is a traitor . . .'

'No. He is a loyal Homanan, serving our *jehan* as best he can. No. I think the intelligence is manipulated before it reaches Wycliff. I think he is given reports of numbers

307

that do not exist; where there are ten men, forty are reported. By the time the news reaches Lestra — and later Mujhara — the number is ten times greater than the truth.'

'Then the Ihlini are *using* us . . . drawing us away from their true objective.' I frowned. 'Hondarth? *Jehan* is there, and Rowan. There were Solindish ships . . .'

Ian shook his head. 'News travels slowly in war — slower yet in winter . . . who can say how things stand now in Hondarth? And each day the weather worsens. Sayre says there will be snowfall before the day is out.'

A winter war. I shivered from the suggestion. 'Is it possible the Ihlini manipulate the Solindish? That there really is little more than *mutters* of rebellion, no rebellion of itself?'

'I am quite certain the Ihlini manipulate the Solindish. What I *cannot* say for certain is if this realm truly does wish to attack Homana.' His expression was grim. 'I have no doubt there are many here who desire independence from Homana — before Carillon defeated Bellam, Solinde never had a foreign overlord — but are they as dangerous as we fear? Oh, aye, there are rebels, raiders . . . zealots—' he did not smile '—but there are always those who seek to throw down the power and take it for themselves. *Regardless* of the competence of the king.'

'*Jehan* should be told.'

'I am sure he knows. He has fought Solinde before.'

'But that was with Carillon.'

He did not answer at once. And when he did, his tone was full of infinite understanding. 'A man learns, Niall. How to fight, how to lead, how to rule.' His face was oddly serene; I saw compassion in his eyes. 'You are learning now.'

I shut my eyes under the cover of weakness from my wound. I knew what he implied: that soon I would lead the army in fact as well as name. For I did not lead it now. Wisely, my father had not expected me to know what a man must know in order to conduct a war. He expected me to *learn* it — and so he had dispatched veteran Homanan captains to lead us through this war.

'Niall.'

I opened my eyes.

'The gods choose only worthy men.'

I grimaced. 'The gods can make mistakes.'

He smiled a little; I had been very decisive. 'Blasphemy?'

'The gods made the Ihlini.'

The smile was banished. 'Aye. They did. And often –
I wonder why.'

No more than I. No more than any Cheysuli, beginning
to wonder if indeed the gods *had* sowed a second crop.

A winter crop, I thought; a deep-winter harvest. There
was no warmth in the air. No spring. No summer. No light.

Only Darkness.

Sayre tipped back his cup of warmed wine and drained it.
He took it away, wiped the excess from his mouth with a
forearm, nodded consideringly. 'You may have the right
of it, my lord.'

It was a concession. Sayre and I got on as well or better
than any of the captains, and I had taken to discussing
strategies with the veteran. He had fought with my father
and with Carillon. He was not old, but his youth had been
spent on the battlefield. He lacked half his right ear; it put
me in mind of Strahan, lacking the ear entirely.

He scratched idly at a reddish eyebrow. A thin pale scar
bisected it. His ruddy hair was liberally sprinkled with
white. 'Complacency would be deadly, but I think the
men are prepared. Fit. When the Solindish come, we will
take them.'

I shifted on the stool. 'This encampment has stood safely
for five weeks, captain. We have fought no one for that long.
How can you be certain the Solindish will *ever* come?' I
put a hand on Serri's head and buried fingers in the lush-
ness of his pelt. 'If they do not, we waste our time. But
if the *Ihlini* come instead . . .' I rubbed my left shoulder.
The wound left by the Tooth had healed well enough, but
the scar was tender still. It ached almost constantly in the
bitter cold.

Sayre rose, thrusting his stool away from the table. He reached for the leather-bound tankard, poured, filled his cup and mine again, though I had drunk only half. He scowled blackly out of his wind-chafed, reddened face, gulping wine again. It set watery blue eyes ablaze.

'Let them come,' he said flatly. 'Let them come. My Homanans will be ready.'

I said nothing. I knew the captain too well. And in a moment he did as I expected: he cursed and sat down again.

'Aye, aye – you may have the right of it. How better to suck the will to fight from men than by frightening it out of them?' He swore again, set the cup down so hard wine slopped over the rim. It splashed against the wooden table and filled nicks, scratches, divots hacked out by steel. Saying nothing, I retreated from the spillage by lifting my arms and leaning away from the table. 'My Homanans are veterans, but they have fought only men,' he said. 'Who can say what they will do when faced with Ihlini sorcerers?'

'Captain—' But I stopped. His eyes had taken on the glazed expression of reminiscence; he was lost in battles long past.

'I recall the night Tynstar came upon us,' he said in an almost eerie detachment.

I looked at him more attentively.

'Tynstar came upon us and took away the moon. He filled it up with blood.' His mouth tightened in a faint grimace of distaste. 'He sent a mist across the land, a *miasma*, intended to swallow us all. And all the army panicked, as he intended, save for Rowan, Carillon, Donal . . . and even the Ellasian prince, Evan, your father's boon companion.' He frowned a little, lost in his recollections. 'He meant to slay us then, to defeat us *before* the battle, and yet he was unable. Donal threw the magic sword at Tynstar, and the sorcery was broken.'

I thought of the sorcery *I* had faced, in the circle of lilac smoke.

'The sorcery was broken,' Sayre repeated. 'But it was by a Cheysuli – the Homanans were too afraid.'

'Then perhaps we should seek out the rebels,' I suggested. 'Perhaps we can finish this war for good.'

'Perhaps we should let them come to us.' Sayre was unsmiling. 'They know this land; we do not.'

I rose abruptly, went to the doorflap of the field pavilion and pulled it aside. Beyond me lay the horizon. The day was cold, windy, depressing. Clouds huddled on blue-frosted plains.

'There is little to recommend a winter war,' I said quietly, rubbing again at my shoulder. 'I think the Solindish will not come. And I think we should go to Lestra.'

'By your leave, my lord – I think I must disagree.'

I smiled. 'You are welcome to disagreement. But I say equally freely: I do not think the Solindish will wage war against us *and* the weather.'

'So you want us to winter in the city instead of here on the plains.' Sayre's tone was eloquent in its careful intonation. 'If we do so, my lord, we leave open the leagues between Lestra and the Homanan border. Open to the *enemy—*' He paused. 'Open to the enemy *and* those men who serve the bastard.'

My teeth gritted. Aye, the bastard. His fame grew each day, and each day we lost one or two Homanans who decided to change allegiances in hopes of better food, warmer bedding, higher pay. I could not openly curse the bastard for leading his growing army in skirmishes against the Solindish borderers – intended ostensibly to *help* me – but privately I cursed him at least once every hour. Those skirmishes mostly helped *his* reputation; word of Elek's murder had tainted my own name and brightened that of Carillon's misbegotten son.

'What profit in taking the borders in deep winter?' I demanded curtly, swinging to face the man. 'I think they *keep* us here for purposes of their own.'

From outside there came a call. Ian's voice; I turned again. With him was a young man all wrapped in winter furs and leather.

'*Rujho* – messages from Mujhara.' Ian ducked through

311

the flap and into Sayre's pavilion, nodding a greeting to the man. He wore heavy furs against the cold and gloves upon his hands. No gold showed, not even in his ear. Against the wind he wore his hair longer than normal, even as I did myself.

The young man entered also. He was hooded, wrapped in woolen scarves. In his hand there was a sealed parchment. 'My lord.' He pulled wool away from his mouth. 'My lord – for you.'

I took the damp parchment, broke the brittle seal, opened it with difficulty – the parchment stuck, tore, nearly came apart in my hands – then looked at the messenger in dismay. 'I can read none of this. The paper is mostly ruined, and the ink has run.'

'My lord, I am sorry.' Weariness made him almost curt. 'It – was difficult reaching you. The Ihlini have fired the land.'

'Fired?' I frowned. 'Be plainer of speech.'

'*Fired*,' he repeated. 'Everything between here and the Homanan border has been put to the torch. People are dead, game dispersed, all winter supplies destroyed. My lord – do you see what they have done? They have cut you off from Homana. You must go farther inward in order to survive.'

'*In*ward.' I looked at Ian. 'So now we know their plan.'

Sayre swore violently. 'An old trick,' he said flatly. 'Drive the enemy homeward and into starvation – or drive them inward to death in battle. I should have seen it. I should have *known* it!' He shook his ruddy head. 'By the gods, I should have listened to you.'

I looked at the messenger. His expression was limned in starkness against the bleakness of the day. '*You* made it through.'

'Aye, my lord. But I was one man. I carried some winter rations with me, and grain. But – an *army* . . .' Uncomfortable with the truth, he shook his head and shrugged. 'What little game is left will die of starvation soon. There is no grass for the horses, no feed or grain stored away. All has been destroyed.'

I turned abruptly and gestured for wine. Sayre acceded

at once, handing over a freshly-poured cup of steaming wine. I put it into the messenger's hands. 'You will be fed. You will be given time to rest. But first — were you given the message verbally as well as written out?'

He sipped. Nodded. Sighed. 'Aye, my lord. General Rowan said parchments may go astray; he gave me the words as well.'

'You have come from Hondarth?' I asked in surprise. 'But this seal is the Queen's.'

'The general is at Homana-Mujhar, *with* the Queen.' He sipped again; color began to steal back into his pallid flesh. 'Two messages, my lord: from the general, from the Queen.'

'Rowan's first,' I said at once. And then, thinking of my sons, I wished I had said the other.

The young man nodded. His brown eyes blanked a little as he sought to recall the words precisely as they had been said. 'There is plague in Mujhara,' he told me. 'It spreads throughout Homana.'

'*Plague!*'

'It slays one out of every family, sometimes more,' he continued. 'The Homanans fall ill of a fever, but most recover, unless they are very young or very old. But — it is the *Cheysuli*—'

He stopped. He looked at Ian, at the *lir*. Lastly he looked at me.

'Aye?' I asked with mounting dread.

He wet his lips. 'For every five Cheysuli stricken, four will die. And — so with the *lir*, my lord.'

'The *lir*—' Ian moved stiffly closer. 'This touches the *lir* as well?'

'My lord.' He stared into his wine. 'Often the warrior recovers. But if the *lir* does not . . .' White-faced, he looked at me. 'If the *lir* does not, the warrior dies anyway.'

'Two-fold,' Ian whispered. 'Slaying one, the plague slays *both*.'

I put a hand on Ian's arm, more for me than for my brother. 'This plague is in *Mujhara?*'

313

'Aye, my lord – and Clankeep. It spreads throughout Homana.'

'My sons,' I said blankly. 'My sons are in Mujhara.'

'And our *rujholla* is in Clankeep, along with other kin.' Ian's face was bleak. 'Gods, *rujho*, how can we stay here?'

'My lord.' The messenger's tone was raised, as if he knew we meant to leave him before he had completed his task. 'My lord, there is the other message. From the Queen of Homana.'

I nodded, still too numb to do much more. *My sons are in Mujhara.*

'My lord, she sends to say the Princess has conceived.'

I gaped. 'Gisella—?'

'In five months, my lord – less than that, *now* – you will have another child.' He paused. '*Ru'shalla-tu.*'

I looked at him more sharply. '*You* are Cheysuli?'

'No, my lord. Homanan. But it seems a wise thing to learn the tongue of those who rule.'

'Thank the gods for a little wisdom.' I looked at Ian. 'You know we have to go.'

'*I* know. But you heard what he has said. No game, no people, no supplies . . .' He shrugged. 'It will not be easy, *rujho.*'

'And if we do not try, we will never sleep again.'

'No,' he agreed bleakly. 'Yet I think I will not regardless, until I know our kin are safe.'

I nodded. *A child. Oh gods, another child. Now three will be at risk—*

I turned to look at Sayre. 'In the morning we will leave. Only Ian and I; it would profit no one to take more. Captain—' I paused, '—do what you can to win this war. However you have to win it.'

'Aye, my lord. Of course.'

Oh gods, I thought, *my children.*

The heirs to the prophecy.

CHAPTER THREE

The land lay in ruin. Although the Solindish plains lacked the heavy forests of Homana, it had boasted its share of scrubby trees, tangled hedges, thick turf, lush grasses. Now there was nothing, *nothing at all* – only charred turf, skeletal remains of blackened trees, ash and grit in place of grass. The land rolled on forever in its funerary finery, stretching eastward toward Homana.

Our horses sluffed through grit and ash, stirring a pall of pale gray dust that filmed our *lir*, our mounts, our clothing. Ice and frost rimed stones, frozen piles of hoof-churned earth, even the naked, twisted trees. Like jewels, ice crystals glittered. Beneath its wealth, the charring lent false glory to ruined wood. Like diamonds, like jet, it blazed and glittered in the thin blue light of an early winter morn, cloaking itself in transient ornamentation.

Though much of my face was hidden in woolen wrappings, my breath still escaped; plumed frost in the frigid air. I was weighted down in hood, furs, leathers, woolens, but still I was cold. Yet I could not say if the chill I experienced was born of temperature or sickened disbelief.

I squinted against the bite of bitter cold. We walked; we did not gallop, did not trot, shadowed by our *lir*, but still the movement stirred our eyes to protest. Tears gathered, spilled over; I scrubbed briefly at my cheeks with a gloved hand, not desiring to let the tears freeze in the winter-chafed creases of tender flesh. For warmth, I had grown back the beard that made me Carillon, but mostly I was *cold*.

'How could they do it?' I asked, though most of it was

315

muffled behind the wool. 'How could they destroy so much of their homeland?'

'Desperation?' Ian, also hooded, shook his head a little. 'Dedication, determination . . . perhaps those and more. I do not doubt it was a difficult decision.'

'But to *slay* people? Their own people?'

His shrug was swallowed by the bulk of heavy leathers. 'If you are engaged in a war to which you are fully committed, and a portion of your own people refuse to join or render aid, perhaps it becomes easier to sentence them to death.'

'Indiscriminate *murder?*' I stared at him in amazement. '*How?*'

Ian pulled the wrap from his mouth. 'I did not say I understood it, Niall — I only offer a possible explanation.'

'Gods.' I was sickened by the thought. 'I could never make such a decision. Determine the fates of innocent people? Never. It is not a man's place.'

'It will be yours, one day.'

'No.'

'*Rujho* — of course it will. What do you think kingship entails? You have attended council meetings, have heard our *jehan* render judgments. He makes a choice, *rujho*. So will you.'

'Our *jehan* would never order a thing as ghastly as *this*,' I declared. 'Murder, destruction . . . *rujho*, look around you! Crops ruined, dwellings burned down . . . even the livestock and wild game stripped of food and homes. How will the land recover?'

'It will. It will take time, but vegetation will grow back, crops will recover, crofts and hovels will be rebuilt, even the game will begin to return.' He looked around grimly. 'This is a waste, a terrible, senseless waste, but it is not complete destruction. The land will live again.'

I shivered. 'Idiocy,' I muttered. 'When we have won this war, the Solindish will see that this benefits none of their people.'

'No, no benefit,' Ian agreed. 'But if you are going to lose

316

a war, you take desperate measures. And if that war is lost regardless of those measures, at least you have left nothing to benefit the victor.'

I looked at my brother. There was little of him I could see, just a shapeless mass atop a winter-furred tall gray stallion. But with the wrappings pulled down, I could see nearly all of his face. Beardless, I thought he looked younger than I. And yet he was so much wiser.

'You should be the heir,' I said finally. '*You* should be, Ian. You are better suited. I think the *a'saii* have had the right of it all along.'

He shook his head at once. 'I am *not* better suited, Niall. You do not live in my skin; you cannot know how I think, how I feel about things. I am not right for the Lion. That task is meant for you.'

'And if I died? If the plague took me, or a Solindish sword – or even a Sorcerer's Tooth . . .' I looked at him with a calm expectation that was as surprising to me as to him. 'If I died, *rujho*, could you accept the Lion?'

The shock made a mask of his face; he stared. And there was apprehension in his eyes. 'Niall—'

'Could you?'

After a moment, he blew out a rushing breath that wreathed his face in fog. 'You have two sons, *rujho*, and perhaps a third yet to come. The choice, thank the gods, will never be mine to make.'

No. It never would be. Unless all of us were slain. And I thought that supremely unlikely.

I looked down at Serri, trotting by my roan. *Unless the plague took every one of us*.

'Why did you ask, Niall? Why is it important for you to know?'

I shrugged. 'But for an accident of birth, it might be *you* who was meant for the Lion. In the clans, there would be no question of it. You were firstborn. And yet, because of Homanan law, only Aislinn's son can inherit. It seems unfair.'

'It is not.' Ian reined his stallion around a frozen

317

hummock of charred turf, searching automatically for Tasha. Against the blackened, frost-rimed earth, her ruddy coat glowed like heated bronze. 'It is what the gods intended, or they would have put us in one another's places.' He smiled. 'I am the fortunate one, *rujho*. My choices will be easier than yours.'

'No.' I disagreed in pointed affability. 'Because I will make you help me with *mine*.'

My brother laughed.

We watered our mounts, our *lir*, and ourselves at whatever streams and burns we could find, although many were frozen solid. Otherwise we drank sparingly of the contents of our waterskins and refilled them at the first opportunity. Food we rationed carefully, along with grain; we could not afford to waste a single pinch because it was unlikely our stores could be replenished. There was no game, no crops, no winter supplies. What we carried was our portion.

I wanted to avoid the charred wreckage of crofts and the remains of other dwellings, sickened by the first two we had visited in search of life and food. But Ian insisted we stop at each one because, he said, a man could not afford to ignore any opportunity. He had the right of it, my brother, but I did not enjoy the discoveries of bodies buried in the wreckage, burned, battered, broken, as if they were only toys. But the enemy had been thorough. There was no food, no water, no stored supplies that had not been methodically spoiled or destroyed.

And so we crossed the charnelhouse of Solinde praying we would reach Homana before our rations – or courage – gave out.

I thought often of the plague. So clearly I recalled how, more than a year earlier – nearly *two* – the furrier in Mujhara's Market Square had spoken of a plague in the north, believed to be carried by white wolves. And I recalled also, but a six-month ago, how the guardsmen seeking me had spoken of white wolves as well, desiring to slay *me* for the bounty. The thing had begun so long ago, and yet we had ignored it, believing it a fleeting thing, a piece of nonsense embroidered with falsehood, a story told at the sheepherders' fires to keep them awake while dogs warded the flocks against wolves of any color.

But now the tale was true. Now the beast was loose.

We crossed the border at last and saw how the Solindish had taken care not to raze any of Homana. With the naked eye a man could see the ragged line of demarcation, the sword's edge that divided Homana from Solinde. Here there was grass, though frosted; here there was life, though sluggish in the cold; here there was the promise of continuance. In Solinde, there was only the promise of ending.

And here there were also men, confronting us on horseback as we rode across the border.

Like us, they were bundled in furs, leathers, woolens. Caps and hoods hid their heads and much of their faces; I recognized none of them. They were Homanans, but that was all I could discern.

Ian and I, with our *lir*, crossed into Homana and the Homanans told us to halt almost at once. Muted light ran the length of their bared swords, but dully; the sun shone only fitfully through the mesh of scalloped snowclouds hanging low across the plains.

One man rode a little forward of the others (I counted fourteen in all) and halted. He looked at the *lir*, then at Ian, marking his yellow eyes. Lastly he looked at me, and he frowned. 'Cheysuli,' he said. 'Both of you?'

'Aye,' I told him, waiting.

He looked at me a trifle harder. But, as was his, most of my face was hidden; it is difficult to recognize a man well warded against the winter. 'There is plague,' he said abruptly. 'Have you heard? All throughout Homana.'

'And are you a patrol sent to turn us from our homeland?'

The other men murmured among themselves. This one did not answer at once. He squinted a little, peering past me toward the ravished plains of Solinde. 'Are you from the Homanan army?'

319

'No,' Ian answered wryly. 'We are from the *Solindish* army.'

The man's brown eyes flicked back to Ian. There was a glint of disapproval in his eyes. Not much of a sense of humor. 'Shapechanger,' he said levelly, 'this is no time for levity. Least of all for you.' A jerk of his head indicated the men waiting behind him. 'We are men who serve the son of Carillon.'

Inwardly, I swore. Outwardly, I did nothing.

Ian nodded slowly. 'We have been long out of Homana. How does the petition proceed?'

The other shrugged. 'The Mujhar is in Hondarth, the Homanan Council divided because of the war. The petition, for now, is set aside, but only for a while. When the war is done, and spring is come, we will set *our* lord in Niall's place.'

'Murderer,' one of the other men said. 'He slew Elek.'

No, he did not – at least, not intentionally. But I did not dare to say it aloud.

Idly, Ian smoothed the pale mane of his dark gray horse. 'This plague – how serious is it?'

'Serious for the Cheysuli. You would do better to stay in Solinde.'

'No,' we answered together.

He eyed us more attentively. 'We will not turn you back. Cheysuli, Homanan, it does not matter. Our duty lies with our lord.'

'Are you recruiting?' Ian asked.

The brown eyes narrowed. 'And are you of the *a'saii*?'

So, even the Homanans knew of the zealots. 'Why?' I asked aloud. 'Have the *a'saii* joined with you?'

'We asked. They declined: our objectives are too different. And so the pact was never made.' He shrugged, rewrapping his dark blue muffler. 'But I think the *a'saii* are finished; too many of them are dead.'

They were my enemy, the *a'saii*. But they were of my race, my clan, my kin; I grieved for their deaths. I grieved for the deaths of their *lir*.

320

'What of you?' Ian asked. 'The plague is not *that* selective. Homanans are dying also.'

I heard murmuring again. A glance at the others showed me furtive looks exchanged; expressions of bleakness and affirmation. No matter what was said, the bastard's adherents also suffered losses. *Many* losses; like the *a'saii*, their cause might be overcome by misfortune rather than anything I might do.

'We will win. We have the gods on our side.'

'*Tahlmorra lujhala mei wiccan, cheysu*,' Ian quoted. 'The fate of a man rests always within the palm of the gods.'

The Homanan turned his horse aside. And we were home at last.

We found little more welcome in Homana than we had in Solinde. Here the land was whole, the dwellings unburned, the crofters alive, the game and livestock healthy, but fear and suspicion also thrived. We were Cheysuli, and Cheysuli carried the plague.

Ian and I learned quickly that it was best if *I* went to the doors and asked for food and water, offering coin in return; for once, my Homanan looks stood me in good stead. But even so, as we drew closer to Mujhara the wary welcomes turned to rude refusals.

And then, with a week's ride left to Mujhara, we stopped at a snowbound croft and were given warm welcome, both of us, and invited in for a meal. The old woman was alone, but did not appear to fear us or the plague. With our *lir* she took us in and served hot food and tart cider, spiced with a twist of cinnamon. And when at last we took our furs off in the heat of the tiny dwelling, our *lir*-gold was bared to a smiling – if toothless – reception.

'Aye,' she said, 'I knew you were Cheysuli. Even buried under fur and leather. *You* have the eyes—' she looked at Ian '—and the animals are more than pets. *Lir*, are they? Aye. Lovely beasts.'

Her white hair was quite fine, thinning; it straggled out of a tight-wrapped knot of braid at the crown of her head.

All the days of the world were in the tapestry of her face. Her faded blue eyes were rheumy, eaten away with the promise of milk-blindness, but even when she could no longer see with them, I knew she would see with her heart.

'Lady,' I said. '*Leijhana tu'sai*.'

She sat in her chair and rocked a little, grinning at my words. 'Old Tongue.' She nodded, knotting her hands in the ends of her faded brown shawl. 'Been so long since I heard it. But even then, it was strange to me. My mouth did not want to shape the words.'

I looked at her in startled suspicion. 'You are not Cheysuli?'

'No, no, not I. Not Cheysuli, no.' She grinned. She rocked. She laughed.

'Lady,' Ian said. 'You know there is plague in the land, and yet you invite us in. You invite *Cheysuli* in.'

'I am old. I have no one but myself, and my cat.' The gray tabby, in the face of much larger kin in Tasha, had retreated to the mantel over the fireplace. 'When my time comes, I will give it good welcome. But I think this Ihlini mischief will not send *me* to the gods.' She nodded. She rocked. She smiled.

'Ihlini.' I exchanged a glance with Ian. 'You say the *plague* is Ihlini?'

'Born of Strahan, aye.' Again she nodded. Her eyes were closed. She rocked. 'It has been coming a long, long time. I remember the days of Tynstar, in Solinde, when he first told Bellam that Homana was his for the taking. And so together they took it, once Shaine was slain in the Great Hall of Homana-Mujhar. Tynstar chased Carillon out of his homeland and into exile in foreign realms . . .' Her recital trailed off. Ian and I stared at her in silence, shocked to hear her repeat so much of our House's history. 'But he came home again, he did, and took Homana back, and then Tynstar stole his youth. Tynstar was strong, but so was Carillon. And in the end, Carillon prevailed.' She smiled briefly; it faded quickly enough. 'But Tynstar sired a son on Carillon's queen, and now that son is loosed upon the land. Like the plague of Asar-Suti.'

322

She said nothing more. In the silence of the tiny room Ian and I waited for her to finish. But she said nothing more.

'Lady,' I said at last, 'how is it you know so much of Tynstar? So much of Shaine?'

'Because I was alive when Shaine was Mujhar.' Her rheumy eyes creased in good-natured humor. 'And Tynstar was my lord.'

'Your *lord*?' I was on my feet at once, hand closing on my knife hilt. 'Lady—'

'Aye,' she said, 'he *was*. And aye, I am Ihlini. But I bid you not to slay me: I am not the enemy. Save your anger for Tynstar's son.'

She stopped rocking. She sat very still in her chair, a small, old, fragile woman, who had suckled at a Solindish breast.

'Why are you in Homana?' Ian asked, genuinely curious as well as wary. So was I.

'Because I like it,' she answered. 'Because now it is my home.' Suddenly she laughed. From some hidden place beneath her shawl, she withdrew a thing that glittered. She held it out in the candlelight, and we saw the stone. A multi-faced crystal; pale, perfect pink. 'Take it,' she said. 'Take my lifestone. If you believe I mean you harm, you have only to crush it, or throw it in the fire. And the world will lack one more Ihlini witch.'

After a moment, I put out my hand and took the stone from her withered palm. I was ungloved; the crystal took on the color of my flesh, altering texture and hue until it was hidden in my hand. Perfect camouflage. It seemed weightless, though it was not. It seemed to have no temperature, though when I first had touched it the stone was undeniably cool.

'Lifestone,' I echoed. 'What does it do?'

'We have no *lir*,' she told me. 'We have a stone instead. It is a locus for our power.' Her eyes were on the stone. 'I have so little, now; I am too old. And I renounced Asar-Suti.'

323

'Renounced him!' Ian stared at her. 'And you were left alive?'

The old woman tilted her head a little. 'Betimes I think I was not. But that is only because I am so old. I lost my youth when I broke faith with the Seker. It was the cost. And now, I wait for the day I will die.'

I frowned a little. 'How old, lady? How many years have you?'

Briefly, she counted on fragile fingers. And then she grinned her toothless grin. 'Only two,' she said. 'Two hundred. Not so old, when you think of how old Tynstar was. Or how old Strahan will be, if no one seeks him out and slays him.' She looked at us both. 'You might,' she said. 'Go to him, seek him out, end the Seker's plague. It is the only way you will save your people. The only way the world will survive.'

She put out her hand. I returned the stone. Before my eyes, it flamed, sent a single tendril of lilac smoke into the air, and then its momentary brilliance was snuffed out. 'If you could take his lifestone, his power would be ended,' she told me. 'If you cannot, at least destroy the white wolf.'

'Gods,' I blurted, 'you wish me to slay *myself*?'

Her hand spasmed, shutting away the pale pink stone. 'You?' she said. '*You* are the Prince of Homana?'

'Aye, lady – I am.'

'Then you *must* go. It is a task you must perform.' Distractedly, she pushed at the wisps of pearlescent hair encroaching into her face. 'Go home, my lord of Homana. And then go to Valgaard, Strahan's fortress, in the mountains of Solinde. It will be Homana's deliverance.'

'And that is what you desire?' Ian asked gently. 'Forgive me, but you are Ihlini. What reason can you give us to believe what you have told us?'

'Reason?' Clearly, she was shocked. 'I have told you the truth. It should be enough.'

Ihlini, my conscience whispered, as Ian and I exchanged dubious glances.

'Reason.' She whispered it to herself. 'I am *too* old; I have

324

forgotten what hatred lies between the Firstborn's children – what prejudice there is—'

'Lady.' Ian's tone was distinctly displeased; I recalled how he had reacted when Lillith had discussed our supposed kinship on the voyage to Atvia. 'We are not blood-bound, lady. Not Ihlini and Cheysuli.'

'No?' She smiled, shrugged, rewrapped her faded shawl. 'No, then. As you wish.'

I looked at Serri. *Lir?*

He remained conspicuously silent. Old the woman might be, and lacking most of her magic, but the link was affected by her nearness to us.

I caught Ian's eye and hooked my head toward the door in a silent suggestion. Equally silent, he nodded once and rose. We put on pounds of leather and fur again, wrapped our faces in wool and pulled up our hoods from our shoulders.

'Lady,' I said, 'our gratitude. *Leijhana tu'sai.*'

Unsmiling, she looked at us. 'I will give you proof.'

'Proof?'

'Reason to believe.' She pressed herself out of the chair. She was tiny, fragile, bowed down with the weight of her age. 'Proof,' she murmured. 'My gift to you – my gift to *Homana*—' And with amazing accuracy she threw the crystal into the fire.

'*No!*' I leaped for her, trying to catch her in my arms as the lifestone fell into the flames, but by the time I touched the woman she was only made of dust. Only *dust* in the shape of a woman, and then even that was banished.

Slowly I opened my hands. Tiny crystals glittered against the flesh of my callused palms. Slowly I tipped them; dust sifted, drifted, settled against the earthen floor.

I looked at my brother in silence.

'*Gods—*' But he stopped. There were no words for this. He turned and walked out of the croft.

CHAPTER FOUR

There were marks on the doors in Mujhara. At first Ian and I stared at them blankly in ignorance, and then the answer became quite clear. A red slash meant plague was in the dwelling. A black one signified death.

All around us was silence, except for the sounds of our horses. Grayish snowdrifts stretched from doorway to doorway, filmed with grime and ash. Down the center of each street was beaten a narrow path of dirty slush over frosted, muddy cobbles. Our horses slipped and slid, pressing slush into horseshoe-shaped crusts of ice. Behind us came Tasha and Serri.

Though it was midmorning, passers-by were infrequent. As they saw us, they huddled more deeply into their wrappings and hastened out of our way. I saw ward-signs made against our *lir*, our horses, ourselves, and realized yet another reason for distrusting Cheysuli had acquired significance. Now they feared us for the plague.

The pewter-colored sky spat snow at us, but fitfully. Flakes no larger than the end of my smallest finger drifted diagonally across my path of vision, sticking to leathers, wool, horsehair, waiting for others to follow. I squinted, burrowing bearded chin more deeply into wool; the path before my roan was quickly transformed from gray to white.

After so many weeks of riding, not knowing what I might find, I discovered I wanted to do it again so the answer would be delayed. I did not want to halt at the bronze-and-timber gates of Homana-Mujhar and see the crimson slash of a plague-house, or the black of a house of death. I did not want to look at all; even as Ian halted before me, I stared steadfastly at the ground.

'My lord!' someone cried.

'My lord prince!' cried another, and the wide gates were opened to us.

I looked up. I saw the leaves of the gate swinging slowly open before me. And I saw the red mark upon them.

'*Rujho*?' Ian waited. And I realized I had not moved to enter the outer bailey.

'My lord.' Someone took my roan's damp rein. 'My lord?'

I bestirred myself to look down at the man. I did not know his name, but I had seen him frequently around the exterior of the palace. One of the Mujharan Guard whose duty it was to tend the gates.

'No soot,' I said. 'No soot upon the gate.'

'No, my lord – not yet.'

'Niall.' Ian again. 'Here is where we part.'

I looked at him in surprise. 'You are not going to come in with me?'

'I will go to Clankeep. Isolde is there, and others.' He reined back the gray who wanted to go home to a stable he knew. 'I will be back as soon as possible, *depending*—' He broke off, looking eastward, yanked wool away from his face. 'Gods, *rujho*, I am afraid of what I will find.'

Snow gathered on his shoulders and on the rim of his hood. There was no sun, only the dim flat light of a winter day, so that most of his face was hidden in bluish shadow. There was tension in the set of his mouth and jaw; in the flesh around his eyes. Freed of the woolen wrappings, his breath smoked in the frigid air.

'No more than *I* am afraid.' I looked past him toward the inner bailey. Patiently, the guardsmen waited to close the gate. 'Go on,' I said abruptly. 'Go on. Come back when you can.' And I rode past him with Serri trotting at the roan's right side.

I did not look back again. And as I passed through the outer bailey into the inner, I heard the gates thud closed.

Boys came running to take my horse, slipping and

stumbling in the snow. I flung them the reins and jumped down from the roan, thanking him with a slap upon one furry shoulder. And then I ran up the steps of the palace with Serri loping next to me.

Gods, lir – what if my sons have taken the plague?

Do not beg misfortune, lir. See if it is true, first.

But even Serri's customary wryness did not make me feel better.

My sons – and who else? My mother?

I thought of everyone as I climbed more stairs inside the palace, but I went to see my sons.

There were women in the nursery, talking quietly as they sat and tended their stitchery. But all talk broke off as I entered; five women stood as one and then dropped into startled curtsies.

'My sons?' I asked. That only.

'Well,' one of the women answered at once, as the others only stared. 'My lord, see them for yourself.'

I was already at the oak-and-ivory cradle, hanging on to the inlaid rim. They slept, did Hart and Brennan, swathed in soft-combed wool. There was no sign of illness about them.

'They thrive, my lord,' the woman – Calla – told me. 'You need have no fears for them.'

'And Gisella? My mother?' I could not look away from my sleeping sons.

'Both well, my lord.'

'I saw the mark on the gate. The *red* mark.' Now I looked at her. 'There is plague in Homana-Mujhar.'

'Aye.' She stared down at her hands. In them she clasped forgotten stitchery. 'My lord, it is the general. The Queen is with him now.'

'Rowan?' *Oh – gods – no—* 'You do not mean General Rowan?'

'Aye, my lord, I do.'

A knife blade teased at the interior of my belly. 'Where?'

'In his chambers. The Queen said to leave him where he would be most comfortable, though others wished to lock

328

him away.' Calla's face was pale. 'My lord.' She followed on my heels as I turned abruptly to leave the nursery. 'My lord – it would be best if you did not go.'

'So I do not risk myself?' Grimly, I shook my head. 'For Rowan, it would be worth it.'

But as I turned, determined to go to him, I came face to face with Gisella.

Once again, swollen with the weight of an unborn child. Or, perhaps, two? This time I could not be certain.

Hands clutched a soft wool shawl over her distended abdomen. 'You did not go *in*,' she said. 'Not into the nursery!'

'Gisella.'

'You did not expose my sons to *plague?*' She was astonished, angry, genuinely frightened. 'Niall?'

'I saw them,' I told her gently. 'Did you think I would stay away?'

'You exposed them!' She wrenched past me and ran to the cradle, even as I turned back from the door. 'Oh, my boys, my little boys, has he visited you with the plague?' Her hands were on the soft wool wrappings, peeling them back to expose sleeping faces. And then, abruptly, she turned on the other women. 'I *said* he was not to come in. I *said* he was not to be allowed. I *said* I wanted him kept away from my little boys.'

'Gisella.' I cut into her diatribe before she could flay the white-faced women with her tongue. 'Gisella, *no one* in this palace has the right to refuse me the opportunity to see my children.'

'*I* do!' she cried. '*I* do – their mother! I do not want you to touch them. I *told* these women you were not to touch the babies.'

She stood between me and the cradle, warding it with her body. How rigidly she stood; how fierce was her defiance. And I could not really blame her.

'I have no plague,' I told her. 'I promise you, Gisella – there is no plague in me. Do you think I would wish to risk them any more than you?'

'White wolf,' she said. '*White wolf*. How can you tell me *you* do not carry the plague. *You* are a white wolf when you take on the shape of your *lir!*'

'Gisella—'

'*No!*' She stared defiantly at Serri, then transferred it to me. 'I – say – *no!*'

Lir, Serri told me, *you cannot battle fear so fierce as this. Give her time. Let her see you do not sicken. She will accept you then.*

They are my sons, Serri.

And she is their jehana. Do you think her fear is misplaced? Do you think she is wrong to guard them with her life?

Inwardly, I sighed. *No. No – perhaps I do not. But I might wish the target were other than myself.*

No doubt. But you have just come through a plague-ridden realm, and everyone knows what your lir-shape is.

'All right.' I said it aloud. 'All right, Gisella, I understand. But when you see that I am well, there will be no more of these demonstrations against me in the presence of my sons.'

Her teeth showed a little. 'There is *plague*,' she said. 'Plague all through Homana. Do you think I will risk my sons? Do you think I will risk the inheritor of the Lion?'

No, I thought she would not. I thought she would risk only herself in order to protect the inheritor and his brother. Even against their father.

Mad she might be, but I could not question her desire to save her sons. Nor would I disregard her loyalty to the Lion.

I sighed. 'Well enough, Gisella. I surrender the battle to you.' Through the link, I asked Serri to stay with my sons; I did not entirely trust Gisella's temper.

And as she sang a song to my sons, I left the nursery to find the sickroom.

Rowan's chamber was full of shadows. The weight of them lay thick upon the furniture and wavered in the corners. I smelled the scent of beeswax and the promise of coming death.

My mother's back was to me as I entered noiselessly. I saw only the chair and the top of her head above it, red-gold hair muted in the dim glow of candlelight. As I approached, I saw how she sat very quietly in the chair, hands folded in her lap. And when I reached her, I saw how rigidly her fingers were locked together.

I heard how she spoke to him.

'—so faithfully,' she was saying. 'He had no one as faithful as you. Oh, I know, you would argue there was *Finn*, as loyal a liege man as could be, but the loyalty did not last. Not as it should have lasted. Not as *your* loyalty lasted.' Fingernails picked absently at the soft nap of the jade-green wool of her skirts. 'I know the story, Rowan: how as a boy you swore to serve Carillon as no other man could serve him, even as he was driven from Homana by Bellam of Solinde. How you never failed your duty to the rightful Prince of Homana. And when he came home again, the rightful *Mujhar* of Homana, you gave him what aid you could. You helped him become a king.'

I looked at the man in the bed. Much of him was hidden beneath layers of heavy blankets, and I could not see his face. I could not see him breathe.

'And when my father was slain by Osric, and Donal became Mujhar, you were there to help him also. To help him hold the Lion.' I heard the minute wavering of her voice. 'One day, my son will need you, as the others have needed you. How can you leave us now? How can you fail Niall?'

'Mother,' I said, and she leaped up from the chair.

'Niall! Oh – *gods*—' She pressed a hand against her breast. And then she shook her head. 'Oh *no*, do not come here. Not *you!*'

'*You* are here,' I told her.

'But I will not be Mujhar. Niall, please go back.'

'I owe this man my attendance. As much as you owe yours.' I stopped beside the chair and looked at the man in the bed. 'He has served the House of Homana longer than anyone I know. It is the *least* I can do for him.' She

331

said nothing. I moved past her to the edge of the bed. 'Does *jehan* know?'

'I had a message sent. But I doubt Donal can come. Not in time. The plague waits for no one.'

Indeed, it did not. Rowan's face was gray and very gaunt. Even his lips were gray, but they were also swollen and cracked. His breathing was distinctly labored.

I looked at my mother sharply. 'Is there no one we can call?'

'Nothing is left,' she told me gently. 'What *can* be done has already been done twice over.'

'Is there no kin to share his passing?'

'He is quite alone,' my mother said. 'His family was all of us.'

Bleakly, I shook my head. 'Gods,' I said, 'what *sterility*. No wife, no children, no clan . . . not even a *lir* to grieve.'

Rowan began to cough. It was a harsh, hacking cough, coming from deep in the lungs. Spittle soiled his chin; his cracked lips split again and bled.

I bent over him instantly, smoothing his coverlet in a futile bid to soothe his pain, though I knew there was nothing for it. The silvering hair was dull and lacking life. Pushed back from his face, it bared the fragility of his skull, showing the bones beneath the drying flesh. There was so little of Rowan left.

And then he opened his eyes; there was more left than I had expected. 'My lord,' he said, and smiled. 'My lord – you have been away so long.'

The voice had been ruined by his coughing. He sounded nothing like himself. 'Aye,' I said, 'but home now. And will stay here, for a while.'

The lids drifted closed, then opened once again. 'My lord—' He drew a rattling breath. '*Carillon*—'

I froze.

'Carillon, I beg you – take Finn back into your service—'

I shut my eyes. 'Rowan.'

'I know what constitutes an oath . . . I know you made one, broke one, according to Cheysuli tradition . . . but

332

make a new tradition. You both need one another.'

Looking at him, I saw how it hurt to speak the words. And yet he continued to try to speak them. 'Rowan, do not trouble yourself—' But in the end I did not finish. It was not for me to tell this man what to do.

His hand was on my wrist. The fingers were so dry, so hot, so oddly insubstantial. Even the calluses were losing their customary toughness. 'Oh, my lord,' he whispered. 'Oh, my lord, it has been an easy service. I could not have asked for a better lord—'

I shut his limp hand up in both of mine. 'Nor could I have asked for a better *friend*.'

Rowan's smile was blinding. Tears were in his eyes. 'Do you recall, my lord? Do you recall the day we met?'

I opened my mouth to urge him into silence; said nothing. I let him tell me how he and my grandsire had met.

'You were in chains,' he said. 'Thorne of Atvia had slain your father and taken you prisoner – and *me*, the same day, but I did not count. I was nothing – *you* were the Prince of Homana.' He smiled a little; blood welled into the cracks in his lips. 'And you spoke to me – to a boy made wretched by captivity – and you called us *kinspirits*.' A tear rolled down one temple to stain the pillow beneath his head. 'But Thorne took you away to his father, Keough, and I thought they would slay you. And then later, when *I* was taken, I thought they meant to slay *me*—'

He coughed. His hand tightened in mine. I felt my mother next to me. 'Rowan,' she began, but he went on when the spasm had passed, and she did not try to dissuade him.

'It was Keough – it was Keough who would have had me slain – when I spilled the wine . . . Thorne would have slain me, but you begged for my life. You *begged* for it, my lord – you offered to take my place . . .' Again, he coughed. His hand clutched mine. 'But – they did not listen. And I was flogged . . . for spilling wine. And when Alix rescued me, I swore then I would serve you all my life – even when you went into exile.' The smile brought fresh blood to his swollen lips. 'How I wished I could have been Finn . . .

when I heard a Cheysuli had gone with you, I wished it could have been *me*—'

Breath rattled in his chest. I thought he could not go on. But he did. 'All those years – all those years I envied him his position as liege man to Carillon . . . and yet by denying my race as a boy – by denying my *lir* – I also denied any chance *I* might have been the warrior you trusted so readily. And when he was gone – when you sent him from your service – I thought I would rejoice . . . but I did not. I was not Finn . . . and you needed him. You needed us *both* . . .' He sighed. 'Oh my lord, take him back into your service. Homana has need of all her children.'

His voice stopped. I swallowed heavily. 'Rowan – *Cheysuli i'halla shansu.*'

He laughed only a little; his voice was nearly gone. 'Cheysuli peace, for me? But I am a *lirless* man . . .'

'*Cheysuli i'halla shansu.*'

He lifted his head from the pillow. 'Carillon—' And then it fell back, and I knew he would not speak again.

I sat there for countless moments, trying to master myself. And when I could, I detached his hand from mine and set it carefully on the coverlet. It was hard to believe he was dead. Hard to believe the hand would never again lift a sword in the name of Homana's Mujhars.

Impossible to believe.

'I am sorry.' My mother touched my shoulder. 'But surely you understand.'

'Why he mistook me? Oh, aye . . . and I do not care. If it gave him peace to believe I was Carillon, it is a gift I would gladly bestow.' I rose. I saw the tears on her face. 'I will see to it arrangements are made.'

'Niall.' Her hand closed on my wrist and held me back. 'It is for others to do.'

I snapped my wrist free of her hand. 'If you think I will delegate the responsibility for this man's disposal to someone else merely because of *rank*—'

'No,' she said clearly. 'It has nothing to do with rank. If I thought it would bring me peace, I would dig the grave myself. But they would never allow me the honor.'

'They?' I frowned. '*Who* would not?'

She looked past me to the dead man in the bed. 'There is no choice. It is a time of plague . . . a time of new − and ugly − traditions. A time requiring measures ordinarily we could refuse. But not even those of the House of Homana may ask to be excused.'

'*Jehana*—'

'They will take him away,' she said plainly, 'to a common grave outside the walls. And there he and the others will be put to the torch so the plague will be consumed.'

'Not *Rowan*. He deserves so much more than that—'

'And if it were you,' my mother told me, 'they would do precisely the same. There are no titles in death.'

No. No titles. Nothing but an obscene *absence* from the world.

I looked at Rowan a final time. And then I drew my mother into my arms even as she locked hers around me. Together we grieved in silence. Together we offered comfort even as it was asked.

Ja'hai, I said to the gods. *Accept this Cheysuli warrior.*

CHAPTER FIVE

I labored over the letter as I never had done before, trying to find precisely the proper words. It would be easy to simply say: *Jehan, Rowan is dead*, but the man was worth more than that. So, I thought, was my father.

I had thought of having a scribe do the work, saying aloud what had happened and letting the other write it down, but that lacked privacy. It gave me no chance to say what I really felt. So I sat at my father's table and wrote it out myself.

And as I signed my name, my brother came into the room.

'Ian.' Quickly, I sanded the parchment, shook it, set it carefully aside. 'How does 'Solde fare? How bad is the plague in Clankeep?'

'I had forgotten,' he said. 'I had forgotten she was to bear a child.'

I sat back in my chair. 'By the gods – so had *I!*'

'Well, it was a boy. Four months ago. 'Solde named him Tiernan.'

I would have smiled, but there was a question I had to ask before I expressed my pleasure. 'A healthy child? And 'Solde?'

'Healthy child? Aye.' He nodded. He shrugged. 'Ceinn said the birth was easy. But the plague has taken 'Solde.'

I did not move. I *could* not. I sat in my chair and stared at the stranger who stood before me.

'Last night,' he said listlessly. 'Last night, as Tiernan cried for the breast she could not give him – the plague had dried her milk.'

Shock was a buffer between comprehension and grief. 'Not *'Solde—*' I said; I begged. 'Ian – not *Isolde.*'

I waited. I watched. I knew he would deny it. Ian *had* to deny it. This was all part of the same obscene jest fostered by Strahan upon us. I waited. I waited for Ian to admit it; to say Isolde lived.

But he did not. He wandered aimlessly into my father's private chamber. Tasha, following, flopped down beside a storage trunk even as Ian sat down on the lid. 'I watched it, *rujho*. I just *watched*. There was nothing I could do.'

No – not Isolde—

'I thought perhaps the earth magic might help to turn the plague away. But nothing answered. Nothing came at my call.' He sounded weary, confused, remote, as if the death had taken away more than just Isolde. 'I *watched* – and knew there was nothing I could do.'

'No.' I saw Rowan's face before me, his gaunt gray face clad in the somber flesh of death. 'No, there is nothing.'

'The baby cried. *Ceinn* cried. But Isolde slipped away.' And then suddenly his listlessness was banished and I saw the ragged blossoming of his grief. '*No* – she did not *slip away!* She was *taken* from us! Like a lamb caught in a bear-trap.'

I shoved my chair back and crossed the chamber to him. But even as I reached out, intending to grasp his shoulder, Ian rose and pushed my hand away. He brushed by me almost roughly; I watched him stalk to the fireplace and stare into the flames. The line of his shoulders was incredibly rigid.

It is not a Cheysuli custom to openly acknowledge grief.

But I had seen him acknowledge other things without a qualm, flouting Cheysuli custom.

He and Isolde had always been close. Closer than 'Solde and I; they had shared *jehan* and *jehana*. And I wondered: *Perhaps it is an indication of how deeply he feels this grief, that he cannot share it with me.*

'Ceinn is inconsolable.'

I saw 'Solde before me, in the rain, clad in crimson wool and the brightness of her spirit. How she had loved the rain. How she had loved the children. How she had loved Ceinn.

337

Still his back was to me. But I knew better than to go to him. 'And you?'

Slowly he turned, but not before I saw the telltale gesture of hand pressing tears away from flesh. 'Forgive me. I have no right to be selfish, *rujho* . . . she was your *rujholla*, too.'

'Aye.' I drew in a steadying breath. 'Rowan is dead as well.'

'*Oh*—' he said, when he could, '—oh, *gods*, but how keenly Strahan strikes!' Like me, he sucked in an uneven breath. 'Niall – it is worse. Much worse than we imagined. The plague has slain half our numbers.'

'*Half?*' All the flesh stood up on my bones. '*Half* of us are dead?'

'At least. They have not counted properly, but they tally what they can. Each day, there are no less than three new deaths. And that is not counting the *lir*.'

It was my turn to sit down on the trunk lid. Half. Half of our clan only? Or of the Cheysuli as a whole?

I asked him. His eyes were bleak. '*Our* clan has lost half. But the others send word of additional deaths. I think we can say half of all clans are dead. Strahan begins his own *qu'mahlin*.'

Half of all the Cheysuli.

I thought of Shaine, our ancestor, who had nearly destroyed a race. I thought of Carillon, who had come home from exile to end a tyrant's reign and end the *qu'mahlin* as well. I thought of how the clans had increased until they had divided, living in freedom again, building Keeps where they wished to build them, raising children in tranquility.

Half of all the Cheysuli.

Taken by Strahan's plague.

Gods, deliver us from the Ihlini. 'The old woman,' I said suddenly. 'The old Ihlini woman. She had the right of it. This thing is born of evil. Born of Asar-Suti.'

'There was another thing she said.' His tone was hard as iron. 'There was a thing she said we must *do*.'

I looked at him. 'We will go to Strahan's fortress.'

In silence, Ian nodded.

338

'His lifestone,' I said intently. 'That, or slay the white wolf.' I looked over at the table. The parchment lacked my seal. But I knew now I would not send it. I would have to send another. 'Ian – it is late, I know . . . but will you ask for the council to be summoned? – those members who are here. If we are to go in the morning, I must name my heir.'

'Without *jehan*?'

I shook my head. 'We cannot wait for him. And even if he *did* come, he would say we could not go.' I shrugged. 'An informal council, perhaps, and a more informal acclamation, but one that must be made. The Lion must remain secure.'

'Aye.' He turned to go. And then he paused. 'What will you say to the Queen?'

What *would* I say to my mother? I sighed. 'I will think of something.'

In the end, I simply said I was going. I told her when. I told her why. I told her what must be done. And I waited. For refusals, anger, tears. But she gave me none of those things.

'Go,' she said. 'Do what you must do.'

I waited. But she said nothing more. In the end, it was up to me. '*Jehana*?' I shrugged a little beneath her calm gray gaze. 'I – thought you would forbid it.'

She sat in a cushioned chair, swathed in a bronze-colored robe. She had prepared herself for bed; the glorious hair, unbound, spilled about her shoulders and gathered in her lap.

'No,' she said. 'The realm is near to ruin. There will be nothing left for Donal – nothing left for you. Something must be done. Strahan must be stopped.'

Still, I waited. Anticipating all manner of remonstrations, I had come prepared. My verbal quiver was full of arrows. But she had stolen my bow.

'Ian, too?' she asked.

'Of course.'

'And the *lir*.' She nodded. 'I can think of no two warriors better equipped for this confrontation.'

I smiled a little. 'Such faith.'

'You are both of you Donal's sons. I think it is not misplaced.'

After a moment, I drew in a quiet breath. 'Ian has called the council. Before I go, I must name Brennan as my heir. And Hart as *Brennan's* heir.'

My mother nodded. Her face was oddly serene. 'You are a wealthy man. *Two* sons to guard the Lion.'

I knew she had always regretted her barrenness. One son. Not enough, not *nearly* enough, when war lives on your doorstep. But the House of Homana had nearly always been poor in sons; she should hardly blame herself.

Two sons. Aye, I was a wealthy man. Perhaps now the tradition changed. I claimed two heirs already, and Gisella was nearly due to deliver another child.

I went to my mother. I bent, cupped her head in my hands, kissed her smooth, fair brow. '*Tahlmorra*,' I told her gently.

She smiled. Squeezed my hands, then let them go. '*Cheysuli i'halla shansu.*'

I smiled. I wanted to laugh out loud; to tell her how accented was her Old Tongue, but I did not. I think she knew. And so, in silence, I went to open the door. And at the door, briefly, I turned back, to wish her a final goodbye; to thank her for her strength.

But I said nothing at all, watching the tears run down her face. And then I went out of the room.

Gisella stared at me. 'Strahan?' she said. 'You are going to find the Ihlini?'

'Find him. *Slay* him, if I can. He must be destroyed.'

Her yellow eyes were very wide and startled; she was a child, I thought, afraid of losing something. 'You are leaving me.'

I sighed. 'No,' I told her. 'No. Not permanently. I will be back, if the gods are willing.'

She sat in the center of her big tester bed, crumpling the coverlet into ruin with rigid, clawlike fingers. 'You are leaving me. Because I am not like Deirdre of Erinn.'

Gods, how she knew to provoke the pain. 'I am going to stop this plague,' I told her harshly. 'It has nothing to do with you. Nothing to do with Deirdre. How *can* it, Gisella? Deirdre of Erinn is dead!'

'And if you go, *you* will be dead.' Awkwardly, she scrambled forward to grab my hand. She pressed it against the mound of her swollen belly. 'Stay here. Stay here. Stay here.'

'Gisella – I cannot. It is a thing I have sworn to do.'

'*Stay here. Stay here. Stay here.*'

I tried to detach my hand, but she hung on with all her strength.

'*—stay here – stay here – stay here—*'

'No,' I told her. '*No.*'

But I knew she could not hear me. The chanting had grown too loud.

Beneath my hand, the child moved.

'*—stay here – stay here – stay here—*'

Gods, my child moves—

'*—stay here – stay here—*'

Child or no, I broke her grip. Because I had to.

I stood up. Moved away from the bed.

The chanting abruptly broke off.

Gisella began to rock. Gisella began to sing.

I closed the door on her song.

I faced what remained of the council in one of my father's audience chambers. It was not the same chamber that had borne witness to the murders of Sarne and Elek, but it was enough like it to instantly set the memories before our eyes. I saw glances exchanged among the Homanans as I took my place in a chair upon the dais, and knew precisely what they recalled. Precisely what they thought.

Ian stood beside my chair. He did not sit, though he had the right; though a second chair stood empty. He stood. As if to illustrate the reality of my rank, and my

341

right to call the assembly in the absence of the Mujhar.

Old men, most of them, or hampered by illness and ancient injuries. Those who were young enough, strong enough, competent enough had assumed their places with the armies. But *these* men were enough, I knew, to bear witness to my announcement.

I leaned forward a little. I felt Serri's warmth and weight against my foot; he lay beside the chair. 'This plague is not happenstance,' I told them. 'Not a cruel test devised by the gods and visited upon us. It is Ihlini treachery, meant to strip Homana of the Cheysuli.'

Once again, sidelong glances were exchanged. And I knew what some of them meant: *strip Homana of the Cheysuli, and the land is Homanan again.*

'In the morning,' I told them, 'I will leave Mujhara. Ian and I are bound for Solinde across the Bluetooth River, across the Northern Wastes. We seek Valgaard, Strahan's fortress. We seek the root of this demon-plague.'

'My lord.' One of the councillors rose. 'What does the Mujhar say to this?'

'There is no time to inform him before we go. He will be told, of course — but Ian and I will be gone.'

I heard murmuring. I heard low-voiced comments made. I knew what many of them were thinking. And I knew I would have to gainsay it.

'You have served the Mujhar well,' I told them. 'And, gods willing, you will serve me equally well when the time is come. But for this moment we must look farther down the road and see another man who is meant for the Lion Throne.'

They were silent now, staring at me attentively.

'Carillon,' I said. 'Carillon betrothed his Homanan-Solindish daughter to a Cheysuli warrior. He did it because he had to. He did it because he was *meant* to, to make certain the throne was secured. And, in time, a son was born to the Prince and Princess of Homana, and the Lion *was* secured.' I drew in a steadying breath. 'A son has been born to the son; a boy intended for the Lion. And I will not leave this place until your loyalty is sworn.'

Another of the councillors rose. 'My lord, this is un-necessary!'

'Is it?' I shook my head. 'If I am slain, there must be an heir for my father. In my place, I put my son. He will assume the title if Strahan takes it from me.'

'My lord—'

'I require it,' I said quietly. 'I am not blind to the knowledge I may be slain, or the threat offered by Carillon's bastard. My first responsibility is owed to my father, my second one to the throne. My third to the prophecy.' I knew they were one and the same, and equally important, but I thought it would please the Homanans if I made each one separate. 'It is not so much,' I told them. 'Surely it is a loyalty you would offer one day anyway. Why not do it now?'

When no one offered argument, I took it for acquiescence. And so I signaled to the guard at the door, who stepped outside a moment, and then the door was opened. Two women came in with my sons.

They brought them to the dais, where I bade the women to face the assembly. Two swaddled bundles, hardly enough to carry the titles I would give them. But I knew it could be done. I had done it myself.

I rose, rounded the end of the table, took my place between the women. One hand I placed on Brennan's head. The other I placed on Hart's. 'Before the gods of Homana and the Cheysuli, I pledge the lives of my sons into the service of the Lion; into the service of Homana. My firstborn, Brennan, I acknowledge as my heir; he will be Prince of Homana. My second son, Hart, I acknowledge as Brennan's heir until such a time as Brennan weds and sires his own. He will be Prince of Solinde.'

I saw the startled expressions; heard the startled ex-clamations. But what better way of stating my confidence in the army than by making Hart prince of a realm we fought?

Beneath my hands the smooth soft brows were cool. 'I request these acknowledgments be formally accepted by

343

the Homanan Council. I request that fealty be sworn.'

They could refuse me, each and every man. I had no power over them; I was not Mujhar. Such a request is more ordinarily made by the king, but my father was not present. If nothing else, my request was a test of their loyalty to *me*. And I think each one of them knew it.

It was Ian who took the oath first. He left his place beside my empty chair and came around the table with Tasha at his side. He stopped in front of the dais where I stood between the women who held my sons. He drew his Cheysuli knife from its rune-worked sheath, kissed the hilt and blade, then bent to kiss each of my sons. He was my liege man, but he offered them his service also. He offered them his life.

He stepped aside. And one by one, slowly, what was left of the Council came forward. My sons were acknowledged my heirs; the Lion was secured.

If the gods see fit to take me, my death will not be in vain.

CHAPTER SIX

Twelve days out of Mujhara, Ian's stallion broke a foreleg. Crashing through crusted snow to treacherous deadfall beneath, the gray snapped his leg and threw my brother as he fell. Ian dug himself out of the snow quickly enough, but the stallion was not so lucky.

I said nothing. I watched, hunched in my saddle, as Ian knelt down and cut the stallion's jugular. And then, as the bright life spilled into the snow, Ian stroked the speckled jaw and spoke quietly to the gray until the life was spent.

He rose. His boots were sodden with blood. He unlaced the saddlepacks and tugged them free of the fallen horse, then pushed through the snow to me.

I reached down to catch the packs as he handed them up. 'I am sorry.'

'Better the horse than me.' But beneath the brutal candor I heard the trace of genuine grief.

I draped the packs across the pommel in front of my thighs and kicked free of my left stirrup. Ian stepped up, swung a leg across the roan's wide rump, settled himself behind me. 'We will buy another,' I told him.

'We will have to,' he agreed. 'Or risk slaying this one with too great a burden in heavy going.'

I watched as Tasha and Serri ran ahead to break a trail. 'There will be another,' I told him confidently.

There was not. It crossed my mind we should turn back, to go home for another horse. But we were two weeks out of Mujhara; the choice had been taken from me. It was unlikely my own horse would survive even the journey home again.

Eighteen days out of Mujhara, the roan died even as we dismounted. Although during the shapechange we could store in the earth such things as clothing, weapons, packs – perishables would spoil. And so we did not bother to carry the packs. In *lir*-shape, we went on.

Five days later, Ian began to cough. And as we neared the Bluetooth he fell markedly behind. I stopped, turned back, looked for two cats and saw only one; saw my brother on hands and knees.

In wolf-shape I ran back to him, but as a human I knelt beside him. '*Ian!*'

He clawed wool from his face and coughed, spitting into the snow. His breathing was loud, labored, rattling in his chest. I heard a sound I had heard before. I saw a face I had seen before.

Rowan's before he died. 'Oh gods–' I said, '–oh, *no*–'

He knelt in the snow, coughing; obscene obeisance to the plague. His face was deathly gray, filmed with sweat; his lips had begun to swell. His eyes were mostly black.

'No – *no*–' I cried. '–*not Ian*–'

He coughed. His eyes glittered with fever. Sweat dampened his hair and dripped into the snow.

I thought of Rowan. I thought of Isolde. Pain enough, in those deaths. More than enough grief. But I could not *begin* to consider what life would be like without Ian.

Not again – gods, not again – I have already done it once. I could not bear it again– 'Serri!' The wolf was at my side. 'Serri – find shelter! Any sort; it does not matter. But let it be warm and out of the wind.'

Even as the wolf sped through the snow Ian tried to call him back. 'No,' he croaked. 'Niall – do not bother.'

'No bother,' I told him. 'You would do the same for me.'

He coughed. It rose from the deepest portion of his chest and brought up foulness with it. Fingers clawed at his throat; freed at last of the woolen wrappings, the swollen buboes were plain to see.

Frenziedly I dragged him up from the ground. Even as he protested, I half carried him to the nearest tree. There I settled him, putting his back against the trunk, and wrapped his throat again.

He coughed. Gods, how he coughed, and it ripped his chest apart. Lips split, bled, crusted, split and bled again. His face was a mask of pain.

Do not take him, I begged the gods. *Do not take my brother. Once already I feared he was dead – do not make me go through it again—*

His eyes were closed, but he did not sleep. He simply breathed, as Rowan had breathed. And each time the rattle stopped, I prayed it would start again.

Oh gods – not Ian – better me instead—

I thought he might be cold, even with Tasha pressing herself against one side. And so I took on the shape of wolf and warded his other side. I waited for Serri to come.

It was later, much later. *A place, lir. A dwelling near the river.*

It took us hours. I stumbled, weaved, staggered beneath the weight of my brother. Ian did what he could to help, but he was so ill and so weak he only made things worse. Tasha and Serri ran ahead yet again, breaking a track as best they could, and at last I saw the glimmer of lantern light through the close-grown trees.

'There,' I told Ian. 'You see? I have brought you to safety.'

'Who would succor a man with plague?' he asked in his ruined voice.

'Someone will. I promise.' *O gods, I beg you – deliver my brother from this—*

We staggered onward. And at last we were free of the trees. The dwelling was very small, a stone hut with thatched roof huddling against the snow-cloaked shoulder of a mountain. Beyond it lay the Bluetooth.

'The ferry-master's,' I gasped.

Ian sagged. I fell as he fell, pulled off balance, and felt myself swallowed by the snow. I was so weary, *too* weary. I struggled up with effort.

My brother was unconscious. Serri and Tasha instantly wrapped themselves around his body as they had throughout the journey to the dwelling, whenever we had stopped. I got up unsteadily and staggered to the door.

'Ferry-master!' I called. 'Master – I need your help!' I fell against the door, banged my gloved fist on the wood. 'Ferry-master—'

The door was pulled open even as I thrust myself aside. I saw a blur of graying mouse-brown hair, brown eyes, a face creased by winter chafing. 'Nae, nae, ye'll nae be needin' me,' the man told me in a thick northern dialect. 'Yon beast be frozen. A man may walk across, wi' nae need o' my ferry.'

'No.' I said. 'No, I need no ferry. I need your *help*—'

'*My* help?' He frowned.

'My brother—' Leaning against the cold stone wall of the hut, I gestured toward the *lir*-shrouded shape of my brother. 'He is ill.'

'Cheysuli,' the ferryman said sharply. 'It be plague, then, aye?'

'I need your help,' I begged. 'Warmth, shelter, food, drink – is it so much to ask? I can even pay you—'

'He'll likely die of't,' the ferry-master told me flatly.

I could barely stand up myself. 'Then let him die in a bed beneath a roof!' I cried. 'Let him die as a man!'

Brown eyes studied me fiercely a moment. Then he stared past me to Ian. At last he hawked, spat out the door, wiped his mouth and nodded. 'Aye. Aye. Ye hae the right of't – isna my place to turn away a sick man. Coom then, lad, we'll bring him under yon roof.'

We brought him under 'yon roof' and settled him in the ferry-master's cot. I shook with a fatigue so deep it nearly made me helpless. As it was, the ferry-master tended Ian more than I myself did. He stripped my brother of his furs and settled hot cloth-wrapped stones against his flesh and covered him up again.

As I bent to look at Ian, the ferryman jerked his head toward me. 'Sit ye doon, boy, afore ye *fall* doon and crack yon head. I'll get ye food and *usca*.'

Lir, do as he says, Serri told me, pressing against my leg. He guided me to a chair near the cot.

Nodding weakly, I fell into the chair. It was roughly made, uncomfortable, but it supported my weary body. '*Usca*,' I said. 'You have *usca* here?'

The ferry-master moved to a shelf pegged into the wall. He caught down an earthenware jug and two dented pewter mugs. 'Aye. Yon ferry be the on'y one on the river road out of the Mujhar's city. There be a road from Ellas as well, and a trade route into Solinde. Most days I see men, I see their goods as well.' He poured, held one mug out to me. 'I hae other drink, but this one warms a man's soul faster. I keep *usca* for the cold.'

Indeed, it warmed my soul, and everything else besides. I slumped in the chair and sipped, taking strength from the bite of the liquor. It burned all the way down to my belly, but it gave me life again.

I pulled myself up in the chair and leaned to look more closely at Ian. Tasha lay just beside the cot, eyes locked on Ian's face. He did not move except to breathe; I heard the rattle in his chest.

Oh gods – I beg you—

'Be bad,' the ferryman said. 'I've seen men die of't afore.'

'So have I.' I thrust one hand into Serri's pelt and tried to take hope from him. 'Master—'

'My name be Padgett,' the ferryman told me. 'Nae *master*, me. Jus' Padgett.'

'Padgett.' I smiled a little and slumped back again in the chair. 'I must trust you with his life. I cannot stay here to nurse him.'

The dark brown eyes narrowed shrewdly. 'I've been on yon beast near thirty years. I've seen a thing or two, but ne'er a man journeying in such weather. What do ye do it for?'

349

The *usca* threatened to put me to sleep. 'The plague,' I said thickly. 'Strahan. I must stop him before he slays more of my race – before he destroys Homana.'

Padgett's surprise was manifest. 'This plague be 'lini-made, then? Not a thing o' the gods?'

'Strahan's,' I said succinctly. 'A thing of Asar-Suti.'

Padgett's brows rose, then knitted as he frowned. He sat down on a stool and picked at a blackened thumbnail in consternation. 'They've ne'er done a thing to me,' he said quietly. 'Oh, aye – a man could say they hae need o' yon ferry, but they be sorcerers. They canna fly, but there are other ways.' He sighed and looked at Ian. 'Folk say the 'lini are evil, and most'y I gie a nod o' the head and go on – because they ne'er done *me* any harm. But – *plague*—' He shook his head. 'Plague be unco' bad. If Strahan turns his hand to harmin' the folk o' Homana – Cheysuli, Homanan, whate'er – I want nae truck with them.' He sighed pensively. 'Go where ye will, lad. I'll do what I can for yon boy.'

Boy. Ian was nearly twenty-five. It made me smile, but then the smile died. I did not want my brother to be this age forever, become only a memory.

'Our coin is gone,' I said, stripping the signet from my finger, 'but there is this in place of gold.' I tossed him the ring. 'If you save him, ferry-master, be certain I will give you more than simple trinkets.'

Padgett turned the ring in the firelight, squinting to study the incised rampant lion. And then he swore aloud. 'Simple trinket? *This?* I know what this is, boy – how did ye coom by it?'

I smiled. 'My father gave it to me.'

'And does he steal from the Mujhar himself?'

'No.' I shook my head.

Padgett stared at the ring. 'I saw one like this on another man's hand. But then I dinna know it – I thought it on'y a ring. 'Twas another man, a soldier in royal liv'ry, who told me what it was.' He turned it; the ruby glowed in the light. 'A long time ago—' He broke off. He looked at Ian and frowned. He rose, went closer, frowned again, and then, in amazement, he swore. 'Hae ye turned back years, then, lad? Hae ye kept the Mujhar young as the 'lini keep themselves?' He looked at me. 'I saw the Mujhar once, near twenty year ago. This ring was on *his* hand – this face was on *his* face.'

'Well,' I said, 'Ian is his son. The resemblance is not surprising.'

Padgett frowned. 'Ye called this boy your brother.'

'Aye.'

'And this ring is from your father.'

'Aye.'

Padgett opened his mouth, shut it. Then he shook his head. 'I canna tak' it, lad. No' from the Prince o' Homana.'

The ring lay in his hand. But I did not take it from him. 'If you keep my brother alive, even *that* is not payment enough!'

'My lord—'

I thrust myself up from the chair and went to kneel by Ian. I did not look at Padgett. 'If *you* will not keep it, give it to someone else. But that is my payment to you.'

After a moment of silence, I glanced back. Padgett's hand shook a little. The ring rolled once in his palm. Then he shut his fingers on it and turned away from me.

I caressed Tasha's sleek head and tried to comfort her. I knew she was in fear. I could see it in her eyes.

If the ferryman can keep my brother alive, I swear, if I could, I would offer him half of Homana.

Serri tucked his head under my elbow and pressed against my side. *You will need it, lir. As a legacy for your sons.*

And if Strahan destroys Homana? What legacy is that?

It is for you to determine, lir. The question will be answered.

I sighed. I rose. I turned away from Ian. 'In the morning, I go on.'

I heard Padgett's indrawn breath of shock. 'So soon ye leave your brother?'

'I have no choice!' I said defensively; the guilt was a weight in my belly. 'Ian himself would be the first to tell me that Homana is more important. That she is worth the sacrifice.' Inwardly I disagreed; I thought nothing was worth the life of my brother. But he would say there was, and so I would respect his wishes.

'What do I tell them, then?' Padgett demanded. 'What do *I* say to them if this man dies, and the Prince o' Homana doesna coom back?'

I looked at Tasha. She lay so still by the cot, maintaining a silent vigil. I thought of Ian, dead, and his *lir* sentenced also to death. I thought of my father, lacking both of Sorcha's children. And I thought of myself, brotherless—

I shut off the thought at once. 'Tell them the truth,' I said. 'They know where we have gone. They know the risks involved.'

'Do *you?*'

Oh, aye, I thought I did. And I was willing to take them. I knew I *had* to take them. For Ian as well as Homana.

CHAPTER SEVEN

'Would you know?' Serri and I stood on the southern bank of the Bluetooth. 'Would you know if my brother died?'

My *lir* stared across the expanse of ice-choked river. His green-gold eyes were slitted; I thought he avoided an answer.

'Serri—'

Not if he died. But if he did, Tasha would also die – that I would know at once.

I turned back and stared at the trees that hid Padgett's tiny hut. All I could see was a smudge of bluish smoke drifting above the bare-branched limbs.

Oh gods – if I leave him – if I leave him and he dies—

Resolutely I turned away and stared blindly across the river. 'Come,' I said, 'we must go.' And I blurred into my wolf-shape.

We went north, fighting the winds and snows. Behind us lay the Bluetooth; we traversed the Northern Wastes. Around us rose bleak walls of slate and indigo, the backbone of the world. Here there were no trees but wind-wracked scrub and brush. No grass, no dirt, no turf, only layers of blue-white ice locked beneath wind-carved layers of crusted snow.

We climbed. Where men could not go *we* could, picking our way through narrow traceries cutting through turreted mountains and wind-honed rock. Our coats thickened, our pads toughened, our eyes remained perpetually slitted. But we knew we would not turn back.

Forests thinned, fell away far below us. The mountains became little more than upward thrustings of barren rock, blank and blue in the howling winds.

Higher. Higher still. And then we were through the Molon Pass and into another realm, climbing down out of the Wastes of Homana into the canyons of Solinde.

Serri, I said, *my brother?*

We are too far for me to ask.

But you would know if Tasha died.

I would know if Tasha died.

Small enough comfort. But it was something; I did not overlook it.

The mountains began to shift their shapes. The slate-blue shadows of Homanan rock took on a darker, more menacing aspect. There were trees again, but twisted, deformed by cruel winds. Roots burst free of the soil. Bare, blackened roots, twisting across stone like a tangle of tapestry yarn. And I began to see shapes in the rocks. Avid faces, gaping mouths, the bulging of eyes in terror.

It made the hair on my neck rise. *Lir—*

Ihlini, Serri said. *They mock us with their stone menagerie.*

Beasts. Hideous, horrible beasts, all locked in blackened stone. I felt my hackles rise; my lips curled back to bare my teeth in a visceral, wolfish snarl.

Serri—

Ahead, lir. Valgaard lies ahead.

Through a narrow defile into the canyon beyond. And there, abruptly, was Valgaard, thrusting out of the earth in a gout of glass-black stone. Curtain walls, towers, parapets, all forming one wall of the canyon. It put me in mind of a massive bird, wings outspread to enfold the world.

How it broods. How it makes the canyon its mews.

Sheer walls jutted upward over our heads. We were small, so small, so insignificant in the ordering of the world. Valgaard crouched before us, cloaked in rising smoke.

My lips drew back. *Gods – how it stinks.*

The breath of the god, Serri told me. *The stench of Asar-Suti.*

It was a field of folded stone, spreading out in all directions. There were waves, curls, bubbles, but all was made of rock. An ocean of steaming stone.

'Serri – something is *wrong*—'
What is right about the Ihlini?

I shuddered. I was not cold; winter had been banished. Behind us lay the defile and beyond that the wind-wracked walls of basalt. But here there was nothing but warmth. A cloying, putrid warmth that made me want to vomit.

Serri— I said. *Serri, the link is fading—*

Too close, he told me. *Too close to the Ihlini.*

We were. I could feel the weakening of the link, the dilution of the power that lent me the ability to shapechange. Even as I concentrated, trying to keep myself whole, I felt the magic fading. I felt myself caught between.

Serri!

I felt the power drain away like so much spilling wine. It splashed against the ground; was turned into hissing steam. And then dispersed upon the air and blown out of Valgaard's bailey.

Abruptly, too abruptly, I was wrenched out of my *lir*-shape and thrown back into human form. But the transference was *too* sudden, too overwhelming for me to withstand.

I cried out. It started as a howl, ended as a scream.

Stone bit into my face. I tasted sulfur, salt, iron. I tasted the spittle of the god. It made me spit out my own.

I pressed myself up from the ground. I was a man again, booted, furred, armed with sword and bow and knife. But I knew – gods, how I *knew* – I needed none of the weapons. This was Strahan's domain, the Gate of the god himself. Nothing but wits could ward me against their power.

The stone was warm beneath my bootsoles. The field stretching before me was pocked with vents that vomited steam into the air. Valgaard was wreathed in smoke.

'Gods,' I breathed, 'look at that. Look at the hounds who guard the lair.'

Hounds? I could not be certain. They were beasts, but none that I could name. Merely shapes. Merely *things*. Extremities only hinted at; formlessness made whole.

Inert, they waited like black-glass gamepieces upon the dark board of Asar-Suti.

I shut my eyes. *Gods – I am so frightened—*

But I knew what I had to do.

'Serri.' I looked down at him, then knelt and swept him into my arms. '*Lir*, I must ask you to stay here.'

Here? Serri's tone was only a thread within my mind, the merest shadow of the link. And fading even as we conversed. *My task is to go with you.*

'Not this time. *This* time, your task is to stay behind. I cannot take you with me.'

Lir—

'I dare not risk us both. This is for me to do.'

He pushed his nose against my neck. *Lir—*

'Serri, say you will stay. Say you will wait for me.'

But if all goes wrong—

'If all goes wrong, at least *you* will retain your freedom. You are young yet, even by human standards; you will not be given to death.'

This is not part of your tahlmorra.

'I *make* it a part of it.' I hugged him firmly. 'There is a chance, albeit a small one. But perhaps it will be enough. Perhaps he will be content.' I unwound my arms from his neck. 'Say you will stay, Serri. Say you will wait for me here.'

Serri's tail drooped. He laid his ears flat back. The tone was only a whisper: *I will wait. What else is there to do?*

Serri— But the link was broken.

I left him. I stepped out from the defile into the field of steam and stone and did not look back at my *lir*. The link was utterly banished; there was nothing binding us now. Only the knowledge of what we were.

Of what there had been between us.

Strahan smiled. 'Somewhat belatedly, you accept my invitation.'

'I thought never to accept it at *all*.'

He nodded. 'People do change. Even princes.' He sipped wine. 'All men eventually grow up.'

356

'Will you?'

We confronted one another in one of Valgaard's tower rooms. The black walls were curved, cylindrical, polished to glassy brilliance. Tapestries cut the chill; one quick glance had showed me I did not wish to see what pictures were in the yarns. Something that shrieked of demons and the god of the netherworld.

Strahan sat. I stood. It was a measure of the circumstances.

'Will I?' the Ihlini echoed. 'Well, perhaps – it depends on how I feel.' He sipped again at his wine. I had been offered a cup of my own, but had not accepted. 'It is not closed to you, Niall: the ability to turn back the years. No more than to anyone else; mind you, I do not make the mistake of inviting you to join me.' He grinned. 'I know better. I know you would never do it. But there *is* an opportunity, for those who desire the power.'

'And how many have accepted?'

'This year? Or last? Or all the years of the past?' He set the cup down on a table and rose, thrusting himself out of his chair. He wore hunting leathers, brown ones, and more than a trifle scuffed. His long black hair, spilling over his shoulders, was glossy and fine as a woman's, and held back by a circlet of beaten bronze. There were shapes in the metal, odd shapes, much as there were shapes in the ill-made stones in the field of the breath of the god. 'So, Niall – you come to me in hopes I will put an end to my plague.'

I watched him. He rummaged in a rune-carved trunk with curving lid. He did not look so much a sorcerer as he did a distracted student, having lost a favorite book.

This is Strahan, I reminded myself, *most powerful of all the Ihlini. Be not misled by the face he wears or the platitudes in his mouth.*

'And I ask you: why? Why should I wish to end my plague?'

My plague. Was he so pleased by it, then? Did he consider it a thing of which to be proud?

Aye. He probably did. 'If ending it gave you something in return, it might be worth it for you.'

357

'But only if the thing was a thing of value.' Still he rummaged through the trunk, only absently paying attention to what I said.

It was disconcerting. He acted more man than sorcerer; more human than demon-born. 'I think it might be,' I told him. 'You wanted it once, though – out of perversity? – you did not take it then.'

He stopped rummaging. Straightened. Turned. Looked at me thoughtfully. 'Willingly you came here.'

'I was not forced – not *physically*. But it was you who brought me here. You did tell me I would come; now, of course, I have.'

'Willingly you came here.' Now he did not smile. 'And – *willingly* – you offer yourself to me?'

I had forgotten how eerie were his eyes, how uncanny in their mismatched brown and blue. He stared, did Strahan; he waited. And I knew not what to say.

He turned back to the trunk. Reached in yet again, drew something forth. I could not see it. He shut it up in a hand.

'Strahan—'

'I have listened,' he said. 'I have heard. But I think you are mistaken.' He closed the lid of the trunk. I heard the catch click shut.

I wanted Serri. I wanted Ian. I wanted free of this place.

I wet my paper-dry lips. 'There was the night you came to Mujhara. For *me*, you said you came. And it was then you told me not to wed Gisella.'

'Aye.' He shrugged. 'I said you should not, but you maintained you would.' He crossed to a heavy book lying open on a stand. 'You know, of course, I might have slain you then,' he said casually. 'It would have been simple enough. But I knew you would be coming. I *prefer* to make men do my bidding before I end their lives.'

I looked at the book. *Grimoire?* I wondered. *The source of so much Ihlini magic?*

Frowning absently, he paged through the book. And as each page turned, I saw the faintest of flames flash out of the red-scripted pages.

'Strahan—'

'You wed her, Niall. You wed Alaric's addled daughter.'

'Aye.' My lips were dry again. 'I will offer you a bargain.'

He did not appear to hear. He stopped turning pages, read something with close attention; then nodded, and closed the book. 'I thought so. Not so hard, I think.' He smiled at me, and the distractedness was gone. He was decidedly intent. 'So, you came here to offer yourself in exchange for the ending of the plague. To offer me something of *value*.'

'I *am*,' I said with what dignity I could muster. 'I am part of the prophecy.'

He nodded. 'Part of the prophecy. A tarnished link, perhaps? Or dross instead of gold?'

He meant to make me angry. And he very nearly succeeded. Inwardly I seethed, but I would not show it to him. 'Dross, gold – does it matter? I am the Prince of Homana.'

'Donal's son,' he mused, 'and Aislinn's as well, which makes you my kinsman as well as my enemy.' Briefly he glanced down at the thing he held in his hand. 'Well, once I might have accepted, when the bargain was a bargain, but now there is nothing in it. Nothing for you *or* me.'

'I give you the prophecy!' I cried. 'Its future is in your hands!'

'Well, no – not precisely.' He shrugged a little, brows raised, and shook his head at me. 'Indeed, it is some measure of sacrifice to offer yourself to me, but there is little value in it. *You* have little value; you married Alaric's daughter. And she has given you sons.'

I opened my mouth. Shut it. And all at once I understood. *Not me. Not me at all. Once, aye, before my sons were born – but now the seed is planted. My link is no longer the last.*

Strahan spread his hands. 'You are too late, Niall. The wheel has turned without you.'

I wanted to sit down. I wanted to *fall* down. I wanted to turn my back on the man. But I could do none of those things.

'Of course,' he said, 'were you to offer me your *sons*—'

'*No*—' I blurted. 'Give over my sons to *you?*'

'But *then* the bargain would be worth the making.' He shrugged. 'You may give them, or I may take them. The choice is up to you.'

So — this is what he has wanted all along; why he did not slay me once he determined my eventual worth — as a sire, if nothing else — like a horse valued for his bloodlines. He wanted the sons I would get on Gisella.

I smiled. 'No,' I told him plainly.

'All right,' he said calmly, 'all right. Then I shall simply *take* them . . . when Gisella brings them to me.'

'*Gisella!*' I stared. 'Gisella would never bring them!'

'But she will,' he said gently, 'when Varien tells her to.'

Slowly I shook my head. 'You are mad.'

'No,' he said, '*Gisella* is mad . . .' He paused deliberately, smiling. 'Unless, of course, she is *not* — and does this for other reasons.'

He had silenced me at last. In the face of Gisella's treachery and deceit I could do nothing but stare at the Ihlini. *Not mad? All of it contrived — an act?*

Strahan watched the play of emotions in my face. And he laughed. 'Something to consider, is it not?' He was truly amused. 'Oh, aye, Lillith is a dutiful sister — she serves me very well. And when Alaric wed a Cheysuli woman, it was Lillith who suggested the children — or *child* — be made to serve as well.'

'Not Gisella. Gisella is *Cheysuli!*'

He made a dismissive gesture. 'Cheysuli, Ihlini — do you think it really matters? We were born of identical parents, the gods who made Homana.' He lifted a silencing hand. 'Cheysuli, aye, she is, and therefore immune to much of our power, but there are tricks that can be taught. Beliefs that can be instilled. *Loyalties* that are secured. I warned you, Niall. That night in Mujhara when your horse had gone lame . . . I warned you not to wed her.' How he watched me, gloating silently. 'But you *did* — and so I devised another plan.'

'You will *not* harm my sons!'

'No, Niall. Of *course* not – I have no wish to harm them; I only wish to *use* them.' He smiled. 'And I shall. One son upon the Lion, one son on the throne of Solinde. And answerable to *me*.'

Alaric. Lillith. Varien. Even, I knew now, Gisella. All serving Strahan's interests? Gods, but how tightly was I bound. How helpless had he made me.

'Gisella,' I said aloud. 'Gods, they are her *sons!*'

'But she has been *mine* since birth. My sister made her so.'

For nothing – everything for nothing – 'For *nothing!*' Overcome, I shouted aloud.

Strahan smiled as I shouted. 'No. Not for *nothing*. You believed in what you did. Some men never have anything to believe in.' He gestured toward the door. 'Now, come with me. There is something I will show you.'

He took me out of the tower into the bailey, and then ordered the gates swung open. Before us lay the field of stinking smoke. The breath of Asar-Suti.

'There,' he said, 'lies your freedom. I think I will give it to you.'

'I am not a fool,' I began. 'If you think I will believe *that*—'

'Then believe *this*.' He held out something that dangled on a chain. A tooth, capped with gold, and hanging from a thin golden chain. I had had one of my own, before I threw it away at Serri's behest.

'Take it,' he said, and put it into my hand.

I did not want it. I wanted nothing to do with it. And as he took his hand away, I threw it into the smoke.

Strahan laughed. 'I thought so. And now the beast is free.'

Out of the smoke and stench was born an Ihlini wolf. His pelt was white, his eyes were blue; he looked a lot like me.

'Illusion,' I said curtly.

'Was it illusion on the Crystal Isle when I slew Finn?' Strahan asked. 'Aye, you know the story – how I slew Donal's uncle. Aye, I see you know it.' He smiled. 'And do you recall what happened to his wolf?'

'Storr – died. He was too old to live without his *lir*.'

361

'He – *died*.' How he mocked me. 'Aye, as a *lir* dies – supposedly there is nothing left when an old *lir* dies. But there was a little left of Storr. Only a *little* – four teeth – and those I claimed for myself once your father and the Ellasian had gone. And with those four teeth I fashioned powerful magic with the aid of Asar-Suti – *powerful* magic, Niall . . . enough to hide Varien's identity, of course – that is easily done . . . but also enough to raze Homana. Enough to purge the land of all Cheysuli.' He looked at the white wolf wreathed in the breath of the god. 'Illusion, you say. Is he? I think not. I think he is the deliverance of Homana.' The Ihlini smiled as I looked at him sharply. 'The plague is born of wolves, Niall. *White* wolves – animals of legend and superstition. All but one is dead now, slain for the bounty offered, but now it does not matter. They have done their work.' He nodded at the wolf who waited, cloaked in hissing steam. 'Slay him, Niall, and you will end the plague.'

'Why?' I asked. 'Why do you give me the answer? Why do you give me the chance?'

He shrugged. 'Enough have died already. I prefer to rule *living* subjects, when I have made Homana mine.'

'I do not believe you,' I said.

Strahan looked at the wolf. 'Go,' he said. 'Your task is incomplete. There are Cheysuli in the world – rid Homana of them.'

The wolf turned, ran, disappeared, even as I cried out. 'Go,' Strahan told me. 'You have knife, bow, sword. It is up to you to stop him.'

I thought, very briefly, of trying to slay Strahan instead. But by then I would lose the wolf.

Strahan's smile was one of subtle triumph, but I saw speculation in his eyes. 'Your choice, Niall. Save your sons – or save the Cheysuli.' The smile grew. 'But which will you choose, I wonder? Gisella . . . or the wolf?'

The chasm opened beneath my feet.

'Your sons . . . or your race?'

I made my voice as steady and cold as I could. 'I can make other sons.'

Strahan laughed. 'But how many on Gisella? How many who will claim the *proper* blood – the blood the prophecy requires?'

I stared after the running wolf. *Without the Cheysuli, without Homana . . . there is no need for my sons . . .*

I ran.

First the wolf – then Gisella—

Gods, how I ran.

The stench filled my nostils. Rising steam veiled my vision. I tasted the tang of sulfur and bile.

I *ran*, threading my way through hissing vents and puddles of steaming water, trying always to see the wolf. But he was gone, made invisible, swallowed by smoke and steam.

Serri! In the link I screamed for help, but the echoes remained unanswered. The task was mine alone.

The ground roared. Vibration stirred my feet. Tongues of flame licked lips of stone; darted out from gaping mouths.

I tripped, fell to one knee, thrust myself up again. Hot water splattered my face.

I ran.

A shape loomed out of the steam. I ignored it – until the shape reached out of itself and tried to swat me down, like a man swatting a fly. I ducked, dodged, nearly fell again as I gaped; the shape was made of stone. Moving, stalking stone.

I ran. And as I ran, I coughed.

—the breath of the god is foul—

Scraping followed; the grate of stone on stone. The gurgle and belch of sulfur; the hiss and roar of vomited steam. And through the smoke-smeared distances I heard the howl of a wolf who sings for the love of it. For the joy of being alive. But not the song of Serri; I know his voice too well. It was the white Ihlini wolf; the demon in the pelt: singing his song of death.

The deathsong of my race.

Gods, how I *ran—*

I was through the defile: out of heat I was thrust into cold.
I shivered. Shivered again; snow still clogged the canyons.
Vented steam was now the plume of breaths expelled. My
sweat shapechanged to ice.

'Serri?'

Lir, I am here. And he was, suddenly, *here*, bounding
toward me out of the snow.

Briefly, I stopped, gasping; preparing to go on. But I
thought now I had a chance. I thought: *now it can be done.*

But I had reckoned without interference; without Ihlini
irony.

Serri saw it first. *Lir — beware the hawk—*

Like a fool I looked at the sky. And the hawk descended
upon me.

Descended—

—and took an eye.

CHAPTER EIGHT

—hands—
  —hands touching—
  —touching me—
Oh gods – the *pain—*
Serri – Serri – Serri—
Hands touching me. Moving me. *Lifting* me.
NoNoNoNo – not with all this pain—
Serri – Serri *– SERRI—*
Oh gods, what has happened?
What have you done to me?

'What have you done to me?'
    The question jerked me into awareness; I realized *I* had asked it. A trace of my voice still sounded in my ear.
    'Be still. Be calm. Be tranquil. The worst is over now.'
    I twitched in shock. It sent a shaft of pain through bandaged eyes. I winced, gasped, hissed; the pain was all-consuming.
    'Be *still*. Do not bestir yourself. Pain is a wolf at the door in winter: fob him off with a morsel or two and he may wait for spring before he comes again.'
    The voice painted pictures with intonations; with subtleties of emphasis. Such a *magnificent* voice. 'Wolf—' *My* voice was more croak than anything else. 'Oh gods – the *white wolf—*'
    'Gone,' the clear voice told me. 'And for now, you must *let* him go. Aye, he must be caught, be slain, but there is nothing now you can do. Not yet. Wait a bit; I promise, you will fulfill your own *tahlmorra*.'

All was darkness. My eyes were sealed shut by bandages.
I smelled the tang of herbs; felt the warm weight of a
poultice against my right eye.

Oh gods – my eye is gone—

'Be still,' the calm voice warned me. A hand was against
my shoulder, pressing me down even as I tried to sit up.

—the pain – the pain – the pain—

'Serri? Serri?'

'He is here,' the voice told me, and I felt the cold nose
pressed against my neck.

Lir, do as Taliesin tells you. His skills will heal you.

'Taliesin?'

'Aye,' the voice answered. 'But you are too young to
know me. And my name is no longer spoken.'

'Where have you brought me?'

'To my cottage. You need not fear discovery; Strahan does
not come here.'

'*You* know Strahan? You know he did this to me?'

'I know Strahan, aye. And I know what he did to you.'
The voice hesitated a moment. 'Not so very different from
what he did to *me*.'

I shut my teeth in my bottom lip. My eye throbbed with
increasing pain. I thought I might swoon from it.

Serri – Serri—

*I am here. I am here. Do not fear I will go. I will not leave
you, lir.*

'Here.' A hand was slipped beneath my head, tipping it
up. Such a strong, wide hand, cradling my skull so gently.
Another pressed a cup against my lips; I drank the bitter
brew. 'It will help the pain,' Taliesin told me. 'Sleep, my
lord – let the herbs do their work.'

My lord . . . 'You know me?'

'I do not *know* you – how could I? But aye, I know who
you are. Be at ease, my lord. Solindish I may be, but I have
no quarrel with Homana. Certainly none with *you*.'

'Your voice—' I was slipping into sleep. 'I am sorry. I
could not say if you are man or woman.'

Taliesin laughed. 'Well, a true bard may be either or both

366

when he sings his lays and sagas. But when your eye is free again, you will see I am a man.'

When your eye is free again . . . How odd it was to know I had only one.

How it twisted the blade in my belly.

The hawk has stolen my eye—

Be still, Serri told me. *Rest. Cheat Strahan of his triumph. He meant to slay you, lir.*

The hawk? Serri – Serri – that hawk—

Dead. Did you think I would let him live?

I shut my hand in Serri's ruff. I wanted to hug him, to pull him into my arms and press him against my chest, to bury my face in his fur.

Mostly I wanted to cry.

But even as I tugged at his pelt, seeking strength and reassurance, I felt myself slipping away. *Serri, do not go – do not leave me—*

I will never leave you, lir.

I slept.

'You said I would fulfill my *tahlmorra*.'

'Aye. You will.'

'But you are Solindish. What do you know of *tahlmorras*?'

'Better to ask: what do I know of Cheysuli?'

I lay on the pallet beneath warm furs. As yet I was a blind man; Taliesin told me the hawk had torn the flesh near my left eye as well as destroying the right. Until the wounds were healed, I would be kept in darkness.

Serri was additional warmth stretched the length of my body. He slept, twitching in dreams; I wondered what he chased.

'*What* do you know of Cheysuli?' I asked obligingly. But my curiosity was genuine.

'I know of *tahlmorras* and *lir* and responsibilities. I know of the dedication that drives your race; the loyalty of the fanatic; the arrogance of a man who believes he is a child of the gods.'

'*Believes!*' I did not like his attitude, regardless how

367

quietly he expressed it. 'We *are* children of the gods.'

'Oh, aye, I know. The word *Cheysuli* means that precisely. But it means other things, as well: zealotry and intolerance, single-minded determination, the willingness to sacrifice many for the sake of a single man: the Firstborn. The child of the prophecy. The Lion of Homana.'

'By the gods, you sound like an *Ihlini*.'

'I should. I am.' A hand pressed me down again. 'Be still, my lord. I am not one of Strahan's minions. That I promise you.'

'Do you set a trap for *me*?'

'Do I? Test it. Test *me*, my lord.' The hand released me. 'Get up from your sickbed and walk out of my hut forever. I will not keep you. I will not call you back. I will tell no one you were here.'

Sweat broke out on my flesh. 'You know I cannot. You *know* I can hardly rise myself without the pain throwing me down again.'

'Then ask your *lir*,' he told me. 'Ask Serri. *Think*, Niall – has the link between you been broken?'

No. Serri and I conversed as we always conversed. There was no weakness in the link, no interference that drained the power away.

'If you are Ihlini, this is not possible.'

'It is. I am not one of Strahan's Ihlini; nor am I one of Tynstar's, though once he was my lord. No. I am Ihlini, aye, but no more your enemy than your *lir*. There is a difference, my lord, a divergence of opinion. Strahan does not rule us all, only those who wish it. Only those who serve Asar-Suti.'

'And you do not.' My dubiousness was plain, but Taliesin was patient.

'Asar-Suti is the god of the netherworld; the Seker, who made and dwells in darkness. But I caution you, my lord: be not so quick to lump us all together. Be not so ready to give me over into darkness when I prefer the light.'

I thought suddenly of the old woman in Homana, the old *Ihlini* woman, who had sacrificed her life to make certain

Ian and I believed she told the truth. She had not done it for us. She had done it for Homana.

'How can it be?' I asked blankly. 'How is it possible?'

'It is possible because the gods gave us the freedom to choose. Even you. Aye, I will admit there seems to *be* no choice when you know you deny the afterworld by denying the prophecy, but there still exists the choice. You could renounce your title, your birth, your blood. You could renounce your *tahlmorra*.'

'I would die!'

'All men die eventually.'

'I have no wish to hasten it!'

I heard him move. No longer did he kneel beside me. I heard footsteps, the scrape of a chair, the sound of him sitting down. But still his voice carried to me as if he knelt beside me.

'I have no wish to shake your faith; to question your dedication. Once, I shared it myself, though I gave it to my lord and Asar-Suti. I *believed*, because Tynstar made certain I did. And I served as well as I could, until I began to question the validity of Tynstar's intentions. Why, I wondered, was it so important for him to have Homana? Why was it so necessary to destroy our brother race in order to claim the land? And so, one day, I asked him.'

My fingers were locked in Serri's pelt. 'What did he say?' I asked tightly. 'What was Tynstar's answer?'

'He said if the Ihlini did not destroy the Cheysuli, the end of the world would come.'

'He *lied!*'

'Did he?' For a moment there was silence. 'Be not so certain, Niall.'

'Tynstar *lied!* How could the world end? Do you think the gods would let it?'

'I speak of perception, my lord, not of absolutes. You know what enmity lies between the races. You yourself are a victim of it; do you not distrust and hate Ihlini? Do you not slay one when you can?'

'Taliesin—'

369

'Perception, Niall: if the Cheysuli are allowed to live and the prophecy is fulfilled, the bloodlines will be merged. The Firstborn will emerge. And, in time – as it is with horses, dogs, sheep – the original bloodlines will be overtaken by the new.' He paused. 'Tynstar spoke the truth: if the Ihlini do not destroy the Cheysuli, the world will come to an end. The world *as Ihlini perceive it.*'

'But – if that were *true*—'

'It is all we have, Niall – our only legacy. And the prophecy will destroy it.'

Survival, Lillith had called it. Nothing more than a struggle to keep a race complete, undivided, *undiminished* by the thing that would destroy the Ihlini: the prophecy of the Firstborn.

How can I blame them for it? How can I hate them for it? They do what I would do; what anyone would do, trying to keep a race whole.

'Oh gods,' I said aloud, 'you turn me inside out.'

'I do not ask you to question your convictions, Niall. I do not say you are *wrong*, or that the Cheysuli are. I say only that when I realized the cost of Tynstar's intentions, I knew I could not afford it.'

'But if we did *not* serve the prophecy—' I broke off. It was unthinkable. It was impossible to envision.

Take the prophecy away and what have we to live for?

I dug rigid fingers more deeply into Serri's pelt. 'How better to overcome the enemy than by removing his reason for living?' I asked bitterly. 'Is this what you try to do?'

'I ask you to make no judgments. I do not intend to shake your faith. I only explain how it was that one Ihlini chose to deny his god, his lord . . . and renounce the gifts the Firstborn gave us.'

'Gave *you?*'

'Aye,' he said gently. 'Not all of us are evil. Not all of us serve Asar-Suti. And when we do not, when we have not drunk of the Seker's blood, we remain only men and women who have a little magic. A *little* magic, Niall . . . the sort *you* would claim if Serri left you.'

370

Serri? Serri? But my *lir* did not answer. It frightened me. 'I would *die* if Serri left me!'

'No. If Serri left you *of his own volition*, you would not die because of it. You would lack the shapechange, the healing – the things the *lir*-bond gives you. But you would not die.'

'There is the death-ritual.'

'Because suicide is taboo. It does not matter, Niall. The ritual is in force only if the *lir* is slain – not if the *lir* deserts you.'

'Serri would never desert me! No *lir* would desert a warrior!'

I expected Serri's immediate agreement; he remained oddly silent.

Serri – you promised you would not leave me!

'Not in your lifetime,' Taliesin said calmly. 'Perhaps it will not happen even while your sons rule the realms you give them. But *some* day – *one* day – when the child of the prophecy is born . . . the *lir* will know a new master.'

No.

' "*One day a man of all blood will unite, in peace, four warring realms and two magic races*," ' Taliesin quoted. 'What happens *then*, Niall? What becomes of the Ihlini? What becomes of the Cheysuli?'

No.

'The races, merged, form a new one. The one that lived before. The one with *all* the power.'

Serri, say it is not true.

'It is what the gods intend. It is what the Ihlini must stop – those who serve Asar-Suti. Because when the Firstborn emerge again, the Seker will be defeated. The Gate will be sealed shut; the netherworld locked away. The Firstborn shall rule the world in the names of other gods.'

'And you renounced Tynstar because of that?' I asked. 'Because you *support* the merging of the races?'

'It means life, my lord, for all of us. I want the Cheysuli destroyed no more than the Ihlini. And the only means for settling our feud forever is to change the face of hatred.'

In darkness, I could not see it. But I doubted anyone could.

Serri? Serri?

Nothing.

Gods, I thought, *I am* afraid — *afraid he tells me lies. But* more *afraid because he may be telling the truth.*

CHAPTER NINE

'There is someone *here!*' I said sharply. I levered myself up on one elbow next to Serri; the pain was mostly bearable now. 'Taliesin.'

'Your ears are keener,' the Ihlini told me. 'Aye, there is someone here, but Caro has always been here.'

'Caro?'

'My guest. My friend. My hands.'

'Hands?' I pressed fingers against the bandages and gently scratched the itching flesh beneath. 'Gods, could you use your hands to rid me of these bindings? I am going mad.'

'Aye, I think it is time. But Caro will unwrap you.'

In a moment I felt hands on the knots of my bandages, loosening, untying, unwrapping. Light crept in, then blazed as my left eye was freed. The right one saw nothing at all.

I shut my left eye. 'It hurts – the light hurts me—'

'Because it has known darkness for too long. Be patient. The eye is unharmed. You will see clearly again.'

Tears ran out from under my shielding lid. I could not stop the watering. 'And my right eye?'

'Gone,' Taliesin told me gently. 'You will need a patch; I will have Caro make you one. I *could*, but he will do it better.'

Caro's big hands were gentle and familiar. All along it had been *he* who tended me, not Taliesin. Not *physically*. But with his voice, oh, aye – his beguiling, beautiful voice.

With a cloth Caro sponged the tears away, then rubbed tender flesh with an herbal salve. Now that I *knew* he was here, I wondered how I had not known it all along.

'*Leijhana tu'sai*,' I told him. 'My thanks, Caro.'

'He cannot hear you,' Taliesin said quietly. 'Caro is deaf and dumb.'

My eyelid jerked open. I squinted as tears welled up again; my empty socket throbbed. But I ignored it. I looked at Caro. Wide-eyed, I *stared*, trying to see him clearly. And when I could, I began to laugh.

It hurt. But I laughed. I *cried*. I could not help myself. Because Caro was myself.

Gods, how I laughed.

'Did you know?' I asked Taliesin, when the laughter and tears had faded. 'Did you *know?*'

He did not answer at once. For the first time I looked upon him as he sat in a lopsided chair. His hair was white, bound back by a thin silver circlet, but his face was smooth, unaged; the face of a man eternally young. His clear eyes were very blue.

I looked at his hands. Twisted, gnarled things, once whole, now not; someone had *purposely* destroyed them, for nothing else could do such tremendous damage.

Gods – who would do that to a man like Taliesin?

I looked again at Caro, who knelt in silence beside my pallet. 'Did you know?' I repeated to Taliesin.

Did you know? I asked my lir.

You were ill, in pain – what profit in telling you before you needed to know?

'They told me his name,' Taliesin said. 'Carollan. They asked me to keep him safe.'

Carollan/Carillon. Not quite the same, but close enough. Like father, like son – except the son was deaf and dumb.

'Safe,' I echoed, looking at my kinsman; at Carillon's bastard son. 'They believed my father would slay him?'

'They were convinced of it. There was nowhere in Homana he would be safe, they said, and so they brought him nearly two years ago to Solinde. To Taliesin the bard, who once sang in the halls of Solindish kings; in the halls of Ihlini strongholds. They knew. They knew I could never harm him. And they knew no one would look for him here. When they need him, they borrow him. But they always bring him back.' He paused. 'It was how I knew you, Niall. This close to the border even *I* hear news of how the Prince of Homana resembles his grandsire; how the bastard resembles his father.'

I looked at Caro in fascination. He was me. But *not*, quite. He was thirty-six, nearly sixteen years older than I. His face was older, as was to be expected; wind-chafed, with traceries of sunlines at the outer corners of his eyes. His beard was more mature. But everything else was the same: tawny, sunstreaked hair, darker beard, blue eyes, almost identical shape of facial bones. Carillon had well and truly stamped his progeny.

I laughed once. But this time it was little more than an expulsion of ironic comprehension. 'And so the Homanans who wish to replace Niall with Carillon's bastard want nothing more than a puppet. An empty vessel upon the Lion, so *they* can rule Homana.'

'Aye, I believe they do.'

I thought of Elek. I thought of Sarne, who had so eloquently campaigned for her disabled son. Gods, but how steadfastly she had insisted Carillon had promised his son a place in the succession. And I thought of the people who had rallied to Caro's standard. Gods, how ludicrous it all seemed now.

I shook my head. 'Surely they understand once the truth is known, the petition will be denied.'

'Surely they do,' Taliesin agreed. 'But I am sure they feel the truth will never be discovered, or – if it is – it will be too late; the Lion will already be theirs. Look at what they have already accomplished, even with him hidden.' He shook his white-haired head. 'Do not forget, Niall, many people never see their king. Many people know only his name, not what or who he is. They toil to pay his taxes, they die in his armies, they celebrate his name-day and the birth of sons and heirs . . . but only rarely do they set eyes upon the man. He is a *name*. And it is possible for a realm to be governed for years by only a name.'

Frowning, I shook my head pensively, carefully. 'But they

were all so *willing* to follow him, to put him on the throne. So willing to slay Carillon's *grandson* to make way for the bastard son.'

Taliesin nodded. 'He is legend, now, as you should know so well. How better to recapture the man himself? By elevating his son. A son is a *son*, and closer than the grandson. And there are those who desire to keep the throne Homanan, to use it for themselves. But mostly I think there are those who desire only to serve the man they believe to be the rightful heir; it is not so impossible to believe Caro is that man. He *is* Carillon's son. Can you blame them? They know only that, nothing more; that he is a *son*, not a grandson – Homanan, not Cheysuli.' His voice was very quiet. 'They believe in what they are doing.'

I stroked Serri's coat. *As so many of us believe . . . Cheysuli, Ihlini, Homanan.*

As so many of you must *believe.*

Aye – *must.* I thought of Strahan and Lillith, serving their noxious god while they also served themselves, desiring to save their race. I thought of Alaric of Atvia, opportunistic Alaric, who no doubt realized he alone could not defeat Homana but that he might come out the victor if he aided the Ihlini by giving his daughter to Lillith. And I thought of the *a'saii*, who sought the purest blood of all and were willing to spill mine in order to get it.

Oh, aye, *all of us*, doing what we had to in order to make certain we survived; to secure the best possible of places in this world and the next.

Serri's tone was warm and wise. *Because, wrong or right, you* believe *in what you do.*

Aye. Every one of us.

Aloud, I said: 'Nothing excuses bloodshed. Nothing excuses the *annihilation* of a race.'

Taliesin's smile was incredibly sweet. This one was also compassionate. 'And do you refer to the Ihlini? Or do you speak of the Cheysuli?'

Bitterly, I glared at him from out of my single eye. 'Both. *Both.* What *else* can I believe?'

He sighed. His ruined hands twitched in his blue-robed lap, as if he longed to clasp them in victory; knowing he could not.

Caro leaned down to rub more salve into my flesh. But I stopped him. I caught his wrist, sat up slowly, confronted him face to face.

I looked for some indication, some *sign* he knew who he was; *what* he was, and what he might have become. But there was only patient curiosity as he waited for an explanation.

I let go of him. 'They told him nothing.'

'No. I think they believe him a lackwit, unable to comprehend. He is not, of course. But neither is he fit to be Mujhar.'

Slowly I shook my head. 'And so the great plan is undone. I have only to announce his disabilities, and the Homanan rebellion is over.'

'So it is.'

Said too sadly; I looked at the Ihlini in sudden consternation. 'Would they slay him? – the Homanans? Would they destroy the useless puppet?'

'I think it more likely they would simply cut the strings. But I will pick them up.' He lifted his ruined hands. 'There is some movement left, I think I can work those strings. Better yet, I will cut them off entirely and let him go without.'

I looked at Caro. I could not tell what he thought. But I knew he was not the enemy, intentionally or no.

I reached out, clasped his arm, nodded to him a little. 'My thanks, Caro,' I told him clearly. 'In the Old Tongue – *leijhana tu'sai.*'

His eyes watched the movement of my mouth; the emotions in my face. I could not be certain he understood. But he smiled. He smiled my smile, returned my clasp, and went to sit upon a stool.

I looked at Taliesin. 'Who did that to your hands?'

'Not Tynstar.' The blue eyes were clouded with memories. 'No, for many years I pleased him with my skill. Instead

377

of remaining an itinerant Ihlini bard, I gained a permanent patron . . . until I asked him why he wanted to destroy the Cheysuli; why he wanted to steal Homana.' The mouth tightened a little. 'But he did not ruin my hands. No. His punishment was of a different sort entirely. He gave me the "gift" of eternal life. He said that if I was truly a man who did not believe in what he and others sought to achieve, he would make absolutely *certain* I was alive to see it when he achieved it. So I could make songs about the fall of Homana and the rise of the Ihlini.'

'Then who *did* destroy your hands?'

'Strahan did this. He felt I was deserving of graver punishment. Once his father was slain by Carillon, Strahan showed his grief by punishing those who would not serve him. And so he destroyed my hands; that I would live forever without the magic of the harp.'

Strahan did this. Aye, Strahan did much to ruin the flesh of others. Retribution for the ear he had lost to Finn?

'I must go,' I said finally. 'I cannot remain here longer. I fear for the safety of my sons, and there is a wolf I have to slay.'

Taliesin rose. He went to a trunk, lifted the lid, drew out a piece of polished silver. He brought it to me and put it into my hands. 'So you will know,' he said.

When I found the courage, I looked. And saw the price of Strahan's humor.

I tried to remain dispassionate, to study my face without emotion. But I could not. All I saw was the lidless, empty socket and the livid purple weals.

All I saw was disfigurement; the ruination of a man. I let the silver fall out of my hand.

Taliesin picked it up with his gnarled claws. 'Caro will make a patch.'

'Patch,' I echoed blankly. *Oh gods, lir, what will the others think? What will the others see?*

What they have always seen, those who know how to look.

Gently, I touched the puckered talon scars. They divided my right brow in half, stretched diagonally across the bridge of my nose to touch the lid of the other eye, reached down-ward out of the empty socket to cut into my cheekbone. There was no question the hawk had known precisely what he was meant to do. But for Serri, he might have done it.

'They will fade, soften . . . in time they will not be so bold.' Taliesin told me. Gently, with compassion. With endless empathy.

Lir, they will heal.

The bard and my *lir* took such care to reassure me. But I *knew* the scars would heal. Of course. I knew that. One day I would grow used to the disfigurement; would hardly notice the scars.

But what they would look like in five or ten years had nothing to do with *now*.

'Maimed,' I said hollowly.

'Niall, you have another eye. Once you are accustomed, you will find the loss of one hardly interferes,' Taliesin said quietly. 'Even as *I*—'

'Maimed,' I repeated. 'Do you know what it means to a Cheysuli?'

He frowned a little. 'Is it – does it mean a thing apart from other races?' He shrugged a little. 'Forgive me, but I fear I do not comprehend your fear.'

'A maimed warrior is useless,' I told him steadily, defying myself to break. 'He cannot hunt food, protect his clan, his kin.'

Taliesin's raised hand stopped me. 'No more,' he said. '*No more.* Forgive me for speaking openly, but I say that is foolishness. What is to stop you from lifting a sword? From loosing an arrow? From slaying deer and others for food? What, Niall? Do you mean to tell me you will give up because you have lost an *eye?*'

I tried to frown and discovered it hurt too much. 'You do not understand. In the clans—'

'You do not live only in the clan,' he told me quietly. 'You will be Mujhar of Homana one day; do you give up the service of your realm and your race because you lack an eye?' He lifted his twisted hands. 'I can no longer play my harp. But I can do other things. Not well, perhaps, but enough to keep me alive. With Caro, it is easier. But as for *you*—' he shook his head '—you are young, strong, dedicated . . . there is no reason in the world you cannot overcome a minor disability such as the loss of an eye.'

'Minor disability?' I stared at him. 'I lost an *eye!*'

'And have another.' Taliesin looked at Caro. 'He has no voice. He hears nothing. And yet he does not give up. Why should you?'

I lost an eye. But I did not say it aloud. I edged back down on the pallet and lay flat, staring one-eyed at the uneven roof of the little hut. But I saw nothing at all.

'It will be difficult,' Taliesin told me. 'You need time, Niall, more time than you have allowed yourself. The loss of an eye requires adjustment. Your perceptions will be different.'

That I had already learned by simply moving about the hut. But I had no more time to spend on myself, not even for needed healing. I had to reach my sons. I had to slay the wolf.

We stood just outside the crooked door. Sunlight spilled through limbs and leaves to make fretwork shadows on the slushy snow. Caro and I were bookends to Taliesin in the middle. Serri stood a little apart, twisting to lick a shoulder into order.

'I have to go. I have – responsibilities.' I smiled a little; too well I recalled his gentle diatribe about Cheysuli intransigence and unshakable dedication.

'The gods go with you, Niall. *Cheysuli i'halla shansu.*'

'*Ru'shalla-tu.*' I resettled the shoulder pouch the bard had given me, filled with rations for when I was not in *lir*-shape. I set a hand on Taliesin's shoulder. '*Leijhana tu'sai.* Not enough, I know . . . but for now the words will have to do.' I looked at Caro. 'You will protect him, Taliesin? Let no one use him falsely.'

'That I promise you.'

Briefly Caro and I clasped arms. He opened his mouth as if he meant to speak, closed it reluctantly. Regret bared his teeth a moment, an eloquent moment, until I pulled him into an embrace. 'It does not matter,' I told him clearly, when he could see my face again. 'I know what you mean to say.'

He smiled. *My* smile.

Serri?

Here, he answered. *Time to go, lir. The white wolf will not wait.*

Then let us go at once. And I blurred myself into *lir*-shape. Shoulder to shoulder we sped through Solindish forests toward the Molon Pass and the border of Homana.

CHAPTER TEN

I lost *lir*-shape as we approached the northern bank of the Bluetooth. Pain lived in my skull, centering in the empty socket, and I could not summon the concentration required for the shapechange. I felt it slipping, tried to rekindle the magic, stumbled even in wolf-shape, lost the shape entirely. On one knee I knelt in the snow, bracing myself against a stiff arm, and waited for the pain to die away.

Lir. Serri pressed against me, but gently, resting his jaw on the top of my shoulder. *Lir, we must go on. The wolf—*

'I know,' I gasped aloud. 'I know, Serri, but—' I sat down awkwardly, sliding over onto one hip, and pressed fingers against my skull. *Oh gods, take the pain away—*

Lir, we must go. I feel *him – he is near the ferryman's cottage.*

Caro's patch warded my empty socket against the bite of cold weather and the brilliance of the sun. I fingered it gently, resettling it; too new, it was uncomfortable. It cut diagonally across my forehead, above my right ear, tied at the back of my head. And though Caro had knotted it gently, at the moment it felt like an iron manacle pressing in against tender flesh.

Lir – Serri again.

'I know . . . a moment.' I gathered my knee under me, waited, carefully thrust myself to my feet. It was all I could do not to vomit.

Lir, the wolf has crossed the Bluetooth.

'Then so will we . . . but I think I shall have to walk.'

Lir, it is your rujholli he seeks.

'Ian!' I stared at my *lir*. 'Finally you can reach Tasha? Ian is *alive?*'

Alive. But endangered. The wolf is seeking him.

Oh – gods— 'Serri – let us *go!*'

The river was still frozen, but the first signs of thaw had begun. I heard mutters in the ice and the occasional snap of cracking floes. Serri ran back and forth along the bank, trying to find the safest way across; at last he plunged ahead. He slipped, slid, fell, got up and ran again. But he had four legs to my two and was unhampered by a missing eye. Carefully I followed his lead, but my progress was slowed by uncertainty of footing as well as the pain in my head.

Slick – so *slick* . . . no matter how careful and deliberate I was, my bootsoles slid on the ice. My arms flailed out as I tried to maintain my balance; I bit my lip and cursed.

Lir . . . come—

Slipping, sliding, jerking uncontrollably. Patches of crusted snow hastened my progress, but treacherous ice often lay beneath.

Lir . . . the wolf—

Halfway. *Halfway.* I set my teeth and refused to look at the southern bank for fear I would lose my fragile balance. One step at a time . . .

And then I heard the howl of a stalking wolf.

My head jerked up. I saw the bank – the smudge of smoke along the treeline – Serri on the other side. And then my balance was lost.

I fell. Landed on shoulder and hip, cracked forehead against the ice. Slumped down and moaned as the pain erupted inside my skull.

Lir – you must come!

My cheek was pressed against the snow-crushed ice. My breath rasped and blew smoke into the air. It tickled my only eye.

Lir—

I moaned. Curled. Rocked a little, back and forth, hugging arms against my belly.

Lir—

383

I heard the sound again: the song of a wolf on the trail of prey.

Ian. Ice and sky exchanged places as I tried to regain my senses. *The wolf is after Ian.*

Up. I pushed myself up, up again, until I was on hands and knees. My empty socket throbbed; I thought my head might burst.

Lir— Back and forth along the bank: silver-gray wolf with green-gold eyes.

Ian. Up. Up again. Standing. Wavered. Stared blindly at my frenzied *lir*.

Ian.

I heard the howl of the wolf.

I shut my eye. I blocked out all the sounds, the sights, the cold and pain and weakness. All of it, gone, swallowed by concentration. I was aware of the great void waiting to take me away, to clasp me against its breast. Calmly I welcomed it, even as I was welcomed.

Lir-shape, I told it. *I need it.*

It examined me. Tasted me. Spat me out again.

I went on in the guise of a wolf.

Serri hardly waited. As I scrambled up the icy bank he went on ahead, streaking through the trees. I followed his lead, on the track of Strahan's wolf.

The hut. It was mostly a blur as I ran: a smudge of gray stone and the weave of careful thatching. And Ian, standing in front of the door.

He turned. Frowned; he had heard the wolf. From out of the trees the wolf exploded: a streak of purest white. Heading for my brother.

Serri – warn Tasha—

Already done— Ahead of me, Serri ran.

Ian saw all of us: two white wolves and one of silver-gray, each running directly at him. He fell back a step toward the hut. Stopped. Half-drew his knife, but did not finish. His confusion was obvious.

'Niall?' I heard him ask.

Gods, he cannot know which one of us is me!

384

One-eyed, even in wolf-shape, it was difficult to differ-
entiate shadows, angles, splashes of sunlight across the
brilliance of blinding snow. I had not yet learned to decipher
all the signals. It would take time, *too much* time – and I
had none of it now. So I ran.

I altered my route, moving to dissect the white wolf's
path. Even as *he* prepared to leap, Serri hit Ian, knocked
him down, turned to protect him. By then I was on the wolf.

Jaws closed on pelt and muscle, locking on his throat.
We tumbled, rolled, were up—

Like me he went for the jugular, trying to tear out my
throat. It was an obscene dance of death, a ritualistic
courtship. We tore, shook, growled, tried to throw one
another down. One-eyed, I was hampered; two-eyed, he
was not.

Ian was up, gone, back. His bow was in his hands; an
arrow was nocked and prepared.

But I saw his indecision. He could not tell which wolf
was brother and which was not.

Hind claws scored my belly – teeth locked in my flesh
– I smelled the stench of rotting meat – the stink of the
charnelhouse – the ordure of the netherworld.

Jaws closed, chewed, tried to tear. I lunged backward,
then sideways, trying to throw him down. Paws scrabbled,
claws ripping into the winter-hard turf . . . he growled and
gasped and choked.

Backward again, again, *again* – then I lunged forward
and took even more of his throat into my jaws.

I shook him, I shredded, I ripped. I felt the tearing in
his flesh. I heard the rattle in his chest and tasted the salt-
copper flavor of blood.

He tore loose. Stumbled backward. Staggered, bleeding
profusely. His tongue lolled, dragged, dangled. He fell.
Scrabbled briefly. Died.

My head hung low. Blood was a mask on my muzzle,
painting me up to my eye. My tail drooped. I turned, saw
Ian's arrow aimed at me, realized he could not know which
wolf had won. And then I lost the *lir*-shape.

'Niall! Oh – gods – *rujho*—' He threw down the bow and leaped, catching my shoulders as I wavered on my feet. 'Niall!'

He broke off so abruptly, staring at me in such horror, that at first I could not comprehend what had happened to him to cause it. And then I remembered my face.

I hung onto his arms. 'Alive,' I gasped. 'Thank the gods – you are *alive*—'

'Niall – what *happened?* Gods, *rujho*, what has happened to you?'

I could not believe I could touch him and know he was alive. 'I feared the plague was always deadly. Gods, but I thought you were dead! Serri could no longer reach Tasha in the link.'

The cat was next to Ian, leaning against one knee. 'I was not nearly as sick as the others. But – *Niall*—'

I put a trembling hand to my head. It hurt. It hurt so badly. 'Strahan,' I said briefly through gritted teeth. 'Strahan sent a hawk.'

'Niall, come in and sit down. At *once.*'

'No. No – first there is something—' I pulled away from him and turned to the wolf. There was no doubting he was dead; his throat was completely gone. I could still taste the tang of blood in my mouth. 'Burn it,' I said hoarsely. 'He is the last of the plague-wolves; Homana will be free.'

'I will,' he said after a moment. 'I will. But come inside. You look near to collapse.'

I was. My head pounded unmercifully; I thought if perhaps I carried it rigidly on my shoulders, I would not stir further pain. Ian took me into Padgett's dwelling and made me sit down in one of the crooked chairs. The hut was empty.

'Gone for supplies.' Ian told me as he moved to pour refreshment. *Usca*, again; I took the cup he gave me, drank, shut my eye. 'He should be back soon. I had planned to leave today.'

'Leave?' I opened my eye as Serri sat down between my knees. 'For Mujhara?'

386

'No.' Ian frowned. 'No, Niall, of course not. I meant to come after you.'

I wanted no more of the Steppes liquor and gave it back to him. 'I thought surely you were dead. And you might have been *yet* – Strahan sent that wolf to carry plague to those Cheysuli who were left.'

Ian squatted before my chair. He looked a little older; the plague had scuffed the edges off his youth. 'Niall—'

'We have to go home at once. The enemy is harbored in the halls of Homana-Mujhar.' I rubbed at my right temple, trying to massage away the pain. 'Gisella serves Strahan. And Varien is Ihlini. They mean to steal my sons.'

'Your *sons*?'

'He means to use them. To *twist* them, then place them on the thrones of Homana and Solinde. And he could succeed, if Gisella takes them to him.' I grimaced, then shut my teeth on the moan I longed to make. 'We have to go *now*.'

'No. In the morning, perhaps. You can go nowhere, now.' He rose, put the cups and *usca* away, asked me if I was hungry.'

'If I eat anything right now, it will only come up again.' I leaned back a little and shut my eye. 'Ian – do you recall what the old woman said to us? The old Ihlini woman?'

'Aye.' He moved around the hut behind me; I could not see what he did.

'Well, I begin to think what she said was true. About Ihlini and Cheysuli being brother races . . . both children of the Firstborn. Taliesin said it also.'

'Taliesin?'

'Ihlini,' I answered. 'Once a bard for Tynstar himself. No more.' I told him then how Taliesin had tended me. But I said nothing of Caro, not yet; another time, perhaps.

Ian listened, then came around to sit down on a stool in front of me. 'It is heresy, Niall. You know that. It goes against all the teachings – what the *shar tahls* have told every child.'

'Perhaps they had reason for censoring the teachings . . . for withholding all the truth.'

'*Why* would they do it, Niall? There *is* no reason for it!'

'There is,' I told him wearily. 'How would *you* react if you were told you were kin to the Ihlini; that once you lay down with Ihlini women?'

He did not answer.

'If you were a *shar tahl* and your duty – your *honor* – lay in defending the prophecy, would you shake the foundations of that honor by tainting it with the entire truth if *part* of that truth had to do with the kinship between Ihlini and Cheysuli?' I sighed. 'Consider it, *rujho* – do you think a Cheysuli warrior would keep himself from an Ihlini woman merely because of her race – if he wanted her badly enough?'

Silence filled the hut. And then Ian broke it. 'I am the *last* one to answer that . . . after what Lillith made me do.'

My eye opened. I straightened. Slowly I leaned forward.

His face was ravaged. There was shame, guilt, disgust; more than a little self-hatred.

'Do not blame yourself,' I told him. 'You believed yourself *lirless* – you *were*, since Lillith used a spell to cut off the link between you and Tasha. Do you think I cannot understand?'

His face was gray. 'I thought *i'toshaa-ni* would help. I thought it would absolve me. But I am still soiled. I remain *unclean*.'

'Ian, stop.' I touched his arm. 'Lillith had a purpose. It becomes clearer even now. Do you see? Merge the blood and you merge the power . . . Cheysuli and Ihlini.'

He looked at me in horror. 'She wanted a *child* of me—'

And I thought it likely she had gotten one. Even Varien had said it: *she has what she wants from your brother*.

'But – it would not be a Firstborn, not a *true* one,' I mused. 'The other blood is needed. Yet if the Ihlini got a child of both our races, they would move perilously closer to fulfillment of the prophecy.'

'But it means their *death!*' Ian cried. 'Why would they do such a thing?'

I released a breath of comprehension. 'If they bred their

own – if *they* controlled the bloodlines, they could control the prophecy. They could make the Firstborn theirs. They could *twist* the prophecy.' I stared at him in realization. 'A Firstborn child in Ihlini hands would be the demise of the Cheysuli. Taliesin even said something about it.' I frowned, trying to remember. 'He said – he said when the child of the prophecy is born, the *lir* will know a new master.'

'Gods – *no*—' He stared at me in horror. 'The *lir* would never leave us!'

'But if they *did* . . .' I looked at Tasha, so close to Ian's leg. And then I looked at Serri. *Lir*, I said, *would you?*

Serri did not answer. And neither, I thought, did Tasha, as Ian asked her the same.

My brother slid off his stool. He knelt. He locked his hands in the plush velvet pelt of Tasha's hide. I saw how rigid was his posture; how tightly he hung onto his *lir*. 'They will go?' he asked. 'The *lir* will go from us?'

'He wants my sons,' I said blankly. 'Strahan wants my sons. As Lillith wanted *your* child . . .'

Ian looked at me. 'Then I will have to kill it.'

CHAPTER ELEVEN

'I think the plague is over,' Ian said. 'People are in the streets again.'

'And they do not spit, do not run, do not make the ward-signs against us,' I agreed. 'Gods, I thought it would slay us *all*.'

We walked through the streets of Mujhara in human form with *lir* on either side. We were warm in our heavy winter leathers; the first tentative tendrils had unfurled from the blossom known as spring, melting the snow and the mud and turning the streets into slushy quagmires. Even the cobbles did not help.

'If you wish to rest, *rujho*, say it.'

I smiled a little. Already Ian knew when the headaches came upon me. Such painful, blinding headaches, some-times so bad I had to stop, lie down, not even *move* until the pain had passed. Sometimes so bad I could not keep food or water in my belly.

I shook my head. 'We are too close, now.' And we were. Even though I was weary and had the beginnings of a headache, I was not about to stop. 'One more corner, and we will be at the gates.' *And Gisella will be unmasked.* 'Do you know, there is a chance she is not mad at all. That she has presented herself so under orders from Strahan through Lillith.'

'*Not* mad?' Ian stared at me in surprise. 'If that is true – if she *has* fooled us all – she is the best mummer I have ever seen.'

'Aye. And it means the choice is taken from me.'

'Choice?'

'What to do with her,' I told him grimly. 'Do you think I will keep her by me? She means to give my children to Strahan. I cannot allow her to remain near them. Who is to say she would not try it again?'

Ian nodded. He frowned thoughtfully. 'What choice, *rujho*? What will you do with her?'

'Either put her on the Crystal Isle, as Carillon did with Electra . . . send her home to Atvia . . . or have her executed.'

'The latter is – serious.'

'But the crime is worthy of it. Giving my sons to the enemy?'

'The Council may disagree.'

'The Council will have no choice. When I tell them about the bastard, they will have no choice at all. They will see that I am the one who is the rightful heir.'

'Tell them *what* about the bastard?'

'What I am intending to tell you.' So I told him, quietly, the truth. And when I was done, we stood before the bronze-and-timber gates of Homana-Mujhar. Both leaves bore the black slash identifying a house of death. It made me think of Rowan.

Ian shook his head as I signaled the gates open. 'After all that – all their plotting and planning . . . it is futile. For *naught*.'

'Thank the gods. And when the Council learns of it, the petition will be dismissed.'

We hastened through the baileys, outer and inner, briefly acknowledged welcoming shouts and good wishes of the men and boys, climbed the stairs into the archivolted entrance. Even as Ian was detained by one of the servants, I went on. I climbed the stairs to the nursery and went in to see my sons before I faced my wife.

But she was there as well.

Squinting a little against the worsening pain in my head, I drew my sword. 'Stand away from my sons, Gisella. Stand away *now*.'

She swung, fell back a step, pressed herself against the

oak-and-ivory cradle. She was cloaked, hooded, patently prepared to leave. In her arms she held a bundled baby.

'What happened to your *face?*' she asked in shock.

'*Put him down,*' I told her distinctly. 'Put him down, Gisella, and stand away from the cradle.'

She was transfixed by my face, until her attention was switched to the tip of my sword as I advanced. Her mouth hung open inelegantly; had she thought I would be slain, and her plans never known?

'Put him down,' I repeated.

She blinked. Shut her mouth. '*Her,*' she declared indignantly. 'Do not call your daughter a *him.*'

'Daughter!' My hand twitched on the grip; the sword tip wavered. I looked at Gisella more closely and saw that beneath the cloak she was slender again. 'By the gods, you have borne the child!'

It should not have surprised me. I could not say how long I had been gone, but certainly long enough; she had only been two months away from the birth when I had come home from Solinde.

She clutched the child more closely against her breast. But she looked sideways at a second cradle. From it I heard the squall of a baby disturbed from sleep.

The tip wavered once more; I lowered the sword. I was diverted from my intent. '*Again?*' I asked weakly.

Gisella nodded slowly, still staring at my face; at the scars and the leather patch. 'A girl. A boy. Three sons and a daughter, now.'

'And all meant for Strahan?' I let the tip drift up again; teased the air before her face. '*All* of them, Gisella?'

Her eyes filled with sudden tears. 'But – I *have* to – I *have* to – Lillith said I *had* to. Varien says I *have* to – I have to do it because all of them *told* me to.'

'Stop.' No more diplomacy. 'Put the baby down, Gisella. Put her with her brother.'

She turned abruptly and did as I told her to. Relief allowed me to breathe again.

'I *had* to,' she said. 'They *told* me I had to do it.'

'Gisella – look at me.'

The tears had spilled over. She thrust a hand against her cheeks and tried to wipe them away. She trembled. She clutched at the cloak and waited for me to sheathe the sword in her body.

By the names of all the gods, how do you ask someone if they are sane or mad? How can you know if they tell the truth?

Must you ask her at all? Serri inquired. *Look at her, lir. What manner of woman do you see?*

'Gisella,' I said helplessly, 'do you understand what they meant you to do? What the result would be?'

'They told me I *had* to do it.'

'Why?'

'Because Strahan *wanted* it.'

'Do you know why? Did they tell you what it meant?'

'They said I *had* to.'

'*Gisella!*'

She trembled even harder. 'I just – I just – did what they said to do. There was the spotted puppy – *two* of them – there was the gray kitten – they said I had to do it. Strahan *wanted* me to do it.'

I stared at her in growing alarm. 'Wanted you to do *what*, Gisella? The puppies – the kitten—?'

She tangled a hand in her hair, twined it through her fingers. 'They said – they said I *had* to – so I did – I *did!*'

'Did *what*, Gisella?'

Her mouth opened, closed. Opened again. Her breathing came very fast. 'I – put the puppies down a well – because they *told* me to!'

I drew in an uneven breath. 'And – the kitten?'

She shrugged one shoulder a little. 'The cliff – the top of the dragon's head.' She shrugged again. 'I let him *fall*.'

'*Why?*' I asked in horror. 'Because they *told* you to?'

She was sobbing now. 'They said I must get used to losing things – losing *live* things – because one day I would have to give up my children—'

'Oh – *gods*—' I sheathed the sword. Went to her. Pulled

393

her into my arms. 'Oh – Gisella – oh *gods* . . . what have they done to you?'

'It was what we *needed* to do.' Varien's voice, so smooth and silken, as he came into the room. 'Do you think it is a simple thing to ask a woman – even a *mad* one – to willingly give up her children? Gisella had to be *trained.*'

'You filth,' I told him, when I could speak again. 'You gods-cursed *filth!* How could you do this to her? How in the name of all the gods could you *do* this to a woman?'

'No,' he said urbanely. 'Not in the name of *all* the gods – in the name of only one. My lord is Asar-Suti.'

'Gisella – stand away.' I pushed her, gently but firmly. And as she went, I drew my sword.

Varien frowned a little. He studied my sword intently. Then his expression cleared. 'A Homanan sword,' he said.

'Still a sword,' I told him. I lunged.

'A *Homanan* sword,' he repeated, and put up an eloquent hand. Easily, so *easily*, he caught the blade in his hand.

Well enough – sever the hand, then sever the neck.

But he stopped the blade dead in his palm. I saw fire explode from his fingers, coat the blade, run down from tip to cross-piece. The steel turned black at once.

As he meant me to, I released the hilt. And *only* the hilt struck the ground; the blade no longer existed.

What is left to lose – he will take the children anyway—

I leaped. Empty-handed, I threw myself across the room and caught handfuls of Varien's doublet, bearing him to the ground. He went down easily enough, but was sinuous as a serpent; writhing, he nearly squirmed away.

We struggled for dominance on the floor of the nursery. I thought of my children, so close to violence. I thought of how I risked them. I even thought of Gisella.

'*Serri*,' I shouted, '*the children!*'

There was no answer discernible in the link. There could not be, with Varien so close. But I knew my *lir* would protect the children. He would give his life for them.

And, of course, give mine.

Varien clawed at my face and caught a corner of my patch.

He tore it away, snapping the leather strap; tried to scrape away tender flesh. The pain was manifest, but it only gave me another reason to fight.

We rolled. My head was slammed against the stone floor. I cried out – the pain of the headache was magnified at once, filling my skull with coruscating light. I felt my belly rise.

Fingers reached again for my empty socket. Childishly, I retaliated by grabbing the stones in his ears and ripping them through the lobes.

Varien screamed. I thought it odd. Torn lobes are painful, I imagine, but hardly enough to make a man *scream*.

Unless, of course, it is not the pain that makes him scream but the loss of the stones themselves.

I clutched both in my fist. I thought of the old Ihlini woman with the pale pink crystal called a lifestone.

Varien was shouting at me, denying me the stones. I was one-handed now as well as one-eyed, not daring to risk the loss of the stones clutched in my fist. Varien was on the bottom, pinned beneath my substantial weight, but now he bucked and twisted and nearly succeeded in flinging me off.

Again, we rolled. I felt an obstruction against my spine; the tripod legs of the nearest brazier. It rocked, tipped, fell, spilled oil across the floor. A sheet of flame followed and set the stone afire.

I laughed aloud. 'Burn, Varien – *burn!*'

I slammed the stones into the fire.

He screamed. Gods, how he *screamed*—

And then the stones were consumed and I was covered with dust that had once been a man.

I scrambled up, ignoring the pain in my head. 'Gisella, your cloak.'

She stood and stared at me. So I ripped it from her myself and smothered the oil fire.

People were in the room. Women ran to tend crying children, men drew hungry swords. But there was no enemy to be slain.

'Niall?' Gisella asked. 'Niall, Varien is *gone*.'

395

'Varien is gone,' I looked at one of the guardsmen. 'Escort the princess to her chambers. Be gentle, but firm. See that she remains there.'

'My lord—' He broke off, nodded, did not question the oddness of the order. Perhaps everyone knew Gisella.

'My lord.' Another man. 'The Mujhar is in the Great Hall.'

I gaped. 'My *father?*' I looked for Serri. *Lir — at once.* We ran.

I jerked open one of the hammered doors, stepped through, swung it shut behind me. '*Jehan?*' I saw him at the end of the hall, on the dais near the Lion. '*Jehan!*'

Ian was present as well, and Tasha. And also my mother, caught in my father's arms. I grinned, strode the length of the hall, opened my mouth to give him greeting — and stopped.

My mother cried. She *cried*, but it was not from happiness. It was the sound of a woman consumed by wracking grief. 'No,' she told him, '*no* — say you will not do it — say you will *renounce* it!'

Ian's face was stark. His yellow eyes were empty. He stood rigidly by the throne.

'Say you will not,' my mother pleaded. '*Say you will not go!*'

His arms were around her, but they did not comfort her. They kept her from harming herself. His eyes, when I looked, were angry, bewildered, lost. They were the eyes of a *lirless* man.

The pain of my head was abruptly swallowed up by comprehension. 'How?' I asked. That only; it was the only word I could manage.

'Plague,' my father answered. 'Taj in Hondarth. Lorn here, two days ago. I should have gone then, but—' He stopped speaking. I saw the grief in his empty eyes. 'Oh, Niall, what has he done to you?'

I had forgotten the missing patch. I put a hand to my face, then took it away. 'He set a hawk on me.'

396

'Gods,' he said raggedly, 'he does not alter his methods.' He touched the old scars in his neck, and I recalled the story. Strahan had set a hawk on my father, some twenty years ago, and nearly slew him then.

But now, he had succeeded.

My mother stared in horror at my face. 'Oh – gods – Niall—'

'I lack an eye, but not my life.' I looked only at my father. '*Jehan*—' But I knew an appeal was useless.

'The war is over,' he told us evenly. 'Solinde has given in. The rebellion was never theirs. Now they weary of the deaths. The realm is ours again.'

'How can you speak about the war?' Ian cried. 'Gods, *jehan*, what of *you*?'

'You know what I must do.' His arms still cradled my mother. 'What every warrior must do.'

'But you are the *Mujhar!*' my mother said. 'Can you not overlook Cheysuli custom even *once*?'

'No.' I answered for him. 'No, *jehana*, he cannot. It is the price of accepting the *lir*-bond.'

Her head twisted on its neck as she glared at me. 'And am I to expect *you* to do the same thing if *you* lose your *lir*?'

'Aye,' I told her gently. 'I am a Cheysuli warrior.'

'Oh – gods – *two* of them—' She turned her face away.

'I have – things,' my father said. 'Something for each of you. It is why I did not go at once, hoping you might return.' He set my mother aside. 'Aislinn, I beg you—'

She shut her eyes. But she did not touch him again.

He turned to the Lion. I saw bundles in the cushioned seat. He lifted one: a blue-suede bag the size of a shoulder-pouch. 'Aislinn.'

With effort, she kept her tears in check. I saw the tremendous strain in the tendons of her neck. She stood quietly before my father.

He lifted her hands, put the pouch into them, closed her fingers over it. 'Duncan made Alix many things. Now I give them to you.'

Her fingers clutched the leather. She stared at the hands

397

that held the pouch: his were firm and bronzed, hers were smooth and fair.

'Do you know,' she said. 'I only realize this now. That even when you were in love with Sorcha, desiring her in place of me, it did not matter. I *thought* it did, then . . . but I know now I was mistaken.' She smiled a little; a sad, bittersweet smile. 'Sharing you was better than not having you at all.'

His hands tightened on hers. 'The things in the pouch are love-tokens from my father to my mother.' He used Homanan deliberately. 'I have always lacked the skill. I can only give you what another has made . . . and swear the feelings are the same.'

He caught her in his arms, lifted her, kissed her as I had never seen him kiss my mother before. For Cheysuli, such emotions are private ones and kept from other eyes, but now there was no reason for it. They did not care who saw.

He set her down again. 'I am sorry . . . *cheysula*, I am *sorry*—'

My mother nodded. She stepped away, hugging the pouch to her breasts, and in silence let the tears run down her face.

'Ian.' My father bent and took another bundle from the Lion. He unwrapped it carefully, and from the folds he took the black-and-tiger-eye Cheysuli warbow he had used for as long as I had known him. 'This was Duncan's warbow. He gave it to Carillon, who brought it home again; who gave it to me on your grandsire's death. Now I give it to you.'

Ian stared at the floor. 'Niall should have it.'

'*No.*' But my father silenced me with a look.

'Niall shall have something else,' Ian was told. 'This is for *you*. This is for my first-born son. The first-born of *all* my children.'

I could not help but think of Isolde. And I knew my father grieved, even as he prepared to give himself over to death.

Ian accepted the bow and looked beseechingly at our father. He said nothing; he did not have to. All the words were in his eyes.

'Niall.' My father took the last bundle from the Lion. He stripped the velvet away. I looked on the scabbarded sword. 'This was – mine,' he told me. 'It served others as a sword is meant to serve, including Shaine and Carillon. It served *me* as my grandsire truly intended when it was forged out of star-magic and other Cheysuli rites. With me, the magic will die, but a sword is still a sword.'

'Hale's sword,' I said.

He put it into my hands. The scabbard was smooth, oiled leather, worked with Cheysuli runes. I knew Rowan had put them there.

I stared at the sword. I heard him strip the gold from his ear and from his arms. He gave them to his *cheysula*. 'Do not watch me go.'

'*Donal!*'

'Do not watch me go.'

She shut her eyes and turned away, clutching my father's gold.

Resolutely, Ian stared at the floor. I looked at the shape in the hilt of the sword: the rampant Homanan lion. The ruby, called the Mujhar's Eye.

I smiled a little. *One-eyed, both of us.*

When I looked up, my father was gone.

I could not sleep. I lay awake in my bed and stared blind-eyed into the darkness, knowing it could not match the darkness of my grief. And when at last I could not stand it, I got out of bed entirely.

There was a thing I had to do.

I drew on leggings, house boots, a winter jerkin. I asked Serri to stay in my chambers; this was for me to do alone. I took up a candle and the sword my father had left me; went alone to the Great Hall with its silent, looming Lion.

I lighted a torch with the candle, but did not take it

399

yet. At the end of the firepit I set the sword down, kicked ash and cold logs out of the way, bared the iron ring. Two-handed I grasped it, prepared myself, wrenched it up from the stone floor of the firepit. The lid peeled back and clanged against the rim.

I hissed, held my breath; the effort had set my socket to aching. In time, the frequent bouts of pain would pass. For now, I had to bear them.

I waited a moment, then took up the torch and retrieved the sword from the floor. I went down into the narrow staircase cut beneath the floor.

The torch roared in the darkness, throwing odd patterns against the shadowed walls. I felt confined by the narrow space, but I descended anyway. All one hundred and two steps.

At the bottom there was a closet. I lifted the torch, sought the runes and the proper stone, pushed, waited as the wall fell open. Flame was snatched from the torch and sucked into the vault.

I took a breath and went in. It had been long since I had been in the vault, *too* long. I had nearly forgotten about it. My father had brought Ian and me here once, to show us the Womb of the Earth; even now, the memory made me shiver.

The walls were of gold-veined, creamy ivory, carved in the shapes of *lir*. I could not name them all. I did not wish to, now.

I thrust the torch in front of me, entered, then set it into a bracket by the door. Ahead of me, mostly hidden in the shadows, lay the oubliette. The Womb of the Earth itself.

I took four steps into the vault. I stood at the edge of the pit. I could not say if there was a bottom to it; no one – *alive* – knew. But legend said there was not.

I unsheathed the sword. In the torchlight the runes ran like water against the steel. I read them aloud into the silence. '*Ja'hai, bu'lasa. Homana tahlmorra ru'maii.*'

I heard the echoes fall into the pit.

'*Accept, grandson. In the name of Homana's tahlmorra.*'

I waited. I heard no sound. Only the song of silence. I smiled. '*Ja'hai, O gods. Homana Mujhar ru'maii.*'

The ruby blazed up in the light of the torch. Such a deep, warm crimson. The Mujhar's Eye was made of blood, as much as mine had been.

'Not my sword,' I said softly. 'Not mine at all — and he will need it where he goes.' I held the sword over the oubliette. '*Accept, O gods. In the name of Homana's Mujhar.*'

I let it go. It fell. Down, *down*, into the hollow darkness of the Womb—

—and was *welcomed*.

EPILOGUE

I stood alone on the sentry-walk along the parapet and let the wind beat at my face. Below me spread Mujhara in the bright garments of true spring: new flowers, new babies, new clothing for the people.

And then I was not alone; I heard the familiar step of my brother.

He came as far as the crenel next to mine, so that only a merlon stood between us. Like me, he leaned against the wall and stared down into the city. 'Do you regret your decision?'

I shook my head. 'No. She will do better in Atvia. There is no place for her here. Let Alaric tend his daughter – he made her the way she is.'

'Some will argue you are too cruel, to separate a *jehana* from her children.'

'I *am* cruel . . . but I would be crueler still if I let her give them over to Strahan.' I looked at him pensively. 'She would, you know, given the chance. Because they *told* her to.'

Ian sighed. 'Poor, addled Gisella . . .' Then he straightened. 'Here – I came to bring you this. I do not know the seal.'

I took the parchment from him. I looked at the seal: a wolfhound in green wax. 'Erinn!' I said in surprise. '*Liam* used this seal!' I broke it, tore the parchment open, read the scrawl avidly. And then I stared at Ian. 'By the gods – they are *alive* – Liam and Deirdre *alive*—'

He snatched the parchment from me and read it for himself. And then he looked at me. 'Only *Shea* was slain, and he took the assassin with him into the afterworld. Liam is Lord of Erinn.'

I sighed. 'For Shea, I am sorry. He was a good lord, a man I admired and respected.' Grief tarnished the moment, then retreated in the bright light of better news. 'But Deirdre is *alive!*'

'And on her way to Homana.' Ian grinned. 'And so I lose my *rujho*.'

'You will not *lose* me! You gain a true *kinspirit*.' I could not damp down my smile. 'Deirdre is not like other women.'

'No,' he agreed with mock gravity. 'Since she is in love with you, she could not possibly be.'

The jest was well-meant, but my mind was on other things. I touched my leather patch in sudden consternation. 'Gods, *rujho* – what will she say when she sees *this?* What if she cannot bear to look at me?'

'You have just said she is not like other women. I doubt she will turn away.' Ian handed back the letter. 'Will you accept the betrothals Liam offers?'

'Since I was the one who originally *suggested* them, aye, I think I will,' I told him dryly. 'My daughter for his son: Keely shall wed Sean. And *his* girl for my heir: Aileen will be Queen of Homana when Brennan inherits the Lion.'

Ian sighed. 'So – it is settled. But what does that leave for Hart and Corin?'

I scratched idly at my right cheek. 'Well, Brennan shall have Homana, and Keely will go to Erinn. It leaves Solinde and, eventually, Atvia.' I nodded. 'Solinde is Homana's now; I will declare Hart its lord – formally name him prince of the realm, to take the throne when I judge him ready. As for *Corin*, I think Alaric of Atvia will leave his island to a grandson. Corin will not be overlooked.'

Ian nodded. 'A just distribution, *rujho*. But what about the Erinnish girl? What about the daughter Deirdre bore you?'

I stared at him. 'Daughter? Deirdre bore me a *daughter?*'

I tore the letter open once again. 'By the gods — I did not *finish!*'

'I thought not,' Ian agreed. 'Well, *rujho*, I think we can safely say the Lion is secured — as well as the prophecy. Four realms in all. Shall I count them out for you?'

I looked up at him blankly. 'What?'

'Homana, Solinde, Erinn and Atvia.' He smiled. 'Four warring realms. If we can just get Erinn and Atvia to stop fighting over a petty island title, we will be that much closer.'

'Oh, aye, but I imagine with Keely as the Lady of Erinn, and Corin in Atvia, the battles will end of themselves.'

Ian's smile widened. 'Or they will *create* the battles out of kinship perversity.'

I reread the letter again. 'Deirdre has borne me a *daughter.*'

My brother sighed. 'Aye, *rujho*, she has. And five is an uneven number . . . I think the battles will be *frequent.*'

Blissfully, I smiled. '*Deirdre has borne me a daughter—*'

Ian laughed.

—Deirdre is coming home.

THE END

APPENDIX

CHEYSULI/OLD TONGUE GLOSSARY
(with pronunciation guide)

a'saii (uh-SIGH) – Cheysuli zealots dedicated to pure line of descent.

bu'lasa (boo-LAH-suh) – grandson

bu'sala (boo-SAH-luh) – foster-son

cheysu (chay-SOO) – man/woman; neuter; used within phrases.

cheysul (chay-SOOL) – husband

cheysula (chay-SOO-luh) – wife

Cheysuli (chay-SOO-lee) – *(literal translation)*: children of the gods.

Cheysuli i'halla shansu (chay-SOO-lee ih-HALLA shan-SOO) – *(lit.)*: May there be Cheysuli peace upon you.

godfire (god-fire) – common manifestation of Ihlini power; cold, lurid flame; purple tones.

harana (huh-RAH-na) – niece

harani (huh-RAH-nee) – nephew

homana (ho-MAH-na) – *(literal translation)*: of all blood.

i'halla (ih-HALL-uh) – upon you: used within phrases.

i'toshaa-ni (ih-tosha-NEE) – Cheysuli cleansing ceremony; atonement ritual.

ja'hai (® French j⅜ zshuh-HIGH) – accept

ja'hai-na (zshuh-HIGH-nuh) – accepted

jehan (zsheh-HAHN) – father

jehana (zsheh-HAH-na) – mother

ku'reshtin (koo-RESH-tin) – epithet; name-calling

leijhana tu'sai (lay-HAHN-uh too-SIGH) — (*lit.*): thank you very much.

lir (leer) — magical animal(s) linked to individual Cheysuli; title used indiscriminately between *lir* and warriors.

meijha (MEE-hah) — Cheysuli light woman; (*lit.*): mistress.

meijhana (mee-HAH-na) — slang: pretty one

Mujhar (moo-HAR) — king

qu'mahlin (koo-MAH-lin) — purge; extermination

Resh'ta-ni (resh-tah-NEE) — (*lit.*): As you would have it.

rujho (ROO-ho) — slang: brother (diminutive)

rujholla (roo-HALL-uh) — sister (formal)

rujholli (roo-HALL-ee) — brother (formal)

ru'maii (roo-MY-ee) — (*lit.*): in the name of

Ru'shalla-tu (roo-SHAWL-uh TOO) — (*lit.*): May it be so.

Seker (Sek-AIR) — formal title: god of the netherworld.

shansu (shan-SOO) — peace

shar tahl (shar TAHL) — priest-historian; keeper of the prophecy.

shu'maii (shoo-MY-ee) — sponsor

su'fala (soo-FALL-uh) — aunt

su'fali (soo-FALL-ee) — uncle

sul'harai (sool-hah-RYE) — moment of greatest satisfaction in union of man and woman; describes shapechange.

tahlmorra (tall-MORE-uh) — fate; destiny; kismet.

Tahlmorra lujhala mei wiccan, cheysu (tall-MORE-uh loo-HALLA may WICK-un, chay-SOO) — (*lit.*): The fate of a man rests always within the hands of the gods.

tetsu (tet-SOO) — poisonous root given to allay great pain; addictive, eventually fatal.

tu'halla dei (too-HALLA-day-EE) — (*lit.*): Lord to liege man.

usca (OOIS-kuh) — powerful liquor from the Steppes.

y'ja'hai (EE-zshuh-HIGH) — (*lit.*): I accept.

SHAPECHANGERS
CHRONICLES OF THE CHEYSULI: BOOK 1
BY JENNIFER ROBERSON

They were the *Cheysuli*, a race of magical warriors, gifted with the ability to assume animal shape at will. For centuries they had been allies to the King of Homana, treasured champions of the Realm. Until a king's daughter ran away with a Cheysuli liege man and caused a war of annihilation against the Cheysuli race.

Twenty-five years later the Cheysuli were hunted exiles in their own land. All of Homana was raised to fear them, acknowledge the sorcery in their blood, call them *shapechanger, demon*.

This is the story of Alix, the daughter of that ill-fated union between Homanan princess and Cheysuli warrior, and her struggles to comprehend the traditions of an alien race she had been taught to mistrust, to answer the call of magic in her blood, and accept her place in an ancient prophecy she cannot deny.

First of an eight-part dynastic epic of a magical race and the compelling prophecy which ruled them!

0 552 13118 0

THE SONG OF HOMANA
CHRONICLES OF THE CHEYSULI: BOOK 2
BY JENNIFER ROBERSON

For five long years the land of Homana had been strangled
in the grasp of a usurper king – its people ravaged by strife,
poverty and despair; its magical race, the Cheysuli, forced
to flee or face extermination at the hands of their evil
counterparts, the sorcerous Ilhini.

The time had come for Prince Carillon, Homana's rightful
ruler, to return from exile with his Cheysuli shapechanger
liege man, free his land from the evil domination of the
tyrant Bellam and restore the Cheysuli to their rightful
position of grace. To claim his birthright he would not only
have to raise an army, but overcome the fear and prejudice
of an ignorant population and answer the call of a prophecy
he never chose to serve!

0 552 13119 9

LEGACY OF THE SWORD
CHRONICLES OF THE CHEYSULI: BOOK 3
BY JENNIFER ROBERSON

For decades, the magical race of shapechangers called the Cheysuli have been feared and hated exiles in their own land, a land they rightfully should rule. Victims of a vengeful monarch's war of annihilation and a usurper king's tyrannical reign, the Cheysuli clans have nearly vanished from the world.

Now, in the aftermath of the revolution which overthrew the hated tyrant, Prince Donal is being trained as the first Cheysuli in generations to assume the throne. But will he be able to overcome the prejudice of a populace afraid of his special magic and succeed in uniting the realm in its life-and-death battle against enemy armies and evil magicians?

Book three of the dynastic fantasy epic of a magical race and the compelling prophecy which ruled them.

0 552 13120 9

THE TRUE GAME
BY SHERI S. TEPPER

including KING'S BLOOD FOUR, NECROMANCER
NINE, WIZARD'S ELEVEN

*In the lands of the True Game, your lifelong identity will emerge
as you play. Prince or Sorcerer, Armiger or Tragamor, Demon
or Doyen . . .*

Which will it be?

The neophyte necromancer Peter embarks on a long and
hazardous quest, to uncover the truth behind the disappearance of the prominent Gamesmen from the lands of the True
Game. As the Wizard's Eleven sleep, trapped by their
dreams, a giant stalks the mountains, the Shadowpeople
gather by the light of the moon, and the Bonedancers raise
up armies of the dead.

The truth unfolds, revealing that magic is science and
science is magic, and Peter, son of Mavin Manyshaped,
must realize his true identity, and become the wild card that
threatens the True Game itself.

Players, take your places. The Game begins . . .

'Very good! It moves with all the precision of a chess game
with fate'.
Roger Zelazny

0 552 12620 9

From the Bestselling author of THE BELGARIAD

BOOK ONE OF THE MALLOREON
GUARDIANS OF THE WEST
BY DAVID EDDINGS

WARNED BY THE PROPHECY THAT A NEW AND
GREATER DANGER THREATENS THE LANDS OF
THE WEST, GARION, BELGARATH AND POLGARA
MUST BEGIN ANOTHER QUEST TO SAVE THE
LANDS FROM GREAT EVIL.

When the Orb of Aldur warns Garion to 'Beware Zandramas!'
the Voice of Prophecy reveals that somewhere in the
unknown land of the East the Dark Prophecy still exists
and that great new dangers threaten.

While Belgarath and Garion seek to uncover the nature of
this threat, Garion's baby son is kidnapped. All evidence
points to the loathsome Bear-cult, which has gained power
once more, and Garion leads an army bent on its destruction. But there are even more sinister forces at work, and
Garion and his followers must look towards the malign and
mysterious evil of Zandramas. Their quest must begin again.

THUS BEGINS BOOK ONE OF THE MALLOREON.

0 552 13017 6

SERVANTS OF ARK
BY JONATHAN WYLIE

'The confrontation, when it came, was cataclysmic. The powers involved were beyond our imagining, but it was a time of great heroism – for men as well as mages. There are many tales of those who fought alongside the wizards. They called themselves The Servants.'

Ferragamo's words referred to the first War of the Wizards, many centuries earlier. Since that time, The Servants had acted as guardians to the islands of their world. Now, after long ages of peace, the new generations of Servants were being called upon the face the resurgence of a long-vanquished evil.

Their story is told in this compelling fantasy trilogy.

'Unlike most trilogies, these books can be read separately; each focuses on a different character and a separate crisis . . . Kings, queens, princes and wizards all live like regular folks, loving and quarrelling and raising their children as best they can in the face of magical war . . . SERVANTS OF ARK is enjoyable fantasy reading, with plentiful light touches that bring a gentle humour to the books . . . With the MAGE-BORN CHILD, Wylie brings the series to a satisfying, truly conclusive end, with plenty of adventure along the way'
Carolyn Cushman, *Locus*

0 552 13101 6   Book 1: THE FIRST NAMED
0 552 13134 2   Book 2: THE CENTRE OF THE CIRCLE
0 552 13161 X   Book 3: THE MAGE-BORN CHILD

THE WIZARDS AND THE WARRIORS
BY HUGH COOK
CHRONICLES OF AN AGE OF DARKNESS. 1:

'I ask all of you here today to join with me in pledging
yourself to a common cause,' said Miphon. Elkor Alish
laughed, harshly: 'A common cause? Between wizards and
the Rovac? Forget it!'

And yet it had to be. Though Alish never accepted the
alliance, his fellow warrior Morgan Hearst joined forces with
Miphon and the other wizards. The only alternative was the
utter destruction of their world.

The first volume in a spectacular fantasy epic to rival
THE BELGARIAD and THE CHRONICLES OF
THOMAS COVENANT

0 552 12566 0

Also available

THE WORDSMITHS AND THE WARGUILD
0 552 13130 X

THE WOMEN AND THE WARLORDS
0 552 13131 8

THE WALRUS AND THE WARWOLF
0 552 13327 2

A SELECTION OF TITLES
AVAILABLE FROM CORGI BOOKS

THE PRICES SHOWN BELOW WERE CORRECT AT THE TIME OF GOING TO PRESS.
HOWEVER TRANSWORLD PUBLISHERS RESERVE THE RIGHT TO SHOW NEW
RETAIL PRICES ON COVERS WHICH MAY DIFFER FROM THOSE PREVIOUSLY
ADVERTISED IN THE TEXT OR ELSEWHERE.

All Corgi/Bantam Books are available at your bookshop or newsagent, or can be ordered from the following address:

Corgi/Bantam Books,
Cash Sales Department, P.O. Box 11, Falmouth, Cornwall TR10 9EN

Please send a cheque or postal order (no currency) and allow 60p for postage and packing for the first book plus 25p for the second book and 15p for each additional book ordered up to a maximum charge of £1.90 in UK.

B.F.P.O. customers please allow 60p for the first book, 25p for the second book plus 15p per copy for the next 7 books, thereafter 9p per book.

Overseas customers, including Eire, please allow £1.25 for postage and packing for the first book, 75p for the second book, and 28p for each subsequent title ordered.